CRESCENDO

BEAUTIFUL MONSTERS BOOK #1

LANA SKY

KITTEN
DANNY

ACKNOWLEDGMENTS

Erica, thank you so very much for taking the time to help me perfect this draft. As always, your feedback and expertise have been invaluable. Thank you, Charity for applying the final touches on this draft, and the many beta readers who provided encouragement along the way.

CHAPTER ONE

Daniela

WE USED TO PLAY TIC-TAC-TOE AS CHILDREN, IN THE dirt with sticks. Now, our game consists of the lives of the two bloodied men standing naked on the ornate rug before us. One can barely see on account of both of his eyes being swollen shut, so he frantically eyes the wall a few inches away from Vinny, while the other stares at the floor, muttering prayers under his breath.

Eeny, meeny, miney, mo, Vinny calls it.

Dressed to kill in a tailored suit, Vinny takes his sweet time observing them both while caressing the pistol he's holding in one hand. "Eeny, meeny, miney, motherfucker," he murmurs in a guttural tone. "Which one should I kill first?" He inclines his head in my direction, ever the gentleman. "Lynn?"

I swallow hard and tug on the sleeve of my sweater. Two hours ago, it was a neatly hemmed number in soft pink. Now, it's bloodstained, the ends of the sleeve ragged and torn.

"Really, Vinny. You don't have to—" I break off and try again. No one tells Vinny what to do—ever. Not even me. "I'm fine. Really."

It would take more than this to ruin my night. This beautiful, perfect night, which should have ended with a nice bubble bath. Not here in Vinny's office, with the scent of blood in the air and the inevitable promise of death tainting the atmosphere.

I glance down at my throbbing hands, surprised by the numerous scratches that mar them. They contradict my lie, and I curl them up into fists, even though I know that it's already too late. *I'm fine.*

Regardless, Vinny doesn't even look in my direction. His thumb greedily traces the trigger of his gun, eager to let a bullet fly.

He's in a mood. Something must have happened even before he caught wind of my little adventure tonight. My heart picks up speed, my spine tensing.

"Really," I croak out against his back. "I'm fine—"

"Sit down, Daniela."

I flinch. My full name is a dangerous sound coming out of his mouth. *Lynn* is his puppy, his favorite toy. Daniela is just a little girl in danger of disobeying her master.

My jaw snaps shut, and I stagger a few steps past him to collapse onto one of the plush armchairs that is positioned to face his desk. His office is one of the few places I hate most in the world. What, in a normal setting, would be designated for stuffy business meetings takes on a broader purpose in Vinny's hands. It's his arena. His showroom. My cage.

I warily scan the oak-paneled walls. They're polished to shine and reflect the rest of the room back to me: hardwood floors and exactly two windows, each one framed by black curtains. There is another leather armchair across from mine, flanked by Vinny's massive desk, which takes up the center of the room. Vinny's reflection is like a dark smudge over the scenery, while the two men before him flicker the way a candle flame does when it's in danger of going out.

"Let's play a game," Vinny declares in a voice that makes me shiver.

I know that tone all too well. Bile creeps up the back of my throat, and oddly enough, the thought of ruining my sweater with puke is even worse than what's already staining it now.

"Tell me again what happened—from the beginning," Vinny says. "The bastard who tells the least amount of lies wins."

There's this painful moment of silence. The men share a look that resembles the wary expressions of two animals shoved into a cage and forced to fight to the death. Which one is the lion, which one the gazelle?

The one with the busted jaw speaks up first, or at least he tries to. "We were just screwing around. We didn't—"

"First lie," Vinny interjects.

I can't breathe. My throat contracts in an attempt to choke down air, but the action doesn't relieve the pressure building in my chest. Lying was another one of our childhood games. It wasn't played quite as often as tic-tac-toe or red rover, but often enough to recognize the way Vinny crouches forward, bracing both hands against his desk. He's got that cold, dark gleam in his eye. The same one that made him seem so powerful, even as a child. His parents may have been immigrants. His family may have been dirt poor. He may have had a slight limp on his left side and a lisp that affected his speech.

None of that mattered when you met his gaze head on. His eyes held a darkness that swallowed you whole. And the worst part? A part of you *wanted* to be swallowed. You were stupid enough to be comforted by the shadows.

"That was the first lie," he repeats. His fingers dance on the surface of the gun until they find the safety. He noisily flips it off so that they hear the clip engage. "Let's make things interesting. Next one to lie gets a bullet through his eye."

The two men don't look at each other this time. They shift on their feet. The one with the busted jaw glances at me as if he wants me to say something. They were just playing around, after all. When they cornered me in an alley and tried to rip my shirt off, it was all just fun and games.

I should be thankful for what will come next. There's a cut on my chin and blood dribbling down onto my scalloped collar. I can taste dirt and grit from when they tried to hold me facedown and pull my pants off.

I should *want* Vinny to blow their brains out all over his priceless, antique rug. Maybe, a few years ago, I wouldn't have cared—back when I'd been younger and stupid enough to mistake his aggression for love or kindness.

But, now, I know the truth. Men like the two sniffling before me are nothing more than predators. They hunt and stalk and gleefully devour their prey in the shadows—but not all predators deserve to be torn apart by the Big Bad Wolf.

"Any takers?" Vinny gives them another five minutes to decide.

The seconds tick by like hours, long enough for stupid, irrelevant concerns to take precedence. I'm tired. All I want to do is crawl into bed and blast Bach until I fall asleep. I want to eat my leftover Thai food with extra hot sauce. I want...

"Time's up." Vinny pulls himself upright to all six feet, two inches of his height. The movement displays the muscles that ripple in his forearms, straining the sleeves of his suit jacket. "This isn't very sportsmanlike. Daniela? Would you like to give us an idea of what really happened?" His tone is crisp with impatience.

"Vinny..." I trail off. My side hurts from having connected with the pavement. There are dark circles under my eyes, I know, from staying up all night and playing until my fingers bled. I'd give anything to play now, to lose myself in the cadence of the music.

"Daniela?" Vinny points the gun in my direction—not at me, exactly. Instead, he trains the barrel over the framed photograph of an Italian villa hanging behind my head. It's a warning. "What happened?"

I fold my hands over my lap, and I try to look anywhere but at the men who are crowding the room. There's a beautiful view of the city from the window across from Vinny's desk, silhouetted by the gap between the curtains. I can see everything highlighted by neon lights and flashing street signs. Against the black backdrop of the night sky, it almost resembles diamonds.

"Daniela—"

"They followed me from the subway," I say, my voice detached. "One of them took my purse, while the other grabbed me. They held me down and tried to... Vinny, I'm *fine*."

"No." The flat of his hand strikes the surface of the desk with a sound that has me jerking upright. "It's not *fine*."

Two quick pops muffled by the silencer and it's over. Two bodies hit the floor with a thud, and Vinny puts his gun down. There's a noticeable release of tension in his shoulders. People like me prefer bubble baths to relax. Men like Vinny go for murder.

"Your cello came," he tells me while wiping something from his chin. "Next time when I send you a fucking car, you be in it, too. The *subway*." He shakes his head, perplexed by the idea of me being so indignant as to shun his hospitality.

In a way, I suppose it's ironic. I cared enough about my cello to have it delivered to the hotel in the town car Vinny had sent for me, but I couldn't bear to climb inside it myself. I walked, traveling two blocks before taking a bus and then the subway.

If I were lying to myself, I'd claim I'd wanted the exercise. In truth, I just wanted to prolong the moment. That freedom. That soothing silence of being alone with my thoughts for once. A world without violence or vengeance or Vinny.

"Lynn?" Vinny snaps his fingers to draw my attention. "Go to bed. Get some rest. We'll do lunch tomorrow. How does Capellas sound?"

"Great," I croak.

Capellas is a restaurant on Fifth, firmly under Vinny's control. The chef's name is Tony. His wife is Maria. For a share of their profits, Vinny ensures their establishment's "protection." Out of gratitude, Tony always serves him one hell of a chicken marinara—on the house.

"Good." He motions for me to get up while he circles the desk to stand in front of me.

I try not to flinch when he touches me and trails a thumb along the corner of my mouth. He observes me like that for two seconds. Then he leans forward and brings his mouth to my forehead, leaving a chaste kiss.

"*Mi Bella.*"

His hand runs down my spine, sensing the curves of my body through the fabric of my sweater, but I don't react. I don't cringe.

I inhale. In and out. Out. In. There's a noticeable tremor in my hands when he finally pulls away. His dark eyes don't miss it and they narrow, homing in on the rebellious fingers.

"Those bastards better have not hurt you," he growls with an intensity that makes my stomach churn.

Fear has a bitter flavor that settles on my tongue. Or maybe it's love?

I run my eyes over Vinny's chiseled features. He must seem handsome to some, with a Romanesque nose and smooth, olive skin. He has a laugh that can raise goose bumps and eyes that gleam like firelight. But none of that can make up for the monster lurking within the beautiful exterior.

"Get some sleep," he tells me before laying another soft kiss on my cheek.

"Goodnight, Vinny." It's a precarious trip over the bodies of the two dead men to reach the door. I manage to keep my balance until I grab the doorknob.

Then his voice rings out behind me, issuing another command. "Send Gino in here to clean up this fucking mess."

"O-okay." I pull the door open and stagger into the narrow hallway beyond it. Two men are standing on either side of the doorway, both broad-shouldered with matching stern expressions. "Gino," I speak to the one with a goatee and heavy-set build. "Vinny needs you to clean... He needs—" I wind up gesturing to the room with a wave of my hand.

He nods once. "Of course, Ms. Manzano."

He brushes past me while I head down the hallway of the suite. It contains ten rooms, all interconnected on the highest floor of the Hirmark Hotel. My room is on the far west corner, but I don't head for it now. Instead, I cross the living room, past four more men lounging on the imported Italian furniture.

One of them calls out to me. "Your instrument is safely in your room, miss."

I glance over and nod, forcing a smile. "Thank you."

"Miss?" He questions when I finally reach the front door. "Do you need anything?"

"No...I—" My grip tightens over the doorknob. "I just need some fresh air. I'll be right back."

I twist the lock and push the door open before he can even rise from the couch. Just outside the suite, another guard takes up his post, but he doesn't say a word when I head toward the elevators. He doesn't have to.

Vinny has even more men watching me from the shadows. Men ready and waiting to trail me from the concert hall and through the subway, there to step in when two thugs try to rape and mug me in an alley.

Vinny has eyes on me everywhere, but after all these years, I know how to evade them for a few precious minutes. Rather than wait for the elevator, I take the stairs. It's thirty-four flights to the bottom level. An elegant oak door leads to the main lobby, while a battered metal one opens onto the street.

It's cold out, and my sweater isn't a good enough barrier against the mid-October weather. Each breath I take paints the air white, but I relish the chill. It's bracing after the stifling heat of Vinny's office. The stench of the city and a dumpster a few feet away almost displaces the spicy scent of blood. I can breathe again, and I take huge, savoring gulps as I stagger two feet down the alley and then turn the corner to skirt the back of another building.

Vinny likes to conduct his business on the Upper East Side. Far away from the riffraff we grew up around, but still close enough to keep an eye on his holdings. It's the perfectionist in him. The same personality quirk that compels him to carefully plan his days around a clockwork-like schedule. The same way he likes to plan mine.

This little detour is entirely my own, however, and I take my time, walking up at least a block until I reach a familiar stretch of pavement. There are a few metal trash cans here, nestled against the side of what I assume is an old office building. Inside one of them is a stack of old newspapers just ripe for the taking.

I scan the faded print in the dim light cast from a nearby streetlamp while I slip my hand into my pocket and withdraw a flimsy book of matches that managed to survive the excitement tonight. My fingers shake when I strike one, holding the flame as close to my face as I dare. The heat it gives off licks at my skin. Orange and amber paint my vision, spilling across the pavement at my feet. It's beautiful. It's terrifying. If I drop this flame into the barrel of newspapers, the fire will spread and become out of control.

Holding it like this creates a precarious balance, similar to the skill required to guide a bow along a narrow row of strings in search of just the right tune. The perfect note. Fire contains a symphony of its own. The crackling embers build to their own silent, destructive crescendo.

"Hey!"

The voice startles me so badly that I jump. The match slips from my fingers and strikes the topmost newspaper. Almost in slow motion, it starts to burn—bright yellow flames at first, then a brilliant orange that dances its way across a headline proclaiming that construction on a new city park will begin next fall.

"Jesus Christ!" A wad of gray fabric smothers the ember's music midsong. The flames hiss as they're beaten down to nothing but embers clinging to a ruined hunk of smoking paper.

Vinny's man is a full three minutes quicker than he was last time. I can't hide the sigh of disappointment that shoots out, tainting the air gray, as I turn to face him, fully prepared to obey the subtle command of, "Let's get you inside, miss."

But I didn't expect the hand gripping my wrist. Vinny's men never touch me—one of the many rules pertaining to the care of his property. Whoever he is, his fingers are callused and rough with grime and dirt. Unmanicured. Unpolished. Unsanitized.

My brain counts the surmounting flaws while my eyes take him in. He's not wearing a suit, just a gray hoodie and jeans, another gross violation. Vinny once beat a man to death for wearing jeans on the job. *"Unpro-fucking-fessional!"* he'd snarled in between the blows of his pistol-turned-bludgeoning weapon.

"Aren't you a little too old to be playing with matches?"

I flinch. His voice lacks a distinct accent. Vinny prefers "imported" men to do his dirty work rather than Americans. I don't know how to process it. Any of it.

My eyes linger on his face—or what little of it I can make out in the dark. His hair is too long. A line of dark stubble covers his strong chin. It's impossible to make out his eye color, but I guess something light. *Blue? Green* maybe?

He towers over me. Almost as tall as Vinny but with none of that imposing bulk. This man is almost lean in build, but his grip is firm. I can't pull my hand away easily, not that I try to. Those thugs in the alley smelled like alcohol and felt like sandpaper. This man smells like...

A sudden breeze glances off the brick walls, displacing his scent before I can decipher it fully. Cigarette smoke. Musk. Cologne?

"You a mute or something?" he asks. He sounds harsh on the surface, but there's an almost amusing note hidden between the words like a soprano almost smothered amongst altos.

Alarm floods my veins. I should scream for one of Vinny's men. Paranoia is one of Vinny's dominant traits, and his money allows him to indulge in it to the fullest. From what little information I've guessed in a few short months, he even posted some of his stooges on the rooftops. A few more work as cab drivers who pretend to be blind to any passenger but his own men.

I wait, holding my breath. Seconds tick by while the stranger still speaks—but no one comes.

"Be more careful," he says while letting my wrist go. "It's no fun getting busted for arson—"

"I wasn't playing with matches." The voice sounds like me, but it isn't a scream. It isn't a plea for Vinny or one of his goons to come running. It was a whisper, almost, as if I didn't want to be heard above the barrage of honking horns drifting from the main street.

"Oh, really? Do you prefer the term 'playing with fire,' then?"

I frown at that. "I prefer playing with...light." My tongue wrestles to convey the words in English. Vinny loathes my accent despite his preference for it in workers.

This man doesn't seem fazed by it. "With *light*, huh? You a pyro or something?"

"P-pyro?"

"Pyromaniac. You know, arsonist." He jerks his chin to the smoldering newspaper. "You like settin' fires or something?"

Piromaníaca? I shake my head. The question doesn't make sense. Who would enjoy setting something on fire? Though...I can't deny the shiver that runs through me at the thought of Vinny's suite, high above the city, doused in flames. How would my room look while consumed by the inferno?

My facial expression must change, because the man laughs, the sound grating against the backdrop of city noise.

"You escape from a mental hospital or something?"

"Something like that," I hear myself reply. *Escape.* My mind gets stuck on that word and won't move on. "Yeah, sure. Something like that."

"Hmph." The man shifts, tucking his hands into the pocket of his sweatshirt. That simple motion violently puts everything back into perspective. This man is way too close, and I move to stand on the opposite side of the barrels.

"Sorry for bothering you," I say, which is as polite a brush-off as I can manage. The smart thing to do would be to return to the hotel without having to be escorted back—but for some reason, I can't move from this spot. The book of matches is still in my hand, and my heart races with the urge to light another. Just one more.

"Oh, yeah. I have some damn nerve getting on a high horse," the man grunts. Rather than leave, he takes a step closer to the barrels between us, and the motion reveals that he's carrying something on his back: a backpack. He opens it up and withdraws a round, cylindrical object. I don't know what it is until he gives it a shake. The can rattles like Vinny's shaving cream, or...

"S-spray paint?" My voice is still a whisper, but the man nods. I think he might have even winked, but it's too dim here to be sure.

"Brick walls always look a little better covered in a layer of chemicals, don't ya think?"

I nod, though I don't know why. Spray paint paired with brick walls typically infers some kind of graffiti. Vandalism. I glance down at his hands again, and what I'd first mistaken for dirt and grime takes on another identity.

"You paint?"

"Well, now, that's one way to put it. Come on." He jerks his head toward the opposite end of the alley from the way leading to the hotel. "I could use your expert opinion, little Pyro Girl."

I freeze solid, digging my heels into the pavement. "You should go." I've been so stupid.

Vinny's man will be here in exactly thirty seconds...twenty-eight seconds. Every bone in my body warns me to walk away before the hound dogs come running, but I *can't*. My brief minutes of freedom were intruded on. It just isn't fair. He'll have to leave first.

"Please."

"Awful strange request to be left alone in an alley with matches, Pyro Girl," the man says. I realize, for the first time, that he's concerned. The line of his gaze travels from the matchbook clenched in my fist down to the barrel of newspaper. "What kind of law-abiding citizen would I be if I did that, huh?"

"Some people are coming," I blurt out, staring down at my clenched left hand. My words come unguarded without Vinny here to filter them, and apparently, the truth is a reckless addiction. "If you're here when they show up, they're going to put a bullet in your head."

"Oh, is that so?" The man seems to mull it over, but shock isn't one of the emotions that crosses his shrouded features. In the end, he laughs. "Well then, that will be one hell of a way to end my night. Come on." He holds a hand out to reinforce the words that seem like a command on the surface. But they aren't. A request? A question.

For five precious seconds, I eye his hand. It's entirely possible this graffiti artist who smells like cigarettes and stale body odor means to lure me down the alley for some nefarious purpose. Would God really be so cruel as to throw me into the frying pan twice in one night? Could he really be so merciful?

My time is almost up, but I don't hear footsteps. Vinny's man is a second late, and I seize the moment by nudging the stranger's palm with one outstretched finger. Handshakes. Hand holding—those embraces most people take for granted. I can't remember how to initiate them properly.

Amused by my attempt, the man laughs. Then he flexes his fingers and captures my entire wrist in a firm grip.

"Come on, Pyro."

I try not to balk when he steers me down the narrow alley and then toward an even narrower strip between two buildings. Like a snake, the man weaves in and out through the tight spaces, bracing his back against the wall. Left with no choice, I copy him, sucking my waist in.

Eventually, we reach another alley. Then another—but we seem to be moving in circles. I bet we're only a block or so away from the hotel, but for some reason, he prefers to take the backstreets. I'm sure the thought should terrify me. Instead, it intrigues me.

"So...do you like art?"

"Huh?" I frown at the question.

"Art." The man chuckles. "Though I suppose I should have asked that question *before* dragging you off to see my mural, huh?"

It seems like a rhetorical question, so I don't answer. It isn't until he glances back at me that I remember what he initially asked.

"So...art. You like it?"

I shrug and then nod. Up this close, the stranger doesn't seem so threatening. He may be tall, but he's nearly as thin as I am. There's a gracefulness to the way he walks, like a dancer, almost—nothing like Vinny's hostile, jerky movements that make me suspect that he's always anticipating the moment someone might put a bullet in his head. This man—or maybe he's more like a boy. His eyes are close-set and definitely blue. There's a line of stubble along his chin, but I wouldn't peg him as any older than nineteen—maybe two or three years younger than I am.

"Is this a stupid question?" he asks suddenly, his mouth cracking to display two rows of slightly crooked teeth. I think he's smiling.

For some reason, I try to smile back. "Yes. I like art... Yes." My mind may have stupidly forgotten the timer on my freedom, but my body hasn't. My skin burns beneath the stranger's fingers, almost as if threatening to betray me. *He'll know. He'll know.*

I yank my hand back, twisting it out of his grip. This time, he lets me.

"So, art," he says quickly, as if trying to postpone the moment I'll turn on my heel and run away. For some reason, it does. Talking is too addictive. Too tempting. Words hold less power here, outside of Vinny's fortress. It's way too easy to let them slip. "What kind?"

"Music," I say on command. I couldn't stay silent, even if I'd wanted to; the answer is ingrained in my soul.

He laughs again and continues to tug me down the alleyway, one slow step at a time. He's savoring this adventure. I'm anticipating its violent ending. Almost two whole minutes, now...

"*Music.* Oh, God. Which bastion of modern music do you subscribe to? Composer Swift or Maestro Bieber?"

I shake my head, not recognizing the references. "Bach," I say. "Yo Yo Ma."

"Ah...a true musician. Singer or player?"

"Cello."

He nods as if the answer had been obvious all along. "So, you make music as well as fire with those magic fingers, little Pyro?"

I don't answer. My love of music is like an old wound that can never fully heal. Some days, I think it's starting to close up, the rent flesh knitting together again. Other days, Vinny likes to cut it open and rub salt into the festering gap. Afterward, he'll always kiss the bleeding sore and murmur, "All better."

Like tonight. Tonight was his peace offering. His gift. My torture. Pain mingles with hope and shame, and it's suddenly harder to breathe.

"You all right?" the stranger asks, cocking his head.

I flinch. Even my facial expressions are suddenly out of my control. I fight to return my mouth to its worn, "charming" smile. Vinny's man can't be far now, but I'd hear him coming, at least. I won't let the man in front of me pay for my stupidity.

"I'm fine..."

"Save the pouting for when you see this piece of shit, okay? It's just up ahead."

We travel ten more steps, though once again, I can't help but feel like we didn't go very far at all. I can still hear the same sounds I heard when I left the hotel—the same concierge yelling for a taxi and the same cadence of honking horns.

Abruptly, the man stops, and I almost run into him.

"Voila," he says, gesturing to yet another brick wall. "Boom, there it is."

"Wow." I take a step forward, transfixed by what's in front of me.

Right here, in the middle of neatly laid bricks, is a whole new world slapped onto the impromptu canvas. A man watches me from amid it all, larger than life, his glowing, red eyes transfixed on my body as if he can peer right through my flesh and into my very soul. Vinny wouldn't call this art. *Vulgar*, he'd say before rattling off something demeaning in Italian. Tailored suits and well-made cigars—*that* was where his appreciation of the word ended.

"Is that supposed to be the devil?" I blurt out while some inner part of me laughs at the notion. The devil lives in a high-rise. He wears suits with custom cufflinks and sips imported champagne from glass flutes.

However, if I still believed in the fantasized version of Lucifer, this mural would depict him well: a dark shadow lurking in the bowels of the city...watching. Always watching.

"Something like that," the stranger says. "Though...a little more abstract. He's missing something. Here."

I flinch when something cold presses into my fingers. They curl around it automatically, and I glance down to find that I'm holding a can of spray paint.

"Maybe you can help."

"I...I can't." I try to give the can back, but he backs away, holding both hands up. "I'll mess it up." My voice cracks. In a world of "perfection," mistakes are harshly punished. "I can't—"

"Put those magic fingers to use," the stranger insists.

I swallow hard at that taunt. *Magic fingers.* "I had an audition today," I say to the wall. I don't know why the words rush out, but it's easy to say them when the man beside me says nothing in return.

He doesn't try to shut me up. He doesn't prod me to go on...

I'm silent for four precious seconds. Then the truth spills free, and it's like a dam breaking. "It was an audition for an orchestra—not a big one." It feels important to clarify that when he lets out a sharp breath. He's impressed, though I don't know if it's by the words I say or by how quickly I say them. "Not a big one. But they wanted me. They offered me a job to play in the strings, second chair. Second chair. It'snotabigdealbut—"

"That's awesome, Pyro Girl," he says quietly.

Awesome. I lock that word away, somewhere deep inside myself where I hope Vinny won't be able to find it.

"I can't take it though. I can't take it. I have..." My throat aches beneath the bigger truths that won't come out so easily. I have Vinny at my shoulder, whispering in my ear. *You don't need to make a living, Mi Bella. I'll take care of you.* He let me audition as a pittance. The fact that he wouldn't allow me to accept my prize was just another game we've played since we were children. Vinny comes second to none. No one. Nothing. "I have...previous commitments."

My voice breaks—a weakness that wouldn't go unpunished in Vinny's presence.

My stranger notices. Even worse, he notices and merely sighs. "That fucking sucks, Pyro Girl."

"Yes," I hear myself croak. My hand trembles and the can still in my grip rattles. "It f-fucking does."

"Wow. Fun night." The stranger whistles under his breath and then waves his hand toward the wall. "Looks like I've picked the best person to take on the devil. Here. Give it your best shot." He nods once at the mural, and I follow his gaze.

Something inside me simply can't resist the allure. It's surprisingly tempting to wield such power over someone else's creation. The paint can drifts upward before I realize it, and my thumb strikes the nozzle.

I jump when a jet of white paint speckles the wall amid a hungry hiss. The "Devil" watches me with burning eyes as I aim in the general direction of his head. I'm too short to clear it completely and the next stream of white hits the top of his carefully coiffed hair. For some reason, it's easier to ignore the guilt this time. I keep spraying. Painting. Defacing.

For exactly thirty-four seconds, Vinny's men are in another universe. There's only me and a skinny stranger and the Devil being doused in white paint. Despite everything, I take my time forming a single shape, though my ineptitude is obvious.

Chuckling, my stranger points it out to me the moment my hand falls to my side. "Is that a halo? Or a...D?"

My mouth quirks into an unusual shape. A smile? "Both," I say.

"Both." He shrugs as if it makes perfect sense. "Well done, Pyro Girl. You've turned my villain into a superhero."

Something inside me twitches, stung. If only it were that easy. My grip tightens over the can of spray paint again. Would Vinny be as easy to shape? The stranger takes it from me before I can settle on an answer.

"Thanks," he says while returning the can to his bag. "You've solved that dilemma. But what exactly does the D stand for? Devil?"

I shake my head. "D for Dan—" My teeth clamp shut, cutting the word off, but I'm too late.

The stranger notices my hesitation. Names are dangerous. Vinny alone has three for me, each one representing a different facet of the person he's shaped me to be. *Lynn* is the good, obedient girl. *Daniela* is a nuisance. *Mi Bella* is the creature I never want to fully become.

"Danny," I blurt out suddenly. "D for Danny."

He nods, once again letting my insecurities go unchecked. It's a small kindness that rubs at something deep inside me. "Cute name, Danny. I'm Espi."

"Espi?"

"It's short for something," he says without elaborating. "Maybe I'll let you know what on our next adventure?" He turns on his heel and fades around a corner before I can say anything in response.

Such as that there won't be another "adventure"? I'll pay for this stolen moment with months of increased security. Little birdies mustn't seek fresh air from their cages for too long. I'll pay for this...

But my body can't quite muster up the urge to shiver as I begin the trek back toward the hotel. Vinny's men are five minutes late, and surprisingly, one of them isn't waiting for me by the emergency exit when I arrive. I enter the stairwell to silence. My footsteps echo off the elegant walls once I reach the topmost floor unaccosted.

I'm panting. A layer of sweat glosses my skin, and something inside me is shaking—but it isn't fear. I can still smell spray paint. I can still feel the stranger's hands on my skin. I glance down and find a smudge of black on my wrist. My first instinct is to rub it away. With every inch I travel closer to Vinny's suite, the more that smudge blares from the shadows like a betraying beacon. My tongue shoots out to dampen my lips, but I tug my sleeve lower rather than erase it. I flinch at the sight of the pink fabric. It's still crusty with blood.

"Are you all right, miss?" The guard by the door is in the same position I left him last. He watches me approach with an unreadable expression. Was he counting the minutes?

I've been out for nearly ten. I'm convinced that his feigned ignorance is a trap. The moment I step through that door, Vinny will be waiting on the other end of it with a stopwatch in hand. *Where the hell were you, Daniela? Whose scent is on you? Who touched you?*

"Miss?"

I blink. The guard has the door open, revealing the grand entryway illuminated by a gleaming chandelier, but there's no one lying in wait when I step over the threshold. Hushed voices reach my ears as I head across the suite. My heart pounds, nearly drowning them out.

"Clean this shit up..."

"Yes, sir."

"Find out who they work for."

Those men. The ones who attacked me near the subway—who knew exactly where a lone, unarmed woman would be that time of night. A traitorous snicker trickles out of me before I can help it while my eyes burn and begin to blur. I can only pray that no one heard me—the living room is empty, at least. Vinny's men are busy tonight. I hear thuds and footsteps coming from the office. They could just be moving furniture—if it weren't for the sickly thud made between the efficient tap of loafers on wood. The door is open, and I can't stop myself from peering at the sliver of the room revealed beyond it.

I can only make out Vinny's desk and a pair of thick hands braced on top of it.

"Lynn?"

I freeze in my tracks. "Yes...yes, Vinny?"

"Get to bed." His tone is gruff, crisp. He's angry. He'd brooding. The glee that fills him at the sight of death has faded to a smoldering lust for revenge. His emotions contain the same wild, untamed energy of a match—only a few whacks with a hoodie won't be enough to put his wrath out. "*Now*, goddamn it!"

"Yes, Vinny."

It takes me exactly twelve seconds to hurry down the hall and pry the door to my "bedroom" open. Vinny designed every last detail: the soft-pink walls, the white lace lining the canopy of my bed, and the plush, ivory floor rug.

It's been a comfortable cage for the last four years. The only object out of place is a wide case propped carefully against the wall beside my vanity. I nearly choke on a wave of disappointment that swamps me, and I tear my gaze away to the window instead. I watch the city silhouetted against the sheer, white curtains as I peel my clothing off and tuck them neatly in the hamper near my bed. A white nightgown has already been laid out for me, resting on the white duvet. I shut the light off and pull it on in darkness. Then I slip beneath the blankets and try not to dream.

It hurts to dream these days. Instead, I close my eyes and picture a devil watching from the shadows.

CHAPTER TWO

Dante

WE ARE SUPPOSED TO STRIVE TOWARD FREEDOM LIKE rats on a wheel working for cheese. Time off for good behavior, they say. Parole is the goal—but, when the unexpected release of a convict is deemed "reintegration into society," it all but implies that we have all been successfully rehabilitated the moment we walk out of the reinforced steel doors.

It's all bullshit, of course. Just a way for the DA to be able to sleep at night, knowing that his inept office allowed yet another monster to slip through the hands of justice. Some poet somewhere probably wrote something deep to describe the cruelty of it, but I'll settle for this: You can't cure rabies with four walls and an armed guard. By then, the beast can't even hear you. It doesn't want to hear you. Why? It's already imagining the uneven cadence of your heartbeat the moment it lunges for your throat.

Once tasted, blood is an impossible addiction to shake, unlike crack or heroin. The stain on your soul left by a death you commit yourself is incomparable to any other human disease. It corrupts your entire being. The aftermath paints the world gray. Crushing a man's windpipe beneath your fingers or striking him down with a bullet you let loose mark the moment you decide to stop being human. Darkness consumes you, and even though a pretty social worker in a clinical lab coat tries to tell you to feel remorse...

You simply don't. *C'est la vie.* That's life.

"Mr. Vialle. Did you hear me?" An orderly is waiting by the door, a clipboard propped in the crook of his arm. "Detective Van Hallen for you." He steps back to allow another man to enter the room.

It's one of the interview rooms the prison uses for meetings with lawyers or impromptu so-you've-been-released well wishes from the cops. Whoever he is, this "detective" is tall. Graying black hair covers his head and matches the neatly trimmed beard around his mouth. Rather than look in my direction, he warily eyes the plastic chair placed on the other side of the metal table I'm already seated at. When he finally sits, he has to spread out his legs just to keep his knees from brushing the table's underside.

"Good morning, Mr. Vialle," he says, finally looking up. "I hope I'm not troubling you too much." He makes a show of placing a battered, leather briefcase on the table. Then he takes his sweet time opening it and withdraws a rather sizeable file. *Dante Vialle* is printed on a sticker taped to the front of it. He makes sure I read the label before he opens the file and shuffles the pages inside it. "You have an...interesting record, to say the least, Mr. Vialle."

I don't answer. This jumpsuit itches. The fluorescent lights affixed to the ceiling are set to the highest setting on purpose—so is the heat that's blasting, though Mr. Van Hallen has enough sense to pretend he doesn't notice. Stupid pigs. You'd think they'd get tired of playing the same old tricks.

"Well, I personally wasn't pulling for your release," Van Hallen goes on. He frowns at something he's reading on one of the pages in my file and begins to recite out loud. "Robbery. Arson. Attempted murder. Assault with a firearm. Assault with a deadly weapon. Felony assault. Possession with intent to sell. Kidnapping—"

"And yet my current charge is 'trespassing,' Detective," I say. "A minor offense."

He flushes, his jaw clenching. Mr. Van Hallen is one of a million. A carbon copy of the same cop to hound my trail since the day I first shoplifted candy from a Quick-Go Mart. They get off on the heroics—making the world a safer place. Little do they know that, when you put one rabid dog down, two more are already ready to take its place.

Surprisingly, Mr. Van Hallen cuts right to the chase rather than climb onto a soapbox. "Vincent Stacatto. Ever hear of him?"

I shrug as best as I can despite the handcuffs securing my hands to the table. "I can't say that I have, Detective."

"Don't worry," Van Hallen assures me. "You'll hear of him soon enough. While you were trading sexual favors for a few cigarettes in this jungle gym they call a prison, Vinny Stacatto's been running roughshod all over your old territory."

I smile without an ounce of hostility in my expression. "I'd say my ass is worth a lot more than a *few* fucking cigarettes, Detective."

Van Hallen grunts. "Let's not play around, Vialle. While your impending release certainly is no cause for celebration...you have a chance to really do some good for this city."

I laugh. I can't help it. My gaze drifts from Van Hallen to seek out the clock hanging on the wall beyond his head. Twenty minutes.

"Oh, I don't know about that, Detective. I can think of a few good things the city might be able to do for *me* though."

Van Hallen struggles to keep his composure. I recognize him from the slew of pigs the DA paraded in and out during my sentencing hearing. Their spiel pretty much followed the same lines. *This man is dangerous—we may not have evidence that he's dangerous, but mark my words. He's dangerous.* How much did the commissioner have to bribe him to come here on his hands and knees?

"Twelve murders," Van Hallen starts. "Three counts of extortion. Human trafficking. Those are the crimes we suspect Stacatto of committing this month alone."

I extend my fingers, observing them in the blinding light. "Sounds like you've been busy, Detective."

"This isn't a fucking game," Van Hallen snarls. He's playing the bad-cop routine without his good-cop wingman. It's an amusing effort.

I smile again and watch as his face becomes an alarming shade of red.

"Let's try another name, huh?" he suggests. "Mathew 'Mack' Spigotti? Arnold Mackenzie?"

"Mackenzie...Mackenzie..." I raise an eyebrow and meet the detective's gaze head on. "Hm... Nope, doesn't ring a bell."

"So, all those years you ran around with those two in the streets never left an impression, huh? What about when you fought for Dino Mulligan?"

"Must be all those favors for cigarettes I had to earn," I say coldly. "My memory's a little fuzzy."

"Okay," Van Hallen spits. He reshuffles his papers and tries again. "Espisido Vialle. You've got to recognize at least *one* of those names."

"One of them," I admit, my entire body tensing the same way the hackles on a bulldog rise when someone gets too close to its territory.

His mentioning of Espi is a dangerous game to play. The bastard knows it. He doesn't make eye contact this time.

"You wouldn't be threatening me, Detective," I say, keeping my voice level. "Now would you?"

Van Hallen doesn't answer me directly. He rummages through the pages of my file and surfaces with three pictures, which he sets out in a line, just out of my reach. One is of a scrawny kid with tousled, black hair barely contained by the hood he has pulled over his head. His blue eyes stare off into the distance—it's obvious he didn't know that the picture was being taken. There's a cigarette sticking out of his mouth, and I scoff at the sight. Little fucker knows better than to court cancer with that shit.

He's grown up, though, in the years since I've been gone. His face has filled out, the baby fat melted down to reveal our inherited bone structure. He has the makings of a mustache budding over his lip. The longer I stare at the picture, the more I can sense something tense inside me. A human might refer to the emotion as guilt. I'll write it off as irritation.

"Are your subordinates into kiddy porn?" I wonder, fixing the detective with an expression that makes him flinch. "That kid's a minor."

"He's nineteen now, Vialle," Van Hallen retorts, shaking his head. "Your little brother's grown up some since you've seen him last. Sadly, he seems to have picked up some of your bad...*habits* as well." He points to the remaining two pictures.

They both depict graffiti that I assume is on the brick walls of the buildings uptown in the city. One of them is an elaborate six-pointed star. The other, the stylized drawing of a man with glowing, red eyes. Even in the grainy photo, I recognize the features.

"The kid's quite an artist," Van Hallen says. "Unfortunately, he doesn't put his talent to good use. Remember Mackenzie? That man you claimed not to know? Well, your brother's been running with him and his gang. The Gardai. Ringing any bells now?"

I flex my fingers, hearing the knuckles crack in unison. Arno really went with that fucking name? Go figure. The bastard loved showing off his so-called "Irish" heritage.

"Get to the point, Detective," I grit out, my gaze on the slowly moving clock.

Van Hallen flashes a grin of his own. "This one"—he taps the picture depicting the painted man—"was found this morning on a building deep in Stacatto's territory. That's one of Mackenzie's tactics, as I'm sure you know. He sends men to mark areas he intends to hit—but if he goes after Stacatto...it could turn ugly. I don't think you'd want your little brother in the middle of it." His voice lowers an octave. The bastard might actually give a damn—which is why his precinct was desperate enough to come crawling to me.

"Sorry, Detective," I say. "I'm not taking any last requests."

Van Hallen has the nerve to seem pissed, though we both knew what my answer would be. "I'll keep in touch," he warns while tucking the photos back into my file. "It's inevitable that you'll be back here within the month. Dogs like you don't escape the pound for too long. In fact, I'd give it a week."

"And let's remember why this dog got loose in the first place," I throw back. The handcuffs click against the table's surface when I lean forward, holding Van Hallen's gaze.

To the old man's credit, he doesn't look away. Yet. There's a twitch in his jaw, however. A bead of sweat forming on his brow. I've been told that my eyes are soulless or some shit. Intimidating. Once you kill a few men, your eyes stop being *just* brown or blue, apparently. Shadows lurk inside them. Evil, they call it. Some days, I can even see it there myself. Van Hallen is no fool, and when I allow him to break the eye contact, he quickly gathers up his briefcase and shoves my file inside it.

"A mistake like that won't happen again," he grunts. "So count your fucking blessings, Vialle."

"Mistake..." I chew on the word. "Is that what they call it when an attorney for the DA has been convicted of... What was it?" I snap my fingers as if I'm searching for the right word. "Witness tampering? And, now, every case that attorney so much as coughed on is being thrown out left and right. Let's just count our lucky stars that the bastard happened to work on mine."

Van Hallen glowers. "I'll be waiting for when you screw up," he promises. "It's only a matter of time, *Kitty*."

I chuckle at the reference to my old nickname. "Do you want to know why they called me that?" I wonder, flashing the detective a wink. "It's because I always liked to play with my food."

I don't know if it's my tone or my expression that has Van Hallen backing away to the door of the room. He raps on the door, and a guard opens it.

"I'll be watching, Vialle," he calls back before shuffling into the hall.

I smile wide and nod. "I'll be sure to give you and your boys a hell of a good show, then."

———

TEN MINUTES LATER, I'M WEARING A GRAY STATE-ISSUED T-shirt and a pair of jeans, standing amongst the armed guards in the lobby of the prison. The clerk behind the counter eyes me up and down. Then he clears his throat and reads the statement he's holding in his hand.

"Dante Vialle. One cross, silver. One wallet, leather. Fifty-four dollars, twenty cents." He places each item onto the counter as he reads them off the list. Then he packs everything into a plastic bag and slides it in my direction. "Sign here."

He hands me a pen, and I sign on the dotted line of the release papers. Just like that, I'm a free man. The world seems to know it. Rain lashes at the windows, and the sky is a weeping, pissed-off gray. Another vicious dog escapes the kennel, but a part of me wonders something right along with Detective Van Hallen: How long will it last?

I'm determined to make a game of it.

I feel nothing when I take the plastic bag of my belongings and head for the main doors. I'm patted down one last time and then turned loose onto a world that seems eager to spit me right back out.

Rain slicks my hair when I step through the electronic doors. "There's a shuttle up ahead," a guard tells me, pointing down a winding road that seems to lead nowhere.

I shrug. "Thanks."

Thunder rumbles in the distance when I finally clear the main gates. I'm free—but that statement takes on a bitter edge. I'm free while Espi fucks around with Arno and his stupid schemes. I'm free while my name has become nothing more than insult slung by some aging pig.

I'm *free*...to return to a city claimed by an entirely new monster. A sane person might feel something like regret for the five years lost behind bars. An animal would relish the challenge.

Vincent Stacatto. I taste the name on my tongue while my boots strike the pavement in tandem. My mouth quirks up into something that might be a smile. Or a snarl.

Due to the result of some stupid technicality, Dante Vialle is free, heading toward a city that only held his memory in the bowels of a police station. Though not for long. Van Hallen gave me a week. I'll take him up on that—gladly.

Daddy's home, I think, picturing the world I left behind—all of those things I hated encased in concrete. *Daddy's home, motherfuckers…*

CHAPTER THREE

Daniela

"Miss." Someone shakes me awake, their fingers warm over my shoulder. "Miss...it's t-time to wake up."

The timid whisper belongs to a woman. Her fear calls to my own, and the recognition makes me huddle beneath the silken sheets. She has to tap me yet again.

"Miss?"

I finally sit up with a sigh, rubbing at my eyes with one hand. When I blink, a pretty face greets me, sporting a strained smile that does its best to seem comforting.

"Good morning, Miss Manzano."

I nod in response while the woman hurries over to the handcrafted wardrobe in the corner of my room and throws the doors open. She flips through hangers, searching for the outfit Vinny planned for me to wear down to the last detail. One by one, she withdraws each requested garment and sets them on a nearby chair. I strain my eyes in the weak daylight spilling in through the windows and observe each piece carefully: a skirt and *that* silk blouse... My stomach sinks.

There's more to the outfit, however.

Frowning, the girl goes through the wardrobe twice, still searching. On the third pass, her hands shake with fear. "L-lace shawl?" she murmurs to herself. "I can't...I can't find it—"

"It had a hole in it," I force myself to say, picturing the garment in question—a shawl custom-made for me by some well-known designer from Italy. "I threw it out."

"Oh." She can't resist rummaging through the clothes one last time before accepting defeat.

She's young, maybe twenty. I don't know her name. For the past four weeks she's waited on me, I've never dared to ask.

Her skin is pale, her eyes blue. She keeps her long, blond hair pinned neatly back, the way Vinny prefers it, but when she coaxes me out of bed and sits me before my vanity, she brushes my dark tresses out rather than arrange them the same way.

I don't know why. I don't ask, not even when she secures the waves behind my ears with an ivory headband I don't even remember owning. Vinny makes me wear white from head to toe today—the blouse and a matching skirt that reflect the shadows of the room as if taunting me when my companion displays them on their hangers and forces another smile.

"Beautiful, yes?"

"Yes," I say as expected, but the look we share contains anything but admiration.

We're grim. We're silent.

With gritted teeth, she helps me out of my nightgown, and we both suck in a breath when my torso is bared. The black lines etched into my flesh are never easier to stomach. Some days, I manage to trace them with a finger, mouthing each letter—but never what they spell out. Vinny tries to erase what he's done to me with high collars and scalloped necklines. *My pure, innocent Lynn,* he likes to murmur into my hair. He thinks the lies flatter me...but there's nothing pure about the girl staring at me from the mirror. Her hazel eyes hold too many secrets.

"Please, miss," my companion urges. Her gaze nervously darts to the clock propped on my nightstand, and she presses the blouse Vinny's chosen for me against her chest. "Let us dress you now?"

I nod and hold my arms out at my sides while she drapes the fabric over me. It's pretty, which in Vinny's world is a term that comprises more than just pleasing to the eye. I look *pretty.* Untouchable. Unspoiled. His.

My heartbeat speeds up. I can't look at myself, so I tear my gaze away to the floor. Vinny demanded lunch, but the clock claims that it's not even ten yet.

"Is... Are we leaving now?" Hope taints my voice, nearly impossible to squash back down.

My companion smiles. It's a fleeting, shaky expression over her pale face, but it's real. "Not yet," she whispers after glancing over her shoulder at the door. "Not for an hour...maybe." She takes a hesitant step across the room, toward the instrument case leaning against the wall. "You play now? For a little?"

I don't hesitate. My fingers shake when I ease my cello case onto the floor, flip the lid, and lift out the instrument carefully tucked inside it. Balancing it on its stand, I carefully maneuver myself onto the chair near my vanity. I swallow hard when I stoop for my bow and ease it into position. Then...I play.

My arm moves fluidly, manipulating the strings while my fingers coax out the proper tune. Notes tumble loose, and then the music floods, drowning everything else out.

The cello weeps for me. It disguises the words I can't say, the emotions I can't feel. The pain weaves a silent thread, hidden beneath the pleasing music. It's one of the few things I have left that Vinny hasn't taken or tainted.

"Miss? Miss?"

I flinch when a hand settles over my shoulder, and the music ends on a harsh note.

My companion stands over me, her face two shades paler than it was only minutes ago. "It's time to go..." She cuts her gaze over to the door.

Gino is standing there in the doorway, his expression unreadable. "Are you ready, Miss Manzano?"

"Yes." I lurch to my feet while the woman rushes to carefully take my cello and my bow.

She doesn't follow when I slip past Gino and enter the hallway. She's lucky in that her imprisonment only extends to this suite. She doesn't have to wear invisible chains wherever she goes.

"It's cold out," Gino remarks, pressing a navy coat into my hands.

I nod and pull it on while we cross the suite and step out into the main hall. Charming classical music drifts from the hidden speakers the hotel has tucked within the corners of the hall. The sound serves as a haunting soundtrack during the torturous descent in the elevator and the grim parade through the front lobby, where I find a black car out front, waiting to take me across town to Capellas.

The sky is weeping; it's such a dreary day. Ice disguised as rain is falling steadily by the time we pull up to the restaurant. It's a beautiful place, really. Small, quaint, and nestled in an older part of the city, away from the harsher realities of the poorer areas—but still a far cry from the posh restaurants that cringe at the thought of serving a crime lord. I think that's why Vinny cherishes it so much.

The brick façade with its emerald-green awning must remind him of the old days, the ones he likes to smear and accolade in the same breath. *We may have grown up in shit, Lynn, but it's nothing like how the world is today...*

"Miss?"

I flinch, realizing that the driver has already opened the door for me. I was staring at the curb with my hands clenched into fists, unconsciously dreading stepping foot onto it. My fingers sting, aching for the feel of my bow and the glossy casing of my cello. I would play forever if it could prolong my precious few moments without Vinny. I'd saw at the strings until my nails broke and my fingers bled. I'd wring every bit of sound I could from the instrument's wooden frame. I'd...

"Miss Manzano." The driver's voice holds a warning now.

I reluctantly obey it, shedding my coat. Time ticks stubbornly forward. Vinny said lunch at noon. It's 12:01. Depending on his mood, I'll either be punished with a warning or...

My throat closes up, but I can't seem to move until the driver finally clears his throat.

"He's waiting, miss."

The staff members at Capellas are well conditioned to Vinny's moods. When I follow the driver through the main doors, a nervous waitress is already there waiting to take my coat. She doesn't smile, and the moment I inhale, I realize that it might be impossible to. Tension laces the air.

Animosity holds an undercurrent that contradicts everything else—the soothing classical music played by the live band at the corner of the nearly empty dining room and the few carefully selected patrons dining at tables spread throughout, their movements stiff. Vinny's men guard the corners, unmistakable in their starched suits. My tormenter himself dominates the center of the room, seated at a table he's chosen for us specially.

When he sees me, his dark eyes remain uncharacteristically flat. "Lynn."

I swallow hard. My footsteps falter, and I nearly trip at the mouth of the doorway leading to the dining room. "H-hello, Vinny." It takes everything I have in me to force a smile, which he doesn't return.

Instead, he unfolds his silverware and snaps the white napkin into the air with a hard flick of his wrist. "Sit."

I hold my breath when I approach the table. Unease ripples through me. My hands shake. I do my best to shove them underneath the table as I sit down, but he notices, and his eyebrows lift ever so slightly.

"Do you want to know what I've learned?" he wonders, his voice the perfect cadence of a gentleman proposing we discuss the news. "About your...*accident* last night."

I can't breathe. I try my best to mime the motion, forcing my chest to contract inward and then outward. But, through and through, I'm already dead. "N-no."

"Someone tipped them off, it seems," Vinny says. He drags his steak knife through the tines of his fork, noisily sharpening the blade. "Those men. They knew exactly where you were. I don't know anyone in my employ who might want to hurt you, Lynn..." His eyes home in on mine, darker than the black lining of his crisp, gray suit. "Do you?"

I shake my head. I don't know anyone in his "employ" who might want to hurt me, but that said nothing for those he kept tethered to him through means other than money. Desperation is a funny thing. It can make a woman reckless. Reckless enough to sell a priceless, designer shawl that may have matched this particular outfit. Reckless enough to spend the money through dark underground channels someone might only learn of after having lived with a man like him for five years. Reckless enough to screw up and manage not to die before Vinny's men could come to the rescue.

He knows. I wait for him to say as much and dole out my punishment. I'm resigned to my fate like a good little lamb.

"Hmph." Vinny shrugs. "You haven't seen Nicolai, have you?"

I cringe at the change in subject, and my brain struggles to process the new information. *Nicolai?* I vaguely recognize the name of one of the guards and a shaky mental image forms. Blond hair. Dark eyes. He's the same one who routinely drags me back whenever I leave the hotel for longer than three minutes. My stomach sinks.

"N-no," I say hoarsely. "I mean...yes? I mean—"

"Hmph." Vinny sits back, but his eyes lose their shark-like gleam. Within seconds, he's bored. Placated.

He snaps his fingers and the band begins to play in earnest, filling the enclosed space with music. Chopin, I think—one of his more obscure pieces. It's lovely. It's haunting. The joyful notes provide an ominous backdrop for the tension seeping through the muscles of the man across from me. I can't help it. My hand shoots out, and I risk taking a sip of water without his permission.

His eyes miss nothing, but he lets me rebel this once. I can't help but feel like it's a gift, and my pulse picks up speed, churning blood through my system. Something's wrong. He's smiling now, and even Vinny's moods aren't this wild. He's angry. In the same breath, he's...excited.

"What would you like?" he asks, gesturing to the menu.

"Whatever you think would be best," I croak out in response.

The exchange is just for show, of course. He claps his hands after setting the menu aside, and a waiter appears with our food already cooked. Vinny is served a steak, medium rare to his exact specifications: a pinch of salt, a hint of cloves, no pepper. He cuts into it and hums with satisfaction when it bleeds, leaving a bloody trail across his porcelain plate.

I'm served a salad, Caesar—also prepared to Vinny's specifications. No salt. No dressing. A splash of olive oil. Two tomatoes cut lengthwise. A handful of Parmesan cheese. Three olives. Four croutons. Twenty leaves of lettuce. Alongside it is a small serving of pasta marinara with exactly a quarter cup of noodles, a serving of sauce, and three mushrooms.

"It's good," I insist after taking a wooden bite.

Vinny nods. "Good. Good..." He watches me eat, his gaze unusually intense.

It's like he's memorizing every motion of my fork. Every twitch in my throat. By the time I finally choke the last crouton down, he's barely touched his steak.

"Is...is something wrong?" It's a struggle to even get the words out. I shift my gaze over to the people trying to ignore us on the periphery of the room.

They're eating slowly, chewing mechanically, and averting their eyes from the man I'm with and me. It used to hurt, this feigned ignorance. I'd never known how alone in the world it was possible to feel until the first night he made me dine with him like this. There we were, amid at least a hundred people who were all desperately trying to forget my face. Back then, I was naïve enough to feel anger. Now, I only feel pity. These people are no different than I was. For however long Vinny needed them, they were prisoners.

"Everything is...perfect," Vinny says. His smile widens.

My heart skips a beat—even more so when his right hand slips underneath the table. *No. No. No.* I hold my breath, clenching my hands into fists, my nails cutting into both palms.

"I wanted to wait until after dessert," Vinny says, his voice uncharacteristically warm.

Oh, God, no. I want to squeeze my eyes shut, but fear holds them open. I'm forced to watch as his hand returns in slow motion and carefully sets a small, black box onto the table.

He flicks it open, and my world ends. "It's finally time."

Time. It slows to a crawl for me. I can't breathe. I can't take my eyes off the object perched on a pillow of black velvet inside that box, either. The light of the chandelier overhead glances off the expertly cut face of a small, polished bit of material. *A diamond,* my mind supplies. It's attached to a metal base that forms a delicate circle. *A ring.*

"You're speechless," Vinny says, grinning. He's happy.

I'm...crying. My vision blurs. I blink too rapidly, and the tears fall, striking my cheeks. I can't even lift my hand to wipe them away, and they slide down my face unchecked, wetting the collar of my blouse.

"It's beautiful, isn't it?"

He holds out his hand expectantly, but I can't move. I can't take my eyes off the ring. It really is beautiful—a beautiful shackle. At the thought of putting it on, pain sears through every inch of my body.

After years of studying Vinny, I know better than to let him catch me off guard, and even this "surprise" was anticipated, in a sense—the inevitable end to the songbird's captivity. I just hadn't expected it to come now. I had another year left, at least. One more year before I had to take his name, become his *wife.*

"Tell me how happy you are," Vinny commands.

I've been silent for too long—emotionless for too long. His fingers flex impatiently for my hand.

"I'm ha..." The words stick in my throat. My arm won't budge.

"Put it on," Vinny urges, nodding toward the ring.

I can't. I can't. I won't do it. I eye the scenery behind his head, chewing so hard on my bottom lip that I taste blood. This is the part of the nightmare when I usually wake up, sometimes with a scream poised at the back of my throat. I can't seem to make any sound now, ironically. I can't speak. I can't cry out.

There's a man at the table behind Vinny. A woman is sitting across from him, but his eyes remain fixated on our table. He sees me, and I wonder if he knows what's happening. If he can see what little life there is left drain out of me. I certainly can feel it leaving. My limbs are heavier. The artificial heat is sweltering. I'm suffocating beneath flimsy lace and luxurious cotton.

"Lynn?" Vinny snaps his fingers, the sound sharp and demanding—but I still can't bring myself to look at him. Not yet. This wasn't supposed to happen yet. "Daniela..."

The man behind Vinny is still watching us. He has short, black hair and a memorable face. There's a scar underneath his left eye, a sight my mind won't let go of for some reason. My gaze drifts downward to take in the rest of him. He's wearing a suit three years out of style. The woman across from him is siting too stiffly. It's as if, even inside Vinny's carefully crafted illusion, they don't belong...

"Daniela, are you listening to me?" Vinny's tone is an ominous growl.

I'm spoiling this for him. He'll enjoy making me suffer.

But I can't take my eyes off the strange diner; he definitely doesn't fit. It's almost as if we're playing a silent game, the two of us. The moment he notices me staring, he reaches into his pocket and withdraws a metal object that glints in the light of the chandelier. He raises it quickly and aims it surely—but there's a split second when he hesitates. I could scream then. Alert Vinny. But I don't.

He realizes that, his mouth twisting into a frown. *Why?* I can imagine him wondering that while Vinny utters something in a dark tone for my ears only. The truth is...I don't care what the hell he does with that gun.

Just as long as he shoots me first.

"Mr. Stacatto! Get down!"

The shout from one of his thugs startles Vinny into turning around—just as the assassin pulls the trigger.

Bang!

The sound is mind-wrenching. World-splitting. It tears through my eardrums, and I can almost taste the resounding silence that comes after. I've never felt freer than in that one pathetic second. There's no one in this narrow void with me. There's only silence…

And then, like a freight train at full speed, reality slams back into me, throwing me out of my chair.

"Stay down!" someone growls into my ear.

Then all I hear is sound. Clashing, clanging, terrible sound. Four more gunshots echo off the walls, followed by shouts and screams that churn into a deafening hum.

I blink, struggling to make out my surroundings. All I can see are polished loafers racing across the room. Silverware crashes down from a nearby table. There's a dark, red substance forming a puddle on the polished floor a few feet away, and despite the confusion swirling around me…I pray to God that it's Vinny's.

"Get up." A heavy hand seizes my collar and drags me to my feet.

I sway. The once beautiful restaurant is in shambles. The tables are crooked, some overturned. The chairs are empty. A few stragglers struggle for the exits, but the only people left are two men I recognize as Vinny's goons and me. And *Vinny*…

He's behind me. I taste his cologne on my tongue, and my throat jerks to swallow it down. I'm choking on the flavor of him, even as he turns me around to face him. Despite a spot of dirt on his lapel, he looks none too worse for wear.

"It's okay," he grunts, pulling me in so that my face is pressed against his chest. "You're safe."

Safe. That word taunts me.

I hear groaning, and I pull away from Vinny and glance over my shoulder to find a man writhing in agony. He's the culprit of that puddle of blood. At first, I assume he's been shot—until I see the knife sticking out of the palm of his right hand, pinning it flat against the floor. He tugs at it, but I know that the effort is in vain. When it comes out, it won't be pretty. The blade has a serrated edge, formed of the finest craftsmanship. Vinny had it made especially with only one purpose in mind. Sometimes he liked to take it out and tell me all the things he'd do with it to the people who pissed him off. *I'll cut the bastard's nuts off with this,* he'd muse. *Slowly...fucking slow, Lynn. There's no point in torture if it isn't done carefully. Precisely.*

"Take that fucker to the hotel," he snaps, sending one of his men into action. "Put him in my office. I want to know who sent him."

I shiver when he turns to me. He grabs my wrist fiercely and pulls me in close again. For once, I don't smother the pain I feel. I don't suppress the grimace that crosses my face or hide the way I bite my lower lip to trap the gasp threatening to break loose. I feel... God, this fear is the only thing I have left. I let it wash over me, and I pray that it's enough to battle the numbness that encases my limbs when Vinny reaches for my hand and shoves something onto my finger.

"It's fate, Lynn," he growls near my ear, as if seeking to dominate the thoughts he isn't a part of. "Nothing or no one can stop what's meant to be. *Mi Bella.*"

He kisses me on the cheek and draws back, frowning at the taste of salt. And only now do I realize that I haven't stopped crying.

CHAPTER FOUR

Daniela

My cello is the most beautiful thing I've ever owned—though I'm not stupid enough to believe I truly possess it. Vinny commands everything. What's his is his, and what's mine is ours. He claims he's done it all for me—built this world, fought these imaginary battles with men no better than he is.

It's why he wants me to be a part of it. It's why he made me drag my cello from my room and set it up in a distant, forgotten corner of his office where even the light doesn't reach. I'm a part of this. His violence is my entire world, and he'll never let me forget it.

"Play something nice," he commands, his words grunted and clipped. His shadow is a stain on the floor, but I don't look up to see the rest of him.

Three men are occupying this room with me. My fiancé, one of his hired slabs of muscle, and the other...

He's a stranger I've only seen once before: while he aimed a gun at my head. He missed. My eyes squeeze shut to trap the tears welling up, but I obediently settle my bow into position blind. *"Play something nice."* I take his loose definition of the word and run with it.

I play something *loud.* My bow saws, spilling out a melody that washes the harshness of the room away. It's Bach, I think. "Cello Suite No. 1." Prelude. The composition doesn't matter either way. I simply perform, hugging the wooden instrument between my legs, and it's *almost* enough to drown out the tortured sounds of the man's moans.

My upper teeth descend into my bottom lip when a gasp mingles with the notes I'm weaving, but I don't stop playing. I am nothing in this moment. I'm just sound. I'm endless. I'm...

"You motherfucker!"

The shouting jars with the melody.

"Who the fuck do you work for?"

I play even harder. Sweat beads on my brow. My arm begins to hurt. Something heavy is weighing my left hand down, affecting the precise movements.

"Who?"

There's a smattering of words in return.

"Fuck you."

My arm slips, and a false note cuts the air. I pant, hesitating, but an admonishment doesn't come. Vinny is too busy interrogating to notice. When I continue, the sound isn't enough to erase what he says next.

"That's enough of this shit. Get his fucking pants off."

Off. My arm takes off. I throw myself into the composition, holding nothing back. Every tone. Every subtle note holds a piece of my soul.

And it still isn't enough to silence the horror taking place in the room.

"Who do you work for?"

"Go to hell."

"Get my fucking knife."

"No! No!"

My fingers are numb. I don't feel them anymore. I don't even register commanding my body which note to play next. Everything just moves, muscle and sinew in perfect sync.

"Ma...MACKENZIE!" The anguished cry battles with my solo for supremacy. "Mackenzie sent me. Arno Mackenzie. Mackenz— "

Everything goes silent but the steady stream of classical music filling every inch of the room.

"Enough."

I keep playing. My left shoulder hurts. The right one is throbbing. My lungs can't seem to hold any air, but I don't stop manipulating the strings while I guide the bow. Faster. Faster. Faster...

"Damn it, that's enough!" Someone yanks on my right hand.

My bow slips from my sweaty grip and goes flying across the room. Just like that, Bach's prelude comes to a screeching halt and only my labored breaths fill the silence.

Blood taints the air I'm forced to pant, haunting and sweet. I shouldn't look over, but I do. A man's body is lying on Vinny's antique floor rug—they didn't even bother to place anything under him to protect the woven threads. His pants are down, bunched around his ankles. There's a bloody, gaping mess where his male anatomy should be. Though I assume that it might be whatever one of Vinny's men is now holding, flaccid and severed, on a silver platter probably fetched from the kitchen.

I coldly register the sight. I don't feel anything when my gaze slowly roves back down to the dead man on the floor. His mouth is open, but there's too much red pooling around his lips. They're painted red with it. Between his teeth is just a gaping hole...

A childish part of me wonders where his tongue is. *Oh,* it perks up, spotting something lying on Vinny's desk amid a puddle of even more blood. *There it is!*

My stomach churns. I only have enough time to bend over and shove Vinny's hand away before my mouth opens and a stream of vomit coats the wooden floor at my feet.

"Jesus Christ," Vinny snarls, backing away a few steps. "Get a fucking hold of yourself, Daniela."

"Get a fucking hold of yourself."

When I'm done retching, I try to wipe my mouth off with the back of my hand, only something hard bumps my lip and cuts it. It sparkles when I brace my fingers against the floor.

"I'm sorry," I rasp while blood wells up, dribbling over my tongue. "I'm sorry...Vinny."

He scoffs in disgust, but once again, the violence has fed his hunger, for now. There's almost a gentleness when he glares down at my puddle of vomit and snaps, "Clean that up!"

I'm on my knees in a second, ready to mop up the mess—with my skirt my hands, *anything* to distract myself so I don't have to look, don't have to smell...

"Not you," Vinny says, and I go still.

In silence, his goon crosses over to me and carefully wipes up my undigested pasta with a handkerchief pulled from nowhere. He wads it up, crosses over to the body, and shoves it into the dead man's mouth with a hiss of disgust. "I'll find someone to help me with this, sir," he promises before leaving the room.

Vinny nods. Then he mumbles curses under his breath, running a hand through his dark hair. "Mackenzie...fucking Mackenzie." This new foe only holds his attention for just over a minute, however. After all, we still have unfinished business. "So...what do you think?" Looking at me, he nods to my hand, and I glance down to find the mocking surface of my ring glinting back at me. "Before we were so rudely interrupted, you were about to tell me. What do you think?"

I swallow hard, wishing that it were possible to choke on a lie. No such luck this time. The words tumble out without difficulty, and I'm still alive. "It's b-beautiful... I..."

I love it, I should say.

"You what?" Vinny questions. He takes a step closer, and I jump, pressing both hands flat on the floor. "Tell me how happy you are. We've wanted this for so long."

He's feeding me all the right words to say. He's making this way too easy. God, it's like he can sense everything I keep locked behind the barriers he's enacted in my own mind.

"I..."

"Lynn?" He takes another step, slow and measured.

"I..."

"*Daniela.*"

"I just... I... Maybe it's too soon."

He says nothing, and the footsteps trail off.

My spine tenses. I can't look up to gauge his expression. "Maybe...we should wait a little longer. Just a little—"

"Longer?"

I don't expect the blow, and it lands without warning. I see a flash of white. When my vision clears, the right side of my jaw burns, but I nearly sigh with relief. Just a slap.

"I've waited twenty-three years for you," he says, his voice dripping with a tumult of emotions he likes to define as love. "I've waited enough. This is what we've wanted our entire lives."

"Yes, yes," I promise the floor. "I know. I know...but—"

"But?"

The floorboards creak beneath his retreating footsteps. I'm stupid enough to think I'm safe. That he'll walk away and leave me here without retribution. As if mocking me, the light flickers off the surface of my ring, disrupted by the heavy shadow that falls over me.

I quake, and my cowardly instincts try to stave off the inevitable. "Vinny, please—"

He grabs me by my collar and heads for the doorway. He's too fast. I can't stand up, and I find myself being dragged down the hallway toward my room. He kicks the door open, startling the poor woman on the other side of it, who seemed to be in the middle of packing away a new outfit packaged neatly in a black shopping bag. It looks like a dress, slender and black: a cocktail dress. My stomach churns with the knowledge that he's planned the engagement party already.

She pales when she sees Vinny, but he shoves her out of the way and yanks me upright before shoving me onto my bed.

I stare up at the man above me. Violent splotches of red paint his cheeks. He's angry. Furious. I school my face into a blank mask so that I don't react when he raises the object he has clenched in his left fist. My bow.

"Turn over," he grits out, his jaw clenched.

My body moves woodenly. I flop over onto my belly, burying my face into the duvet. My eyes shut. Like always, my teeth catch the tip of my tongue so that I won't make a sound.

"Spread your hands out," he commands.

My heart sinks, but I do it anyway, digging my fingers into the blanket, clutching fistfuls.

"Yeah...like that. Now, tell me you love me."

The woman in the corner of the room whimpers, even before I feel a firm hand begin to tug at the back of my skirt and lift it over my hips. My panties are peeled down next, just far enough to reveal my ass. I flinch when he palms the left cheek.

"Say it," he urges as his fingers curl, sending his nails into my flesh.

I inhale and exhale my soul, leaving the rest of my body limp in his grip. With my last ounce of will, I turn my head just enough to free my mouth so the words come out clear. "I love you."

The air hisses. I hear the slap of wood against flesh first before I feel the sting. It's not quite as sharp as it could have been. He hit me too far up, and the wooden spine of my bow struck me through the barrier of my skirt.

"Say it again."

He's toying with me, and dread makes it harder to speak.

"I...I love you."

He aims true this time and hits nothing but tender skin. My entire body jerks with the force of the blow. Fire burns along my lower back, but I don't scream. I squeeze my eyes shut, instead. I will myself far, far away...

I'm not here. Not really.

"Say that you need me."

He hits me twice when I don't answer quickly enough, and the threat of a sob chokes the back of my throat when I do speak.

"I need you."

He growls, unsatisfied. Once again, I've done it wrong; the words came out too breathlessly.

"Say it again." Another blow.

"I—" My teeth clatter together when he hits me again, unexpectedly hard. A real moan drips out onto the bedspread before I can smother it. Without even having to look, I know he broke the skin. Raw agony sears through flesh and muscle. "I..." I fight to suck in enough air. "I n-need you."

"Damn right, you do." He hits me again, the force unrestrained.

The resounding thud echoes in my bones. My entire body jerks when he strikes again. Again. He's grunting with the effort, bracing his other hand on the small of my back so that I can't wiggle away—not that I try.

I float beyond the pain and just listen. The sound my bow makes whenever it connects is almost beautiful. A violent, staccato rhythm that would sound lovely when paired with a few notes from my cello. Something low and haunting, in G-major. I can almost hum it—it sounds so real. *Da da. Da dum...da da...*

"Look at me." Snapping me from the melody, Vinny grabs my collar again and flips me over.

I can't smother a groan that breaks loose when I land faceup on the mattress. My backside is on fire. Vinny staggers back at the sound, his nostrils flaring—but he's not ashamed. He breathes in my fear like it's a potent narcotic. It fills him with every deep, heavy breath he takes until he's drunk on me.

"Do you know how much I've done for you to scoff at that fucking ring?" He jerks his chin toward my hand.

A part of me wonders if he'll go get his knife and cut the offending digit off. Maybe he'll take the whole hand—both of them. Fervent desperation flares up so sharply that I have to squeeze my eyes shut against it. Maybe this time he'll lose his mind and kill me in the process. *God, please...*

Let him do it.

"Look at me, Daniela."

I obey, but my eyes are painfully dry. It hurts to keep them open like this, but I don't dare close them for a second. I don't even blink.

"Do you?" he questions. "Do you understand everything I've given up for you?"

I don't answer, and not expecting one, Vinny stalks forward. I don't react when he bends over me and harshly undoes the clasp to my skirt. With one hand, he yanks it down while the other wrenches at my blouse. I'm not wearing a bra underneath, and my breasts are bared. So is the message he himself etched into my torso.

He inhales sharply when he sees it, and his eyes shoot black. "You are mine, *Mi Bella*," he breathes out while his thumb traces one of the letters, smearing his possession into my skin. "Mine."

The hand that attacked my skirt moves over to his waist. He tugs impatiently at the buckle of his belt, and something inside me goes numb. Dies. His ring becomes a lead weight. Is this the *real* reason why he wanted me to wear it? Can he justify "spoiling" his promised fiancée more than he can his pure, perfect, virginal Lynn?

I can see him wrestling with the decision as he lets his pants fall down to his ankles. He observes me carefully while twisting his fingers around the waistband of his boxers. I hold my breath when he tugs them down his legs, revealing toned hips. There's a tattoo etched into the skin of his left thigh. The shadows of the room obscure the script, but my mind fills in from memory. *Victory.*

"Look at me."

I do. My eyes are glued to him. He looks ghoulish in the dim light spilling in from my window. When did it get so late? The moment the thought crosses my mind, my fingers throb. How long did I really play? How long was that man tortured? How long?

"Is this why you don't want to marry me?" he wonders, his voice dangerously soft as he gestures to my body with a wave of his hand. "Are you afraid?"

He palms his cock with one hand...but I don't look. I eye the ceiling instead, counting the flourishes in the speckled ceiling. *One. Two.*

"Answer me, Daniela."

Threefourfivesixseven—

"Look at me, damn it."

My neck cranes down slowly. It seems even darker than it did seconds ago. Vinny is a specter standing at the foot of my bed, formed of shadow—my nightmare come to life, getting off at the sight of my pain. The veins in his neck pop while his right shoulder pumps up and down...

"Don't you know how much I love you?"

"Yes, Vinny," I chant on cue. *Please don't. Please.*

"I love you, Lynn." He takes a step forward...and then he lashes out, grabbing the woman who's pressed herself against the wall instead.

She doesn't shout when he wrestles her to the floor and tugs at her neat blouse. He strips her torso bare, leaving her in nothing but a bra while he positions her on her hands and knees.

It's a familiar game, but this time, I forget the rules. "Vinny, don't!"

"Lie down," he growls before I even register sitting up. "You get off that fucking bed and I'll break her neck. You just *watch*."

I go limp. The back of my head strikes the pillow just as the woman cries out. The sound is so brief and so sharp. It's like the howl a dog makes when you step on its foot. The rest of her cries are smothered, however. She'll bite her lip. She'll grind her face into the floor if she has to. Anything to keep from rewarding him with a scream.

Vinny's low groan scratches against my eardrums when she falls silent. There's a sickening sound like that of flesh striking flesh—hard. Again. And again.

"What's your name?" he demands of the woman on the fourth thrust. His hand fists into her hair, yanking her head upright when she doesn't answer quickly enough.

Her eyes are glassy. Drool runs down her chin. I don't think she heard him until two broken syllables tear from her lips.

"Ol...ga..."

He grunts and lunges against her, rutting like an animal. He doesn't give a damn about her name—but he knows I do. He knows why I've avoided learning it for over a month.

Olga. Her muffled cries haunt me, a painful melody until the moment Vinny finally pulls out with a groan. He shoves her down and braces his hand against her back to find enough leverage to stand. Then he turns to me, still erect.

Shut it off, I tell myself. I'm not seeing him. I'm not here. I'm not...here.

"I love you," he tells me over Olga's whimpers.

She tries to crawl away from him, but her arms tremble too badly to support her weight, so she tumbles onto her side and just lies there.

"I love you, Daniela..." Vinny hisses, palming the length of his erection. His hand moves violently while he braces both feet flat against the floor. "Look at me."

My eyes meet his, but I don't see the irises. I'm staring far beyond his head. There's a stage. Bright, beautiful lights that create a puddle of light around a single chair. There's a cello there, too... It's perfectly crafted. The elegance of it makes tears sting behind my eyes. Not this. I'm not here. Not here.

"I love you—fuck!"

Hot liquid hits my thighs in burning lines. Once...again. Being marked with the evidence of his lust aches worse than the marks he left with my bow. I'll never erase them. He's marking my soul; it's just a plaything to sate his cruel desire.

"I love you," he insists while pulling his pants up. "Tomorrow, you wear the fucking ring. You smile. You will be *proud*." He spits that word at me while he steps over Olga and staggers through the doorway. The door slams shut after him, and then there's only silence.

Olga and I don't dare commiserate together. We simply exist...staring at the ceiling while darkness consumes it.

CHAPTER FIVE

Dante

A RABID DOG CAN LIVE FOR A WEEK ON NOTHING BUT scraps. It knows which kennels to scratch at. Which favors to call in. Who to intimidate when it needs a bone to nibble.

Some habits are impossible to shake, as the good detective subtly hinted at. But, if I wanted to keep my nose clean, then the rumors that swirl wherever I go certainly don't help. Nothing lures a mutt into trouble like the scent of another alpha's piss trail, and Vincent Stacatto has figuratively lifted his leg over the entire city. Arno's mark is fainter, but still there, from the Lower West Side, all the way down to the docks. There seems to be no fire hydrants left for an ex-convict to mark all over.

Good. Blood is a better marker anyway.

"I don't know who you're talking about," the bartender insists while tucking the twenty I slipped him into his pocket. His gaze shifts from one corner of the narrow room to the other as if checking for spies lurking under the shitty pool table in the back. "Mackenzie? Never heard of him."

"Okay." I turn on my heel and head for the door only to pause somewhere in the middle of the room.

The bar's a shithole. The prison cafeteria had a better setup than the mismatched chairs surrounding rickety card tables. Torn posters of irrelevant bands line the walls, but one piece of artwork sticks out. Between two shots of the Beatles, someone painted a six-pointed star directly onto the wood paneling. Each arm of it alternates in silver and black paint.

"So, you don't know him?" I call over my shoulder. "Just for the record."

"I told you, asshole," the man snarls back. "I never heard of no fucking Mackenzie."

"Right." I nod while turning on my heel. I return to the counter in two steps and snag my empty shot glass before he can take it away. "Give me another."

I nod to the rack of bottles behind his head, and the bastard makes a show of pouring the shot of whiskey. I bring the rim of the glass to my mouth and inhale the burning swill inside it. Then, when I'm sure he's watching, I tilt my hand and allow a drop to land on the counter.

"Hey, watch it—"

"Imagine this is my patience," I explain, cutting over him. "Imagine that it's running out." I allow another drop to strike the counter, melding with the first. "And let's imagine that, when it does, this glass is going to become part of your fucking eye socket."

He flinches, shaking his head. "I...I'd love to see you try, asshole."

"Don't tempt me." The words come out closer to a plea than I care to admit. My fingers shake. To hide the motion, I twist my wrist and half the glass splashes onto the countertop while the bastard shouts in anger. "Just riddle me this: If you don't know Mackenzie...then why the fuck is his symbol hanging in your bar?"

The man swallows. His skin goes a shade paler, but to his credit, he doesn't flinch when I make eye contact. At least, not at first. The fucker's a good liar—but not good enough. Arno must have grown some balls in the five years I've been gone to earn this kind of loyalty. His thugs don't lounge on street corners these days, conducting business in full view of the pigs. He doesn't own the twitchy addicts getting high in alleyways anymore. He's into *distribution* now. My little puppy's grown up into a mad dog of his own, and I can't fucking wait to rub his goddamn nose into the mess he's created.

"Where is he?"

The bartender frowns, trying to suss out more than he can from my plain shirt and jeans. My tattoo may give him some clue, but he doesn't seem to recognize the name.

"Who...who are you?"

I chuckle and take a sip of whiskey. *Who am I?* My prison docket says case number 09-05962. The good, Christian name on my birth certificate is even vaguer. The bastard I face in the mirror every morning gives the best answer, I guess. The identity was etched right there on the side of my neck. *Kitty.*

"Don't worry about me." There's barely a drop left in the glass when I set it down. "Let's say I'm looking for an old friend." I even manage a smile, but there's no warmth in it.

The fingers of my left hand shake. I form a fist until the knuckles whiten, but they still tremble all the way down to the goddamn bone. I take deep breaths and count them— that bullshit they taught us in group therapy—but it doesn't make a dent in the anger swirling through my blood like poison. Like heroin. I'm addicted to that fucking high. I want nothing more than to take that glass and jab it into the bastard's face until his nose breaks. Until I can feel his orbital socket crunch beneath my fingertips and his blood speckles the floor. I want to send my fist through his fucking smart-ass mouth so that his teeth decorate the walls along with the fucking Beatles. I want...

Stop. I inhale sharply and blink until my vision becomes less red. The counter turns brown again. The glass is still clear with only a drop of amber liquid left in the bottom of it. Maybe that anger management shit works after all.

"Just tell me where Arno is," I say once I regain control of my voice. This time, it only wavers slightly.

That's a good thing. Not beating this bastard into kingdom come—that's a *good* thing. No need to take Van Hallen up on his bet so soon. The party hasn't even started yet, and I still need an invitation.

"Look." Something in my expression makes the man clear his throat. His gaze darts around the dim barroom, but it's empty this early in the day. I made sure of that. "I can't just give out that kind of information freely. He'll...he'll kill me."

I grunt out a sound that might be a laugh. "And what do you think I'm going to do?"

The bell above the door chimes before he can answer. I don't turn to face the newcomers, but I sense two, both men. One is taller than the other, and his footsteps make a firmer thud as he swaggers inside.

"Here, Kitty, Kitty," he croons. "That's no way to make new friends."

My jaw twitches. The smile might actually be real this time when I glance over my shoulder and meet the gaze of the man standing in the doorway. He's grown some since I last saw him. Bulked up. His reddish curls have become a full mane that drapes his shoulders. The puppy's grown into a lion, but he still has enough fucking sense to show respect to another predator.

"Dante." His eyes narrow in recognition, but he's still wary.

I haven't been exactly subtle in my search for him—but subtlety was never my thing. He's never been much for it, either, though I suppose some things haven't changed in five years. Arno Mackenzie is just as fucking reckless as always.

"Jesus Christ, *Dante.*" He takes a step forward and raises his left hand. A scar crosses the center of it, a single line identical to the one that mars my right palm.

Espi and I might have been born sharing my blood, but Arno has earned it.

"It's about fucking time." I step forward, slapping my hand against his. The violent *thwack* echoes throughout the piece-of-shit barroom, more intimate than any hug or handshake.

"Shit," Arno grunts, shaking his fingers free of the sting. "Tell me I'm not high and you aren't some fucking hallucination. They put your ass away for twenty years."

I shrug and let my hand fall back to my side. "You probably *are* high, but I'm here. Try picking up a fucking newspaper. The merits of 'good journalism' got me out."

"What?" Arno scratches at his chin with a broken fingernail. He's grown out the start of a beard, and it makes him seem older than twenty-seven. "You mean that shit at the DA's office?"

I shrug again. "That same shit, but...I'm not here to catch up on old times." I take a step closer, invading the invisible bubble of space every man creates around himself.

Given the situation, it's a bit like bringing a knife to a family reunion. Arno tenses, but to his credit, he doesn't step back. He holds my gaze, and for the first time, I notice the man he's strategically placed near the door, who has one hand hovering near his jeans pocket.

So, the puppy's learned a few tricks.

"Espi," I say. "Where is he?"

Arno snorts out a laugh, his posture relaxing a fraction of an inch. "Is *that* what this is about? I hate to tell ya, but I don't keep tabs on the kid—"

"I told you to keep an eye on him," I interject, my tone catching on a growl. "An *eye*. Not involve him in your shit, Arno. So, do you want to tell me why a cop saw me today, shoving proof in my face that you have Espi working for you?"

Arno shrugs, but the motion serves to open up his stance. He's built up a few more muscles than he had last. So have I. My left hand flinches. There's blood welling at my fingertips, and a muscle in my jaw aches. *Shit.* I turn away, shaking out both hands as if lashing out at the air might quell the urge to smash them into something. Something breakable, made of flesh and bone...

Fuck. Arno stares back when I look at him from over my shoulder. He keeps his hands out at his sides, his expression blank. I know that fucking look on his face. It's the same one the guards wore on patrol, always waiting for the moment one of the beasts might lunge.

"You asked me to look after him," he says carefully. "I have. But he's not a kid anymore. I don't tell him what to do. He likes to paint. And if he just so happens to do that in the territories I'm looking into, then that's his business. Not yours."

Not mine. I inhale. Exhale. My fingers still shake. They burn. I have to clench them up so tightly that the knuckles pop. I pace, slamming my heels into the fucking floor. I breathe. *One. Two.* There's a buzzing working through the back of my skull. It itches when I notice it, irritating the inside of my head. I crush the fingers of my right together with an audible crunch. Then I slam the fist into the palm of the left—hard. The pain jolts through my system, clearing my thoughts for a split second, but it's like taking a bone from a mutt. The relief is only temporary.

When my vision clears, I face Arno again, and he has enough sense to pretend like he didn't notice the slip. "Where is he?"

"He's safe," the man says carefully. He knows me too well. He doesn't move an inch. He gives me no excuse to react. I'm a caged animal, but Arno knows too damn well how to hide the key. "I wouldn't let him in the crew. You know me better than that—"

"Do I?" It's an animal's howl, barely constrained by a raspy tone I force my voice to keep.

"Yes, you do," Arno says without hesitation.

There's something in his heavy Brooklyn accent that muzzles the beast inside me. My fingers flex again, and the burn subsides a little. It wouldn't be a good idea to lose my shit here anyway. Can't let the cops come running too soon. Can't lose control yet.

Not yet.

"Okay, then." I shake my head like I'm trying to clear it of water, and I can't shake the feeling like I really am submerged underneath something—not water. Something heavier. More suffocating. Addicting.

"I'll take you to him," Arno suggests. "But let's get some alcohol in you. The good stuff." He glances at the bar behind me in disgust. "None of this cheap shit. Then we'll talk. Catch up, and maybe you'll tell me why the fuck you *really* aren't in prison."

I don't miss the way his voice lowers an octave on that last part. In five fucking minutes, Arno's proven that he trusts me. He still knows enough to tread carefully around Dante Vialle—yet he isn't stupid. Men don't just crawl out of prison, skirting a twenty-year sentence. He's afraid I made a bargain or licked some police commissioner's ass to get a deal.

I'll prove him wrong at some point. Right now, it seems more important to accept that promise of a drink. If I'm to stay out of prison for longer than seventy-two hours, I'll need it.

"Okay." I nod once. "Deal."

Arno breaks into a smile, cutting years off his age. He's a teenage boy again, with a batch of heroin in his pocket to sell. "Good, good. I'll introduce you to the crew, starting with ol' Francisco here." He nods to the man behind the counter, who's watching us, clutching a bottle of booze in one hand and a dishrag in the other. "You won't find a more loyal man on this side of town."

"Happy to help," Francisco says, inclining his head, all transgressions forgotten.

Still smiling, Arno heads for the door, jerking his chin for me to follow. "Welcome back, Kitty," he says. "Let me show you around my corner of hell."

————

ARNO'S SET UP SHOP IN AN OLD PUB ON THE CORNER of Finch and Horn. The name on the storefront reads *Mulligans*. It's a decently sized place—a far cry from the run-down gas station where we used to set up shop. The Gardai logo spans a banner hanging on the wall behind a well-stocked bar—that six-pointed star. Dark walls and hardwood floors create a spacious barroom with a color scheme designed to disguise any bloodstains. Reds. Greens. Blacks.

The puppy's chosen his doghouse well. His human bloodhounds rise to attention the moment we walk inside. There are maybe ten of them gathered. They sniff around, their hackles rising at the sight of me. I recognize a few. The rest are all new blood. Arno's been building himself quite the army.

"Friends," he says, his voice booming. "This is my brother, back from the dead." He slaps my shoulder once, but the display of friendship doesn't seem to put his men at ease.

These aren't the run-of-the-mill punks he used to command. They look rougher. Some of them are sporting expressions I recognize from prison—a look I know I wear myself. It's a mask, hardened by anger and reinforced with bitter hatred, worn at all times, even in your sleep. It's the mark of a wild dog who's been locked in a cage one too many times.

"Friend?" one of the men pipes up. He's about Arno's size, with a sizeable mass of black hair growing out in all directions. His eyes are brown, but they surprisingly aren't hostile when they meet mine without fear. Good fucking choice on his part. "Does this 'friend' have a name?"

Arno opens his mouth, but I speak for myself.

"Dante. *Friend.*"

A few men started forward to circle my position, but they quickly step back now. It can't be helped. I tend to have that effect, whether I say my name or not. Dogs can sniff out other dogs, after all, and even the average mongrel knows when to submit to a bigger, more brutal beast.

The man who questioned me doesn't flinch, however. There's a grudging bit of respect that flares up before I can smother it.

"I'm Dall," he says. "Any *friend* of Arno's is a friend of mine."

"Now, don't go busting out the fucking friendship bracelets now," Arno grunts, placing a hand on my shoulder. He steers me toward the bar, and I allow him to, remembering the promise of that drink. "At least let me get wasted first."

"Where's Espi?" I wonder. Scanning the bar, I don't find him anywhere. My gaze lingers on a small, scrawny figure hunched over a stool, but they're too short to be Espisido. The blond hair spilling from beneath a ratty hoodie gives me another clue.

"Is that my Kitty?" The figure stirs, lifting her head, and her green eyes seek mine out. They're bloodshot and caked in a layer of black makeup. She's high. Judging from the half-empty bottle in front of her, she's drunk *and* high.

I smell her from here. Fuck, it's a wonder what five years can do to a person. She's twenty-three but looks twice that much.

"Parish?"

"As I live and breathe." Her smile is uncomfortable. It's like her mouth has been too busy being stretched around a cock for cash to buy drugs that she can't even form the expression right. At some point in her life, she used to be pretty, with Arno's nose but paired with softer features. Now, she just looks tired. "I thought you were in prison?"

Apparently, Arno's not the only one who doesn't know how to fucking turn a television on.

"They let me out for good behavior," I say.

"Good behave—" Parish laughs. "My ass. You're a bad boy, Dante. Prison tends to not like to part with bad boys."

"Well, they parted with this one."

"I can see that." She looks me up and down, her eyes focused on my pockets. Desire flickers across her gaunt features, but it's only for cash. She needs a fix, and even being the sister of a dealer doesn't come with the perks of an unlimited supply, I see. "Got any dollars you can spare?"

"No." Arno muscles his way between us and grabs his sister by the shoulder, manhandling her from the stool. "You're going to beg for cash in my bar? Get the fuck out." He shoves her to the door. "Come back when you don't smell like piss and some old man's jizz, Rish."

"Yeah, yeah, yeah." She makes a talking motion with her right hand. "Fuck you, *Arnold*."

He scoffs and tosses back, "Only when Mom's not around." Despite his tone, there's concern in his expression as he watches Parish stagger through the main doors.

"She's still using."

It isn't a question, but he nods anyway and takes a seat at one of the stools, gesturing for me to do the same. "Still using. Still a pain in my ass. Not all of us lucked out in the family gene pool." He glances at me, his expression unusually serious. "Espi's a good kid, but he won't be happy that you're back. Mark my words on that."

I grunt in response. My brother is my fucking problem.

"So, what now?"

The bartender is a woman with tattoos draped over her arms, her black hair pulled back into a bun. When Arno snaps his fingers, she's ready and places a bottle of something dark and tempting down before him.

"Now?" Arno rips the lid off the bottle. "Now, we play, Kitty. Welcome back."

CHAPTER SIX

Daniela

SOMETHING IS WRONG. IT'S BEEN TWO DAYS SINCE HIS proposal, but Vinny's kept his distance. I've spent those days inside my room, playing until the calluses on my inner thumbs blister and bleed. It's a welcome reprieve, but the anticipation chills me more than the freedom from him gives me peace.

Time gives Vinny a chance to brood. A brooding Vinny is more likely to leave scars, like the kind that I know will mar my backside for at least a month. The pain mingles with dread as I fidget on the seat of my vanity and eye the reflection facing me. The woman in the mirror reveals none of Vinny's secrets. She's curious. Too many questions battle for supremacy in her eyes when a sudden knock rattles the door.

I'm shaking too badly to even call out a reply.

Is it him?

What does he what?

What will he say?

Do?

"I'll get it, miss."

My fiancé's absence is joined by Olga's. The morning after the proposal, a new companion shook me awake. I haven't bothered to learn her name, and I can only pray that I never have to.

She's younger than Olga, slender, with red hair that gleams as she crosses over to the door and pulls it open.

"Mr. Stacatto requests your presence, miss," Gino says. His tone is flat, revealing nothing. "Eight o'clock tonight. He suggests that you wear the new dress."

"Th-thank…" My lips are too dry, and it takes several swipes with my tongue before I can form a coherent response. "Thank you."

"Miss." He's gone, closing the door behind him, and it's a painful waiting game until night rolls around with all the finality of a tolling death bell.

The dress is silk. Lace adorns the sweeping neckline, and I'm alarmed to find that it plunges between my breasts, displaying a teasing V of cleavage. It's an upgrade from my usually demure wardrobe, but it's not an improvement.

Vinny only likes to show off the toys that he knows are his. *"You are mine, Mi Bella."*

"Your hair, miss."

My new companion expertly styles it, pinning the dark waves up to display my neck. The illusion pays off. I seem whole despite my healing wounds and the battle scars etched into my flesh beneath black silk. Vinny's chosen word haunts me. *Nice.*

"The car is waiting, Miss Manzano," Gino calls from the hallway.

I believe that all is well until I enter the hallway. There are only three men in the suite tonight—Vinny's taken the bulk of his detail with him, it seems. Their eyes chase me across the room, but on my way through the foyer, I catch sight of the grandfather clock perched against the wall. The time is displayed in emblazoned numbers, and I freeze in my tracks.

8:15

"It's late." Fear chokes me. I think I'm going to be sick, but even my churning stomach knows better than to ruin my new dress. *Oh, God. Oh, God.* "C-call him! Please." I turn to Gino, and for a second, I forget myself. My hand shoots out, seizing his collar. "Tell him! *Please.* It wasn't me. It's not my fault. I can't be late."

The room spins. Gino has to physically pry my fingers loose, but he lets me go just as quickly and backs away, leaving me to sway on my feet. His hand darts into the pocket of his suit jacket, withdrawing a slim cell phone.

"I will," he promises, bringing the receiver to his ear. The words he speaks are barked out in another language, but he assures me that everything will be okay in English when he finally hangs up.

I believe him as he ushers me into the elevator and leads me across the lobby below. I have to believe him.

Out front, the car is idling, unconcerned by the danger its driver has placed me in. I think of the girl in my room, fearfully organizing the clothes in my closet. Will I learn her name tonight? God, the thought of it is too much. It swallows me whole, locking me within a prison that seals me up tight, cutting off all oxygen.

Gino leaves me at the curb. I'll travel to this nightmare alone. I'll face Vinny alone. The thought has never terrified me more. *I can't. I can't.*

I'm a shell of a woman, sitting in the back seat of the car, my hands neatly folded on my lap. My heart is a pathetic ball in my chest, incapable of churning blood. I can't take my eyes off the scenery darting past, muted by the car's tinted windows. I'm sure I'll die before we reach the venue —suffocate.

But my pulse keeps thumping. My lungs continue to fill with oxygen. My body won't obey me, so conditioned it is to following Vinny's will.

My fiancé's will.

My *husband.* The thought sends hot tears trickling down, but I don't hold them back. I'm too tired to wipe them away. He'll be angry when he sees. I'll be punished.

Yet they continue to fall throughout the entire journey and still linger when the car finally comes to a stop and the door is opened from the outside. A sob hitches in my throat. My ring weighs me down. Whoever the unlucky goon is to greet me, he'll have to carry me inside.

I wait for him to utter the usual line. *He's waiting, miss.*

I don't expect for whoever he is to climb inside instead and shove his body against mine. I don't expect to hear a gun cock or feel the icy ridge of a barrel graze my temple.

It's like waking up from a dream. This new rush of fear that jolts down my spine is another flavor from the kind Vinny inspires.

"Keep driving," a gruff voice commands as the door is slammed shut again, but with me trapped inside. "Keep fucking driving."

Dante

Being Arno Mackenzie's "guest" comes with the perk of a fully furnished apartment above the pub. It's small but clean, something I've learned to appreciate after the shared quarters of a maximum-security prison. It's a rare luxury to have your own toilet to piss in. Even rarer to take a shower without jostling for a spigot with twenty other men.

Arno himself claims to have his own place close by, but after the first night, I'm in no mood to reminisce. I spend the first night alone. Back before, I'd troll the city, keeping an ear to the ground for information, or scrounge up old allies who might not run at the sight of me. For what it's worth, I avoid the bar, but I don't have to for one fact to become crystal clear.

Arno wasn't embellishing shit, for once. Espi doesn't want to see me. He lives at Mulligans as well, from what Arno would tell me, but in twenty-four hours, I've had a better chance of forming a relationship with the roaches that scuttle in the corners than I do of reconnecting with my suddenly "adult" kid brother.

The brush-off leaves me antsy. Espi knows better than anyone that I hate to be ignored. I prefer a man to face me head on rather than sulk in the fucking shadows. Van Hallen. Arno. They don't know shit. Espi is still the same punk kid I left behind, pouting in the corners.

I've given him long enough. Impatient and restless, I head down to the bar just after midnight, descending the single rickety staircase that separates the two levels. It opens onto a back room behind the bar counter, beside the kitchen.

On the previous night, I heard enough noise seep through the floors to know that Arno likes to keep a full house, but tonight, the pub itself is nearly deserted. Only Francisco and Arno sit at the counter. The latter rests his head in his hands, but I know enough to suspect—despite how much he likes to knock back—that the man isn't stupid or suicidal enough to get drunk out in the open.

"What's wrong?"

Spotting me, Francisco rises to his feet. "Arno..."

"Leave him." Arno raises his hand, slicing the air with it.

Like a good dog, his man falls back, but not without fixing me with a hostile glare, which I graciously return.

"What the hell is going on?" It isn't too often that a man goes from a "brother's" welcome to spooking the puppies overnight. Typically, that kind of swift change comes on the heels of a murder or two. "Where's Espi?"

"Espi." Arno releases a harsh bark of laughter as he pulls himself upright. His eyes are red. Bloodshot. Even back in the day, he never sampled his own product. The only other explanation is that the bastard has been...crying. "Where's Espi. Where's *Parish*?" he growls.

"Parish?" I frown. Only twelve hours ago did the man kick his sister out on the street when she tried to ask me for money. "In an alley somewhere?" I guess, taking a stab in the fucking dark. "Getting high? I don't fucking know."

Arno laughs again, but the sound comes out dangerously unsteady. He's the mad dog gnawing at his leash this time. "Getting high," he snarls. In one smooth motion, he's on his feet, facing me with his stance open, his hands clenching into fists. "You want to take that back, Dante."

"Arno." Francisco, the dog, has enough sense to step back. "Arno. Try to keep a clear head. You don't—"

"The fuck if *you* know what I don't want to do." Fire gleams in the redhead's eyes. He's burning—itching—for a fight. To beat something or someone bloody with his fists. To bare his teeth. Growl. Bite.

Don't I fucking know the feeling? My blood boils. My fingertips burn. They ache. I can't stop flexing them. I'm hungry for a battle. Fuck that; I *crave* it.

But I'm not an idiot.

"Listen to him, Arno." I jerk my head in Francisco's direction. "Sit back down."

"I will," Arno growls, the muscles in his arms straining. "Just as soon as you take back that shit you just said about my goddamn *sister*."

I don't hesitate. "No."

With an unrestrained roar, Arno lunges, and I'm ready for him. My fist tightens eagerly, and I let it fly into his stomach, driving every ounce of air from his lungs. The blow lands harder than I meant it to. Harsher. He wheezes and swipes at my head with an open palm. It's child's play to duck it, and I land another blow on the center of his chest that sends him backward and sprawling against the counter.

"Stop!" Francisco steps in between us. His stance isn't hostile to me as he places a restraining hand on Arno's shoulder, but it's almost too hard to silence the blood lust that rises up so fierce and so hard that I can feel it taking shape around me.

The buzzing begins at the back of my skull, swelling to a deafening hum that won't be silenced until I beat Arno's face into a pulp. Until I smash his fucking face into the counter. Until I feel his blood on my hands. They curl, hungry for that slick, intoxicating heat. And I want—*need*—to feed that itch.

"Dante."

I shrug off the voice that battles with the steady pulse taking residence in my brain. It's a chant, almost. *Fight. Punch. Bleed. Kill.*

"*Dante*." It's Arno calling me this time. There's blood on his chin, but I'm not sure how or why.

My knuckles ache. I only registered two punches, but the twinge in my shoulder warns me that it was several more.

"Dante," Arno tries again. He spits out a mouthful of blood onto the floor, which is dark enough to obscure the violent coloring. "Parish...she's... Fuck, Dante, she's dead. Parish is dead."

"What?" I shake my head, desperate to clear it. It's too confusing to jump from violence to blood and then death.

"She's dead," Arno says almost as if to himself. His hand fumbles along the bar until he finds a discarded glass, and he downs whatever is inside it. "How the fuck am I supposed to tell our mother? Those bastards didn't even..."

"Who?" My voice ripples over that familiar, low tone. Clarity returns in snatches, but my fingers aren't shaking at least. "What happened to her? Mack?"

"No, not him. These other bastards—" Arno breaks off, and something cold fills his gaze. "I didn't want to bother you with this. I know this isn't your fight, but—"

"I'm in."

Parish. Stupid fucking Parish. So busy trying to act older than she was, but still too fucking young to die. If it's Mack who got her, then some other drug dealer probably gutted her when she couldn't pay—if she hadn't put a needle in her arm first. It's cruel, but not unexpected, though I don't know why Arno seems so caught off guard. He understood the fire his sister liked to play with. Hell, some might even say that he was the one to inject it into her veins in the first place, considering the business he dealt with.

But no. Arno seems too raw. Too broken. Parish wasn't killed at random.

"I'm in," I repeat, giving the word a vicious edge. "Whatever you need."

"Good." He nods once. Then he turns and heads for the back of the bar, jerking his head for Francisco and me to follow. "I'll *need* someone to help me clean up the mess."

———

ARNO HEADS TO THE BASEMENT OF MULLIGANS. There's a door off the rear entryway near the fire exit. One of his men is standing guard. There's a Glock in one of his pockets and a knife tucked in the other. He doesn't attempt to disguise the telltale bulges of either weapon, and his gaze is icy. Parish may have been a nuisance, but loyalty to Arno makes her death everyone's burden to bear.

"It came a few hours ago," Arno's saying as he leads the way down a wooden set of stairs. "Fuck. S-she..." He shakes his head, squaring his shoulders as if preparing to barrel through the closed door awaiting us at the base of the steps. Instead, he knocks on it once with the broadside of his fist, and the door is opened almost immediately from the inside.

"She's here," a man says as Arno moves past him, ushering Francisco and me into a large, open area where more men are lurking in the corners like guard dogs.

The only light comes from rows of fluorescent lights attached to the ceiling. The walls are gray, nothing more than painted cement. The floors appear to be poured concrete. There's none of the comfort or care that decorates the upper interior of Mulligans. The barroom is for show. This place is for business.

"Well, where the fuck is she?" Arno demands. He cranes his neck and makes a show of glancing around the room on a scavenger hunt for a woman hidden among the slew of men.

I follow his gaze. He has about ten bodies here—for show, I suspect. Whoever this guest of honor is, Arno wants to make quite the impression.

The only furniture is a metal folding chair placed in the center of the room, beside a matching table and a laptop. It's flipped open, the screen displaying a blank blue desktop.

"They're on their way in," one of the men says, and Arno begins to pace, raking his fingers through his mane of hair.

Maybe five minutes pass before the door leading to the stairway finally opens.

"Did anyone see you?" Arno demands of the figure at the door before they can even enter the room. "Were you followed?"

His voice prickles with suspicion. He's on edge. His hair gleams like a flame, and the man himself seems just as untamable, liable to set everything he touches on fire.

"No one saw," another man replies, his voice gruff. "I got her. The driver's been paid off. It went as planned."

I'm expecting a man to appear from the shadows of the doorway. Not a woman. She's small, slender, and dressed as if for a party. Her black hair is piled on top of her head, displaying a slim throat. Her dress is short, paired with a cleavage-baring neckline, but if Arno has decided to mourn his sister by ordering a high-class call girl, she doesn't seem to be the type. She looks too young, for one. Her lips are painted red, but they do little to combat the smattering of freckles across her nose or the innocence that wafts from her skin like perfume. I'd peg her at twenty, tops. The color of snow, her skin gleams beneath the fluorescent lighting, though I figure the paleness of it has something to do with the gun being pressed against the back of her head.

"Arno...what the fuck is this?"

He doesn't bother to answer me. Instead, he grins as the woman is marched across the room by the gun-wielder, who I recognize as one of his men. Dall. "Sit her down," Arno commands, jerking his chin at the table.

The woman is shoved down onto the metal seat, though she does her best to regain her composure. Her legs cross politely at the ankles, her hands settling primly on her lap. She could be at a fucking tea party if it weren't for her expression. Fixated on the laptop screen, her eyes are dead, staring far away at something that isn't there.

"Arno..." I don't know whether to intervene or merely watch. There's something hypnotic about the entire scene. Something intoxicating. And I fucking hate having to admit it to myself. The urgency calls to the beast inside me, who stirs hungrily, sniffing at the air. The threat of violence is as irresistible as it is disgusting. "What the fuck is going on?"

"Language, Dante," Arno playfully scolds. "We have a guest." His eyes continue to smolder. He's amped up on something more potent than alcohol—it's rage.

Like venom, it taints his every word, and I stare down at the seated woman on whom he seems to project most of his wrath. She doesn't seem capable of murder, but I know without even having to ask that whatever is going on has everything to do with Parish.

"Play the fucking tape," Arno snarls, but his voice slips an unsteady octave. His bottom jaw trembles and he clenches both tightly in an attempt to hide it. "Now, damn it!"

The man with the gun keeps it trained on the woman with one hand while he leans over her and fiddles with the keys on the laptop with the other. The screen turns black, and then the still image of a woman appears. Over her face hovers a white, sideways triangle enclosed in a circle: the universal symbol for play. The moment the video begins, I know why Arno's so unsteady. Why his men are sporting the looks of wolves eager to hunt.

The video's star stares dead into the camera. Her hair hangs dank and limp down her shoulders, and her green eyes are vacant but steady. She's high, but not to the point where she can't feel any fear. "Arno..." She inhales, her voice trembling. Someone behind the camera must have been holding up something for her to read, because she squints. "Th-this is what happens..."

"Keep going," someone grunts, their face unseen.

Parish flinches. Her tongue shoots out to wet her lips before she tries again. "Arno, this is what happens when you—*oh, God.*"

A hand seizes her hair, yanking her head back, and the camera pans out to reveal the figure standing behind her. He's tall. Parish, hunched over on her knees, barely comes up to his waist. Dressed in a black, tailored suit, he doesn't seem like the sort to solicit the favors of a coke whore. He's young, maybe thirty, but there's an agelessness in his dark eyes. Brown, slicked-back hair frames a broad forehead anchored by a square jaw. His nose is crooked—like it's been broken one too many times. Behind him is a nondescript backdrop of white walls and tiled flooring. I scope out every detail, but it's no use. They could have been anywhere.

"This is what happens when you fuck with the wrong man," he says. The line is cliché, but his delivery is almost enough to erase the corny-ass phrasing. An accent lurks in his words, but it's like a knife's edge, honed sharp and impossible to place. "Enjoy the show."

He shoves Parish forward, and another man enters the shot. His back is to the camera, but with a chuckle, he undoes his pants and lets them fall around his ankles. Parish whimpers when he waltzes over to her, but her cries are soon muffled when he takes her by the back of the head and...

"Jesus Christ, Arno!" I'm moving forward, reaching for the laptop. "Turn it off—"

"No!" Arnos's shout mingles with the woman's.

She's sitting straighter, her eyes glued to the screen. Arno doesn't seem to notice when he lunges for her and grabs her by the nape of her neck.

"This little bitch is going to watch. Every fucking minute of it." He shoves her forward, nearly throwing her out of the chair.

With a grunt, she braces her hands against the table, but she doesn't take her eyes off the screen as the bastard continues to shove his cock down Parish's throat. Seconds into it, Parish struggles. She chokes when he goes too far. Laughing, the man pulls out of her mouth only to stand behind her. Bending down, he tugs at her jeans, winking for the camera.

I memorize every inch of the bastard's face. My blood hums, singing its bitter melody. I feel rage burn slowly through every nerve in my body, centralizing in my fingers —but, without anyone to take it out on, it builds like the pressure in a teakettle.

"Arno," I manage to grit out before my vision goes fully red. "Don't watch this shit."

"I need to," he says hoarsely, but his eyes are unfocused. Unsteady.

I can only imagine how many fucking times he's "watched" it, playing this scene over and over in his mind.

There are more men in that room, twelve of them at least. They appear from the periphery, circling Parish while the first bastard succeeds in getting her pants off.

"Fuck."

They show no mercy. They're ruthless, like the animals we all pretend to be. At one point, Parish screams so loudly that the sound comes through the speakers only as static.

"Arno."

He doesn't look at me, but he's no longer facing the screen, either. He shoves the woman forward until her nose is nearly brushing the screen while his eyes remain fixed on the wall. They're red and welling up with moisture with every pathetic cry his sister makes—but he grits his teeth rather than let them fall. The rest of his men fare no better. In fact, the only one who seems to be at rapt attention to the gruesome movie is the woman in the black dress, her face a mask.

The man with the gun to her head has his eyes averted from the screen. His hand shakes, his finger quivering over the trigger.

"Give me the gun." I snatch it from him before he can comply. "You'll blow her fucking head off."

The woman doesn't seem to notice or give a damn as to her impending death. She watches the men take turns abusing Parish. She doesn't flinch. She doesn't cringe. Her eyes are almost thoughtful; it's like she's taking fucking notes. How much abuse can another woman take before she starts screaming for her mother?

It's unsettling, watching her. Almost as unsettling as it is to watch Arno. His fingers tighten around the woman's neck. He has her nose brushing the glass now. There's too much fire in his eyes. When Parish moans his name, it's like tipping a gallon of gasoline on an already raging blaze.

"Don't," I say, and he glances down in shock.

It's as if he didn't even realize that his fingers have encircled her throat entirely, pressing into the white flesh. The woman makes a strangled sound, but her eyes never leave the laptop screen. On her lap, her fingers flutter, but then she laces them together tight as if fighting the instinctive urge to resist the suffocating pressure. She's entirely willing to sit there patiently while he kills her.

"Arno..."

He flinches. His knuckles pop, turning white. Then he lets go, and the woman slumps forward, gasping for air.

"I can't..." He stares down at his hands.

For a second, I don't even recognize him. He's a stranger silhouetted against his sister's screams and the curses and jeers of the men who torment her. It's a dark game we play: this tiptoe around sanity. Arno's close to losing whatever shred of it he has left, and some sick part of me almost wants him to. Misery fucking loves company, after all.

"Stop." It takes more effort than I'd like to admit to stalk forward and brace my hand against the back of the laptop's lid. "Turn this shit off—"

"No."

The protest doesn't come from Arno this time. The woman on the chair clutches her throat with one hand and bats my fingers away with the other. There's something almost regal in the motion. She's a fucking little queen, unwilling to be denied her entertainment. I don't know whether to be pissed or impressed by her tenacity. Who the hell is she?

Arno doesn't seem capable of giving me any answers. His gaze is on the floor. He's shaking his head slowly from right to left. Then left to right. "I've never asked you for anything," he says heatedly. "Never. But, Dante—"

He doesn't even *need* to ask.

"Go." I cut my gaze over to the door. Then I cock the gun and aim it in the vicinity of the woman's head. "I'll watch her."

He staggers toward the stairs without question, but when his eyes meet mine again from over his shoulder, the lion stares back. "Make sure she watches every fucking bit of it." He palms the doorknob and gestures to the rest of his men. "Everyone out."

They leave, though it's hard to register the movement when my eyes are focused on the girl. She's leaning forward again, her ass nearly out of the chair completely. Her prim little lips are pursed, her gaze steely. It doesn't seem to bother her one fucking bit, the sight of two men using Parish's limp body at once.

For what it's worth, I can't fucking watch it.

Two hours. That's how long the video lasts. The laptop's almost out of power by the time the final man takes his turn with a motionless Parish. The machine protests its overuse with a steady beep that cuts through the guttural sounds issuing from the video. I turn to the screen just as a prompt warning *2% battery remaining* flashes across it and the video cuts off on a still of Parish's body lying naked and lifeless on the floor. Someone threw syringes onto the floor in front of her, each one filled with amber liquid.

Slamming the screen shut so hard that something cracks is the only thing I can do to preserve her dignity. The violence of the motion makes the woman seated before me jump. She blinks as if snapping out of a trance. Her mouth opens for a sharp intake of air. Then she laughs. The sound trickles out of her, low and unsteady. Then louder. High-pitched. Her body jerks with the force of it, and she winds up slumped, facedown against the table, giggling hysterically. Helpless, her hands flutter at her sides, the fingers circling and uncurling as if she doesn't fucking know what to do with them. With herself.

It's as chilling as watching a pack of hyenas cackle after a kill. She's drunk on the violence and high off the bloodshed. Every brutal, violent image is etched onto her skin, and the bitch just can't stop giggling as she takes it all in.

It's only when she seems to run out of air that the sound finally dies off. She inhales brokenly instead, writhing with each breath. Her face tilts until she's looking at me, her eyes bloodshot, her hair a mess. There are tears rolling down her cheeks and snot on her chin.

"Is that... Is that what you're going to do to me?" she asks when she's caught her breath. Like the first man on the video, she has an accent I can't place. "Is it?"

I don't answer her. Arno does for me.

"Yes." He's returned, guarding the doorway to the stairs like some beast straight out of Hades itself. There's a cold, icy gleam in his eye I know well. Hell, I helped put it there. The puppy and the kitty cut their teeth on the same bones back in the day, honing their shared lust for blood. "I'm going to do exactly that and send it to your fucking fiancé. But not without giving him a little appetizer first."

He flexes his right hand, and the knife he's holding in it catches the light. It has a wicked edge, and when he reaches the table, he shoves the computer out of the way and stands directly across from the woman.

"Hold her still," he tells me.

I can't fight that part of me that bristles at the order, but even I can forgive a grieving bastard for forgetting his place. I reach down, bracing one hand on the woman's shoulder, not that she struggles. Slowly, she pulls herself upright, sitting pretty once again. Her eyes trace the blade Arno's waving in her face. She doesn't flinch. It's only when he reaches for her arm that she moves at all, jerking out of his reach.

"Not my hands," she says hoarsely. "Not my fingers." She accompanies the command by reaching up to brush a strand of dark hair behind her right ear. Then she tugs pointedly at the earlobe. Her message is simple but crystal clear: *Take this instead.*

Arno grimaces. I don't know if it's in shock at her brazen request or the fact that the little princess just took all the fun out of his torture. She doesn't seem scared shitless by the threat of the blade. She merely requests we not cut off her goddamn fingers first.

Once again, a single question crosses my mind, more fiercely than before. Just who the fuck is she? *"Your fucking fiancé,"* Arno said to her. I picture the man in the video again, the one in the suit with the crooked nose. Was that him?

The girl has a ring on her left hand. The diamond in the center of it almost spans the width of her entire finger. Whoever her fiancé is, he certainly isn't a poor motherfucker.

"You don't make the fucking rules of this game, bitch," Arno snarls. But it's increasingly apparent that he can't make good on his threat. His hand is shaking too badly. The rage is back, consuming his gaze and swallowing him down whole.

Before the girl can react, he lunges across the table and snatches her forearm. He yanks her forward, nearly dragging her across the table. Her feet dangle in the air, the black heels scraping the floor.

Grunting, Arno eyes her skin, hefting the knife. I doubt he'll be satisfied with just a finger. No. He'll take her whole hand. Her arm. And something tells me that he'll want her alive long enough for her fiancé to get the message.

"Give me the knife." I hold my hand out, forcing Arno to make eye contact.

He shakes his head. "This is *my* fight, Dante—"

"Give me the knife."

Something in my tone makes him back down. He lets the woman go, shoving her onto the chair. Then he slams the knife against my palm blade-side down. I hiss at the burning pain, but I curl my fingers around the blade and switch it to my dominant hand.

I'm like a butcher, hunting for the finest cut of meat when I trail my gaze along the woman's fingers. They're slim, slender, and she curls them up tight beneath my gaze. In the end, I don't know what makes me seize her earlobe between my thumb and my forefinger instead. She has a diamond stud in each one, and the gleaming head serves as the perfect guide for when I start to cut.

I make it quick. One firm slice and her earlobe is in my fingers. She whines, smothering the sound beneath a pale hand before it even seems to fully leave her throat.

"Here." I throw it onto the table, toward Arno, who just stares down at the severed bit of flesh.

His fingers shake, but after swallowing hard, he reaches down and captures it in his fist. "Take her," he says while circling around the table, his gaze on the door.

"Where?"

Arno shrugs. "With you. Any-*fucking*-where but here. Take her upstairs. My men are too riled. I need her alive, and…" He stops in his tracks, and his entire body rises with the force of his inhale. "You're the only one I can trust. It's only for a few hours anyway." He shrugs and looks back at me, his expression the grim mixture of a smile and a grimace. "She'll be gone tomorrow."

———

I force her to walk up two flights of stairs and into the apartment Arno lets me crash in. She staggers, leaving a trail of blood the entire way, but I don't bother to disguise it. Let Arno get the mess. I hope he has to get on his fucking hands and knees with bleach to erase every trace of her. Maybe then he'll remember that "babysitter" isn't listed on my fucking résumé.

She's silent when I shove her through the narrow living room without bothering to turn the light on. I sense her body stiffen. She's pale enough to glow in the dark when I shut the door behind me and twist the lock.

A true monster would get off on her fear. The pain makes her sway. Blood dribbles down her neck, emanating from her like perfume. A part of me can't resist breathing it in. Then I surge forward and shove her down the hallway before she can bleed all over the fucking floor.

"Get into the tub." I grit the command out while I flick the bathroom light on and drag her into the narrow space by her forearm.

It's a tight fucking fit. She has to practically climb over the toilet in order to obey me. With one hand, she clutches at her bleeding ear and eyes the basin of the tub with a wary expression. Her free hand slides down her hip to tug at the hem of her dress, and I imagine her trying to decide the most ladylike course of action to climb inside it.

I make the decision for her and ram my open palm against her shoulder. She goes down hard, smacking her chin off the tiled wall, but she curls up on her side, small enough to fit inside the coffin-like space with room to spare.

Blood wells up beneath her. Already, her eyes are unfocused, her gaze drifting up to the ceiling. Frowning, I snatch a towel from the nearby rack and throw it toward her.

"Put pressure on it," I tell her while I crane my neck back to take in the mess she's already made all over the floor.

Arno won't be the only one forced to scrub tonight. Fuck.

The girl obediently curls her fingers around the edge of the white towel, but she doesn't move. She eyes the ceiling instead, and I leave her there, cutting off the light before I slam the door shut. Her blood spots the carpet. I can see it even in the darkness. I can smell it. I can smell her.

Ignoring both, I turn and enter the flat's single bedroom. Then I slam the door shut and try to get some fucking sleep.

CHAPTER SEVEN

Daniela

THOUGH I WALK THROUGH THE VALLEY OF THE SHADOW OF death, I will fear no evil. It sounds good enough in theory, but no one tells you that, when you're taken from that valley, all you fear is the pain. Your body aches with it. For so long, it's put up with the torment. The agony. Fear is a pathetic emotion, but pain rules all.

It's haunted me ever since I left the hotel, lapping at the horrific memories that have only chosen now to surface. It chases my every breath, and at some unguarded moments, I know that it's close to winning. I can hear its hungry growls as it awaits my soul.

Not fearing death is one thing. Welcoming it is another entirely. Though I may not fear that valley...I'd rather die than be forced to travel through it again.

The world without Vinny is quiet. There's only the hiss and rattle of faulty plumbing to fill an otherwise endless silence. Sometimes I hear footsteps. Sometimes I swear I hear Vinny himself whispering into what remains of my ear. *You think you can escape me so easily, Mi Bella? Think again.*

I flinch when a very real sound breaks through the delirious fantasy: a door opening. A sliver of light escapes through the crack. Then the light to my cell itself is switched on, though it's not really a cell. I'm in a bathroom. My body is lying lengthwise in a tub that catches all my blood and feeds it to a hungry drain. He gave me a towel to staunch the worst of it with, but I'm lying on it and staring out instead.

He's shirtless. God, he's tall, too. Taller than Vinny, even. Certainly bulkier. Muscle weighs his bones down. It's the type of strength evil men love to employ to carry out their dirty work. Though I don't think he works for the red-haired man.

His blue eyes cut across the room and find me watching him. The sight of me doesn't affect him in the slightest. With a sigh, he sheds his boxers and stoops for the lid of the toilet. With one hand, he palms his cock, aiming surely as he relieves himself.

It's something a *nice* girl wouldn't watch. So I greedily stare. I always assumed that all masculine anatomy was one in the same, but his cock looks different from Vinny's. The head is smooth, almost naked. *Circumcised,* a part of me suspects. It doesn't draw my attention nearly as much as the rest of him, however. His skin is drawn taut against bulging muscle like copper hammered over stone. There are scars on his hips, a row of jagged, semi-straight lines that travel nearly to his knee. With one last tug, he wrestles himself back into his boxers. Then he shuffles over to the sink and begins washing his hands.

I wonder if he'll be one of the men who will rape me like the girl in the video. That beautiful girl. She is Olga...and Amelia, and Violetta, and Sabina, and Lina, and Allessandra, and Tiffany, and Sarah.

She is *Daniela*. Just another soul for Vinny to use. Another stain on the bottom of his shoe. It won't bother him in the slightest if I'm dead—or if my body is used and abused before the final bullet is driven into my skull.

My soul is all that matters to him, and it is already tainted black and tattooed with his name. I'll never erase the damage he's done to me. It's more permanent than the missing part of my ear or the pieces of me he's marked black.

I am nothing but a shell. Yet some part of me just can't help adding to my misery.

"Her name..." My throat is so dry that it aches. I'm dizzy. Blood loss paired with trauma has probably sent me into shock, but none of the physical ailments really matter. "The girl in the video." It takes effort to get the words out, and the man barely looks up as he scrubs his hands clean in the sink. "Her name. What was her name?"

If Vinny has taught me anything, it's that a name is a powerful weapon. I've avoided learning them out of self-preservation ever since he used the very first maid he'd appointed to me as a tool in my punishment. She will haunt me forever. They all will. Regardless, I still can't resist adding one more ghost to the ones I already carry inside me. That girl with the haunting, green eyes can't be forgotten. Vinny won't own all of her soul; I'll keep part of it.

"Please."

The man at the sink shuts the faucet off and takes his time shaking the water from his fingers. Then he carefully dries them on a gray towel hanging from a rack beside the mirrored cabinet. I know he can hear me. He knows *I* know he's ignoring me on purpose.

It's a silent game we play. In the end, he eyes his reflection in the mirror and then heads for the door. I flinch when he turns the light off. The darkness should be a welcome friend by now, but it's suffocating. It hides too many unknown variables lurking just out of reach.

The man closes the door behind him, but I don't hear the latch lock. His heavy footsteps retreat away from me, down a hall maybe? I don't remember enough of the layout of where he brought me to make a proper guess.

I'm too tired to sleep, however. So I wait.

———

MY CAPTOR RETURNS JUST AS GRAYING DAYLIGHT drifts in through the bathroom's only window. It's built into the wall, high above me—too high to reach. Or so he seems to think when he appears in the doorway and eyes it with a frown. Maybe he's just cursing what I assume will be another rainy day?

He provides no answers. There's an intention conveyed in the way he moves, however. Fluidly. Self-assuredly. He knows I won't run. He knows I won't fight. I think I bore him. Perhaps that's why he sighs when he finds me curled up in the bathtub where he left me last.

He's fully dressed now, wearing jeans and a faded, gray T-shirt sporting the name of some band Vinny would smear as vulgar. His feet are bare, and I eye his overgrown toenails as he pads to the center of the narrow room and comes to a stop at the center of a fuzzy, blue rug.

"Get up."

The tension in his voice stirs something in my blood. The part of me that obeys Vinny without question stirs sleepily, recognizing the power of a man with the potential to be just as brutal a master. He's not used to taking orders—he prefers to give them. I saw a glimpse of it last night when he interfered with the plans of the red-haired man. A wounded doe knows a dog when she sees one, and this man is no different from Vinny. They even stand the same.

"Get up," he repeats. There's no glimmer of concern in his eyes for the fact that I'm still dizzy from the blood loss. He's impatient, and I'm too tired to tempt him.

My body screams in agony when I attempt to sit upright. It takes me three tries before I can get a good enough grip on the rim of the tub to haul my upper body from the base of it. *God.* My ear burns when I lift it from the towel. The terrycloth tries to cling to the ruined skin. Fresh beads of blood drip down to coat my neck, but I don't bother wiping them away. It's only when I try to stand on trembling legs and climb out of the tub that simple physiology overcomes sheer will.

I'm too weak. My knee slips and I go sprawling forward. My elbow strikes the tiled floor while one of my legs remains caught in the tub. My ass is in the air, my dress bunched up around my waist. If I'm expecting the man to help me, I'm sorely disappointed. He merely stands there, watching and waiting.

The world swims while I wrestle to regain control of my limbs, and I somehow manage to hook one of my hands underneath me and push off the floor. My other knee crosses over the rim of the tub and catches the end of the fuzzy rug before I can fall. I've almost managed to raise myself up on both hands when I vomit. Foul liquid splashes mere inches away from the man's toes. The next torrent bathes them in it.

I stiffen in grim anticipation. Vinny would hit me for daring to soil him, even by accident. This man... Well, this man just sighs.

The floor creaks beneath his weight as he turns and exits the room, his footsteps slow and unhurried. I press my cheek against the icy floor and try to imagine what might happen if he never comes back. I could bleed out. Die here. It would be peaceful. No Vinny. No violence. No lies.

My delirious brain plays tricks on me. I start to drift off. When something jostles my shoulder, I believe that it is Saint Peter finally here to wrench me out of this world and into the next—but it's another entity shaking me awake. I blink my eyes open and shudder at the sight of the filthy foot nudging my shoulder. My captor has returned. He drops something onto the floor in front of me, missing the messy puddle of my vomit by inches.

"Change."

The command tickles old nerve endings of fear that I'd thought living under Vinny for so long had snuffed out. At least until I notice that the garment he's given me is an old cotton T-shirt that smells like cigarette smoke and musk. He's worn it. He hasn't washed it. A part of me trembles at the thought of slipping it on over my dress. Vinny's carefully selected scents and this man's don't mesh. It's two different worlds clashing together with an aroma that scratches at my nostrils.

Groaning, I struggle to pull myself upright. My support arm wobbles while I reach for the shirt with the other. My captor watches me observe it as if I'm checking the thread count. How long has it been since I've worn something that hasn't been hand-sewn or purchased in a fancy boutique?

Is it sad that my body trembles, aching to find out? Shifting sideways, I spread the shirt out in front of me. It's plain, sporting no markings on the front. When I finger the wide collar, my first plan changes. Rather than pull the shirt on over my dress, I tug on the lacy collar of it instead. It's fitted too close to my body for me to easily slip off. A prison made of silk and satin.

There's a zipper at the back, and I can sense something dark swell on the horizon when I scuttle around so that my back is facing the stranger. With one hand, I pull aside the mess of hair that drapes my shoulders, and then I pose a simple request. "C-can you unzip me?" My voice cracks.

Vinny's specter lingers over the shadows of the room, always watching. My maids have been female for a reason. He's never even let one of his men touch me, whether when I'm alone or in his presence. An insane trill races down my spine when the floor shifts as the stranger comes closer. I *want* him to touch me. I only wish Vinny had some way of knowing. Reckless abandon makes my head spin more dangerously than the pain from my severed ear does. Is this what freedom feels like?

My captor has no idea as to the gravity of the situation. When he crouches behind me and brutally tugs at the zipper nestled between my shoulder blades, he doesn't seem to realize he's just committed sacrilege against the church of Vincent Stacatto, violating his heavenly Lynn. He doesn't seem to understand why I shiver and flinch into his coarse fingers, desperate to feel every broken, dirty nail graze my skin. Even if I return to hell, the sensation of his hands on me will be a dark souvenir. Vinny's control doesn't extend across the entire world the way he'd like to think. He's powerless here. I let another man touch me. I even *wanted* him to.

"Damn it."

My zipper struggles against him though. If I don't care about the potential backlash of this situation, then this priceless dress does. He has to bunch the fabric in what feels like two fists and tug. The back of the dress tears and I shiver when icy air tickles the bared flesh revealed within the gap. This is real. I could hunch over, I suppose, and attempt to shield my naked body from him. I could ask him to leave.

I do neither. I shift my shoulders instead and let the dress slide from them with the same casual ease he used to undress in front of me. He's watching. His eyes paint a burning trail from my ass to the top of my head—I feel it even though I don't turn to see him there. I inhale. Then I take my time bunching his shirt in my hands before lifting it above my head. The motions feel so strange, and I snicker with the realization that it's the first time I've dressed myself in five years. In the end, when I finally tug the hem of the shirt down over my knees, I think I've put it on backward— as well as inside out.

If my captor notices, he says nothing. I hear him sigh again, which is followed by the telltale groan of strained metal. He's sat on the toilet, I see when I glance over my shoulder. His pants are still on fully, and he's seated on the lid. With one hand, he reaches out and flips on the faucet to the sink, which he can easily reach. Then he snags the gray hand towel from the rack and wets it. His eyes darken with concentration as he drags the rag along the tops of his feet and then between his toes, erasing all traces of me from his skin. I should apologize, but my lips won't budge.

I fidget with the fabric of his shirt instead, twisting the itchy, cheap material between my fingers.

"Get up," the man says when he finishes cleaning himself. He stands, and I attempt to, using the rim of the sink for balance.

My aching head doesn't like being upright. The world tilts under me, and my knuckles turn white from how tightly I'm forced to clutch the sink's basin. I wish the mirror weren't there, throwing my pathetic reflection back at me. Vinny's Lynn is a bloody mess. A drying layer of it coats the right side of my neck. My ear...it's missing the entire lower lobe. All that's left behind is a jagged, bloody edge clinging to cartilage. For some reason, the state of my hair strikes me as more pressing. Half of it has remained carefully coiled the way Vinny wanted. The rest hangs loose and wild almost to my waist.

I frown, straining my features. With one hand still clutching the sink, I tug at the elegant knot until my hair is completely free, violating another one of Vinny's rules. The thought makes me smile, a ghoulish expression in the dim lighting. He would hate to see me like this, filthy and pale —but I can't deny myself of every basic necessity he would approve of.

"D-do you have another rag?" I croak out to the man standing near the doorway.

He doesn't answer, but after a quick search of the room, I spot the towel he gave me the night before. Most of it is soaked red, but there's a sliver of untouched white about the width of my hand. I'm less unsteady when I stoop to grab it, and I almost don't sway when I return to the mirror.

Licking my lips in concentration, I wet the clean part of the towel and then use it to wipe at my throat. I can't silence a whine when I nick part of my ruined ear. The pain...it makes splotches of color splash across my vision. *Blue. Green. Yellow.* With effort, I ignore them and attack as much of the dried blood as I can. Then I set the towel aside and run my fingers through my hair. Shapeless bobby pins litter the floor, too mangled to be of much use. With nothing to tie it up with, I settle for leaving it down—another silent sign of disobedience.

My ear starts to bleed again by the time I finish. A wad of toilet paper staunches most of it, though it burns like hell to press it against the wound. My eyes streaming, I risk asking the man another question he'll probably ignore. "Do you have peroxide?"

No answer.

"Tape?"

He turns on his heel and retreats down what seems to be a darkened hallway. In his absence, I manage to open the cabinet behind the mirror with one hand and find a bottle of hydrogen peroxide there. It takes more mental preparation than I'd like before I can gather enough nerve to wet a fresh wad of toilet paper with it.

It's funny how Vinny can beat and terrorize me, but I've trained myself not to scream—only, when I inflict pain upon myself, such as by attempting to sanitize my wounds, I can't stop myself from crying out. The harsh whimper echoes until I shove my free hand into my mouth and bite down on the knuckles. That newer pain combats the rest while I hold the peroxide to my ear for thirty agonizing seconds. I'm panting when I let go, and the ruined flesh of my ear bubbles and sizzles beneath the cleansing fluid. It's not bleeding anymore, at least. I take a carefully measured strip of toilet paper from the roll and begin to wrap it around as much of the wound as I can. I barely notice when my captor returns and places something down on the counter before me: a roll of silver duct tape.

My fingers tremble while I consider my options. Left with no other choice, I carefully bite a square of tape off with my teeth. When paired with a wadded piece of toilet paper, it makes for an impromptu bandage. The sight isn't pretty, but it will have to do for now.

When I open the medicine cabinet to put the alcohol away, I spot a toothbrush lying on one of the shelves, beside a half-empty tube of toothpaste. My hesitation lasts all of five seconds before I grab it and wet it beneath a drop of water from the faucet. My captor watches on stoically as I prime the bristles with a bead of toothpaste. He says nothing as I attack my mouth with the borrowed instrument. Irrelevant concerns flash through my mind. This is unsanitary. Unhygienic. Rude.

None of it really matters a damn anyway. When I spit, the remains of whatever meal I had last circle the drain, and at least some part of me feels cleaner. *Besides,* I realize as I place the toothbrush and the tube of toothpaste back into the cabinet and close the mirrored door, *if these men plan to do to me what was done to the girl in the video, they should appreciate the courtesy.*

"Okay," I breathe out, observing my ramshackle reflection. With both hands braced against the counter, I turn to watch my captor from my periphery.

He's watching me as well, but his expression gives me no clue as to what he thinks. I wait, keeping my posture as still as possible so that he knows I'm ready to follow him now.

Five seconds pass. Then he turns on his heel and retreats down the hallway once again, but this time, I creep after him. It's cramped and narrow wherever we are. Not even a few feet down from the bathroom is another doorway that opens onto a minuscule bedroom. There's a mattress, which looks unmade, on the center of the floor. Nothing more than what appears to be a bedsheet nailed above the frame covers the only window. There's something chilling about the space when the stranger enters it, leaving me at the threshold.

He stalks over to a pile of what appears to be clothes in the corner. On one knee, he crouches and rummages through the pile. When he stands, he's holding a black jacket in one hand, which he casually slips on over his bulky frame. I hate that I flinch when he heads toward me, his posture unreadable, but he only pushes past me and heads down the opposite end of the hall. Before I can follow, his voice reaches me on a grunt.

"Stay here."

Here. My bare toes flex against the rough carpet, though I don't know where my shoes might be. I don't even remember taking them off. I don't find them when I give the room another passing glance. An alarm clock on the floor near the makeshift bed proclaims that it's barely seven a.m., and I laugh just once out loud, wincing at the pathetic sound. I've been free from Vinny for nearly twelve hours. It all seems so surreal.

Dizziness paired with exhaustion is the only reason I enter that damn room. My body has a mind of its own. My legs give out, pitching me forward, facedown on the mattress. I groan when my ear connects with a wall of pillows, but for some reason, I can't seem to pull myself upright.

I'm simply too tired. Twelve hours have aged me twelve million years. Common sense can't make a dent in the instinctive, overwhelming need to close my eyes and stop moving. So I do. The mattress is lumpy. The blankets smell like musk and a man. *Him.* His essence permeates the air—so different from Vinny's chosen aroma of cologne and intimidation. Maybe it's the simplicity of it that lures me asleep?

It's so strange to lie in the den of an animal that doesn't try to disguise what it truly is.

CHAPTER EIGHT

Dante

THERE'S SOMETHING INSTINCTIVELY SOOTHING ABOUT holding a beer bottle in one hand and a weapon in the other. It appeals to both of a man's baser instincts in one go. Words can't explain the tremor that runs through me as I take a swig of booze while testing the weight of a pistol in my grip. It's a comforting heaviness. Familiar. My head feels clearer when I set it onto the counter and finally glance at Arno from my periphery.

"So, who is she?"

The man sighs. I doubt he's slept. He reeks of booze and sweat. Dark circles line his eyes like shadows. Nursing his own beer, he takes a sip of it. "Vincent Stacatto's whore," he finally says.

Whore. Something about that word doesn't fit when applied to the girl upstairs. Someone's pet? Maybe. A debutante mob-princess? Perhaps. But whore? No.

I picture the way she moved, even when half dumb with pain. She never let her posture slouch. She kept that pert little nose high in the air. She never flinched away from meeting my gaze, and the way she pampered herself in the bathroom was as if she'd been at the fucking Ritz-Carlton.

That woman is no whore.

"What's her name?" I don't know why I care. This time tomorrow, she'll be dead anyway—if she's lucky.

Arno grunts. "The fuck if I know." He raises his bottle to his lips again and takes several long pulls, draining it in seconds. With a belch, he slams the bottle onto the counter and wipes at his mouth with the back of his hand. "I just need to get this shit over with," he growls. "That fucking bastard... He *will* pay."

"Parish—"

Arno flinches at the sound of her name, and I feel something that could be guilt burn through my chest.

"The video didn't... How do you know for sure that she's dead?"

It's no use beating around the bush, and Arno shrugs, his expression grim. "The video came with the address of a morgue. She was one of their Jane Does. Dead three hours by the time we found her. Apparent overdose."

I exhale sharply. "I'm—"

"Don't," Arno snarls. He curls one of his hands into a fist and slams it hard against the counter. "Don't say anything. Just fucking *help* me."

"All right." I take another swig of beer and face the row of shelves behind the bar.

It's decently stocked. Arno wasn't kidding when he boasted about having good booze. He's done well for himself, it seems—but every mad dog knows that a nice pile of bones has to come from the body of another beast.

"Who is Stacatto?"

A dangerous sound rumbles up in Arno's chest. "A dead man," he says. "Some asshole punk who fell into good fortune. He used to run with Capella, back when the bastard was living. Was his little pet prick. When Capella's 'organization' folded seven years ago, Stacatto took over the shitstorm that remained, and now, the asshole thinks he runs the fucking city."

"Capella." The name holds a flavor of recognition. I picture a face: old and worn with a mole on the chin. "I remember him." An Italian bastard who liked to think of himself as the last bastion of the old mob.

"May he rest in Hell," Arno growls, spitting onto the floor. "Vinny used to be content with his side of the fucking river. But, now, he's starting to overstep his boundaries. Needs to be taught his goddamn place in the pecking order."

I nod. Arno not only got territorial—he got greedy.

"What did you do?"

"I..." He clenches his fists and shakes his head. "I sent him a little *present* that he didn't take to kindly to."

"You tried to kill him." I scoff and take another sip of my beer.

He doesn't deny it. "It's business. But the asshole crossed a line with Parish. You don't—" He breaks off, gritting his teeth so fiercely that I can hear them grinding together. "There are just some fucking lines you don't cross."

It's all bullshit, of course. Something he tells himself out loud to relieve the burning sting of guilt he feels for his sister. But, if he were given the chance to do it all over again, I know that Arno wouldn't hesitate. A mad dog has to fight for his share of the junkyard, after all.

"So, your idea of revenge is torturing his fiancée." While not exactly my method of choice, I can't fault the bastard for flair. An eye for an eye; a woman for a woman.

Arno chuckles darkly and swipes a mass of red hair from his face. "It comes with the territory."

Vincent Stacatto. He's the same man Van Hallen was bitching about, apparently for good reason.

"I guess there's a reason why you haven't shown that video to the cops?"

Arno gives me an odd look. "Stacatto owns the fucking police. The bastard's even got judges in his pocket. They'd arrest my ass for possessing illegal pornography or some shit without even touching Stacatto."

"Hmph." I digest that newest tidbit of information while downing another sip of beer. Van Hallen didn't bother to mention that.

"So, where is she?" Arno asks suddenly. He stands up and begins to pace. Something tells me that part of what kept him up all night is plotting ways to use her to make Stacatto suffer.

I jab my thumb at the ceiling. "Upstairs."

"Alone?" Arno raises an eyebrow. "You lock her in a closet or something?"

I shake my head, feeling no need to lie. "She's in the room."

Arno comes to a complete stop. "You left her unguarded?"

"You told me to keep an *eye* on her," I point out. "She won't run."

My voice comes out self-assured. Despite not being restrained or beaten or threatened, the woman won't run. I know that without being able to explain it. Besides, to leave the upper level, she'd have to march right through this very room on her way out or take her chances by jumping out the damn window—and suicide isn't very ladylike.

"You better fucking hope not," Arno mutters darkly, but he has enough sense to keep the words from becoming a threat. "I'll do it today," he swears. "I'll gather the boys. Make a game of it. Tie the little bitch up like a pig."

"Where?" I ask purely out of curiosity. Arno has my loyalty, but I won't stick around for his little party. There are more important bones for this mutt to sniff at. Other old hydrants to check for new piss. First and foremost, I need to find Espi.

"The basement," Arno says, but he doesn't sound sure. It's like he's pulling the details out of his ass, too blinded by rage to come up with a solid plan.

"And what if her man comes looking for her?"

The thought makes him chuckle. "He can try, but he won't find her here." He shoots me an icy grin from over his shoulder. "Don't forget: Even you couldn't sniff me out when I didn't want you to, *Kitty*."

Fair enough. I stare up at the ceiling and picture the woman whose fate is about as fragile as the bottle in my fist. How a woman like that fell into the hands of a man like Stacatto, I'll never know. Maybe boarding schools don't keep a tight enough grip on their budding debutantes these days? She has to be some rich man's daughter. There's an air of aristocracy about her—though definitely the degenerate kind with more debts to their name than money. Her mask is similar to the ones worn by disgraced stockbrokers or vengeful widows who were desperate enough to seek out a man like me in order to enact their "due justice." Every little breath she takes is a carefully crafted lie. A part of me wants to dissect it—the meaning behind those scars on her ass or the dark hint of a tattoo that crosses her torso. The fact that I'm curious makes me clench my jaw, and I drain my beer of every last drop. Everyone knows what happens when curiosity meets the fucking cat.

"You gonna stick around?" Arno doesn't seem surprised when I shake my head.

"I have business to take care of," I say.

"You mean finding Espi?"

I don't deny it. I don't exactly use the opportunity to have a fucking heart-to-heart, either. While I trust Arno with my life, some things are best kept only between brothers.

"I'll try to keep a low profile." It's the least I can do.

Van Hallen's countdown is still going. I have three days left to make a full week free from bars. Maybe I'd send the bastard a thank-you card when I finally pass that deadline. On the other hand, maybe he'd gloat over my ass in a prison cell by that time.

"Can..." Arno hesitates. He won't make eye contact. "Can you at least bring the bitch down to the cellar? I'll have one of my boys watch her. I know you're not a fucking babysitter," he says before I can respond. "But I can't... I'll kill her, Dante. With my own fucking hands." He flexes the limbs in question as if imagining them wrapped around her throat. "It's best if there's a fucking camera around when I see her again."

I nod. "No problem."

My muscles protest when I stand and stretch both arms over my head. How ironic. I thought that it might take longer than four days to fall back into some semblance of my old life. The shackles of the animal I am have found me again without my even having to seek them out. It's one thing I've always been good at: letting trouble find me first before I even begin to hunt for it.

With a sigh, I leave Arno and head for the stairs. It's a short trip to the upper level, where a handful of doors lead to separate apartments. Mine is the third from the right, and when I brace my hand against the knob, I'm surprised to find that I left it unlocked. Entirely by accident or out of some sick test devised for the woman within? Even I'm not sure. Not really.

An unexpected tension tightens my spine when I push the door open and enter the narrow entryway. Excitement? Anticipation? The thrill of the hunt never ceases to amuse a rabid dog, after all—but I don't find her in the small living room or the tiny kitchen nook that branches off it. The entire level is silent. The little bitch could have truly pressed her luck and run, if I couldn't still sense her scent, even from here. It's faint, but with a pull like that of a fishing line dragging me forward, down the hall, and to the doorway of the only bedroom.

She's on the bed. Scratch that—she's passed out, deep-as-fuck asleep on the bed. Her hair is a nest around her shoulders. One of her legs is twisted within the navy comforter and something that could be drool dribbles from her slightly parted lips and onto the pillowcase. Her chest rises and falls heavily. It's like she's sleeping on a fucking cloud. Hell, it's almost ironic: She's Goldilocks, curled up on the bed of a killer.

"Get up." I cross over the mattress in two strides and kick the edge of it—hard.

She jolts awake, blinking as she struggles to get her bearings. She mumbles something, and her right hand flies out toward me, the fingers outstretched. It's a silent but universal command. *Help me up.*

That act more than anything proves that the little bitch is old money, used to having someone wait on her hand and fucking foot. She seems dazed when I don't take the hand she's offering. I see her eyelids flutter as she slowly registers the unfamiliar scenery of the room. Then she sees me, and her hand flies to her side, the fingers clenching tight.

It takes her three tries to stand upright on her own, but she's already steadier than she was less than an hour ago. I know she'll follow when I jerk my head toward the doorway and turn on my heel, leaving her to catch up. She staggers after me, clinging to the wall for balance. The steps are tricky. She takes her time, and I have to wait at the foot of them for nearly five minutes before she finally descends the bottom step.

The little princess's modesty is showing now that we're on the lower level. Her nostrils flare like a wounded doe sensing the inevitable stench of nearby predators; she can hear Arno pacing just a few feet away. Her fingers flutter to the edge of my shirt, which hangs down past her knees. She flattens her hands out as if to glue the fabric in place as I lead her to the basement door.

I don't wait for her to descend the stairs this time. She flinches when I take her wrist and haul her forward; I ignore how she pants as she's forced to keep up. The basement's already fully lit. Either someone was here before us or no one bothered to lock up after last night. The table and the chair are still there. So is that fucking laptop.

"Sit," I tell her, cutting my gaze toward the center of the room.

She takes her time, moving with such regal little steps. It's as if no one's told her yet that she's no longer in her high palace. A part of me wants to ruin the fantasy for her. My hands twitch at my sides, aching to shove her forward just to see how she'll react if she's pushed onto her knees. Arno's invitation makes for a sick temptation. I never got off on violence against women, but something in me just can't fucking resist the curiosity of what she'll do when those men surround her. How she'll react. What kind of pleas will that haughty mouth form in order to save her own life?

"It won't work."

For a moment, I think I've conjured her voice—but it's too hoarse, even for my twisted imagination. Her accent is a rare weakness she fights to rein in.

"It won't work."

I shouldn't respond at all, but the question is instinctive. Fucking curiosity. "What?"

"This." She directs the word to the wall as she sits, tucking her bare feet neatly beneath her chair, her hands settling on her lap. "Whatever you plan to do to me...for Vinny. It won't work." The words seem pleading enough, but she doesn't *sound* like she's begging. Her voice is too coldly detached. Factual. "Violence doesn't faze men like him." Her eyes seek mine out from over her shoulder, unexpectedly steady. "He'll see it as my honor to die for him."

"He'll get his wish," I say.

She nods, accepting her death with the same grace with which most people accept the weather report. She doesn't resist her fate. The doe accepts that it's merely a doe caught in the middle of a rift between wolves.

In silence, she faces the wall again, her back toward me, and for the first time, I realize just how small she truly is. Just a sliver of a woman who seems liable to melt through the gaps in the structure of the metal folding chair she sits on.

Whatever her purpose, I hope Arno finishes with her quickly. I don't want to see her when I return, and I don't look back when one of his men descends the stairs not even a minute later to silently take my place keeping "an eye."

In five minutes, I'm out on the street. The scent of the city calls to me, beckoning with countless toys to amuse an old dog. I'm eager to seek out every last one and discover what I've missed out on for five damn years. After all, Arno's not the only one capable of learning new tricks.

I'm back in Mulligans by noon. There's no sign of Espi among the few patrons who crowding around the bar —but the kid's only partly the reason I've returned. Irritation sings through my blood. The kind of itch you can't scratch. That buzzing impulse you can't shake—you can only surrender to it. It's the same urge that drives a junkie to get high or a dog to bury its bones. That fucking burn that makes a mosquito bite sting. There's an unbearable need to just dig at the infected wound until it bleeds; only then can you satisfy that craving.

Stacatto's bitch is a drug—and not even the good shit like dope or coke. She is nothing more than nicotine, addicting only when it's set on fire and left to burn.

Arno's men pay me no mind when I barrel through the main room of the pub. It's only when I head for the door to the basement that someone puts a hand on my shoulder, his voice a warning octave.

"I wouldn't go down there if I were you, *friend.*"

I don't waste time on words when I shrug him off. Then I reach for the door and wrench it open. I'm down the rickety staircase before anyone can try to hold me back, but when I enter the room, I merely take a spot against the wall and watch.

Arno's finally descended into hell to meet his captive. Green eyes clash with hazel ones—they're an odd match. He towers over her, his standing body positioned above her seated one. He leans down so that his mouth rests beside her ruined ear, but she doesn't seem to flinch. Not even when he curls his hand beneath her chin and forces her to make eye contact. It's not long before I realize why. Her gaze is distant again. She's anywhere but here in this room.

"Smile pretty," Arno says, his voice a chilling murmur. "Let's give that fiancé of yours something to keep him up at night."

He draws his hand back and then slaps her. A choked sound rips from her throat at the impact. I assume that it's a moan. Then it comes again and there's no mistaking the faint haunting sound for what it truly is: a giggle.

Arno's "boys" don't seem to know whether to laugh or growl. Their master is stoic; he merely watches, analyzing every inch of his prey.

"It's not enough. It won't bruise," the woman explains, her eyes glassy. "You'll have to hit me harder than that—"

Arno fulfills her request. He forms a fist and smashes it against her cheek—not hard enough to break bone, but enough to knock her off the chair, onto her hands and knees. She'll bruise, all right. One of her slim hands flies up to her mouth, catching the blood that trickles from a torn corner of her lip. She's quick and efficient about it, and the scarlet gleams against her pale skin when she braces her fingers against the floor.

"Wait for it to show," Arno commands, slamming a digital camera down on the table. "Then take a picture. Make it *pretty*."

He's gone before he notices me standing here, so consumed by his plans for revenge. While he stomps up the stairs, one of his men approaches the girl. He chuckles and reaches out to finger a strand of her black hair.

"Don't bruise up too badly," he tells her. "I want to put that mouth to good use."

She flinches, and for the first time, something that could be fear flashes through her dark eyes. The next second, it's smothered, whatever it is, and her gaze is blank again.

"Get up." I take a step toward her.

Almost as if she's moving in slow motion, she turns her head in my direction. She cranes her neck, sending that curtain of hair over one shoulder. It takes her eyes a few seconds to focus on me, regaining clarity like a camera's lens is forced to adjust and dilate.

Say cheese.

She gets up slowly, wincing with every movement. One of her hands flutters as if she's fighting down that ingrained habit of sticking it out to demand assistance. Stacatto kept her well maintained, it seems. His influence is obvious in the way she reacts even to Arno's men. She's a deer desensitized to the horrors of the wolf den.

"Sit," I tell her when she finally stands, facing me.

She does so obediently, folding her hands on the table in front of her. She winces when her tongue shoots out to staunch the blood dribbling from her mouth. Already, the skin is starting to redden. Oddly enough, she doesn't seem to mind the pain. There's almost a cat-got-the-mouse expression that flits across her features too quickly to pin down. She's like a kid who's been smugly rewarded with an extra scoop of ice cream after asking for it politely.

Arno's men can't leave her alone though. Varying levels of anger distort their features, but I'm not impressed. How many of them fucked Parish or gave her money for drugs? How many of them treated her like shit and called her as much to her face? Her death has made her a saint. Arno's sister will be avenged, all right.

One of the men steps forward, tugging at the clasps of his pants. "How about a little preview, sweetie?" Once his limp prick is revealed, he palms it, gasping out, and gives her an impromptu performance.

The princess doesn't even spare a glance in his direction. I'm grudgingly curious as to why—especially when she didn't seem to shy away from my own dick. She's staring off again, her features blank and empty. It pisses me off, that look. She's far from the pain. The indecency. No one can touch her wherever she flies off to, and deep down, some part of me acknowledges why that dazed expression lights a burning in my fingertips. I fucking *know* that look.

Arno's man jumps back when I approach, his jeans still bunched around his fucking ankles. I ignore him, my focus solely on the girl. She doesn't react, but a part of her returns to observe me curiously the closer I come.

I expect her to wince when I reach out and seize her chin in the palm of my hand, but she doesn't. Not even when my thumb presses into her split lip and then slides along her mouth, painting it with her own blood like a canvas. I can see her chest rise and fall from here, but the movement is steady. She's not afraid. When I lean down, close enough to bring my mouth alongside her ruined ear, her breathing doesn't even hitch. She's flying off again, steeling herself for whatever I'm going to say. I don't feel the urge to whisper, but I find myself speaking gruffly anyway, for her benefit.

"Tell me about Stacatto."

I withdraw just in time to see her eyes flash with interest. We've hit upon her favorite topic of conversation, it seems. Apparently, nothing gets a bitch to talk like her own fucking love life.

"This won't work," she says. She meets my gaze fully, and I don't know if it's amusement or despair that I see there. "Hurting me... It won't work. Vinny will expect me to suffer." She shrugs as if the threat of pain is just a messy business she'll have to just endure. "He thinks I'll die for him."

It's the second time she's spoken like that. He *expects* her to be honored to die for him. He *thinks.*

"So, what *doesn't* he expect?" I wonder.

Arno certainly seems to be in the mood to try all new kinds of torture. The princess doesn't seem capable of giving me an answer though. She frowns, her expression thoughtful. I guess she hasn't considered that side of the scenario. Her gaze drifts down to the ring sparkling on her finger.

"You're wrong," I tell her. "What Arno plans to do to you…" I trail off, shaking my head. Something that could be a smile shapes my mouth, and I watch her carefully to see how she reacts to it.

"You don't know Vinny," she replies, her voice steady and assured despite the tender hint of a bruise that's already blooming over her jaw.

"Well, I certainly wouldn't want to see those things happen to *my* fiancée—"

"He's not human," she counters as if it's as simple as that.

I frown, not liking the way she assumes I'm not in the same boat. *We're all monsters here,* I think, looking her up and down. Even her to some degree. She's seen things—her eyes hold the scars. Whatever shred of humanity she might have once had has already been tainted, long before Arno's men snatched her.

"Well, what *would* piss him off?" I wonder for the second time.

She laces her hands together, seeming to think it over. "I'd have to…disobey." She frowns as if confused by the possibility. Her ring catches my eye again, and I can't resist imagining what drew her to such a man. Perhaps the little princess gets off on power?

"Disobey?" I repeat, curious despite common fucking sense.

She whispered the word like a prayer—one of those naughty ones we mutter internally so the priest won't hear, those imploring pleas for God to smite whoever wronged you. To hurt that bully on the playground or strike a wayward offender down with fire and brimstone. I knew those prayers well, back when I still believed in them, that is.

"How?"

She shrugs, and her gaze begins to glaze over.

But I'm not satisfied, and I snatch for her wrist; she won't fly off so easily. "Disobey how?"

She doesn't answer me, and rather than press the issue, I let her go and reach for the camera Arno left. It's small but easy to use.

"He wanted a picture," I remind her. A part of me bristles at doing Arno's dirty work, but something tells me his men won't let her pose alone. Intervening isn't my main goal, however—once again, I'm fucking curious.

"Disobey," she said. As if the man controlled her by a leash and not a priceless diamond ring.

When I raise the camera and capture her face on the screen, it's utterly expressionless, dangerously pale. With the wad of duct tape over her mangled ear and her hair a mess, she cuts a striking image. Despite what she claims about the man, a mad dog can guess the reactions of another mad dog—and there isn't one alive who wouldn't growl when another beast steals his toy.

"Smile, sweetheart," someone goads from the sidelines.

When my finger hits the button and the flash goes off, I assume she ignored the taunt. With the swelling shaping up nicely on the left side of her face, Arno will have a very *pretty* snapshot regardless. But, when I glance down and scroll through the gallery, something rises up swiftly, knocking me full in the chest. *Shock?*

The zombie-caricature of a woman stares at me from the camera's screen. She *smiles* back. The grin contorts her mouth, plumping up her cheeks and giving life to her eyes. She looks like a party girl, exhausted but having the time of her fucking life. She isn't imploring help or begging her fiancé to save her with puppy-dog eyes. She taunts him, her bitter smile a twisted message: *I'm bruised and broken and bloody, but I would rather be.*

Disobedience, I think, looking up to face the woman in person. She entertains a much different definition of the word than I do. I let the camera fall back onto the table. A part of me wonders if I should make her take another one—force her to look pathetic—but I don't, and she stares blankly ahead as if she had never reacted at all.

I keep her secret and return to my place at the wall, watching her. Arno's men are anxious. They loudly discuss what they'll do when Arno finally gives the go-ahead. How many ways they can make a "bitch scream."

If she hears them, the girl's face offers no indication. She's ice cold, her expression a carefully composed mask. I'd admire her if I weren't almost as impatient as the other dogs were. The waiting game never was my forte, but Arno seems to relish making her sweat. I wish he would fucking get it over with. I want to see how the little princess keeps her head held high when she's forced to pleasure an entire crew of brutal, violent men. Something tells me she's been through worse, and I fucking hate the part of me that wonders exactly what.

Maybe an hour passes by the time Arno finally returns, his hair streaming behind him like fire. He scan the room, spotting me near the corner. "Dante." He doesn't seem surprised to see me back early—he sighs, apparently more relieved instead. "Something came up. I need these assholes to help me...take out the *garbage*." He gives the words a meaningful edge that make his men lurch to attention. I can fucking hear them sniffing at the air, eager to cut their teeth on fresh meat. "Can you watch her? It won't take long."

He leaves the matter up to me, but I shrug rather than answer. The little princess has stiffened up in his presence, and I don't miss the slight slip in her otherwise impenetrable armor. Despite her shit about disobedience, she truly is afraid. I can't decide if I'm amused or not.

"Dante?"

I shrug again and run a hand through my hair. The fingertips burn slightly, and I'm not sure why. "I'll stay."

"Good." With one look, Arno musters his men into action, and they follow him up the stairs.

The ceiling trembles with their combined weight as they march across the length of the bar and exit out of what I assume to be the main doors. God help whichever bastard pissed Arno off today. The girl might get a reprieve after all. If she's lucky, the worst of his murderous lust will be rubbed out by the time he comes for her. Though I doubt it will do much good. She may be better at hiding it than most, but her body can't stave off the lasting impact of pain and exhaustion for very long. She's already trembling, rattling the metal legs of the chair. Her skin is icily pale, and a sheen of sweat glistens over her forehead.

I give her an hour, maybe two, before she fully goes into shock—and she certainly won't be laughing by then. The desire for something to pass the time drives me up the basement steps, leaving her there. She won't follow, and I doubt she has enough strength left to run. I take my time when I head across the now nearly empty barroom to the counter. The bartender gives me an odd look when I ask for something "strong as hell," but she tosses me a bottle of dark, nearly black liquor, and I accept it with a nod.

I sip at it while I return to the basement. Whatever it is, it burns like hell. I drain nearly a third of the bottle by the time I finally approach the woman.

"Drink," I tell her, placing the bottle down in front of her—though I don't fucking know why.

If she's stupid, she'll hit me with it and try to run. If she's smart, she'll ignore me. I can see her wrestling with either decision as she warily scans the label.

"W-why?" she asks.

I cock my head and shove the bottle closer. It flirts with the edge, only about an inch from spilling onto her lap. "Drink."

Her fingers tremble as she clutches the neck of the bottle with one hand. Her eyes dart to mine and then flit away again. She knows she won't find any comfort in them. She gets her reassurances from the drink instead, taking a small, pursed-lip sip. It's fucking pathetic.

"Another," I command, bracing one hand flat against the table so I have enough leverage to position myself above her.

To her credit, she doesn't flinch or sink into her seat. She keeps that debutante posture, her fingers clutching the edge of the table.

Slowly, she reaches for the bottle and wraps her lips around the opening. She tosses the bottle back and almost immediately lurches forward, sending drink spraying across the table. Her eyes water as she sputters. I bet her lip is burning, along with her throat and her internal organs. The little princess has never sampled good booze before. She winces at the taste. Then her cheeks redden, and I don't have to prompt her to take another taste. This time, she gets most of it down, though some trickles down her chin. Her eyes meet mine again, still hesitant, as she should be.

"Another," I tell her. I mime drinking from a glass when she doesn't comply and make my tone harder. "Take another sip."

She wipes at her mouth with the back of a shaking hand. She doesn't want to. I can see it in her eyes, but she makes a show of taking another measured taste.

"Again."

"How much?" she counters. The defiance in her gaze becomes questioning.

Something in me bristles at that. I'm an asshole, getting the sacrificial lamb drunk before her slaughter to see if she'll make even more of a mess. Arno's plans for her don't faze me in the slightest, but when she takes her hand off the bottle, I don't know what makes me reach for it.

"Drink." I press the opening to her lips, ignoring the way she flinches back. "More."

"W-why—" She breaks off and rephrases the question, her eyes meeting mine. Probing. "How much more?"

I consider holding her down and pouring the liquor down her fucking throat. It certainly would make for one hell of a prelude to the main event Arno has planned. In the end, I set the bottle on the table. She's not expecting it when I reach out for her wrist and manually curl her hand around the bottle's neck.

"Drink," I tell her, my gaze settling over the blood welling from her cut lip. "Drink...until you stop feeling the pain. Until you don't feel a damn thing."

Something flickers across her expression as she swallows hard. I'm sure she'll resist. I'm just about ready to take the bottle for myself when she lifts it and brings it to her lips again. When she throws her head back, most of the liquor is wasted on sputtering coughs as her body rejects the bitter taste. But, when I no longer have to command her, I know she's gotten enough.

CHAPTER NINE

Daniela

I think I hate *him* the most of all. The bastard with the blue eyes—he's watching me even now.

The other men are mere dogs like Vinny. They don't understand anything but violence and bloodshed. But he... This man is different. He's colder. He's calculating. He is a snake circling the carnage and swallowing down his chosen prey before the poor soul even knows what's happening.

Though maybe it's the alcohol that makes me so angry. My head drifts. My thoughts are harder to grasp, and sanity is like a rudder struggling to propel me through the darkness. The bottle is gone; I don't know what he's done with it or if it was really there in the first place.

Delirium likes to play tricks on an already exhausted mind. My head is on a cloud. My right ear is miles away, and everything else feels like distant pulses. I can see my other limbs when I crane my neck down, but controlling them seems about as easy as telling smoke in which direction to float.

I can't help feeling like this is his own selfish pittance; make the poor girl so drunk that she won't be able to feel her own rape. Hell, maybe she'll pass out during it. Whatever helps him sleep at night.

Silly, silly bastard. Didn't he know how impossible it was to sleep with the souls of others weighing you down? They whisper in your ear at night, right before you drift off, and they haunt your dreams, turning them into nightmares. I haven't slept in five years. I cease to exist at night. I go numb right until the exact moment slumber takes me. Then I open my eyes again, wide awake, and it's torment.

On second thought, he doesn't seem as tired as I am. He drank more than I did, yet his posture is stoically erect. He watches me unashamedly. He's counting the hours down.

"Vinny." I don't know why I speak. My voice is a hollow whisper that slithers to the farthest reaches of the room—he can't pretend like he doesn't hear me. "Vinny. You want to know what would really make him angry?"

My tormentor doesn't answer, but I know I've piqued his interest.

"If I willingly f-fucked another man... That would make him *anggrrrryy*." My tongue fumbles with the words, and then I end on a sudden hiccup. "*That* would make him want me back."

If only so he could kill me himself.

The man doesn't seem impressed by what I've said. He's unamused by the unfiltered Daniela, but she suddenly feels desperate to have an audience.

"I would do it, too," I tell him. Virginal Lynn's deep, dark secret. I would take anyone over Vinny. The red-haired man. Any one of his thugs. The man with blue eyes.

Anyone. I'd deny him the one thing of value I had left. No matter how tonight will end, Vincent Stacatto wouldn't claim all of me.

"I'd do it," I say out loud, just to make it sink in. My confirmation to the universe if not to the man himself. Vinny would never have me fully. The thought makes me snicker, and the blue-eyed man pulls away from the wall, bored of me already.

I watch him head to the doorway that leads to the stairs. There, he pauses, and this is when I realize that someone else is already in the process of descending them.

"It's showtime," the red-haired man declares in a guttural rumble. His eyes burn with a sickening mixture of rage and excitement.

Slowly, my gaze drifts over to focus on the wall. I'm not here anymore. I see a stage...a cello. I'm playing Bach. My mind spins the invisible notes. I focus hard on crafting the melody, its soothing cadence. But I'm too dizzy. Words break through the song.

"What the fuck is wrong with her? Is she drunk?"

The words dissolve into countless syllables that bounce across the room. My head throbs. A million thoughts and fears leak through the cracks these men have beaten and cut into—I can't hide them anymore.

A hand grazes my shoulder, and I flinch. Then the entire chair is wrenched out from under me, and I land hard on the floor. My knee smarts. More pain joins the symphony of it that fights with the rising stream of voices for my attention.

"Set up the camera—"

"Where?"

"Any-fucking-where!"

I bite my lip to silence a scream and squeeze my eyes shut, blocking out the room and the men who are crowding it. I'm not here. I'm floating...flying...playing. Bach's melody fills my ears again. My bow is in my hand. I can feel the tension in the strings.

"All right... Get her clothes off."

A hand seizes the collar of my borrowed shirt and tugs. I hear ripping. There's cool air on my back, and the laughter and jeers of countless men battle with my attempts to ignore them. My cello is too heavy to lift. The bow breaks. The music dies off.

All at once, I'm lying on an ice-cold floor, clothed only in a pair of underwear, which someone attempts to drag down my legs while they croon what a "sweet ass" I've got into my ear.

"Wait."

The hands stop tugging, but the callused fingertips still graze my skin. Whoever speaks...he has a voice that makes the entire room go silent. The roar of a lion is heeded by all predators. A part of me flinches in recognition. I *know* that voice, but my mind is too busy spinning to place it.

"Think...Arno... Another method." His words come in bits and pieces like the clues to a puzzle I'm too dumb to solve.

"Don't tell me you've gone and grown a heart on me," someone snidely retorts, but his tone is cautious. There's a true monster in this pit of beasts, and even this animal knows when to tread carefully. "Want me to give her back to fucking Stacatto on a silver platter?" He's shouting, and I shudder at the words *give back.*

I'd rather die than go back.

I arch into the hands at my sides, hoping that their owner will let his lust override any objections. Use me. Kill me. I *can't* go back.

"...just want...to think about other options. Use this to your benefit. There's another way to make him pay."

"How?" It's a violent, bellowed plea that a part of me seconds.

Tell me how. *How can I win? How can I screw the devil himself?*

I don't hear what is said next. The panting of the man crouched over me drowns out all else. He strokes me sloppily, grazing my hip with his nails. It feels like an eternity before another softly spoken word breaks the monotony.

"Your choice. Don't say I never gave you business advice."

I'm unsure just what makes me peel my eyes open. He stands out like a panther in a jungle of weeds. Tall, broad shouldered. Fearless, he heads for the stairs as if he doesn't have a care in the world. I'm just a speck on his peripheral vision, too insignificant to merit a passing glance. With my eyes, I follow his ascent through the door and up the narrow staircase beyond it. Then the man at my backside shifts.

"Arno? We...we, uh, doing this or what?"

The red-headed man's reply comes without hesitation. "We're doing it. Who's first?"

My eyes drift shut again. I will my head to float and separate from my body. I need to be far away. I'm not here. I'm not here. I'm...painfully trapped inside my skin, forced to feel every inch of the hand that dips into my panties and plunges between my legs.

Panic dances through my skin, riding the sharp tendrils of pain. My stomach, overflowing with alcohol, rebels. *You're not here, Daniela. You're not here. You're not—*

"Ah, fuck! Stop." There's a sound like that of flesh striking flesh, but it isn't violent—more as if someone slammed a hand into their own fist out of frustration.

I can taste it, this dangerous tension building in the room like poison. Then a man somewhere grits out a harsh sigh, and it all scatters at once.

"Let her go."

The hand between my legs doesn't abate its cruel, searching thrust. I can't silence the cry that slips loose, verging on the edge of a scream. I can survive anyone but Vinny...anyone. But my aching body isn't as willing a sacrifice.

"I said let her go."

The hands recede, and I slump to the floor, trembling and floating and panting. My eyes open once again, and I see him there, lurking just near the mouth of the staircase. A part of me wonders if he ever really left, but his voice isn't the one that put an end to the party.

"Jesus—fuck, *one* day, Dante," the red-haired man snarls. "One fucking day. You come up with nothing and I'll fuck her myself and send her in pieces to Stacatto. Understood? You fuck this up...and Parish's blood is on *your* hands."

The blue-eyed predator accepts the challenge with only a nod. He is uncaring, his face revealing nothing. I wonder what he's promised. What he wanted. Why the men are leaving, spearheaded by a furious red-headed man, who slams his boots against the floor with every step.

"You can leave her here if you want," he tells the man, Dante, before pushing past him for the stairs. "But I won't lock the door. If anyone wants her, they are free to have her."

I shiver, pressing my throbbing cheek against the floor while I try to find my melody again. *"If anyone wants her, they are free to have her..."* I hear footsteps approaching me. They're steady, unconcerned when I try to shift out of reach.

My new attacker catches me easily. He seizes my panties in a fist...and then drags them back up to my hips. The next second, I'm in the air, and the world spins for a terrifying moment before coming to a sudden stop—only I'm upside down. My eyes open to a hazy view of the cement floor. It shifts and writhes right before my eyes like a vibrant, gray body of water. My arms sway, dangling before me like pendulums. I'm moving.

Though, on second thought, it's more like moving *with* someone. They're carrying me, whoever they are, across the basement and up the stairs. My nose hits something firm, which I assume to be a muscular body shielded by cheap cotton. I inhale sharply before I can stop myself. A mixture of musk and sweat and alcohol.

CHAPTER TEN

Dante

SHE WEIGHS ALMOST NOTHING. I'VE WORN COATS WITH more give to them. It's almost entirely too easy to carry her up two flights of stairs to the apartments. It's a bitter sort of irony fit to kick someone in the ass; her weight reflects none of the burden she brings.

I should have let Arno have his way with her. His men would have wet their appetites and Arno might have been able to sleep a little easier. Nothing mended a broken heart like a bit of sweet, twisted revenge.

In theory. But men like Vincent Stacatto didn't play by the rules of normal men—or even the average asshole who liked to think of himself as a monster. They abided by the laws of their own twisted games, and the technicalities were all a mystery to outsiders. The only opponent with any chance of beating them was usually one of the victims they toyed with for fun.

Though she may have been wearing his ring, the girl harbored no love for Stacatto. It was all in the way she spoke about him. She came alive, for once. Her hazel eyes seared at the thought of hurting him, even at the cost of her own pain.

Not that I gave a damn. Her pain meant nothing to me. After all, the world was a bitch with plenty of agony and unfairness to dish out in spades. Nothing about it was fair. Though, hell, maybe I just liked the thought of putting her little drunken boast to the test? *"If I willingly fucked another man...that would make him angry."* There were plenty of bastards who would pay to see something like that. Though something tells me that she wasn't lying. Maybe it was that hard, desperate gleam in her eye. Some might call it insanity.

I know that look well, too. I face it every day in the mirror. I've even grown to appreciate it for what it is: a cold reminder to never be weak again. I'd bite and scratch and kill if I have to—no one would ever control me.

The thought shakes a dark memory loose, though I push it back to the recesses of my mind where it belongs. *She* did this. My fingers throb, trembling beneath the urge to punch something. Someone. Rage paints my vision red, but then a pathetic moan scratches my eardrums, and it fades to the dingy light of the hallway.

Goddamn, she's drunk. I'll be lucky if she doesn't puke down my back. I can hear her moaning, the sound aimless —though, on second thought, she's trying to form words. They trickle out of her, garbled and meaningless.

"Shut up," I tell her while palming the door to my apartment with one hand. I'll be lucky if Arno doesn't kick me out for daring to interrupt his grand little scheme. A part of me wants to take her back to the basement and leave her there for whichever horny prick happens upon her first. I toy with the thought, prodding it with more conviction than I'd like. I turn...

And then I'm staring into a mirror. The other Dante stands at the mouth of the staircase. He's wearing a hoodie that barely contains the dark hair spilling out from the hood—the first clue that I drank too much of Arno's shit and I'm hallucinating. He has my nose. My eyes. They even reflect the same hatred I reserve only for myself and a few other choice bastards.

"So, you really are out." He doesn't sound like me, at least. His voice is softer with a higher pitch.

Recognition hits me like a punch, and I stagger a step forward. "Es...Espi."

The kid's all grown up. It's more jarring to see him in person than only in a picture. Espisido's taller now. Give him a few extra inches and he'd tower over me. It's a humbling, irritating realization. There used to be a time when I'd tuck him into bed. Fight his bullies on the playground. Kick his ass when he dared to get out of line.

Now, he runs around with men like Arno. His picture is in a police file with my name on it. So much has changed in only five damn years, but some shit never does. His eyes narrow when I take another step toward him. Then they flicker over the woman I have slung over my shoulder. The half-naked, drunk, groaning woman who can barely lift her head up.

"You've certainly wasted no time," he says.

There's a backpack hanging off his shoulder, stained with a million splotches of different colored paint. The zipper is partially undone, and I can make out metal cans filling the bag to the brim. He's been out tagging, but his little hobby takes a back seat to the hostility lurking in his words.

"What is that supposed to mean?" I know what it fucking means. Fuck, I wonder if he knows—if Arno told him about his sick little revenge plot. If he knows about Parish. With a grunt, I set the woman upright and let her stumble against the door to my apartment.

She flinches, bracing both hands against the wooden surface. "The walls..." she mumbles, her accent strangling her words. "The walls are *bleeding*."

"Quite the charmer, she is," Espi says snidely, eyeing her bare back as she struggles to keep her balance. At least the theory that he knows is shot—the kid was never malicious enough to mock a dead woman.

From the back, at least, she looks like the average party girl who had too much to drink. I can only hope that he doesn't get a good look at her mangled ear, her face, or the blood that speckles her skin in all the wrong places.

"I've been looking for you," I say, changing the subject while I shift sideways just enough to block the woman from view. I scan the hallway with narrowed eyes. Which door belongs to his apartment? How long has he scuttled in and out of the pub, trying to avoid me?

Espi shrugs, adjusting his backpack. "I know. Apparently, you can't take a fucking hint."

"Hey." I take a step forward and grit my teeth, cutting a violent remark off. *Focus.* "We need to talk," I say instead, sounding somewhat calmer.

"Talk?" Espi meets my gaze and scoffs. "It's about five years too late, Dante. I don't—"

The sound of retching cuts him off. We both turn and find the girl slumped over on her hands and knees. She gags, but her stomach has nothing left to spit up.

"I think she needs you," Espi says, nodding to her.

But she can wait. "Espi—"

He turns and races down the stairs before I can stop him. I start to follow, but the damn girl tries to gag again, making herself choke.

"Fuck..." I waver between the two of them for all of three seconds. Concern for Arno's floor wins out. I'll track Espisido down again, and next time, I'll *make* him talk. For now, I content myself with kicking the fucking door to my apartment open and dragging the woman inside by her arm.

I let her go the moment her feet are clear of the doorway, and she slumps over the placemat.

"Get up," I tell her once I get the door shut and wrestle the locks into place.

Her body twitches as she attempts to move. The only part of her that succeeds is her left foot, which jerks against the floor. Sighing, I leave her there and take off down the hallway, peeling my shirt off when I enter my room. I toss it onto the floor, and then I fish out another from the pile of my stuff in the corner. With it clenched in a fist, I kick my shoes off and switch the light on. It floods the room, chasing away the shadows and serves as a buffer against the anger raging a silent war at the back of my mind. For now.

The girl's still where I left her when I return to the hallway. She doesn't react when I toss the clean shirt at her. She's still curled up on her side, her back facing me. That mane of dark hair encircles her limbs like ebony netting.

"Get up," I snap, my voice catching on the edge of a growl. "Get into the bathroom and change."

The walls have a better chance at obeying me. I nudge her shoulder with my foot, and she whimpers. A string of words trickles from her throat, but they're impossible to make out. Clenching my jaw, I sink to one knee and wrench on her hip so that she's facing upright.

Then I stiffen. Her body *alone*, that's what I focus on. She's got nice curves for a stuck-up little princess. Her hips are narrow, but they flare out from a slender waist. Her breasts aren't too bad—not too large, but not nonexistent, either. The curls between her legs match the same fucking shade of ebony as her hair. She's shapely, though a little on the scrawny side. She has a mole on her hip. There's a bruise on her thigh. A scar on her left ankle.

It's wrong. It's sick. But I ogle. I stare. I shamelessly eye every part of her body but the section that calls to me the most. I can't ignore it for long, and true disgust is harder to swallow. The bastard marked her: Seven indigo letters are etched into the skin just under her breasts—tattooed there.

VINCENT

They're uneven and sloppy as if hand-carved. Some of them are a deeper shade of ink than the rest. It's hard not to picture someone holding her down when she struggled and digging the needle in even harder as punishment. She guards her imperfection well, even when drunk out of her mind and half conscious; one of her hands scuttles across her chest to shield the letters.

"Get up," I snarl, drawing back, though I wind up lifting her anyway.

She moans when I drag her into the bathroom and maneuver her into the tub. Her eyes seek mine out, vacant and empty as I flick the showerhead on with one hand and reach for her waist with the other.

Her gaze drifts down toward where my fingers aim. Her lips move. Sound comes out. *Da...dum...da...la...* She's fucking humming. It's a frantic sound like the kind a kid makes when things are in danger of not going their way. *I can't hear you. This isn't happening.*

I snatch my hand away and turn my back on her, leaving her beneath the spray. Hopefully, some of the blood will run off her. Some of that stench along with it. Nothing spoils the mood like the aroma of pain, fear, and desperation—she reeks of all three. The stink floods my nostrils while I enter the hallway on a hunt for a spare towel.

I find one in a small closet, along with a bar of soap and a stack of spare washrags. When I return to the bathroom, she's still curled at the bottom the tub, drowning beneath the shower spray. Her hair clings to her body, shielding most of it from my sight like a makeshift cape. She barely stirs when I grab her wrist and yank her upright. I can only force her to sit, but somehow, I manage to wrestle the soap into one of her hands and a rag into the other.

Her eyes are glassy, and she mimes the motions, washing more of the air than herself. Either way, I'm satisfied when the last drop of what little suds she managed to work up wash down the drain. Then I cut the water off and turn for the door, aiming to leave her there.

The fuck if I know why I don't. Maybe it's the threat of one of Arno's men potentially taking his boss's words as an open invitation to get some free ass. She's safer in the bedroom, where I can keep an eye on her, than here. It's the only course of action that makes sense. No one is going to invade my space on her account and catch me off guard.

The light paints a harsh picture when I finally carry her down the hall. Her face is a mess—Arno might have held back from causing serious damage, but not by much. Too many of her secrets are bared to me when I let her fall onto the mattress. The letters on her chest stand out in stark contrast against her pale skin. There are other bruises and marks on her legs, too old to have been caused by Arno or myself. The duct tape on her ear glimmers silver. I can still see it even when I flick the light off and take up a position by the door, my back braced against the wall.

Arno gave me a day. A day to come up with a better way to torture Stacatto. A day to avenge Parish's death. Another day to play nursemaid to the little bitch in the black dress.

I sigh, gritting my teeth, and close my eyes. I should have stayed in fucking prison.

CHAPTER ELEVEN

Daniela

I WAKE UP IN THE LAIR OF A BEAST. HIS SCENT irritates my nostrils, though for some reason my lungs heave to breathe him in. I'm nauseated by his flavor, but my belly is a shriveled ball, devoid of anything left to force out through my mouth in protest.

I don't know how long I lie here. How long before my eyes manage to peel open one by one and light stabs at them like jagged pieces of glass. I'm naked. Damp sheets create a shocking sensation I can feel against nearly every part of my body. My head throbs, and it's almost ironic—my fingers prefer the strings, but my brain apparently has taken up percussion. It hammers out an unsteady rhythm against the inside of my skull.

I can't decide if I'm alive or if this is that eternal torment in Hell that the Bible warns about. An agonizing few seconds pass, but I still don't know which destination seems more appealing, Hell or Vinny. Then I see him. My vision is a colorless blur, reducing him to nothing more than a splash of shadow against an otherwise gray surface—but those eyes shine through, unsettlingly clear. Through the chaos of my thoughts, a single name comes tumbling out. *Dante.* A part of me scuttles away from it the way a roach escapes the light. It's a terrible thing to learn the name of a monster. I'll settle for choosing a made-up one to call him instead.

I blink until his dark features form into more solid lines. In the pale light that comes in through the window, he almost seems harmless. *Lucifer.* He used to be an angel, I remember. God's favorite before he fell. I'll call him that.

Lucifer doesn't react when he sees that I'm awake. He eyes me coldly, and then he turns his gaze to the empty wall behind me instead. Broken women are such a poor way to start the morning off, so who could blame him?

He sits a few feet away, his back braced against the wall. There's something on the floor beside him. Two almost invisible cylinders...white caps...light-blue labels. Before my mind can settle on an identity for them, he bats at one with the flat of his hand and it rolls toward me.

Water! I lunge for it, bringing a million different agonies to life. I try to ignore them as I capture the bottle in a trembling hand and wrestle the cap off. I'm too exhausted to pull myself upright, so I tilt my head instead and allow the water to pour into my open mouth like a funnel. More of it winds up dribbling onto the sheets than going down my throat, but I manage to drain most of the bottle in seconds. Before I can choke the last drop down, Lucifer nudges the second bottle toward me.

I reach down to trap it in a fist while easing my body upright this time. *God.* The world pitches and sways beneath me. It's like I'm on the merry-go-round my brother and I used to frequent as children. My throbbing head even manages to tap out a lively beat.

Staring down at the blankets twisted around my legs, I inhale. Then I bring the bottle to my lips and greedily take in every last drop. The moment I do, Lucifer stands and inclines his head toward the doorway that leads out into the hall. The command may be silent, but it's no less authoritative than one of Vinny's shouts. *Come. Now, Daniela!*

I glance at my pathetic, bruised body. I'm naked except for a pair of black underwear that survived my trip from Vinny's town car. Other than that, pale skin and numerous imperfections paint a morbid picture. I hate the fact that he's seen me like this. His eyes have traced Vinny's brand without a shred of emotion. If only I could be as indifferent to it.

"Come on."

He's impatient, lingering on the threshold of the bedroom like an animal uncomfortable with being locked in a cage, even one of his own making.

I eye the gray carpet while my tongue shoots out to trace my bottom lip and returns with the flavor of blood. Standing has never felt like a more impossible task. A part of me just wants to ignore him and lie here until these men finally settle on a use for me. I'm so tired. At least Vinny rarely delayed his punishment. Retributions for breaking his rules came swiftly—he didn't like to play around with his food. Unless, of course, he was in a mood.

Setting the empty bottle aside, I brace one of my hands against the floor and attempt to push off that way. I manage to clear the mattress about an inch before my arm gives out and I land on my side, croaking out a gasp of pain before I can smother it. Lucifer watches as I grit my teeth and try again. God...the pain... I can taste it. The left side of my face aches. The room's still air assaults the tender flesh there like a repeated blow. My eyes water. *Focus, Daniela.* For a second, I imagine that Vinny's here, sneering down at me from the man's position.

Get a fucking hold of yourself, Lynn.

I hate myself for the fact that even the imaginary threat of him is enough to marshal my body into action. I crawl over to the wall and then use the surface of it for leverage to slowly climb upright. For a moment, I think I'll lose my balance again, but my trembling knees hold up. I succeed in taking a step in the man's direction, and he enters the hallway without a word.

It's a slow, agonizing shuffle down the hall to enter what seems to be a small sitting room. I have to cling to the wall the entire way before choosing to crawl on my hands and knees to a couch, which I scramble onto.

"Here." The man throws something at me while I settle on the uneven cushions.

They're upholstered in a faded material that seems to sport blue-and-white stripes. At some point, the colors must have been vibrant. Now, they're worn and gray in places. I picture the leather furniture that decorated the suite I called home for five years. Vinny certainly wouldn't approve of this abode. The furniture is minimal. There's an armchair matching the style of the couch a few feet away, against the wall. There's a small television as well, and a plain coffee table is in the center of the carefully assembled selection. Someone's tried their best to make it homey, I think. But furniture and blue curtains can only go so far to displace the otherwise charged atmosphere. I feel like I'm in a pot, dangling above a pit of fire—while I may not be able to see the flames through the metal prison, I can still smell them. Their heat tickles my skin.

Lucifer's eyes burn like that inferno. He nods to a wad of gray fabric that has appeared on the couch beside me. "Put it on," he says. Each word is pronounced slowly and deliberately. It's like he knows that my brain will take twice as long to process them.

Put it on? Oh, that's right. I'm naked. My hand drifts out, and my fingers seize a handful of cotton. Another shirt, apparently. This one doesn't smell like him, but I pull it onto my lap, fingering the hemmed edges. I glance up and find him watching, and then I set the shirt aside.

There's no use in donning another garment that will wind up being torn off. I'm too exhausted. I'll make it easy for these men. Lucifer frowns at the disobedience, but he says nothing. His eyes drift over me, lingering over the center of my torso, and I realize he wants me covered for his own benefit. No man likes to be reminded of the power of another, but I'm too tired to humor his pride. His gaze can't violate me any more than Vinny's hands already have.

He blows out a harsh sound the way a penned bull does when it paws the earth, right before lunging for the bullfighter egging it on. Then he turns and approaches a refrigerator that is separated from the rest of the room by only a row of counters. He rummages through the cabinets and then turns to face me.

"What do you want?"

I stare blankly until he raises both of his hands, revealing what he's holding in either one. The right contains a bag of bread. The left has a colorful box sporting a grinning chipmunk in the process of shoving round bits of cereal into its mouth. *Chunky Bites.*

"What do you want to *eat?*" he demands again. His voice deepens when he's losing his patience, I notice. It's a chilling sound.

My mouth opens. *Whatever you think is best.* Those words are on the tip of my tongue, but I wrestle them back at the last moment. My hand rises from the couch and a trembling finger points toward the *Chunky Bites.*

He slams the box down onto the counter and then grabs a bowl from one of the cupboards. I watch his fingers move, almost studiously, as he tilts the box, allowing a pile of Chunky Bites to fall into it. Then he douses it all with milk from the fridge. My mouth waters. My greedy hands shake as he crosses the room and shoves the bowl toward me. I bring the rim of it to my mouth and sip at the strange concoction before I even notice the spoon he's offering me next. It tastes like sugar, and my eyes drift shut as I swallow.

How long has it been since I've eaten cheap, commercial cereal? How long has it been since I've chosen for myself what to eat at all? Those two combined luxuries explode the moment I shove the first spoonful into my mouth and chew.

It's good. I'm shoveling more into my mouth, more quickly than I can get it down. It's like I blink and the bowl is empty, and Lucifer is already snatching it away. Before disappointment can really descend, he returns. The bowl nearly overflows with more, and I take my time with the second helping—or at least I try to. I devour every last bit of chunky, sugary "bites," and then I down the milk so quickly that most of it winds up running down my chin. I'm greedy. My tongue shoots out, tasting the remains of sugar that coat the rim of the bowl.

I hold it out to Lucifer, licked clean, but he isn't as gracious with the servings this time. "You'll get sick if you eat any more," he says while marching over to throw the bowl and the spoon into the sink.

I think he's right. Already, my stomach is trying to adjust to painful emptiness, sudden fullness, and the poisonous effects of alcohol. I draw my knees up to my chin and bury my face between them, just in case, but it isn't long before the nausea dissipates.

"Last night." Lucifer uses the two words to draw my attention back to him. He stands behind the counter, bracing both of his hands on top of it. "You said that you had an idea to pay back Stacatto."

He's prompting me for something, but my memories are a tangled ball that hurts to unravel. I grimace. Last night...

Oh. I remember now. I claimed that I'd willingly sleep with a man, on camera no less, just to make Vinny seethe. God, I wish I'd been lying. Alcohol is a powerful truth serum, it seems.

"He won't care," I say haltingly, trying to justify the boast, "if...if I'm r-raped—" My teeth chatter over the words. "He'll expect it. But if I was willing..."

Vinny's perfect Lynn would never be so brazen. He'd be furious—more than that. For all of my bravado, I can't even imagine it. I rest my head on my knees instead and shut my eyes against that violent truth.

"He won't negotiate otherwise."

"Negotiate?" Lucifer's voice is an almost-amused drawl. "What makes you think that Ar...*we* want anything in return for you?"

I lift my shoulder in an artless shrug. So it is true—these men only aim for revenge. How pathetic. It's such...such a waste. Vinny will be able to make his Lynn a martyr, justifying more of his madness, and these men will just suffer a grisly end for their defiance.

It's all enough to make me sigh, which rustles the loose ends of my hair.

"You need a shower," Lucifer declares, his tone wrought with disgust.

"Why?" My voice is a tired croak. My body prefers to wallow beneath a layer of misery and pain. It smells better on me than Vinny's false perfume and cologne. I just want it over with. If these men want me, they'll just have to contend with the blood.

"*Why?*" Lucifer doesn't like being questioned. He turns each one of mine into a verbal missile that lands with an impact that makes me wince. "Because, when you plead for your life, you might want to look like less of a used-up coke whore."

A part of me stings beneath the harsh assessment. Then I register the rest of his words with a frown. *Plead?* I groan with the effort it takes to lift my head and meet his gaze. I intend to contradict him—hell, he could kill me himself, here and now. It wouldn't matter.

But he's ready for me. "You want your revenge against Stacatto? Then do what the fuck I say." He cuts his gaze toward the hallway. "Clean yourself up."

Gino would never talk to me like this. It's such a stupid, senseless thought, but there it is, shining on the edge of my periphery. Obeying anyone other than Vinny is a strange sensation. It's almost like sleepwalking. A part of me wants to deny him, shut him out until the merciful end finally comes. But Lucifer knows his prey well, and he's paired a carrot with the whacking stick. *You want your revenge?*

"W-what do you mean?" I ask, fumbling with my sore jaw and my swollen lip.

He doesn't answer. He crosses over to me instead, and I know I can't hide my fear when his hand shoots out. Giving me an odd look, he snatches up the shirt and then heads down the hallway. Even in the absence of a verbal command, his orders ring clear. *Follow.*

I linger for a few precious seconds, wavering on the sweet edge of surrender and curiosity. The latter one wins, and I find that Lucifer is waiting for me at the mouth of the bathroom when I stagger toward it.

The shower roars, already running. It's only a matter of stripping what remains of my underwear and climbing into the tub.

Lucifer watches me, his gaze shameless. He's easy to ignore once the water pelts my body, however. I gasp, the harsh sound catching at the back of my throat. The heat awakens old nerve endings that flare beneath a mixture of abuse and sharp pain. Gritting my teeth, I manage to stoop for a rag and a bar of soap that already litter the basin of the tub.

Washing myself is a slow, mechanical dance. For a moment, I'm far away from this apartment. From Lucifer. I'm safe inside my head, going through the motions. I wash my hair. I clean my skin with a rough bit of friction until I realize that most of the spots of "dirt" I'm rubbing at are really bruises. I still feel marginally better when I wring the last bit of blood out of the rag, though I school my face into a blank mask rather than let Lucifer suspect as much.

He watches me shut the water off. Then he tosses a towel at me and continues to stare as I dry myself off. I don't know if it's lust in his gaze or disgust. His expressions are nearly impossible to read. I try anyway, probing them mercilessly.

At some point, he must become bored by the scrutiny, because he approaches the sink. He washes his hands and then fishes his toothbrush from behind the counter. He brushes swiftly, but I'm not prepared for the moment he rinses it off and then offers it to me.

My hand shakes when I take it and stumble out of the tub to stand before the sink. There's an almost compulsive need to erase the taste of alcohol, blood, and sugar from the inside of my mouth. I brush twice, scrubbing until the water I rinse with comes out tinged red.

I'm a skeletal figure who dominates the mirror when I finally glance up to observe my reflection. Lucifer is standing behind me, his face a mocking contrast from my bruised, swollen one. I reach out, tracing my bottom lip with the pad of my thumb. It stings in protest. Vinny would scowl at the sight of me—he always made sure never to strike me on the face to ensure that his transgressions against my skin could always be covered up for the days he liked to pretend he still loved me.

It's a bitter thought. My soul aches beneath the smarting sting, and I can't hide it. My eyes are wide open and empty, spilling out emotion to circle the drain along with the mess I wash off the toothbrush.

"Here," Lucifer says when I turn away from the mirror. He hands me the shirt again.

My fingers tremble...but I take it and slip it on over my head. His borrowed clothes work like armor when I gather up the nerve to face my reflection again. The roll of duct tape rests on the top of the toilet, and I bite off another square and replace the bandage over my ear. The ruined flesh stings, but already, it's starting to heal, scabbing over into a jagged, rust-colored edge.

I wet my fingers and use them like a comb to run through my ragged, tangled hair. I manage to claw most of it into submission. Then I wet another washcloth and carefully dab the traces of blood from around my mouth.

I must be decent enough, because Lucifer finally pulls away from the counter with a sigh and heads back into the living room. I follow him, feeling naked beneath his shirt, which fits me much like a shapeless dress.

"Wait here," he commands before undoing the locks of what I assume to be the front door. Then he's gone, slamming it behind him so fiercely that a piece of chipped paint breaks off and hits the floor.

Dante

"Ah...there he is. The big man."

It's barely eight a.m. and Arno's already drunk. His bloodshot eyes glare as I cross the bar. He has two bottles before him. One looks half empty. He pours some of the liquid from the other into a fresh shot glass and knocks it back, hissing at the taste. "You wanted to fuck her first. Is that it?" he demands. "I would have let you have the first bite. You only need ask—"

"She has a plan." The words seem ripped from my chest against my will. Frowning, I approach a barstool and sit.

Two of Arno's thugs linger around the edges of the room, pretending to play pool, but their suspicious gazes irritate the back of my neck.

"The girl," I grunt when Arno doesn't react. "She has a plan of her own for getting back at Stacatto."

Arno laughs and pours himself another shot. "Let me guess." He props a finger beneath his chin and pretends to mull it over. "We send her back with a pat on the ass and she'll beg her fiancé to apologize for treating my sister like a fucking whore?"

"No," I say, my gaze on the counter. Something that might be...fuck, *admiration?* It swells in my chest before I can swallow it down. "One man. No chains. The camera. She says she'd do it willingly." Even I have to admit that it's sadistic as fuck. No man would stomach watching his woman being raped by other men—but if she willingly *sullied* herself just to erase his touch? Screwed a stranger on camera for no reason other than to prove that, despite wearing his ring, she owed him no loyalty?

That's the kind of shit that fucks with a man's head. It sets the fires of rage that can't be easily smothered. It's the kind of twisted mind game that starts a war.

"Bullshit," Arno grouses, but I have his attention—his hand stills on the bottle of liquor, and he cocks his head, his emerald eyes mean and mistrustful. "You've been talking to her, eh, Dante? Lapping up her fucking lies. I know you're picky about your women, but Jesus Christ—"

"She'll do it." My voice resonates with conviction, though I'm not sure why. For all I know, the little bitch could be trying to merely prolong her own life, but...ah, fuck. She wasn't lying. I saw the desperation on her. "She'll do it," I repeat. "And, when Stacatto wants her back, you use this as an opportunity to extort whatever you want from the fucker."

Arno frowns down at his still-full shot glass. "What makes you so sure he'll even want her back? If *my* girl fucked another—"

"He'll want her back."

There is something inherently cruel about possession—that dark, brutal need that drives a man to draw his own name onto his victim's skin. She could leave on his terms. Die with his say. Bleed at his hand.

But if she dares to make that choice on her own? Well...it won't matter what the hell Arno asks for. Stacatto will entertain paying it—if only for a second—to have his disobedient toy back. He'll make her suffer for having dared to exert her own will.

"He'll want her back..."

Arno's thinking. He does so loudly, fumbling to lift his glass. He drops it and liquor sloshes across the countertop. Some of it wets my fingertips, but I don't attempt to wipe them. Her blood is on my fingers as well. Literally. Figuratively. She willingly put it there, and I fucking let her.

"You sure she'll do it?" Arno asks finally.

I nod. "Yes."

"Hell, even if she doesn't, I'll still let my men have a go at her anyway." He chuckles darkly, relishing the idea of torture as an appetizing side dish to his liquid breakfast. "But...let's say she does go through with it. Who will be the lucky man? You?" His gaze pierces me as if seeking out any ounce of lust I could be trying to hide.

"No." I shake my head. "Maybe you or one of your men." That would be an interesting sight, seeing them all fight over who gets to screw an easy lay.

"He'll have to wear a mask, I guess," Arno suspects, already arranging the details in his head. "Stacatto will make whoever the bastard is a target. And she'll need something sexy to wear. None of that pathetic T-shirt shit." He nods and then glances over at me, his smile gruesome. "Ask her to make a list of what she'll need. And tell her to get specific —if she doesn't ask for condoms, she won't fucking get any."

"When do you want her?" I ask, rising to my feet. I don't waste time on the stupid questions. Arno's mind is already made up, and that's one good thing about the bastard. He rarely lets emotion cloud his fucking common sense.

"Tonight," he says. "Maybe. I need to fucking sleep." He eyes the bottle as if it holds the answers to nights without memories of Parish. "I'll probably need to move her too. Stacatto won't find her here, but that bitch isn't good for morale." He sniffs the air as if tasting her scent along with that of his own stink. "I'm putting you in charge of this, Dante," he adds while I head to the back of the pub. "Get our little movie-maker whatever she needs..."

The mocking request chases me up the stairs. The hallway is empty. There is no one here to see me barge into the apartment and face the woman still sitting on the couch. Her hazel eyes watch me cross the room, but she doesn't react. Her head lolls against the back of the couch. She's fighting to stay awake or maybe just conscious. Her skin is paler than the milk I left out on the counter. I reach out for the bottle and then march over to the fridge.

"Will you do it?" I ask without turning around. I shouldn't have to fucking elaborate as to what.

"Yes."

I turn and find her watching me from the couch still. There's no hesitation in her gaze. No questioning.

"I'll do it…but—"

"What?" I chuckle darkly, steeling myself for some silly, childish request. *But the man has to treat me nice first. I need to be drugged. I need you to tell him that I didn't really mean it…*

"When it's all over…you can barter whatever you want for me, but after that, you kill me. I go back to him dead. Promise me."

There she goes, commanding again. Her princess nose juts high into the air, her eyes seeking mine. The haughty act is almost enough to counter the shocking truth in her words. She's that damn sure the bastard will be willing to trade for her.

"I don't make promises," I grunt.

"Make this one." She sits forward, her hair draping her like a cape. Her hand flies out, the fingers aimed like an arrow for my chest.

I stare at it, and slowly, she brings it back down. Her face is dazed.

"Vinny does handshakes…" She sounds horrified that she's driven to use the same tactics he does. Then she shakes her head, clearing it. "You have to promise me."

The next few seconds hang between us, a silent draw. I don't tear my eyes from hers, and she doesn't so much as flinch. The bitch has honed her poker face. How many times has the bastard hurt her while she's struggled to keep her face blank? How many horrors has she watched be committed right under her nose without batting so much as an eyelash? Something catches in my chest and makes me grit my teeth before I can help it. Holy fuck, I think I'm *impressed*.

"I..." My fingertips burn at the subtle hesitation. Dante Vialle never fucking hesitates. "I'll strangle you myself," I tell her, curling my hands into fists.

"Thank you." She exhales sharply, her eyes closing in relief. The emotion deflates her, and she falls back against the headrest of the couch. "Thank you... Thank you."

Her gratitude stings. I've signed up to be her murderer, and she looks ready to kiss my fucking feet.

"It'll be my pleasure." I put as much fucking violence and hate that I can into the words; they become a cutting whip that glances off her skin with barely a nick to show for it.

"Thank you."

"Make a list of what you need," I tell her, turning to face the door.

"N-need?"

"Make sure you add condoms." I leave her there and enter the bathroom. I piss, gritting my teeth as irritation seeps into my veins.

There's a buzzing at the back of my skull, harder and harder to ignore the longer I breathe the same air as Stacatto's whore. I stand before the toilet for minutes. When I wash my hands, a fucking stranger glares at me from the mirror's surface—some bastard who promised to murder a woman in exchange for a sex tape. Parish will be avenged, all right. I hiss and flick my wet hands in the air, watching drops of water distort my reflection.

When I return to the living room, the bitch is still on the couch.

"I'll need new un-underwear, I guess," she says softly. "And c-condoms. And..." She recites her list blankly while her eyes focus on the far wall. "I'll need...video—" She licks her lips as if the word is too dirty to leave there. "Tapes. S-so I c-can..."

Oh. I nod sharply. She wants to study a porno in action and see what it takes. Again, I don't know whether to be impressed by the cold, calculating way she's planned her fiancé's humiliation or just...disgusted. The man sure did a number on her. The princess knows what's expected to make her show look real. She's unafraid. I can see the determination in her gaze from here. It burns like fire, smoldering and quiet.

"And," she starts, meeting my gaze, "the man...he'll... I'm a virgin."

I feel myself frown, and I turn away before she can discern the shock I'm too fucking stupid to hide. A virgin. My eyes find her again and seek that ring out. Vincent's Stacatto's virginal little fiancée is willing to dance with the wolves just to keep some part of her out of his reach. It's sick. It's twisted.

It'll make for a good fucking show.

CHAPTER TWELVE

Daniela

Lucifer doesn't talk much. He leaves me again but returns before I can really notice the silence his absence creates. Under one arm, he's carrying a laptop—the same one that displayed the video of that girl.

He places it on the coffee table and lifts the lid. There's a crack jutting through the center of the screen, but the man plugs it in anyway, and it comes on without difficulty. When he circles around to place his hands on the laptop's keys, I shift over, making room on the couch, but he remains standing. I can't see what he does or what icons he clicks, but when he steps back to stand beside the couch, there is a website dominating the screen. *Girls! Girls! Girls!* proclaims the blazing headline that flashes across the header. A small video window floats amid a sea of obscene pictures of nude women in various poses. When Lucifer hits play, the scene opens with a shot of a busty blonde watering the lawn. Spotting the handsome gardener across the yard, she decides to take her skimpy bottoms off. Then…

God. I grit my teeth and dig my nails into my palms. I don't look away—I won't. I shut a part of myself off, and then I take notes. I observe every obscene gesture. Every position and every forced moan. It all seems so fake. The two "leads" spend more time staring at the camera than they do each other. One would think that I wouldn't need the extra research after all of the "performances" Vinny's put on for me, but at least these women aren't writhing in pain and biting their palms to silence their cries. They smile widely. They "ooh" and "aah." They don't flinch when the man slaps them on the ass and tells them to take it like a "good, dirty slut." They manhandle him right back, palming his cock until he winces before attempting to shove it down their throats.

I don't find any joy in it. No pleasure. When the video ends, Lucifer steps forward to hunt for another, and I find myself watching him more than I do the screen—a selection entitled *The Laddie and the Sexy Tramp.*

Does this arouse him, Lucifer? His posture reveals nothing. He stands straight. He doesn't flex his hips when he's erect the way Vinny does—if he even is…

After that video ends, he finds another. And yet another. By the tenth clip, my mind swims with vulgar phrases. I've seen a cock go into more places on the human body than I'm comfortable with. Silly, nonsensical questions form before I can help it. *Anal or vaginal? Missionary or doggy style? Which one would piss Vinny off more?*

I'm so caught up on the logistics that I don't even notice when the laptop screen finally goes black. Lucifer's been watching me, though I'm not sure for how long. His expression is almost easy to read for once. He thinks I'm disgusted.

I'm determined. "When will it happen?" I ask.

He shrugs. "When—"

There's a knock on the door. I jump at the sound, but Lucifer's already across the room.

"Who is it?" he demands in a tone that makes something inside me quake.

"Arno."

The door opens, revealing the red-haired man.

"I do have a key for this fucking place, you know," he says, but his playful smile dissipates the moment his eyes leave Lucifer and focus on me. "It's showtime, princess," he snarls while he throws something at me over Lucifer's shoulder: a box that bounces across the floor and lands at my feet. It's black, with *Trojan* written across the sides in gleaming silver script. *Ribbed for her pleasure* proclaims the tagline. "We do this now," Arno says.

Now. I blink and only now do I seem to realize how dark it is. The laptop's screen casts a bluish light that paints everything in a morbid glow. It reflects off Lucifer's back, emphasizing the muscle straining the cotton of a shirt nearly identical to the one hanging on me.

"Take her across the hall," Arno tells Lucifer, who seems to stiffen at the request disguised as an order.

There's an uneasy truce between these two men, I sense. Lucifer isn't one of his lapdogs, and yet helps him out of a reason other than fear. *Loyalty?* It's such a strange contrast to the way Vinny interacts with his goons. They are loyal to his money but obey him solely out of fear.

Lucifer sighs a violent sound. Then he cuts his gaze to me and jerks his head toward the doorway. "Come on."

I scuttle from the couch and bend to grab the box of condoms. They weigh me down as I enter another hallway lined with several closed doors. Only one is open now, displaying what appears to be another apartment, but the layout is different from Lucifer's. I swallow hard as I creep up behind him and toe the edge of the doorway.

In the space meant to serve as the living room, someone placed a bed. Black sheets hang from the walls, obscuring the windows. Perched on a tripod in the far corner is a camera, its lens centered on the mattress.

"Change." The red-haired man, Arno, shoves another object in my direction. It's a bag. *Victoria's Secret* is written along the side.

My fingers shake when I take it. Then I force myself to step over the apartment's threshold. It smells different than Lucifer's. There's the lingering scent of cigarette smoke and the faint odor of the men who most likely set up this little showroom.

I don't let myself picture which of those men might be chosen as my costar. I'll survive. I'll live long enough to at least make a dent in the shackles Vinny has enslaved me in for so long. I will...

But my traitorous body isn't as easy to reassure. It tenses as I creep across the room and find a narrow bathroom nearly identical to the one in Lucifer's apartment. I strip his shirt and then fish my "costume" from the depths of the shopping bag. It looks like something the women in those videos might wear: panties and a black bra that seem to contain more bits of revealing lace than they do fabric. My nipples show through the bra, and Vinny's brand is a blazing reminder of the man and his rules. The panties are just a triangular strip and then a slender line of string that I guess is meant to separate my legs. I pull them on woodenly, observing my reflection with a frown.

Lynn is a disjointed mess. Her bruised face serves as a harsh reminder of the duress she's under. I'll have to do my best to pretend—no, to *act*. I want this.

"You want this," I tell myself, though my trembling voice has trouble even reaching my own eardrums—let alone Lucifer's.

He's waiting on the other side of the door when I come out. His face is expressionless, though a part of me shivers with the grim knowledge that he heard what I said.

"Are you the one—"

"No," he says coldly, and I can't smother a relieved sigh.

Some nameless, faceless man who smells...I can handle. Not Lucifer. His eyes see too much. His body is too big—too much like Vinny's. My act won't hold up around him. It's a good thing if...

I shake my head. "Who, then?"

He focuses his gaze down the hall, toward the main room, as if wondering that very thing himself. "Wait here."

Dante

"So, who is it?" I demand of Arno.

He's seated on the bed. Both hands are braced on his knees, and for the first time since Parish...I see a hint of the old dog peeking through the haze of grief.

"Why?" he snaps. "You want her?"

"Cut the shit," I snap. I picture the girl—I can't help it. Wearing the shit Arno bought for her, she looked like a child hooker. I know she has to be legal if she's legally engaged to Stacatto, but still... There's something inherently creepy about seeing her tits bound by a push-up bra, her eyes wide and empty in porcelain sockets.

"I know the perfect man for the job," Arno insists.

"Who?"

He holds my gaze for a second, his eyes narrowed. Then, all at once, his shoulders slump, weighed down by exhaustion. He looks ten years older, and something tells me that, despite that promise to sleep, he hasn't laid off the drink since this morning. "You," he says.

I whirl on him. "The hell I am—"

"*Please*, Dante." He stands and starts to pace. He moves his hands through the air as if to illustrate the fucking insanity his mind must be entertaining if he thinks I'll agree. "I've been thinking," he starts. "You're right. If we play our cards...Stacatto will be willing to negotiate for her. And, fuck, I want... I *need* to make the fucker squirm." His eyes glow with an unsteady gleam. Stacatto will pay, all right—and dearly—if Arno has any say in it. "But this shit has to go down properly. I can't trust one of those other fuckers to do it right. To let her... I would ask Francisco, but he's gay." He breaks off suddenly, his eyebrow raised. "Unless you're..."

I roll my eyes and bunch my hands into fists, trying to ignore the infernal itching. It creeps up again, inching toward the first knuckle of every single finger. "I'm not."

"You've just... I've never seen you take a girl," Arno says quickly. "And, even if you *were* gay, that would change nothing between us."

I don't know whether to be irritated or honored by the fact that he seems to mean it.

"But if you *aren't*..."

"No."

"It's free ass, Dante."

"No."

"I'd do it myself, but I'll kill her." His eyes are desperate. He can't seem to stop flexing his fingers as if already wrapping them around the girl's slender throat. "I can't...I can't. *Please.*"

I grit my teeth and turn to face the wall. My hands shake fully. The familiar buzzing eats away at the back of my skull. The only way to silence it is to punch the wall so hard that I feel the impact in my fucking bones. With my throbbing knuckles still pressed against the dented plaster, I force out, "Why me?"

"It has to look good. The bitch needs to be willing or whatever the fuck she wants. I know you loved Rish, but you don't..."

"I don't what?" The words come out riding a growl. The beast is nibbling away at his cage, hungry and restless; it takes more effort to rein him in. I blink and my vision's red. Blink again and the wall is white.

"You don't get...emotional," Arno says as if it's as simple as that.

Emotional. I laugh, only the sound trickles out of me more like a wolf's jagged snarl.

"You *don't,*" he insists. "You don't let shit get to your head. You can think clearly when all I want to do is..."

Kill. Bite. Fight. Fucking rip. Tear. Destroy. I swallow hard. Ruby-colored light seeps across the room. The buzzing surges into a deafening hum.

"Do this for me," Arno says, sounding miles away, "and I'll get Espi to talk to you."

"What?" I turn, shaking my head to clear it. Arno flashes from normal to scarlet and back again.

"Espi," he says, drawing the name out. "I'll talk to him. I'll get him to at least listen to you. He won't be happy about it, but if you do this for me...I'll make it happen."

My jaw clenches around another refusal. My eyes narrow, but I swallow hard and push it down—just like Arno knew I would. "I've been looking for him," I say coldly.

"I know."

"Then why do you fucking wait until now—"

"Because he doesn't want to talk to you," Arno says quickly. "He made that very, *very* clear." He rubs at his jaw as if the kid had punched him there. Fuck, maybe the little shit did. "But I know of a way to make him. Though, like I said, it won't be pretty."

I inhale, squeezing my eyes shut. *Fuck. Fuck. Fuck.* My fingers are on fire, aching to punch something. Or maybe *gouge*—starting with Arno's fucking eyes. I don't need a middleman to talk to Espi. It could take time, but I know that the kid will come around on his own. Blood is thicker than water and shit. I cycle through my options. When I open my eyes again, the walls are a pale off-white. Arno's the same albino asshole he's always been, and the buzzing has gone silent.

"You get me a talk with Espi, and—"

"I'll bend over backward in a little pink skirt if you do this for me. Brother?" He takes a step forward, his hand outstretched. The jagged scar we made as teenagers seems to lurch against the dusky skin of his palm, and I feel my own hand twinge in answer.

I don't say a damn word when I slap my palm against his. I don't say a damn word when he gives me a brief rundown of how to work the camera before racing from the room as if that might keep me from changing my mind.

Standing here, while the girl finally creeps out down the hall...I don't say a damn word.

Daniela

I expect to find my costar when I finally gather up the nerve to enter the "bedroom" again. Not Lucifer. He's standing tall, silhouetted against the backdrop of black sheets like his fallen, angelic namesake. He's angry. His body ripples with tension, and something in mine tightens in response. When his eyes finally focus on me, I'm unprepared for the venom I find spilling out of them.

"Come here." He crooks a finger—such an unusual gesture coming from him that I find myself inching forward. His hands are heavy when they fall over my shoulders. He uses the grip to marshal me toward the end of the bed. Then he manually steers me around to face the camera. He makes sure I'm still watching when he crosses over to it and hits a button that I assume turns it on.

"Show us what you've got, sweetheart." His voice is a cold, mocking parody of its usual emotionless baritone. His eyes are dark coals. There's no shred of lust in his posture—it's too tense.

My heart starts to race. My palms are slippery. Words race up my throat, but only a few trickle out. "I thought...you said..."

"Well, I fucking lied," he snarls, taking a step toward me.

I flinch back. His hands are shaped like manacles, and his expression...it's so much like Vinny's. I can't breathe. The room is too small. The floor buckles underneath me, and I somehow wind up perched on the edge of the mattress, clinging to the black sheets for balance.

"N-no..." I don't know if I'm talking to him or myself. *No, you can't waste this chance. No, it can't be him. No. No. No.*

Lucifer hisses out a laugh and staggers toward the wall. His fist strikes it once—hard enough to make the entire surface tremble. "The fuck if I even *want* to."

Something in his voice shakes me awake from the fear. There's no lust in it. No desire. No sadistic need to intimidate. *He doesn't want me.* Somehow, that fact is enough to give me the strength to stand. My knees tremble.

Once again, my body goes against my mind's conviction. I can do this...

"The...the camera is still on." My voice scratches at the silence, fighting with the mechanical whirl of the machine in question.

Lucifer stiffens. He flattens his fist against the wall, his shoulders hunched away from me. I have to grit my teeth and fight to maintain my resolve when he finally turns to face me. His eyes are an unsteady shade of indigo. Blue fire—that color at the base of the flame. They watch me coldly while one of his hands drifts down to the buckle of his jeans.

"Don't sound so eager," he scolds, his voice an acidic taunt.

But there's something inside his gaze so unexpected that it makes my heart stop. I'm panting when my pulse catches up again. I blink rapidly, but there's no mistaking it.

For a minute...I swear his expression almost resembled Olga's right before Vinny bent her over on the floor. That same helpless plea. *I don't want this.*

"Why...why you?" I ask, and suddenly, I don't know if I'm referring to making the video or...*everything.* Of all the men, he was the only one who interfered with the red-haired man's original plan.

Lucifer grits his teeth rather than answer. In an instant, he's cold and collected again, my angel in the flesh. With one hand, he undoes the fastenings of his pants while the other reaches into his boxers for his cock. He isn't hard, I see when the boxers finally come down and he's fully bare before me.

Even so, his size is impressive. I can't help but wonder how large he'll be once fully erect. His hand tightens over the shaft as if he senses my train of thought and doesn't like one damn bit of it. He eyes the ceiling and strokes himself slowly. Then harder. Faster.

It's no use. He's still not aroused despite the friction. He doesn't want me.

I step forward without thinking, my hand reaching out. "W-what can I do?"

He bites out a growl when I take a step too close. It's like approaching a caged animal, one that is mortally wounded and doesn't give a damn whether I'm friend or foe. It'll chew off its leg rather than admit its own weakness. For so very long, I was that animal. I know the bars of that cage well. You will never convince the beast to come out on its own; you can only climb inside.

He flinches when I reach for him again.

"T-tell me what to do—"

"Get the hell away from me." He continues to stroke himself and then groans when the action fails to produce any results. Those icy-blue eyes settle on my cleavage. For nearly a minute, he watches me until he finally crooks his finger again, beckoning me closer. "Come here."

I obey, my heart pounding. My throat's dry. I don't know why I choose to sink to my knees, just out of his reach.

Lucifer watches me warily. Then he grounds out a sigh and inches forward. His hands fall down to his sides, and he's at my mercy.

Dante

She palms my cock with all the care of a snotty little socialite handling her tiara. I can't deny the softness in her fingers. Heat stirs in my blood at her touch, something I couldn't accomplish myself.

I hate watching her. Her wide eyes drift up and down the shaft. She licks her lips. Then she curls her fingers around me fully and guides her hand back and forth. *Damn*...she studied those videos too fucking well.

One of my hands shoots back to find the wall, and I brace my palm flat against it while tension gathers in my abdomen, shooting down my spine. She's not like the other handfuls of women I've had. She takes her time. She's slow. Careful. Her pampered, prissy hands lavish attention on every inch of my length, and the greedy fucker's hungry for it.

I inhale and breathe out through my teeth. I try to imagine that it's anyone but her. Not Stacatto's stuck-up whore. I don't want her. I don't want to taste her skin or bury myself between those stick-thin little thighs. I don't want to rake my hands through her hair and hold her goddamn mouth in place while I pummel it. I don't want...

I flinch when her other hand settles against my hip, using it for leverage while she increases her pace. Holy...fuck. She's too fast. Not fast enough. I glance down and find that she's already looking up, her gaze meeting mine. I don't find shame stretching across that pale, battered face. There's hell in her eyes: the inferno Stacatto put her in and the new flames she herself is willing to set. She's beckoning for me to join her, become swallowed by the fire.

Espi. Espi. Espi. I chant his name like a fucking prayer to counter her. I'm doing this for him. Not because I want her. I don't. She's...

A fast learner. Her mouth twitches in only the slightest clue of her hesitation. Then she parts her lips wide and leans forward to take as much of the tip of me into her mouth as she can. Her tongue cradles the underside. She bobs her head slightly, mimicking the motion she's only seen performed by porn stars. It works, however. I stiffen. I'm thicker. Her entire body trembles as she realizes what she's done, but it's too late. The hell she wants to burn in so badly...I'll give it to her.

My entire vision goes red when I fist my hand in her hair, dragging her closer. She takes me deeper with a startled gasp, and the pathetic vibration travels all the way to my brain. My hips jerk, my cock twitching, aching to plunge into the wet heat of her mouth. Every stroke of her tongue paints my vision in slashes of red and amber.

Clenching my jaw, I shove her away, staggering against the wall. My cock twitches angrily in protest. Desires I've suppressed for too fucking long flare up, unwilling to be locked in their cage again. *Five years. Five years. Five years.* It's a mantra that guides me when I reach down and clench the base of my shaft in a fist before I come too soon and end this fucked-up little party.

It's been five years since my last roll in the hay. It's the timespan that makes me react—not her. Not those goddamn fucking eyes or the faint glimmer in them that flares up as she falls back onto her ass, her lips parted and wet. It's harder than I want to admit not to move forward and shove myself between them, rubbing out this searing, stupid physical reaction.

Arno can take his deals and shove them up his ass. I won't go through with this. I open my mouth, aiming to tell her as much... "Get...get the condoms."

She obeys on her hands and knees, nearly lunging across the floor to reach the box near the base of the bed. Her fingers shake as she gets the top open. She withdraws a square of foil and glances back at me.

I thrust my hand out, but before she can move, I jerk my chin toward the box again. "There's lube," I grit out. A customary sample size, according to the box.

It's a simple courtesy I'm not sure why I grant to her. Her comfort or dignity don't seem to matter to her one damn bit, but she fishes it out anyway, tucking the small packet in her other hand. I try not to react when she approaches me again, still on her fucking knees. She places the condom onto my palm, and I tear it open with my teeth. I have it on in seconds, held in place with one hand. It's like I have to hold my fucking *cock* in place. It stirs while she eyes the lube in her grip.

Slowly, she nibbles a hole in the corner of the packaging with her teeth; those pornos taught her another trick. She lathers the substance onto her fingers and then brings them to the waistband of the thong Arno gave her to wear. She hesitates, uncertainty distorting her features. Then she tugs on the elastic with one hand and slides the two fingers of the other underneath...

"Fuck." My head rears back, my eyes shutting as heat unfurls swiftly and centering between my legs. I'm thicker. Harder. My eyes fly open again and I find her carefully slicking the entrance of her cunt. In three unsteady steps, I'm in front of her while she scrambles to her feet. I reach out, intending to shove her back onto the bed, but she bats my hand away.

"No." Her hand is on my chest before anger can even flare up. The fingers tremble as she pushes me back, causing her nails to graze the skin beneath the cotton of my shirt. I stiffen, prepared to shove her off. "I...I need to be in control."

That's right, a part of me remembers. This is *her* little game. I'm just a guest at this twisted tea party, merely meant to be manipulated into position for the best possible effect. She takes another tiny step toward me, her scent heavy on the air: blood, pain, and desperation. Then, before I even know it, *I'm* the one herded back onto the bed. My knees bend automatically when she flicks her wrist. Seconds before the curtain rises, Vinny Stacatto's little whore gives me one last appraising glance.

Then she turns to the camera—her true costar—and it's showtime. People say that men like me can change within the blink of an eye. We can go from contained to uncontrolled with little provocation. We shed our skins eagerly to become the monsters we only *pretended* not to be while out in public. It's like hitting a switch almost; it's that fucking simple.

Stacatto's girl flips her own switch. She stands taller while her eyes home in on the camera's lens. She doesn't hesitate to shed her underwear, revealing an ass stained blue, purple, and green with healing bruises. She inhales, and her entire body seems to recoil with the breath she takes.

That pathetic little princess is gone when she turns back to me. The creature staring out from behind a sea of black hair is a completely different animal. I can't ignore the part of me that stiffens and howls out in welcome as she mounts the bed on her hands and knees and waits for me to do the same. There's a hint of recognition in the way she takes her time slinking toward me, imagining her fiancé watching every move. There's no shame. No barely concealed self-deprecation of a porn star. She's in control. Hell, she's drunk on it. A part of me knows exactly what she's feeling: the instinctive need to scratch this dark, dangerous urge that won't be satisfied until she's sure Stacatto is punished. I can almost hear the insistent buzz emanating from the back of her head, swelling to a hum.

After all, it takes a wolf to know a wolf.

CHAPTER THIRTEEN

Daniela

He feels like glass under me when I finally straddle his broad waist—unbreakable, bulletproof, thicker-than-steel glass. It's a fragile, terrifying game to balance myself over hard muscle and twisting sinew. His erection stabs at the air. His eyes set the room on fire. He's calculating my every move, and it's a good thing the camera won't be able to catch his expression from this angle.

My ruse would be over before it's even begun.

I try not to tremble when I reach down to place the flat of my hand against his chest while I shift my weight to bring myself closer to his hips. I can feel his heartbeat—it rails against me, fierce and brutal. For a brief, faint moment, I consider scrambling away and insisting they find someone else. Anyone else.

Lucifer is too...*everything.* His cock aims away from me, and I swallow hard while I try to entertain the notion that he could ever fit inside me. It will hurt. Some sick part of me even craves that pain.

Not Vinny. He's not Vinny, this little voice at the back of my head screams. Vincent Stacatto would never lie back and let me mount him like this. He wouldn't merely stare while my shaking fingers reached for his cock. He wouldn't dare me with his eyes, issuing a silent challenge to just do it. Fuck him already.

I press my knees into the bed to find enough leverage to lift myself off him. He's steel in my grip, and it's almost a struggle to place the head of him against my entrance. Lube won't be enough to ease him inside me. I know it, and it's nearly impossible to swallow the wave of fear that washes up, threatening to pull me under...

But I do. My gaze drifts above Lucifer's head and finds the ever-watchful eye of the camera. I stare into it while I lower myself onto him, trying to force him inside me. He grunts. I gasp. There is burning tension already. He's too big. Too much. He's...not Vinny.

I let that single thought drive me as I flex my hips and sink down *hard*. God...it burns. He's an inferno inside me, swelling and raging against the confines of my body. I'm consumed by the feeling. I see black; the pain is so much. Grunted sounds tear from Lucifer's throat. He strains, twitching inside me, begging for more friction.

My vision is a blur when my eyes open again. My head's thrown back, my gaze on the ceiling. One of my hands is at my lips, trying to smother the sound of pain I made—and a sudden, terrifying realization batters me down. Vinny owns me even here. Even with another man inside me, I can't erase the damage he's done, the reactions he trained my body to perform instinctively.

I can't. I can't...

"Fuck."

The coarse sound yanks at me like a tether. I glance down and find Lucifer staring up at me, his dark eyes hooded. He wants me to move...on him. I can see the need in his eyes even though he tries to counter it by clenching his jaw.

I flex my hips ever so slightly, feeling my body protest at the intrusion of his. The blue fire grows hotter. Searing. Biting my lower lip, I move again, bracing my hand against his stomach for leverage. *Again.*

His pupils dilate. His hips jerk beneath me. I swivel harder, gasping out when he nudges inner parts of me, as hungry and brutal as a battering ram. With every sick, painful movement, Vinny can't touch me. I move faster, rocking an instinctive rhythm back and forth, forth and back. Up. Down. The faster I move, the better I feel. Oh, God, he feels...

The bed shifts. He's arching up, changing the angle of pressure. I hiss between my teeth, but I don't resist. I gasp again. Colors spot my vision. My fingers curl, snagging a fistful of his shirt, yanking him closer...and then shoving him right back down. I almost forget Vinny in the dizzying rush. Then my eyes spot the camera capturing every moment.

It's like surfacing from an eternity spent underwater when I rip the ring off my finger and throw it into the corner of the room. I'm drunk on the feeling. *Freedom?* It prickles all over my body, gathering between my legs and traveling up my stomach. I feel him everywhere, Lucifer, even though he digs his nails into the bedsheets rather than touch me.

And I need him to. I need Vinny to see. I need to feel. I need, need, *need,* and for the first time in my life, I just take what I want. My hands grab his wrists and I place the callused fingers on my hips, my breasts. *Touch me.*

He doesn't want to. I can see the challenge blaring from his eyes. He wants this over. I *need* this to continue.

"Please." I don't recognize the woman who calls out. Her voice is a plaintive little howl, but Lucifer's nails graze my skin as he starts to grope, punishingly and brutally at my flesh. My hands clutch his wrists, manipulating his touch. Here. There. I want every part of me raked raw by his fingers. I want him to mark every single inch of me.

My eyes drift shut, and my body moves of its own accord, driving him in, *deeper, deeper, deeper. Harder. Faster. Harder. More. More.*

I'm not prepared for the heat that swelters. Sweat slicks my skin. He roils beneath me, too strong and heavy to fight, but he lets me stay on top. He lets me set the pace. He lets me keep control.

And I'm drowning beneath that power.

We fuck for Vinny. We fuck each other. We *fuck*, and there are no pretty words to describe it. I'm a base, primal creature hungry for only one thing. He gives it to me, holding me in place for several brutal, hungry thrusts that claw noises out from my chest. His own growls echo mine, tense and strained. They reveal the secret he didn't want me to know—when he finally throws his head back and groans out his release, I feel the truth hit me like a kick to the gut.

He *wanted* this.

It's a bitter victory some part of me gloats over. I let him grip me. Bruise me. Use me. Hold me up while he thrusts out the rest of his release and fills the condom.

I'm laughing when it's all over, and Lucifer relaxes beneath me if only for a second, his body devoid of that animalistic tension. I laugh when he shoves me away and peels the bloody, sweaty, filthy used condom off. Our desperation marks it, mine and his.

I laugh and laugh until I don't even notice the tears that fall down my cheeks as I lie limp and used on the mattress. I've never felt dirtier than I have now. I've never felt cleaner. I've never felt better. For the first time in my life, I truly feel free, if only in this moment...

A stranger between my legs had to give me this, driving the sensation into my body like a nail.

The devious thought makes me stop laughing. It makes me hate him—how many women experience this with him?

But, for some reason, *that* thought only makes me hungry for more.

It isn't fair.

Dante

My head's still separated from my body when I stand and toss the used condom onto the floor. The camera flashes a red light to let us know it's still fucking recording. Still watching. Still waiting for us to put on a good show.

I nearly knock it over when I jab my thumb against the button to shut it off. It trembles on its tripod, that ever-watchful eye swaying back and forth, threatening to turn Vincent's princess's little exploits into nothing more than smashed metal and film.

Oh, but no princess I knew of could fuck like that. She's a little predator wrapped up in the skin of a lamb. It takes one to know one, though my disguise was shredded long ago in favor of my true form. I wear it when I face her again. She's slumped on the center of the mattress, her eyes swollen, her chest heaving, her nipples stabbing at the air, her legs still parted.

The rules of her little game were simple. We play nice for the camera. We put on a good show for her big, bad fiancé. I let her ride me like a cheap circus attraction.

But the show's over now. It's time for the dancing animals to be shoved back into their cages behind the stage. There's a mess that needs to be cleaned up. Fresh tickets to sell.

The little bitch doesn't react when I grab her by the ankle and drag her to the edge of the bed. She watches me, a grim smile playing over her mouth like she knows the thoughts circling through my head when I sink onto my knees and pull her legs apart, throwing one over either shoulder. She doesn't even flinch until I seal my mouth over her cunt and shove my tongue inside her.

She makes a sound she didn't learn from those porno videos, however. Her hands claw at my shoulders. Then my hair. She whines when I find her clit and graze the bundle of flesh between my teeth. Her taste floods me, more potent than any of the shit Arno has stocked in his bar.

One hand on her waist keeps her pinned down while I taste the little bitch inside and out. She's sweet, if it's even fucking possible. Sweet like liquor. Sweet like heroin. She's an addict's kind of bitter taste—my own personal hit of dope.

I take every dose until she's writhing. Until the sounds she makes cease being sounds at all, and she's merely grunting beneath the brutal, twisted fuck. I taste every single goddamn inch of her. Then I use my fingers to finish her off, trapping her clit beneath my thumb and rubbing until her back bows and her nails break my skin. It's only when she's limp and panting that I come up for air.

I don't take the time to observe her flushed body when I spot my jeans lying in the corner and I shove them on. With single-minded determination, I rip the camera from the tripod. When I toe the threshold, I finally look back and find her watching me, her eyes unsettling...

And I slam the door behind me so hard that it shakes on its fucking hinges.

———

ARNO'S SEATED AT THE BAR, WAITING FOR ME. HE doesn't react when I drop the camera onto his fucking lap. He doesn't make eye contact. There's a full shot glass on the counter in front of him, and he merely shoves it toward me.

I take it and knock it back, grimacing at the bitter taste. It's a dangerous fuel to add to the fire already consuming my fingertips. The blaze grows hotter, lapping up my wrists and surging through my blood with every unstable beat of my pulse. *She* did this. Her taste mingles with the alcohol. I swipe at my mouth with the back of my hand, but she clings to my lower lip, stubborn and vile. I rub at the spot, nearly stripping the skin raw. Then I take the second shot Arno offered me and down it.

He says nothing when I leave and slam the door on my way out. It's dusk. A spreading night sky battles with a resistant, orange sunset that scars the horizon like a burning fire. I scowl at it. Then I head down the street, going wherever my fucking legs take me. I'm unfamiliar with this part of the city. After five years, street names have changed. New buildings have crept up on top of the ashes of the old ones. Even the people are different. Tougher. Stranger. Louder.

They don't offer me one fucking moment of silence to clear my head. One moment to find the familiar beast that I know dwells in my skin like a parasite. The barrage of sound doesn't even succeed in drowning her out. I still hear her moaning. Panting. Begging. Pleading. The sounds form a noose around my cock, which is so fucking greedy after having been denied for so long.

Trolling the streets like a dog off its leash is a bitter way to brace myself for the wrath that will come once Stacatto sees what his fiancée's gladly done. But the fucker can come for me. I'm ready.

Oh, the fuck am I ready.

I almost believe that fate's playing some kind of cruel, twisted joke when a man staggers into me the moment I turn a corner. For the first time in his fucking life, Dante Vialle finally gets his goddamn wish...

"You got a problem?" the man demands, his head cocked. He has a five-o'clock shadow stretching over his jaw and wears the dirty jeans and the oversized sweatshirt of a punk with too much time on his hands and too much dope in his brain to know when to back down.

"Yeah," I tell him. "I've got a big fucking problem."

The bastard doesn't hear the warning note in my voice. Tt's the jarring crunch of a bulldog breaking off its leash; it's the second when the wolf realizes there's blood in the air and releases a howl; it's a danger even I sense, and my fingers clench, fighting to ignore the way they burn. Throb. *Ache*, still slick with her.

The stupid fucking bastard doesn't know how close I am to losing control. How much I goddamn *want* to lose it. I need any excuse. Any fucking one.

And he presents it by stupidly stepping closer. His hot breath fans my cheek, mingling with the sweat from her skin. Her taste is still on my tongue, even as the bastard says, "I suggest you apologize. Friend."

It's like lighting a match above a pool of gasoline. Fire erupts, spreading wild and ravenous, and there's no fucking way to contain it. My skull breaks open and something evil spills out. It stains my vision the color of blood, and my fist goes flying.

Flesh and bone reverberate beneath my knuckles. Again. Again. Again. There's shouting. I'm in the middle of the street in near broad fucking daylight, but none of it fucking matters. I can hear each sickening blow I land. Maybe the bastard managed to get some in himself, because I'm not sure whose blood I taste when hands paw at my shoulders and finally pull me back.

Under...arrest... The words come in slow motion. Pieces of my vision return like puzzle pieces. The conflicted sky. A confused sea of faces. A body lying motionless in front of me.

My mouth's open, I realize. I'm laughing as icy metal encircles my wrist and some asshole reads me my Miranda rights while sirens wail in the distance.

I can't fucking stop.

It's been nearly a week, right on the dot. Van Hallen was right.

———

General lockup isn't like being in prison. You're herded like cattle into a cage with other vicious mutts. They size you up, warily wondering which dog has the biggest dick—who you just don't want to fuck with. Maybe it's the blood on my knuckles. Or the look in my eye. Hell, maybe it's the subtle scent of I-don't-give-a-fuck wafting from my skin. Whatever the reason, I'm left alone. It makes for an interesting way to pass the night. Arno might want to try it sometime when he's not drinking himself to death on liquor.

Nothing says "fun" like waiting for the inevitable.

"Vialle."

I stiffen at the sound of my name mangled by a Brooklyn accent. An officer stands before the holding cell, reading from a clipboard—but his uniform isn't the royal blue of a patrol officer. He's wearing a tan trench coat over faded-gray slacks. He sure takes his job seriously, down to every last fucking cliché.

"Vialle," Van Hallen reads again while his eyes seek mine out through the bars. "You're free to go."

Free? I don't question it. I hold my tongue when an actual officer enters the cell and undoes my cuffs. He and Van Hallen lead me to the front of the station, where I sign a piece of paper. Just like that. I'm "free."

"You've been bailed out," Van Hallen explains when I start to head for the door. "Seems you've got some powerful friends out there, Vialle. The man whose jaw you broke won't even press charges. Says it was all just a 'misunderstanding'—or he *wrote* it, at least. There are even corroborating witnesses who've stepped forward to say that he started it first. It was self-defense."

I should keep walking, but I don't know what makes me slow near the glass doors to the station and glance over my shoulder. The only other person around is a clerk behind the front desk who does her best to busy herself with paperwork and pretend to be invisible.

"There a point to this, Detective?" I ask.

Van Hallen, the prick, merely smiles. "If you were out on parole, you wouldn't even have the option of bail. You'd be sent right back where you belong."

I shrug. "But my record's sparkling clean, Detective. The DA saw to that."

"Don't fuck with me, Vialle," the detective says gruffly. "We both know it's only a matter of time before you're hooked up on something that intimidation and nice connections can't wriggle you out of. Tell me something. A man loses his temper and nearly beats someone to death right in front of a passing patrol car containing officers just about to start their break. Talk about coincidence."

I raise an eyebrow, dissecting his words. "You've got a detail on me..." I spot a name tag stuck to his chest and play off the fitting name embossed there in gold. *Richard V. H.* "*Dick?*"

He shrugs, but there's something smug about his expression. The buzzing at my skull perks up, but it's only a dull whisper, sated by enough violence for now.

"Let's be serious now, Vialle," Van Hallen says. "A man would notice if he were being followed, wouldn't he?"

I grit my teeth, irritated by this interesting new bit of information. "That he would, Detective."

"A man would also try to keep things in perspective," Van Hallen adds, and I suspect that this is the real reason why he cornered me here. Not to gloat about the fact that he had men watching me, but to spew whatever is about to come out of his mouth next. "I've been going through your old case file. Interesting stuff."

I turn on my heel and head for a door, not giving a damn as to how it looks.

"You beat a man to death with a hammer..." The bastard keeps up with me. "But do you care to explain why there were no fingerprints? No hard physical evidence? Nothing we could pin on you, not even with the fuck-up at the DA's office. A man who's reckless enough to kick someone's ass in broad daylight can't even leave *one* bloody smear on the end of a ball peen—"

I barrel through the glass doors and allow them to slam shut behind me. Van Hallen's not stupid. He doesn't follow me out of the precinct, but I feel him watching me. Then I have enough fucking sense to scan the block for any patrol car or cop who seems to be on my trail. It's late. Pedestrians crowd the sidewalks, heading home or looking for trouble, while traffic churns through the streets.

It'll be a long walk back to Mulligans, and I can only assume that's why Arno didn't send one of his thugs to collect me. He wants me to sweat it out. Clear my head. The bastard's known me for way too long.

CHAPTER FOURTEEN

Daniela

They leave me here. In this room. On this bed. Drowning beneath his scent and mine. The sheets are a prison. The ones hanging from the walls drape me in shadow. I'm a twisted, shallow shell of a creature who doesn't truly know what she even is anymore.

My head swims with him. The things he made me feel. What I wanted to feel…

I'm sore and throbbing between my legs. When I slide a hand down my stomach, there's only wet skin, still burning from the heat of his mouth. My eyes slam shut while my fingers do things I don't tell them to. *Rub. Twist. Touch.* They mimic him, but the feeling isn't the same. It's a slow, painful burning that only intensifies when my mind pairs my own ministrations with dangerous, twisted thoughts. Images, really. His face. Those eyes. The sounds he made when sheathed inside me to the hilt.

My head goes back as my fingers quicken. My stomach bunches and tightens into knots. My eyes roll within their sockets. I cry out once and then drive my teeth into my lower lip to silence the sound. Breathless and shaking, I rock against my own hand, forced to picture him. Taunted by him. Haunted by him. Then everything in me loosens again, all at once, and I unravel.

My eyes are wet when my body finally goes limp, and the only thing I can do is pant. I draw my hand away and let it fall to my side, aching and pathetic. My lungs heave for air, struggling to push out the unwanted stench of musk and rage that taints a man like Lucifer.

I almost succeed. Almost. Then I move and my body flares to life with the aftermath of being filled by him all over again.

I hate him. I hate him more than Vinny. More than the red-haired man. More than Gino and Nicolai. More. More. More. No matter the evil comparison, it still isn't *hateful* enough.

The only course of action I have left to take is to crawl from the mattress and stagger into the bathroom. The lights are already on, and they illuminate everything about me in harsh clarity. My bloodshot eyes watch me accusingly from the mirror's surface. I'm dressed like a whore. Part of the duct tape on my ear is starting to peel off, revealing the gaping wound underneath. My hair is a mess. My lips are bloody. Angry little crescent-moon-shaped marks dot my skin, left by...nails. Fingernails. Greedy, grasping fingernails...

My head swims when I turn my back on the mirror and yank the lacy bra off. Then I stagger into the shower stall and turn the water on as hot as possible—the highest setting. Steam drifts up, distorting everything beneath its presence. My skin is on fire, but bit by bit, the pieces of himself that Lucifer left behind circle the drain along with everything else.

I strip myself of every inch of him. Then I recollect my thoughts, centering them around the only thing that matters: I was free. Vinny would see the video and…well, whatever happens after, I most likely wouldn't be around to see.

The sobering thought drives me to shut the water off. With no towel in sight, I settle for drying myself off using the bedsheets. Then I re-don my video "costume" and sit, bracing my back against the wall. Then I stand. I tap my foot against the floor. I pace. Despite the restlessness, I'm fine until I misstep and my toes cringe away from something rubbery…wet. I glance down and the world sways.

The next second, I'm backing out of the room and then the apartment altogether. The hallway's deserted. It's late, I assume. A flickering light bulb casts unsteady illumination and even harsher shadows. The door to Lucifer's lair is across the hall. I wonder if he's there. Can he sleep? Does he remember his promise?

My finger drifts up to graze a burning trail across my throat. It's not that hard to imagine it. With his strength alone, he could make it quick. With his icy temper, he could make it slow.

I'm not sure now which one I prefer.

My finger still trembles when I reach back and find the doorknob to the showroom. I should go back inside. Who knows what the red-haired man plans to do with me next. Until Vinny sees that tape, I'm still at his mercy. The fact that he went along with my little plan means nothing. Revenge taints things, even deals between enemies.

My foot twitches against the floor. I *need* to go back inside. I *shouldn't* stagger forward, trailing my hand along the wall for balance while the other tugs the apartment door shut behind me. It is a long, slow journey to Lucifer's red door. My heart falters the entire way. When my fingers finally brush the wooden door, I can only sense silence on the other side of it. Curling my fingers into a shaking fist, I knock once to no answer.

My knees curl instinctively, and I slide down to the floor, leaning against the wall. My hair shields the rest of the hall from me. Staring at a sliver of red paint, I can almost imagine that I'm truly in hell, at the mercy of my very own custom devil.

———

I'M SHAKEN AWAKE WHEN THE WORLD SHIFTS UNDER me. Something slams into my elbow, and I blink my eyes open in confusion. The red door is gone, revealing a portal of darkness in its place. A demon stands over me as if prepared to shove me through it, and I glance up into an icy-blue gaze.

He has his arm extended above me, clenching the doorknob in one hand while the other dangles by his side, curled into a loose fist. There is blood on his fingertips. Even more speckles his shirt. Fear mingles with dread, and I shift back against the doorjamb. Only now do I realize he already has the door open.

He tears his gaze away from me and steps over my curled legs. I wait for him to slam the door in my face. Maybe a part of me even wants him to—but the bastard leaves it open, and I can't resist the part of me that scuttles over the threshold and kicks it shut with my foot.

We stay like this for what feels like an eternity. A million questions well in my throat to fill the silence. *Where was he? Was the tape sent? What will happen next?* My teeth lock them away, however, so I settle for watching him instead. His back is turned to me. He doesn't move an inch, and the shadows drape us both as if struggling to conceal the naughty little secret we share.

Tension swallows me down whole. I wonder if he's affected, but almost as soon as the thought crosses my mind, he's already headed down the hall and into the bedroom. The door slams shut behind him, hard enough to jar the entire damn building, it seems like.

Sighing, I slump against the wall. My borrowed lingerie itches. The shower did little to ease the all-consuming ache that encases me from head to toe. It doesn't diminish any when I curl my knees up against my chin and rest the good side of my face on top of them.

It just lingers, seeping into my bones like the tendrils of fear sown by Vinny that will never ever fully leave. The devil's made his mark on my skin for all of eternity.

Whether we both like it or not.

Dante

I wake up hungover and painfully hard. My soul is hard. My resolve to find Espi, whether he wants me to or not, is even harder. My *cock* is steel...

It's a defect I struggle to ignore, gritting my teeth until I taste the damn enamel being ground away. When I lift my head and shrug the blankets off, I don't find Stacatto's whore lurking within one of the corners. I vaguely remember leaving her by the door, but for all I know, she could have run. Or maybe Arno's men had gotten bored and decided to "borrow" her for the night?

It's not the thought that drives me to my feet, and I wince as blood rushes to my throbbing head—both of them. I have to piss—maybe brush the fucking taste of that woman, blood, and booze from my mouth while I'm at it. *Those* are the concerns that drive me into the hallway.

I don't notice that the bathroom light is already on until I'm over the threshold, nearly running into the slim figure leaning against the sink. Her ass juts out, her pale hand clutching the sink's basin like it's the only thing capable of holding her up. She has my toothbrush clenched between her teeth. Apparently, she's as eager to scrub away the taste of my cock as I am to erase her. Her eyes meet mine as she woodenly manipulates the toothbrush before removing it from her mouth and spitting. Wordlessly, she turns the faucet on, washing her mess away. Then she holds her hand out, presenting the toothbrush to me.

I take it, easily muscling her body away from the sink and against the tub. My eyes narrow as I make a show of sticking the bristles beneath the running water and grinding them beneath my thumb, chasing her essence out. But it's as futile as picking up a dropped piece of food from the floor and pretending that unseen bacteria haven't already tainted it. I take a leap of faith when I slather the brush in toothpaste and shove it against my tongue. One hard scrub and I know I failed; she clings to the surface, and I'm grinding her taste between my teeth.

I don't let on though. I spit, rinse the bristles, and then return it to the cabinet. I use my hands to splash water onto my face, scrubbing at the crust that's formed around my eyes. I shut off every sensation but the mechanical motions. I almost succeed in blocking her out completely, but when I turn for the shower, she's still there. Her eyes home in on the moisture sliding down my chin. I don't think she notices my hand shoot past her to wrench the shower faucet on until the water switches on amid the squeal of rusty plumbing. Then she scuttles out of reach while I strip my bloodied shirt and jeans. Her eyes trace my calves as I shed my boxers though, and I know she's making note of the scars on my hips.

Fuck her.

The rag I gave her is near the drain, and I stoop to make use of it myself. Her blood is on it, but I pretend not to notice the pinkish stains and drag it over any part of me I can reach. I pay her no attention as I douse myself beneath the shower spray, taking my damn time. Only when the water goes cold do I step out of the tub. Naked, I pad across the floor and enter the hallway, pretending that she isn't watching my every step.

I slam the door behind me, cutting her view off. Then I take my time fishing for a fresh pair of jeans and a T-shirt. I don't bother to towel off, and the moisture causes the clothing to cling to my damp skin, but anything is better than the inevitable question of what will happen if I use any sort of friction on a certain part of my anatomy.

It's a pain in the ass to get the zipper up. It's more uncomfortable to move. It's harder to walk. My cock is a stubborn, ignorant, greedy fuck, and I almost entertain the idea of attempting to get myself off alone. I run a hand down my thigh, but my dick doesn't react. I think of a pair of pink, broken lips parting for me and it fucking *jumps.*

My fingers curl, strangling the air. Fuck her. *Fuck* her.

Arno can take her from here.

I have myself convinced of that when I enter the hall and barrel straight toward the kitchen. I snatch the milk from the fridge and drink right from the jug. Then I fish out a carton of eggs, crack two, pour them into a glass, and knock them back raw. I wash the gruesome mixture down with chunks of bread ripped right off the loaf. It isn't until I start to clean up the mess that I realize she's watching me from the couch.

I stiffen, but I don't understand what makes me shove the bread across the counter, though I never voice an invitation to her out loud. She rises anyway. She stole the shirt I left in the bathroom and is wearing it over the shit Arno gave her. I don't react as she comes closer. I swallow the rest of the milk and tear off another slice of bread just as she cautiously prods the loaf with slim fingers. She observes the substance carefully, turning it over in her hands.

I imagine that she's used to better breakfast options: omelets and shit shoved right down her fucking throat, served on a silver spoon. Just when I think she'll refuse, she takes a delicate bite and swallows. Her expression is guarded, but she doesn't hesitate to chew off another small piece.

"If you want eggs, you can make them yourself," I tell her, pushing past her to stand on the opposite side of the room.

"I don't know how."

I cock my head, eyeing her over my shoulder. A part of me wants to sneer at her admission; of course a pampered bitch wouldn't know how to cook. But then I remember my own limitations—what it felt like as a kid to be too terrified to use the stove, so I'd force myself to eat the eggs raw instead and be fucking grateful for a full stomach. I don't like relating to her, even on such a small, superficial scale.

"Then don't eat them," I snarl.

She nods, unconcerned by the venom in my tone. Then she skirts around the counter to gather up the carton and return it to the fridge. Her back is to me, but I can almost count her heartbeats by the trembling ripples that shake her back. "D-did you send it?"

"Arno has it." I face the wall, eyeing the nicks and dents left by only God knows how many previous owners. "I don't know if he has yet."

"He'll kill you, you know," she says, her voice cold and matter-of-fact. "You didn't cover your face. He'll—"

"He can get in fucking line." Someone like Stacatto is the least of my worries. The only bastard I fear these days lived within my own skin.

"You're not afraid."

Well, give the woman a medal. I turn to face her, expecting to find her gaping at me wide-eyed. She stares me down instead. There's no clue as to whether or not she's impressed by how easily I blow off a man she seems to fear. In fact, I'd stake my life on the guess that she isn't one damn bit.

"No," I say, searching her gaze for any hint as to what she thinks of that. They're guarded up tight. She's not so brazen when she's not in front of a camera, it seems.

"He's killed for less," she says simply.

"In front of you?" I don't know what made me ask. The princess hides bloodied hands beneath her kidskin gloves.

Maybe some sick part of me gets off on making her relive it. The horror. The pain. If so, the jagged emotion that runs through my chest when she flinches doesn't travel down to my cock.

"Yes..."

I don't expect her to elaborate, but she leans back against the fridge, crossing her arms over her chest.

"He's killed in front of me before. Sometimes, he makes me play for him while he does it."

"Play?" I clip the word, so it comes out less of a question, but she answers me anyway. It's almost like she can't resist the urge to talk—or at least do something besides sit and wait for the inevitable.

"Cello." There's a hoarse, aching note in her voice I can't miss.

Cello. I picture two instruments resembling the basic shape of a violin, but I'm not exactly sure which is which.

"I taught myself," she adds, and an unmistakable hint of pride colors her tone. "Where I grew up...we used to live near a community theater, and some days, they offered free lessons. My father was a janitor there, and when I went with him to work, I'd sneak into the music storage rooms and play when—" She breaks off, her lips sealing shut. Her gaze drifts to the corners of the room. She said too much.

"So, this man," I hear myself say once she's been quiet for over a minute. "You'd rather die than go back to him."

She nods, though we both know that it wasn't a question.

I feel my eyebrow lurch. "So, why marry him in the first place?"

When her cheeks redden, I expect the usual superficial reasons women like her use to excuse their own greed. *He took care of me. He wasn't always like this. I love him.*

Instead, she swells up, almost seeming to rise up onto the tips of her toes, and both of her hands clench the rim of the counter behind her. "I had no choice." The words tear out of her and echo off the walls. It's the loudest I've ever heard her speak. The little lamb's braying almost holds the edge of a growl now. "If I didn't, he would—" She stops herself again. Then she cradles her forehead in the palm of her hand, and her body deflates, leaving her about two feet tall. "I used to run away. Before. Sometimes I'd break away in public, where everyone could see. I'd try to leave. I *wanted* to run." She shakes. Her voice quickly deepens to a moan, but she can't seem to stop the flow of words that overtake her. "Then he brought me 'gifts.' Maids. Girls who could barely speak a word of English and were only meant to wait on me hand and foot. If I disobeyed him...he would use them to punish me."

"How?" I know even before I see the expression that crosses her face that the bastard didn't employ very orthodox methods.

"He'd...hurt them," she says as if struggling to get the words out. "The first girl, her name was Sabina. He slit her throat when I told him that I didn't want to go out for lunch." She chokes on a strangled sob and then swallows it back down. Her eyes gleam. The memories may torment her, but she won't let him control her here. "I tried to avoid learning their names after that. It was easier... And I tried. I tried to obey him. I tried to keep them alive. God, I tried. I *tried*."

"It wouldn't have mattered anyway," I tell her. A mad dog can only control its impulses for so long before the leash begins to chafe—a fact I know better than most. The sky could be too blue one day or the wind too chilly. If he feels the urge, a true monster can come up with any reason at all to take his rage out on someone else.

"H-he didn't like my hair," she stammers, proving my point. "My clothes. My face. My posture. Nothing I did kept him happy for long. And, when he gave me his ring..." She bites her lip as if to trap the painful revelations inside. She lasts for about a second before they spill out regardless. "I thought he might finally do it. Rape me." She lifts her shoulder in a casual shrug as if the thought of violence no longer even fazes her. "God...a part of me almost wanted him to. Maybe then he'd finally grow bored once I had nothing left."

She stares back at me, a ghost of a woman with soulless, empty eyes. It's such a stark contrast from the vixen who starred in her own sex tape less than twenty-four hours ago. There is nothing remotely comforting I can say, so I don't say anything. We merely stare, two dark, twisted animals who refuse to shy away from the brutality revealed in the other's gaze.

"What about you?" she asks suddenly, like a jackal

demanding I let her feed off the carcass of my own suffering the way I fed off hers. "The red-haired man. You defer to him, but he doesn't own you. Why?"

My eyes narrow at her word choice. *"He doesn't own you."*

"I'm not someone you can own," I tell her coldly.

"Vinny's men are," she counters. Her eyes dare me to prove that I don't have the name of some master tattooed into my skin.

"If you haven't noticed, I don't exactly work for your *fiancé.*"

She flinches, and I feel an echoing twinge in my chest that I write off as satisfaction.

"Who is he to you?" she asks, trying to rephrase the question, and only the softness of her voice keeps it from seeming like another haughty command.

"My brother."

She raises an eyebrow but doesn't challenge the designation —and a part of me almost bristles as that. It almost wants to see her challenge me. I'd gotten a taste of the little wolf lurking beneath her lambskin... One more peek of her couldn't hurt.

Oh, yes it can, a part of my anatomy warns. The front of my jeans was becoming a vise grip. *Death,* I chant inside my head, forming a list of the most disturbing shit I can think of. *Blood. Gore. Screaming. Gaping. Wounds...*

Like the one on her ear. She doesn't seem to notice that one is sporting a delicate diamond stud while the other is adorned by a wad of toilet paper and duct tape. It's like she's conditioned herself to shut the pain off. I've seen grown men barely cope with less of an injury. Color the predator in me impressed.

"So..." I inhale and switch to another topic of burning interest. "If Stacatto does want you alive, what if he specifies that we bring you to him first before any trade can be made?"

If I've poked a hole in her flawless plan, she doesn't let on. "You promised me," she says, refreshing my memory. "A man owned by no one should be very good at keeping his promises."

The little bitch has a point. "I warned you," I say rather than admit as much out loud. "I don't make promises."

Something dark taints the hazel of her eyes. I don't know what to think when she turns and opens the nearest drawer. She rummages through it, carefully searching. Opens another. Pulls out a knife.

I can't help the laugh that bellows out of me. My fingertips itch. The buzzing starts at the back of my skull. My cock throbs.

"Then I'll just kill myself," she says, pressing the blade to her throat. It's little more than a butter knife, but anything can make for a weapon if you're determined enough. Case in point was the ball-peen hammer Van Hallen cited in my own fucking case file. "Here and now. You should have nothing left to lose if I do."

The words aren't a threat because she knows she has nothing left in her arsenal to barter. The tip of the blade presses into her flesh. Her hand is steady. Her gaze doesn't leave mine once.

"So do it," I tell her. I shift my weight as if I'm turning for the door. I see her fingers tighten their grip. Then I move.

Vincent's little whore has never held a weapon before. It easily flies out of her grip when I bat her hand away and wrench her arm behind her back before she can even break her own skin. I force her onto the counter facedown and position myself behind her. She hisses in pain. It's a position designed to immobilize—but the seconds pass and I don't let her go.

I fully intend to, but my cock seems to have other intentions. She's too close. I can sense her heart beating frantically through her skin. The smell wafting from her is that of soap mixed with the artificial flavor of mint. She's warm...so fucking warm. And her ass avoids brushing the front of my hips by mere inches.

I don't want her. My fingers twitch, aiming to let her go, and she forces her body to go limp, making it easier to do so.

More seconds pass. Minutes. I know that her arm must have gone numb, but she doesn't complain. She doesn't resist. The little lamb has overcome her inner wolf as if resigned to a life of being prey.

Or so I think until her words reach me, muffled against the counter's surface.

"You are owned by no one," she says. "Vinny doesn't own me anymore, either... So go ahead. Take what you want. Kill me. Hurt me. I won't stop you."

It's a dare, though I'll be damned if I know just what she is taunting me to claim.

"Stop me from what?" I ask. Another minute passes without an answer, and I can't stop my free hand from fisting in her hair and using the grip for leverage to yank her head back, lifting her face from the counter. "What do you think I want?" I growl into her good ear.

She stares ahead, her mouth set in a stubborn line as if she knows a dirty little secret she won't tell me.

"What do *you* want?" I demand, tightening my grip until she winces.

"I want..." Her eyes threaten to go vacant. Then she twists her head around so that she's staring at me directly. "I don't want to be his."

CHAPTER FIFTEEN

Daniela

LUCIFER MAKES IT TOO EASY. TOO EASY TO FORGET THE words branded onto my skin. Too easy to forget the unsettling sensation of Vinny's touch. The man casts a shadow—not as wide or as twisted as Vinny's, but potent enough to outlast him here.

And I want to drown beneath the swell.

I want him to dredge out the old memories he replanted into my head. With violence. With hate. I want him to mark over my scars like graffiti. I need for this man to taint and violate every single part of me so that, if I do go back to Vinny alive, there will be nothing left for him to destroy.

Lucifer will kill me in one way or the other—even if I have to make him drive the knife into my chest myself.

When he lets me go, I press my forehead against the counter and brace my hands on either side of me. They shake, and it takes me two tries to be able to finally push up and turn around to face him. He doesn't back away when I do. He violates my personal space, gauging my reaction the whole while.

I scan his face: the black stubble along his chin, the faint scar slicing through his left eyebrow, the mole on his neck, the anger in his gaze.

I recall the night when the artist accused me of "playing with fire." Matches and old paper were merely a child's game. *This* was the true definition of that peculiar saying. I was playing with Lucifer the same way a suicidal thrill-seeker might play Russian roulette.

Which part of him contains the bullet? I will only learn through trial and error.

He doesn't react when I cut my gaze over to the knife, but I sense a slight shift in his posture. He'll stop me from reaching it, though I have enough sense to know that it's out of the fear that I'll use the blade on him rather than myself. And maybe I can. I'd slash a jagged wound across his face. His neck. I'd goad him into killing me, even if by accident.

The thoughts swirl in my mind, and a laugh trickles out of my mouth before I can bite it back. I'm dizzy beneath my own insanity. There's no true identity lurking beneath the shackles Vinny's used to conform me since the day we met. I'm a puddle of nothing but rage and desperation, melting the moment I'm cut loose from my cage.

And Lucifer... He's watching me like he isn't hungry to do every violent thing I know he's capable of. Control is a drug to him—I can sense it. He prides himself on maintaining it, no matter the temptation.

My right hand skims my thigh, drifting down to curl around the hem of my borrowed shirt. I finger the bloodied, sweat-soaked fabric while Lucifer watches. He pretends not to notice or care when I begin to drag the fabric up to my waist. My other hand comes down, and within seconds and a few stiff motions of my arms, I have the shirt over my head. Then it hits the floor at my feet.

Fire begins a dangerous dance down my spine. Lucifer doesn't enjoy being played with. His jaw clenches, and he doesn't allow his gaze to travel down to the cleavage bared by the lacy bra. I don't know why I decide to take it off, fumbling with the fastenings as if I have all the time in the world to strip myself naked before a monster.

Maybe I want him to fuck me again—split me open, ruin me utterly for any other man. Or perhaps bash my brains out against the cupboards? Maybe I want him to do *both*?

I don't know, and it's a terrifying, suffocating sort of tension to watch him watch me as I take two steps back until the rim of a counter juts into my spine. I brace both hands on either side of me, and then I haul myself upright so that my ass hits the surface.

Lucifer glowers. I think he'll opt for the second of my two twisted scenarios as I spread my legs wide, allowing him to see what little the patchwork of black lace and silk attempts to hide. Deep down, I know that it's insanity to taunt a man like him. Maybe this hollow shell of a woman is who Vinny's reduced me to. Only the newer pain keeps him at bay now...and I need Lucifer to blind me. Smash my skull so that I don't have to think. Cut my throat out. Tear my soul apart. Fuck me until I bleed.

Anything to prove that, as long as I can feel again, I'm not *there*. Vinny's specter, lurking in the corners, isn't real. He won't ever own me again.

The floor creaks when Lucifer finally moves. I expect him to walk away. He doesn't. His gaze holds mine as he stalks forward like a bored, exhausted wolf unable to resist the willing throat the sacrificial doe presents.

His grip is hard when he seizes my wrist and drags me from the counter. I stagger forward, and he uses that momentum to shove me into the main room. I don't stop moving until my hands hit the back of the couch. The force sends me to my knees, and my chin smacks off one of the seat cushions.

Lucifer is already behind me. He fists his hand in my hair so hard that I can't silence a cry. A scream. The pain floods my system, a powerful narcotic. My vision blurs, obscuring those haunting shadows.

To block them out completely, he shoves me forward as if he means to suffocate me against the cotton and padding. The act forces me higher on my knees, and the fingers of his free hand are there to seize the waistband of the panties and drag them down my legs.

He doesn't prepare me this time. I hear his zipper come undone. I hear him groan. I feel him. I'm impaled by him. On him...

My entire body screams to life at the invasion. Everything feels different when I'm not the one setting the pace. I moan, digging my nails into the couch's upholstery, breaking some of them, and Lucifer doesn't hold back. He slams his hips into me, forcing me to accept him. There is no more room for any dark memories. I'm stuffed to the brim, and it hurts the same way the burning alcohol did when poured onto my ear. Darkness dies screaming...and with every brutal, harsh, violent thrust, new shadows are forced into the spaces Vincent Stacatto used to infest.

I go numb beneath the assault. My brain is a slave to the sensation. I don't even register the act for what it is—sex. This is demolition.

Lucifer growls into my ear, the sound part pleasure, part aggravation. He's a beast, feasting on a fresh kill he never really wanted to hunt. He gorges himself on the feel of me anyway. The taste. I don't flinch when his teeth rake my neck as if biting is the only way he can prove his lack of attraction.

I shiver and shudder beneath the feeling, his teeth grinding my skin between them. Marking me. It would be so easy to just let him take me. All of me. Corruption is best delivered in steady, mind-numbing doses—Vinny taught me that. I shouldn't be so greedy for it. So impatient.

I bite my tongue when he thrusts again, his hips slapping my backside, pressing my stomach against the edge of the couch. It's searing friction; he's impossibly deep.

But it's still not deep enough.

My sweat-soaked hands fumble against the cushions, finding enough leverage to allow me to push back. *There.* My mind swims. The walls of the room shift and shatter. I'm falling and then flying, my stomach churning too quickly to make out which direction is which.

I taste blood on my tongue as a craving for more goads me to flex my hips when he shoves himself into me again. Again. *Again.*

I can't smother the sounds I make: desperate, pathetic, triumphant, bitter, brutal, animalistic sounds. Lucifer doesn't appreciate my little bid for power. He shoves his hand down on my hip, holding me steady while he pounds his essence into me, every naughty little drop. I swallow it all down. I'm choking on him. I'm drunk on him.

My knees flex against the floor. My hips swivel, chasing an even deeper, darker sensation. I want to feel him everywhere. Everywhere...

And then I do, but his presence doesn't inspire pain. The fire burns hotter, spreading too quickly and turning ravenous. I want the agony, not the pleasure, but it drives the most tortured sounds out of me. Moans. Squeals. Whimpers. It, more than anything, takes control of my body, forcing me to throw myself at him. Arch my back.

Reach for him with my hand, plunging my nails into the side of his ass. He flinches at the contact and bends the offending arm against my back. I'm at his mercy again, and I expect to feel that same fearful desperation that gnawed holes into my soul while living with Vinny.

Instead, all I feel is...

Hungry. I want *more.* I need him to hold me tighter. Force me down. Force himself inside. Bite. With every depraved thought, the heat surging through me gets even hotter. Higher. My skin crackles and burns. My blood boils. Then it bubbles over, and it hits me like a wave: pure, aching, smoldering pleasure. Too much. Not enough. I gasp as if I can catch more of it on the air. I breathe him in. He's swelling inside me, branding the shape of his cock onto my inner walls.

And it still isn't enough.

"S-stop," I rasp.

Lucifer stills his brutal pounding, and I don't let myself dwell on how sudden—how easily—he listened to the plea. I don't care that the monster heeds the commanding pull on his leash. I twist out from under him, hissing as he withdraws, still impossibly thick. I'm transfixed on the gleaming, swollen head of him—wet from me. Throbbing for me.

I flip over until my back is pressed against the couch, and I dig my heels into the floor, spreading my legs wide on either side of him, and lift my hips. He stares at the offering between my legs, and his eyes shoot black. One of his hands catches the side of my waist, wrenching me forward, and he sinks deep. To the goddamn hilt.

My head falls back as my eyes shut and my teeth clatter against the carnal, incredible pleasure. *Yes. This is better.* I throw myself on him, feeling resistant parts of me spread easily, letting him in even deeper. Harder.

Yes.

My knees tighten, trapping his hips between them while he continues to thrust. My heels dig into the backs of his thighs, urging him on, driving him deeper still. I'm gasping, staring up at the ceiling as my eyes flutter open when he hits some soft, inner part of me that makes sparks shoot through every single nerve ending. My toes curl. My hands find his shoulders, using the grip for leverage to thrust against him. Fuck him back.

"God," I hear myself croak, clawing at his shirt. "Damn. F-fuck. Sh-shit." The curses come like candy, another display that would be forbidden around Vinny—but even they aren't enough to describe it. I have to dig deeper into my arsenal of words. "Fuck. *Fuck. Bosta. Filho da puta—*"

Lucifer's growl swallows up my voice, and we both spiral. I'm exploding. My blood is pure gasoline, thrown onto an untamable flame. It's too much—pain, pleasure, everything. I lose myself. Daniela Manzano is finally annihilated, and she relishes the carnage made of her own skin.

I'm still on fire when Lucifer pulls out of me a second time and flips me onto my belly so that I'm lying flat on the carpet. He strokes himself—there's no mistaking the audible glide of flesh against wet, tender flesh. I hear him groan, and then I feel the mark of his release, burning ropes of it, lash against my lower back.

My heart races. I can't shut out the memory of Vinny doing the same, and I expect the same disgust to flare up. But it doesn't. Lucifer seems to like the sight of his semen on my skin though. He leans over me, his weight grinding my chin into the carpet amid a stinging ache. Something sweeps up from the side of my belly over to my spine, and I flinch in surprise. His hand. He's marking me, rubbing his seed into my skin.

It's the worst thing he could possibly do to me.

The substance is an antiseptic against the festering wound that I'd forgotten dwells there. I go limp in shock and just listen to the startlingly wet sound as my skin accepts him. My body quakes against his callused fingertips, chasing that relief. It hurts that I crave this base, violent claiming almost as much as I craved the violent sex. Tears sting my eyes, and I can't blink them back. My throat contracts around the hint of a sob, and it's like a dam breaking. Within seconds, I'm writhing, choking on gasping, wrenching sobs as my eyes stream and the fire he set slowly consumes the rest of my body.

CHAPTER SIXTEEN

Dante

THE FUCKING BUZZING WON'T BE SILENCED THIS TIME. It hammers away at my skull, even as my cock finally deflates and Stacatto's whore is painted with my cum. It's ironic how her skin still glistens beneath the obscenity; she'll wear a man's mark just as easily as silk. Though her new accessory comes with a high price. She shows more emotion now than when I severed part of her ear.

I suppose some part of me should feel proud at breaking her, but all I feel is irritation: the heat, the insatiable prickle in my skin, the goddamn *buzzing*. Even her strangled gasps aren't enough to smother the sound ripping through my head. It's instant. It's pounding. It's...

Someone knocking on the goddamn door.

"What the fuck do you want?" I growl while my hand flies out for my jeans. I yank them on one-handed and stagger for the door.

When I wrench it open, I expect to find Arno or maybe one of his men on the other side of it. Though, these days, who knows where the kid's loyalty lies anymore? There's no hint of it now as Espi watches me coldly, his eyes raking over my bare chest and my unfastened jeans.

"Am I interrupting something?" His gaze cuts to the woman he only catches a glimpse of, her naked body contorted by her muffled cries. Shock tightens his mouth before I can force myself through the doorway and slam the door shut behind me.

"Espi..." I observe him from head to toe.

He's wearing clothes similar to the ones he was wearing in Van Hallen's snapshot: a dark hoodie and filthy, paint-stained jeans. The expression on his face is a little different though; instead of looking fierce and determined, he stares right through me.

"Having fun?" he wonders, jerking his chin toward the door.

Fuck.

"It... That isn't what it looks like." I shouldn't have to explain shit to him, but I can't shake the urge to defend myself against the accusations I can see forming in his eyes. That bruised, broken woman had nothing to do with me.

"Oh, I'm sure it isn't," he says, spitting the words at me. "You... You're no different than *him*."

"What...what did you just say?" Rage smothers everything. My ears pop with the clarity it brings. Ruby taints the edges of my vision, and it takes every ounce of concentration I have to blink it back. "Don't you ever...ever compare me to that bastard—"

"Why not?" Espi eyes the door to my apartment again. "Like father, like son—"

I see scarlet. I fucking taste it. The rage breaks loose from its chains for only a second, but it's long enough. My knuckles burn and Espi's clutching the left side of his face.

"Nice one, Dante," he grits out along with a harsh chuckle. His jaw won't bruise, but he still winces as he pulls his hand away. "Yeah, you're *so* different."

He spits out blood before turning for the stairs, but I'm right behind him.

"Espi, wait."

I'm still on his heels when he enters the pub. Arno and his men are seated at the bar, but they pretend not to notice as Espisido darts across the room and barrels through the main door, out on the street.

It's only when I start to head after him that Arno speaks up. "Let him cool off."

"What the fuck do you know?" I toss back. I can see Espi's dark hair bobbing amid a crowd of pedestrians across the street. He's headed south. I flatten my palm against the main door before it can fully slam shut. I start to shove it open again when a hand falls on my shoulder. Only sheer force of will keeps me from sending my fist through its owner's skull.

Arno knows better.

"Let him go," he says, withdrawing his hand the moment I whip around with both of mine already curled into fists. He backs up a step, holding his palms out flat toward me. "I'll try talking to him again, once he's calmed down."

"I don't need your help," I snarl.

Arno says nothing, but his expression reveals what we both fucking know. *I do.* The bastard just has enough sense to not rub my nose in that fact.

"I'll send the tape tonight," he says, changing the subject. "I thought I'd let the fucker stew for a few days. I hear that he didn't react very nicely when he got her ear." He flashes a wicked grin, his eyes gleaming. "Let him see what happens when you fuck with my family."

"What will you do to her?" It's a dumbass question. I tell myself that he could string her up for sport and I still wouldn't give a damn. Then my fingers twitch, sticky.

Arno shrugs. "Nothing for now. If you're bored of her, you can send her down to the basement—"

I leave him there, heading for the stairs, and Arno doesn't follow me to the upper level. There's no one to witness when I throw the door to my apartment open so hard that it ricochets off the wall and nearly closes again. When I finally step into the living room, she's still on the floor. She lifts her head when I come closer though, her eyes glassy and distant as they attempt to focus on me.

Staring her down, I wait for the rage to resurface. My fingers curl in anticipation of that irritating heat. I blink, expecting to find her drenched in red any fucking second. I'm ready for the violence; I won't resist the impulse to take out every bit of frustration I feel on her pale skin. She'll get her death wish after all...

I wait.

She keeps still, almost as if she knows what's coming. Her hair drapes her back, strands of it mingling with the substance still drying there. Her body is limp, resigned. I know now that she won't fight when I attack her.

Hell, she'll relish the assault.

My head throbs, but for a different reason as I reach back to slam the door shut behind me. I stalk down the hallway, my gaze on the doorway to the bedroom. I don't know why the hell I pause to direct two words at her over my shoulder.

"Get up."

She does so noisily, staggering against the couch to catch her balance. I hear her let out a low groan as she registers the pain she'll feel for the next few days. Any smug pleasure I may have felt at hurting her is washed away by exhaustion. Arno's not the only bastard who's been deprived of sleep. I need to wash these past forty-eight hours from my brain, and I consider heading down to the bar to seek out some liquid assistance to do just that.

Instead, I enter the bedroom and take up a spot on the floor.

"Lie down," I order when the woman staggers to the doorway and clings to the wall for balance.

She found my shirt, and she's wearing it, the filthy hem brushing her knees. Her eyes flicker with uncertainty when she spots the bed, but she crosses over to it and sinks down without question.

Pressing my head against the wall, I close my eyes, blocking her out as she lies stiffly on the mattress. I'll make a new plan to talk to Espi, with or without Arno's help. I'll find a way to make that bastard Van Hallen pay for putting his babysitters-in-blue on my trail. I'll repay Arno for posting my bail.

It's a long list, and I grit my teeth in irritation.

A wolf never sleeps.

———

"Going somewhere?" I grind out, my eyes still shut.

The quiet rustling that jarred me awake goes silent, followed by a softly whispered word. "B-bathroom..."

I sigh and consider ignoring her. Hell, if she wants to sneak out of the apartment on her own and risk running into one of Arno's men, that's no concern of mine. After a minute of silence, the rustling starts up again as if she's settling back down against the mattress, and I finally open my eyes to near darkness.

10:00 flashes on the alarm clock, illuminating the room in hints of neon red. "Make it quick." I stand and make a show of stretching my arms above my head, knowing she's watching and imagining the difficulty she'll have if she tries to run. When I head for the door, I hear her scramble to her feet.

I don't follow her into the bathroom, entering the kitchen instead and flicking the light switch. Arno had it stocked with food the day I showed up on his doorstep, but what little there was is nearly gone; there are just two eggs and a rind of bread left over. Sighing, I run a hand along the side of my jeans and feel the crunch of a few crisp dollars in my left pocket.

"What do you want?" I turn to find her creeping up the hallway, rubbing her wet hands on the front of my shirt.

She looks like a zombie in the shadows; a blood-stained, bruised, violated corpse animated only from her eyes. She cocks her head. "What do I—"

"To *eat*," I clarify. "What do you want to eat?"

She still looks confused. "Whatever you think is—" She cuts the words off, clenching her jaw—something I notice she does whenever she's trying to break a habit she learned from *him*. Handshakes. Polite words. Prissy little posture.

Stacatto trained her well for life as the whore of a crime lord.

"I want..." Her eyes narrow in concentration as if thinking for herself is a hard skill to master. "Thai," she says finally. Her own frown reveals that she knows that it's a stupid request—one I definitely won't obey—but she can't seem to stop herself from saying it anyway. She needed to hear it come out of her own mouth. *I want Thai.*

It's a haughty little request. I want to write it off as a byproduct of her living in the lap of stolen luxury, but I can't. It's something Espi would ask for. He used to make a game out of how many exotic foods he could try in a week. Living off takeout was the skill of a kid who'd grown up without a mom to cook for him and an idiot like me to scrape his meals together.

I don't answer when I head for the door and enter the hallway, but I lock it behind me, tucking the key Arno gave me into my pocket. The pub is packed when I head downstairs. Arno's throwing a party, it seems, but I don't find his red hair mingling through the crowd by the time I reach the door and head out onto the street.

It's a slow, cold walk up a nearly deserted block in search of any food place open this late. I won't get fucking Thai. Maybe Mexican or some cheap-ass fast food.

If she doesn't like it, then the little bitch can starve.

CHAPTER SEVENTEEN

Daniela

Lucifer returns, bearing gifts in a brown paper bag. My body aches from sitting on the floor, waiting for him. The couch is a hostile domain lording over the other side of the room, so my new perch is in a corner near the fridge with my back braced against the wall, my legs stretched out over the linoleum.

He doesn't see me at first when he comes in and sets the bag down on the counter that conveniently shields my position. I start to stand, but something makes me take my time and observe him safely from my hiding place.

He is a cold, dark shell of a man. Humanity is a mask he wears to keep the mere mortals around him from panicking at the sight of the evil smoldering within his skin. His eyes are predators hunting beneath a jungle of dark hair. His mouth is a cage—he rarely says anything he doesn't mean. An unusual display of restraint and of freedom. So many people are forced to parrot whatever lies they pretend to believe in order to earn money or stay alive. His brutal honesty is as rare as it is dangerous.

"I belong to no one."

"I'm here," I say, rising to my feet when his eyes begin to stalk the corners, his body tensing.

I raise my hands, revealing that I don't have the knife. It's still on the floor, and he makes sure by spotting it there, beside the wall. Then he open the bag rips and places his offering on the counter between us.

I blink, my nose twitching to register the exotic, spicy scent of *gaeng daeng* and *shrimp pad Thai.* I don't let myself register the fact that he obeyed my request. I snatch up a plastic set of silverware instead. Verbal thank-yous are for humans, so I show my gratitude by stabbing at a piece of food and choking it down.

It's good. I'm leaning over the counter before I can help it, shoveling more into my mouth. Hot, spicy, fragrant, messy. Sauce and loose noodles coat my chin, but I don't bother to wipe them away. Vinny wouldn't approve, and every bite tastes even sweeter from knowing that.

Lucifer watches me, however. I know that it's rude that I don't stop to offer him any, but I can't seem to regain control of my body until the last greasy morsel goes down my throat and all traces of it have been licked from my fingers.

The dangerous silence that falls between us doesn't require anything to fill it. It's almost better if we maintain the lethal tension that determines the boundary of captor and captive. I have every intention of playing my role—I *do*. Until I look up. Questions cloud the devil's gaze before he can hide them. They distort the blue of his eyes. He almost looks human.

"We lived near a Thai restaurant when I was growing up," I say, allowing my plastic fork to fall against the countertop. "My parents got food from there at least once a week. My father said that it reminded him of the food back home, but I think he was joking." My throat aches. Talking about the past hurts worse than reliving my hell with Vinny. Some wounds are too deep to risk prodding. I'm bleeding out words, and I just can't stop. "We came from São Paulo when I was eight. My mother got a job at a factory, and my father worked construction and cleaned for a contractor at night. I went to school in the city, but I knew very little English, and the kids liked to tease the strange Brazilian girl."

I laugh at the memory, though the treatment stung at the time. Back then, the world of Daniela Manzano only consisted of two dolls with cornflower hair—Maria and Isabelli—a small apartment in the slums of downtown, her *Mãe* Ana, her *Pai* Daniel, and a younger *Irmão* Christoph. She liked the color blue and loved reading books from her father's lap, hearing him translate the words in his native *Português*. The world was smaller then. Simpler. Happier.

"I didn't have a lot of friends," I admit, compelled to keep telling my sordid tale, even though he doesn't want to hear it; he stoically eyes the wall behind my head. "Then, one day...I met a boy. His family members were immigrants too. He was older than I was, but his English was better. I think he took pity on me, at first... He would walk me home. Help me with my pronunciation. We'd play games in the street until my father had to come and drag me inside..."

Lucifer listens in silence. I don't know if he's already guessed the identity of the new character introduced in the story when I finally reveal it.

"His name was Vincent. His family had come over from Italy, but he didn't like to talk about it. America was his home now. He liked green. He liked to read. He loved classical music." It's a simple list I used to repeat to myself before my soul became numb to his violence. Back when I wanted to believe that boy was still there, lurking somewhere within the monster's skin. "When he was fourteen, his mother was murdered buying groceries. A man working for some local gang had tried to rob the place. He used her as a hostage and killed her when things got out of hand. I think...I think all the good in him died that day."

I wrinkle my nose at the memory, trying to pinpoint the exact moment the boy—my dearest friend—became a stranger. "He tracked down the gangsters on some stupid plan for revenge, and they broke his legs in five places with baseball bats. He still has a limp," I add, my voice falling flat. "After that, a man by the name of Antoni Capella found him in the streets and took him under his wing. He was from Italy too and had mob connections in the city." To hear Vinny tell it, the man was a god, a more admirable father than the one he'd left behind grieving with a bottle of whiskey in the ghetto. "After that..."

I trail off. There is a whole new chapter of the story to tell, but I'm too exhausted to turn the page. I stare down at the empty food containers instead. I suffer Lucifer's careful, silent scrutiny and pretend not to notice—but it's a much harder game to play now than before. Too many smells taint the air between us. Too many stains. Too many secrets. Too many lies.

"What about you?" I glance up at him through a wayward fringe of my hair that does little to block out the ice in his gaze. I don't specify just what I'm prodding to learn—I'd take anything.

Or maybe I knew all along that the question would send him turning on his heel and marching down the hall, leaving me alone and in silence once again...

———

LUCIFER STORMS OUT OF THE APARTMENT AGAIN A little after dawn. I don't lift my head from the floor to see for myself. His anger paints a blazing trail detectable through scent alone—and the sound of the door slamming shut provides another clue of his departure.

I pretend that his leaving doesn't worry me. I pretend that my first instinctive urge isn't to creep over to the door in order to make sure it's locked. I pretend that, even if he does turn me over to the other men, it wouldn't matter.

I pretend, and I pretend until my sore muscles have gone numb and another sound jolts me awake again. The noise—a careful tapping—comes from the door, but I doubt Lucifer is the culprit this time, cautiously demanding entry. After four more quiet knocks, the sound stops and I almost believe that whoever the unwelcomed visitor is has changed his mind and gone away.

"I know you're in there."

I tense at the sound of a man's voice, but...it's not quite as guttural as it should be. He sounds a few pitches higher than Lucifer, and his tone lacks the murderous lust of the red-haired man or one of his men. Confused, I flick my gaze over to the knife only a few feet away from my outstretched toes. Lucifer's arrogance is an interesting puzzle I'm not sure I'd ever want to solve. Instead, I take advantage of the fact by easing myself upright and crawling for the blade. I move slowly, striving to make my every motion silent against the uneven flooring, but the moment my fingers brush the knife's handle, the "visitor" knocks again.

"He's gone," they say, their voice low and deceptively neutral. "Open up. Unless...he has you tied up. In which case I should call the police."

I swallow hard and drag my thumb over the edge of the blade. It's dull, unwilling to cut even the pad of my thumb, but I press down and force it through the skin. The pain is white-hot, waking up my sleepy nerve endings and electrifying them with fear.

"I have a cell phone," the man warns. "If you don't answer, I'll just have to assume that he has you incapacitated."

Lucifer? My fingers shake, and I dig my nails into the palm of my free hand to counter the reaction. Whoever this man is, he apparently isn't in on the intentions of the red-haired man. He's hostile to Lucifer. Opening the door would only incite my devil's wrath, but if this man really does call the police...Vinny would know. He would find me, and my charming fiancé would love to put on a caring show for the police officers before taking me up to that damn hotel suite and killing me slowly.

I could always take myself out of the equation, I realize while my blood continues to speckle the surface of the blade at my fingertips. How easy would it be to hack my wrists open and bleed out before anyone could ever reach me? I consider it...

But Lucifer's infected me. It's no longer just enough to imagine Vinny's reaction to my little tape. It's not enough to estimate the extent of his rage. I want to see it. I want to feel the heat of the fire I've set before I die.

"That's it. I'm calling them—"

"I'm f-fine." I struggle to inject calm into my voice, but my sore jaw disrupts my attempts. I sound garbled. I sound tired. I sound...under duress. "I'm fine," I repeat, making my voice louder as if volume alone can counter everything else. I stand, leaving the knife behind, though I'm not sure why.

Fear demands attention, commanding my body into action. I should be cautious. I should carefully heed the threat of Lucifer. I... That voice shouldn't sound so familiar.

"Oh, really?" the man counters. He copies my tone, losing the cautious murmur. "Then open the door. Let me see that for myself."

I shake my head, well aware that he can't see the reaction. "No. I'm fine—"

"I'm not asking out of concern for *you*," he says bluntly. "I need...I need to see that he hasn't... I need to see for myself."

Once again, I suspect that he's referring to Lucifer. *I need to see that he hasn't...*

Kidnapped a woman and held her hostage? If he's looking to be reassured by my appearance, he'll be sorely disappointed. My back feels sticky. I'm still wearing Lucifer's stolen, bloodied, filthy shirt, and I felt no desire to shower or change when he left. I'm a false martyr relishing in the ashes of her destruction, but I tug on the hem and contemplate how much worse it might seem if I open the door wearing nothing at all.

"I'm waiting." The voice holds a flicker of impatience along with a dare: He'll call the police.

My hand reaches out, my fingertips brushing the doorknob. A million reasons to let Lucifer's house of cards come crashing down race through my mind, each one jostling for supremacy. In the end, I force myself to undo the lock for only one reason alone—self-preservation. Any humiliation is better than being hand-delivered to Vinny in a squad car, already wearing handcuffs.

At least, with the lack of a strong accent, I know that this man doesn't work for him.

"I'm fine," I insist while I pull the door open merely a fraction of an inch. I peer through the crack, and if I hoped that my words alone would counter the effect of my appearance—namely the bruises on my face—I'm sorely disappointed.

The blue eyes watching me from the other side widen, but not entirely with shock, I realize. Before I can react, a hand smudged with dirt slips through the crack in the doorway and bats the door open wider. I'm forced to step back while a taller man—almost as tall as Lucifer—forces his way inside. His blue eyes are too familiar. *Lucifer himself, after all?* No...

He blinks, his gaze darkening with recognition at the same time I realize just who he is, and I feel the world start to crumble from underneath me.

"P-Pyro Girl?"

CHAPTER EIGHTEEN

Dante

"I want in."

Arno glances up as I circle around him and take up a stool at his side. He's nursing two different bottles of liquor today. Does the bastard *live* at this counter?

It's only when I meet his once again bloodshot eyes that I realize that—at least for the past few nights—he probably has. Wherever he does stay, he most likely shared it with Parish.

"So, the Kitty wants to jump back into the litter box." He pours a shot of something clear that smells like varnish and nudges it over to me. "I was wondering when you'd run with the wolves again. Frankly, shit's been boring without you—"

"Give me a job," I insist rather than reminisce. "Anything. I'll do it."

Preferably something nasty. Something violent. Something to get me away from *her*.

"Eager to sharpen your claws?" Arno eyes my hands with a smirk.

I ball both into fists and don't answer. I'm not in the mood for games.

"All right, all right," Arno sighs. He takes the glass in front of me and downs it himself. Then he sips from the second bottle and winces. "There is a small...*irritation* you could handle for me. There's this bastard on South who runs a cushy little operation smuggling weed out of a bookstore. 'Special order' books on exotic plant life, you see." He chuckles, but when the sound dies off, his eyes are a little clearer. His hands grip his next drink a little steadier. Nothing sobers him up like plotting the pitfall of another rival. "It's a low-level piece-of-shit operation, but I want you to make a point, more or less. The man who runs it used to work for me, but lately, his judgment's been off, and he seems to believe that he takes his orders from Stacatto now. I want you to jog his memory—but you don't work for me, Dante. When you bring that asshole into line...make him answer to *you*."

I raise an eyebrow and consider taking one of his bottles of liquor for myself. "Why?"

Arno flashes a lethal smile and brings a newly filled shot glass to his lips. "Because, when that fucker Stacatto is nothing more than a memory, I'll need a true ally to help me take back this shithole of a city." He downs the shot and slams the empty glass onto the bar. His eyes seek mine out, and for a second, he's *Arno* again. "Welcome back, Kitty. Let's see if you've still got that nasty bite."

———

IT'S A COLD, DARK DESCENT INTO THE CRIMINAL underbelly that people like Richard Van Hallen like to pretend doesn't exist. The shadows rejoice in my return, swallowing me whole. I'm home, amid the muck and violence and chaos men like Arno hone for profit and, on a more basic level, simple entertainment.

Prison taught me better than anything else that a wolf is never truly at ease until it's back hunting on the outskirts of a pack, bathed in the growls and the musk of its own kind.

The man Arno sent me to see conducts business in a seedy part of the city that's seen better days. The sidewalks have weeds growing through their cracks. Even the police don't patrol here, preferring to skirt the outer perimeter of this forsaken shithole.

The man, a dealer by the name of Andre, has set up shop in a dilapidated storefront that calls itself a bookstore. A sign, handwritten on cardboard, proclaims *All Shakespur 50% off!* When I shove open a battered metal door and step inside, I'm greeted with the telltale stench of cigarette smoke and weed.

"We're closed," a man snarls. He's about half my size, wearing an outdated "Welcome to 2000!" T-shirt. His hair is matted.

I guess that it used to be naturally curly. At one point, this man probably didn't *naturally* reek of piss and body odor.

"I've got nothing to sell," he tells me smugly as I pick my way through metal shelves piled high with old magazines and books that seem decades old, as if picked from the remains of a library.

"I'm here to see Andre," I say once I am close enough to his perch that he can't run without crossing my path. My fingers flex.

The room's narrow layout is fairly open—there are no witnesses. Even for as shitty a dealer as he seems to be, the lack of protection is just plain stupid, and I intend to teach him that lesson through example.

"Who the fuck are you?" he slurs, his eyes bloodshot from sampling his own merchandise.

"I'm your new best friend," I say while I try to decide which part of his face I'll bruise first. "Arno Mackenzie says hello."

Daniela

Like any good conundrum worth solving, my Lucifer apparently possesses two sides. One half is the beast I let crawl into my skin—a man who doesn't seem to give a damn about anything or anyone. The other half is a figure so similar in appearance that he could be his twin: a stranger who cared enough about the welfare of some random waif of a woman that she had to beg him out of going to the police.

"I'm just dirty," I lied. "I haven't showered yet, just a lazy girl lounging in."

He didn't believe me, of course. Regardless, he let me spin my tales and babble something about being "just about to take a shower" as any non-captive would. Hell, I almost believed I'd convinced him.

Then he surprised me by crossing the center of Lucifer's lair and perching his lanky frame on the very edge of that hated couch as if he had no clue that he'd just ventured into hell.

"Go ahead," he prompts while I try to approximate just where he's sitting. Where the tips of some of my nails were still embedded within the upholstery? Or where I smothered my moans into the padding? "Go ahead," he repeats when I don't react. "Change. I'll wait."

It's an ironic dilemma: Lucifer's angelic twin wants me to implicate his darker half. Give him any reason at all to...

What? My mouth twists into a frown while I try to decipher the relationship between the two men. *I need to see for myself that he isn't...*

"That's not a good idea," I say finally, forcing myself to meet his gaze.

The artist merely shrugs. "Afraid he'll come back?"

I flinch, caught in my own web. Afraid of Lucifer? Not really. I am merely concerned by what might happen when the wolf returns to his lair to find another creature sniffing around the carcass he keeps hidden in the back room. By opening the door, it feels like I've unknowingly tipped over a domino chain miles long. Where would the final one land?

Only God knows that.

"Take a shower," the artist says. His voice is softer. He's looking at my legs, trying to avoid the bruises and marks that mar everything else. "Danny. It's...it's Danny, right?"

I force a nod, surprised that he remembered my name.

"Then, Danny, *please*. If you're here of your own 'free will' and all, then take a shower. Change into the fresh clothes that I'm sure you have in a suitcase somewhere." He raises a skeptical eyebrow. "Just, please. Prove to me that my brother isn't a...freak." The word is a fill-in for a darker insult he can't say. *Monster*.

I would hate to be the one to spoil that secret. Before I'm forced to, I register the rest of his words—*brother*—and flinch again, seizing my lower lip between both rows of teeth. I bite down once, hard enough for the pain to flood my system and counter any emotion that could cross my expression and give me away. Lucifer has a brother—a man who likes to paint the devil on the streets.

It's almost *too* poetic.

"Okay..." I shake my head to clear it and head for the hallway—or at least I pretend to. I take the exaggerated route, skirting around the counter, and then I pretend to trip so that he doesn't notice the knife I tuck into my hand.

The rest of Lucifer's dwelling seems to repel my presence when its master isn't there. I shiver when I make a detour into that lonely bedroom and approach the pile of things he keeps in the corner. It's such a meager set of belongings. Plain. Simple. Durable. Vinny wouldn't survive on such a lifestyle. Lucifer doesn't require tailored suits, gold watches, and thousands of dollars to cut an intimidating presence, it seems.

All he needs are those eyes. I can almost feel them watching me now as I reach out and bat aside a pair of gray boxers to find three more plain T-shirts lurking underneath. I settle on a navy-blue one—as feminine a color as I'm likely to find. After a moment's hesitation, I grab the boxers too, hoping they might pass for shorts, if I can even get them to fit, that is.

I'm ice cold when I creep into the bathroom and run the shower at full blast. The pelting hot spray doesn't do much to ease the ache in my limbs or quiet this insistent whisper in my head warning me to just take my chances and run. Damn Vinny. Damn Lucifer. At least I'd spend my last moments of freedom...*away* from some form of bloodshed.

I let the fantasies goad me into some semblance of peace. It's only when I finally climb out of the tub and reach for one of the damp, used towels on the floor that I realize I never let the knife go. It adds a mocking shimmer to my reflection when I finally gather the nerve to turn and face it.

Lucifer's brother has been humoring me. There's nothing remotely "fine" about the woman staring back at me with dry, soulless eyes. They've been sucked clean of all emotion —she's a robot, merely going through the motions. I'm that pathetic automaton again, the one Vinny molded and corrupted me into being. *Lynn.* She traces her broken lips with a pink tongue, already anticipating the next beating.

No. I grit my teeth and shake my head. Then I use Lucifer's toothbrush to chase every ounce of her away. Daniela returns when I blink, her exhausted expression a welcome sight. I scan the wet, black hair clinging to her skull and warily drag my fingers through it. I manage to shift most of it over to my right shoulder, shielding as much of my damaged ear as I can. There's no help to disguise the black bruise around my left eye, however. I try to counter it by making the rest of me seem as whole and as comfortable as possible.

It's a laughable endeavor as I pull on Lucifer's clothes. The shirt swallows me up like a child playing dress-up in her father's clothes, but I manage to roll the waistband of the boxers until they fit somewhat snugly. I'm clean at least.

When I finally tiptoe back into the hall—with my stolen knife hidden safely in one of the boxer's pockets—I do my best to appear at ease. As if I've willingly encased myself within these four walls—though, in a way, I have. Squalor gleams like paradise when compared to Vinny's luxurious prison. It's easier than I would have thought to let my shoulders lose some of their tension. I don't smile though—that would be a step too far, even for a delirious captive.

I try to seem neutral instead, as if it's completely natural for me to leave the shower dripping wet and wearing Lucifer's clothes.

"You have a strange taste in wardrobe, Pyro," the artist exclaims on a sharp exhale once he spots me near the mouth of the living room. "What happened to the cashmere sweaters and silk pants?"

I wince at the reminder of just how much control over my life—my identity—Vinny had. "I don't have any clothes," I say, choosing not to waste energy on a lie. "He..." Lucifer has a real name, and I struggle to remember it. Something with a D. "D-Dan...*Dante* is helping me get back on my feet."

"Bad breakup?" the man asks. I can't tell if he's humoring me or making a logical guess.

"The worst." For a second, I let the full horror of Vinny's memory wash over me. That fear seeps into my blood, pooling within every muscle. Nothing about my reaction is faked, and the man takes notice.

He sits straighter, bracing both hands flat against his knees. "How do you know him? Dante."

I reach up and fiddle with a strand of my hair as a distraction while I try to come up with a plausible lie. There are none. In the end, I spit out the first scenario that comes to mind. "He...he found me crying. He bought me something to eat." I nod to the corroborating empty cartons of takeout on the counter behind me. "He gave me a place to crash while...while I get back on my feet." The appendages in question shuffle uneasily against the floor, and I have to dig my toes into the carpet before he notices.

"Hmph." The man—I struggle to recall the name he gave me. Espi?—nods along with my tale. "So he found you naked and drunk on the street corner and didn't call the police or take you to a hospital?"

I frown. I don't remember telling that part of the story.

"I saw him," the man adds, "carrying you up the stairs drunk out of your mind. You only had on a pair of—"

"D-do you want me to just say it?" I demand, injecting a false bit of shame into my voice. My heart races as I run out of options and just wing it. I'm drawing on a movie Vinny made me watch with him once. *Pretty* something. "My...my profession?"

His eyebrows shoot up into a fringe of black hair. "You mean...you're a h..."

I say nothing, allowing him to draw the conclusion on his own. *Prostitute. Call girl. Whore.* How very fitting to describe it—in the end, that's all I really ever was to Vinny. The explanation even ties in nicely with my bruised face and lack of proper clothing as well.

"Dante's helping me," I say, and for a second, I almost believe my own lie. "So I'd really prefer if you didn't call the police..."

The devil's brother says nothing. He merely watches me, and I can't decipher any conclusions he comes to when he finally stands.

"Wait here," he says before turning to the door.

"But—"

"Don't move," he says without turning around. "I'll be right back."

He leaves the door to the apartment open, allowing me to see him dart across the hall and open one of the other doors that appears to branch off the hallway. It's about two doors down from the "showroom," and I can't suppress a shudder while my mind conjures what other secrets he might pull from this new Pandora's box.

A bag, apparently. It's small, made of plastic, and sporting the name of a grocery store on the front.

"It's not much," the man tells me while letting the handle dangle from his hand. "Just a few things I could bother sparing for now. I can bring more over later when I—"

"L-later?" I reach out for the bag as if taking it might be enough to make him leave. "You can't—"

"I have some...business to take care of now," he says with a wary glance over his shoulder. It's the first sign of unease I've seen from him. Spraying graffiti in Vinny's territory or even waltzing into Lucifer's lair didn't affect him as much. "But, when I'm done, I'll come see you again. Seeing as how you're here of your own volition, Dante shouldn't have a problem if you have visitors. Right?"

It's like he's daring me to tell the truth, and for the life of me, I don't know why I don't. Lucifer's nefarious intentions should be no concern of mine. The red-haired man doesn't deserve any protection against a stranger who might not be able to stomach the idea of a tortured woman kept in the wings for his amusement.

I have every reason to come clean.

In the end, I wrap my fingers around the handles of the bag and carefully pull it toward me. It's heavy. I hold both ends open to peek at what's carefully packed inside it—what appear to be two sweatshirts, one red and one black, and a pair of jeans, which just may be small enough to fit around my waist at least. There's also a pair of sandals and a canister of men's deodorant still partially wrapped in packaging that sports the words *Two Pack!*

Something foreign pools into my stomach. Gratitude? It's been so long since I've felt it. While the items might not seem like much to anyone else, I suspect that they were what few things in the world he had but was still willing to part with.

His generosity leaves me feeling greedy.

"Thank you."

He shrugs. "Don't mention it—seriously. Don't say anything to Dante."

For the first time, I notice the hard way he pronounces the name. Crisp...almost the same way in which Vinny utters *Daniela*. Lucifer's near-twin doesn't share any love for him, it seems. He doesn't want the wolf to know our secret.

But he doesn't have to tell me twice. I aim to give the clothing back though—I have nowhere to hide it. But, before I even move to offer it to him, he's already heading down the hall, his backpack hiked over one shoulder.

"See you around, Pyro Girl," he calls back to me.

I don't know how long I stand here, his bag in hand, before I finally gather the nerve to creep back inside.

CHAPTER NINETEEN

Dante

"I didn't kill him." I utter that declaration as I slam a wad of cash onto the bar while Arno watches me from across the room, a pool cue in hand. Admittedly, some of the blood that drips from my fingers onto the bills might counter that statement, though no one in this room seems to give a damn either way.

"Is that what I'm supposed to tell the police when they come looking for you?" Arno's almost smiling as he twists a block of chalk onto the end of his cue. Closing one eye, he lines his shot up—a yellow ball toward the corner pocket. He shouts when he makes it and brandishes his fist toward the man who steps up next. "Top that, you son of a bitch! Your secret's safe with me, Kitty," he grunts in my direction, his grin giving way to a colder expression. "Dead or alive. I don't really give a shit—just as long as you got my point across."

"His...memory's been jogged," I say while I hunt the bar counter for something to drink.

Rock music pulses and the bartender taps her foot in tune to the beat. Her dark eyes glance me over, lingering over the spot where my hips disappear beneath the edge of the counter.

"Can I get ya something?" she asks, her voice low and throaty.

"No." I grit my teeth. My fingers flex, their sore knuckles throbbing, but the buzz at the back of my skull continues to grate on my nerves. Beating up some punk for petty cash barely made a dent in the itch that demands to be scratched. I consider asking Arno for another job or finding another asshole to pummel on the streets—anything to silence it.

"I told you to make that fucker into *your* man," Arno says, sounding closer.

I turn and find him stepping beside me, up to the bar. He snaps his fingers at the bartender, and she smiles before turning to fish a bottle from the shelf, swaying her hips with every step.

Arno licks his lips at the display, but his mind is still on business when he slaps his hand over the bloody wad of bills and shoves it firmly toward me. "Take it. This is your spoil."

I shove the money back toward him. "Don't want it."

When the bartender returns, I jerk my chin at the bottle she's holding, and she silently pours two shots. Arno knocks his back with a grunt, but I sip mine slowly, savoring each burning rush of liquid down my throat.

Neither sip is enough. She's in my veins—in my head—challenging every drop of liquor. My body hums, demanding something that won't be satisfied no matter how many times I pound my fist into the face of whatever fucker Arno wants intimidated or whichever bastard is unlucky enough to cross my path.

"Another," I choke out, and the woman's barely topped me off before I down the next shot. Then another. My body burns with the aftereffects when I finally stand and snatch for the money, leaving Arno there to flirt his way into the brunette's pants. I barely hear a word he says to me when I push my way through the men crowding the bar. I take the stairs two at a time, gritting my teeth in lethal anticipation.

The blood already on my hands isn't enough. My skin craves more—specifically hers. I could tear her from limb to limb, and I bet her eyes wouldn't even widen in shock. That lamb's already been nibbled at—she's used to the snarls of the monsters who prowl the edges of her pen. Even when I finally reach the door to the apartment and throw it open, she doesn't flinch from her position on the couch.

She merely draws her knees up to her chin. Cautiously, she watches me slam the door and approach, but there is no fear in her gaze. Even when my hand lashes out, the tips of my nails grazing her wrist, she doesn't make a sound.

I don't expect her to stand when I miss though, placing herself directly into the line of fire from my fists should I decide to hit her. I don't know why the hell I *don't*. My eyes flicker over her body instead, and my nostrils flare to register her scent. She's showered. Her hair is wet. She's stolen another one of my shirts, and underneath it, I can make out the edges of what I think are my boxers.

I have to clench my teeth together and flex my fingers to send my blood surging again. It flows through my heart and then straight down to where I need it the least. Her eyes watch me the entire fucking time. It's like she can sense the way I harden, thicken, and strain. She's as smug as she is empty.

Something flashes through her gaze before I can name it. *Disgust?* Her nose juts a little higher into the air. The princess doesn't enjoy being commanded, but her knees bend regardless and she lowers herself onto the floor—but it's entirely of her own volition. Through the shadows that paint the room gray, she stares me down, unafraid.

"Get up." I turn on my heel and tear down the hall before she can obey. The room is nearly dark when I enter it, and I don't bother turning the light on as I strip my shirt off and toss it in a random direction. My right shoulder twinges—a result of being overworked while beating a man half to death on Arno's say-so.

Though, if I want to be honest, the bastard was merely a distraction. A toy. Fun. I want to take my rage out on something...real. Something that might scream when I go too far. Beg. Plead.

I want *her* to bleed.

As if following some cruel cue, she appears in the doorway uninvited. Apparently, the bitch just couldn't save herself, and I certainly won't do it for her.

"Come here." I leave no room for hesitation this time when I beckon her with a finger as if toying with the invisible trigger to my own sanity. I shoot, and the bullet goes flying, delivering a dose of hatred right into the center of her chest.

Her eyes are wary now. She's uncertain of just what I want. To strangle her? Get off by shoving my dick down her throat? She seems to mull over each possibility, her lips pursed. I want her to struggle, but I can almost sense her uncaring shrug. *Either one works for me.*

Damn her.

I step back when she starts forward until I hit the wall. She's paces away when my arm shoots out, sending her sprawling flat onto her ass, half onto the mattress and half off. Her eyes widen, but her teeth seize her lip as if to hold a cry back. Her gaze goes glassy, and like a true caged bird, she flies off... But she's not fast enough. Her soul smacks off the ceiling when I crouch over her, and she blinks, landing back down on the filthy cage lining. She's trapped inside her skin again, forced to watch as I bring my mouth close...grazing the tip of her nose before homing in on her ruined ear.

She smells like a mixture of old blood and cheap soap. These past few days of filth have seeped into her pristine skin, dulling its luster. Regardless, she still glows, still seemingly untouchable. I can't seem to even make a stain when my fingers encircle her throat and begin to press into the supple flesh.

She gurgles something unintelligible, turning her gaze up to the ceiling. I can almost sense the fight rise and then die within her. She wastes more energy on forcing her limbs to give up their instinctive urge to resist than she does trying to breathe. She's like a child, holding her breath and counting to ten in anticipation that the "scary time" will soon be over.

It's such a fucking stupid comparison, but for some reason, I don't squash it down as I finally let her go to sputter and wheeze beneath me.

Espi compared me to him. *"Like father, like son."* Maybe I fucking am some sick fuck who can only feel in control at the expense of someone else's pain. My thoughts swim, threatening to crack the shell of my skull and escape. Red drenches my vision. My hands sear with the need to punch, hit, attack, and the only way to ease it is to reach out and grasp the first thing I touch.

I'm not like him.

Old memories hitchhike on the air, sneaking into my lungs and clawing through my thoughts like roaches. He used to tiptoe into my room, trying his damn hardest to be silent— as if I hadn't already been lying awake. I think he thought the stealth was doing me a fucking favor...

A lone moan scratches the air, too soft to be one of mine. I grabbed *her*, my nails biting into the skin of her arm. Scowling, I let go, swiping my hand against my hip as to wipe her off. It was like some part of me instinctively needed an anchor—something to tether me to reality.

"Turn over," I growl.

Before she can, I flip her over myself and position her on her hands and knees, presenting her ass to me. Her head dips low, her forehead pressing into the twisted sheets. From between her legs, I can see her eyes squeeze shut, her bottom lip once again skewered by her teeth.

I pull back, exhaling sharply. Air hisses in and out of my lungs, weighed down like smoke. The stench of her blood, sweat, and tears in the sheets is a bitter smell. It chafes my nostrils when I try to ignore it and sink back down within the rage. I want it to consume me. I want to take every violent emotion out on her.

But, when I glance down, her eyes hold me captive. Wide. Clear. Unafraid. We have both seen the devil and lived to tell about it—not that we fucking do. It's not enough to merely bitch about evil; you emulate it.

"You think your fiancé is so terrible," I tell her, my words landing with flecks of spit against her back. "You think you're the only woman in the world to experience the pain of an abusive prick? Think again." I chuckle darkly while she calmly stares back.

In the end, I'm the one forced to look away, but I settle for eyeing the steady rise and fall of her chest. The bitch may have aced her poker face, but her body gives her away. Her pulse is ten beats too fast. She flinches every time I exhale, though she makes her limbs stiff in an attempt to disguise the reaction.

She's not afraid of me... No. But she is wary, and I intend to go from there. Inspiring fear is like stoking a flame into a full-fledged inferno. All you need is a spark.

When I reach down and graze her breast through the fabric of the borrowed shirt, it's like striking a match. She was expecting pain—not this. Not soft, gentle, squeezing motions. I can see her eyes flicker as she struggles to process the sensation. *Pleasure?*

Though the bastard may have held back from fucking her, he never *gave* to her, either. He never ground his presence into her skin with his bare hands. Never tasted her cunt on his tongue. He never made her writhe, wanting his cock. I know better than most that pain can be withstood and faced with gritted teeth—pleasure isn't so easy to resist.

Her body tenses when I lower myself against her back like a wolf aiming to deliver the killing blow. I continue to stroke her while my mouth grazes the nape of her neck, my tongue attacking the line of her pulse. Her nipples rise sharp to attention, greedy and demanding, practically grazing my palm through the layer of fabric. From the corner of my eye, I see one of her hands flutter as if she means to shove me off before she braces them both flat against the mattress.

When I tease her with my teeth, she jumps, and an answering jolt shoots through my cock. This game is a double-edged sword, but I intend to win.

"Get...on your knees."

I pull back and watch her consider disobeying. Her eyes stray, fighting to return to that distant place—but she can't, and she resigns with a slow, deliberate shift of her ass. Suddenly, she's on her back, looking up at me. She pulls herself upright and then leans forward on her hands, arching her spine...

Fuck. I shift backward, dismounting the mattress altogether. Her eyes glow through the shadows, daring me with a silent taunt. *Make me bleed. Scream. Do it. Erase him. Make me yours...*

I don't want her. I don't, but I'm reaching for the buckle of my jeans anyway. I'm hard, a shock I ignore in favor of watching her gaze drift down to find me erect and straining. She inhales, the broken sound playing like some fucked-up melody. Her tongue shoots out, dabbing her bottom lip as if in anticipation of my taste.

"Open," I grit out, rising to my feet.

She obeys, parting her teeth, her tongue lying passive in the center. I use the pink flesh as a bull's-eye as I shove my cock deep into her mouth. Her cheeks contract automatically, trying to force me out, but before I can, she relaxes, and fuck... It's like the bitch tries to swallow me down whole. She's sloppy. She's never sucked a man off before me—I can see it in her eyes as they meet mine, taunting me to make her stop.

My fingers grip the back of her skull instead, using the contact to guide her, steer, control. Once again, she proves to be a fast learner. Her tongue strokes the underside. Her teeth graze the shaft. The tension ratchets up, coiling in every muscle until I'm rocking onto my heels, grunting out curses through clenched teeth. *Damn. Fuck. Shit.*

Too soon, I have to shove her back, panting while my body struggles to regain control. I clench my cock at the root, tightening my grip until the impending release gathers in the pit of my stomach and stays there. I consider just jerking myself here and now, pelting her with the evidence. Her owner would surely like that.

But *she* wouldn't. She'd want me inside her, deeper than the fucker could ever reach. She wants to be tainted, owned, and destroyed—but I'm not sure if I want to be her pistol this time.

I don't know how long I fucking stand here, about to boil over into my own fist. Maybe it's the sound she makes when I start to turn away? It's a gasp—a protest, a plea. Words are beyond this little lamb now.

"Take the shorts off—"

The command is barely out of my mouth before she has the boxers shed and tossed onto the floor. She lies back when I step forward, her eyes roving up to the ceiling while her hands grip the sheets until her knuckles turn white.

I can feel her breath on my neck as I mount her. She doesn't make a sound when I find the opening to her cunt and thrust balls-deep. Her head falls back. Her toes curl. She clenches, her thighs tightening around my hips. Her breasts heave against my chest, and then I just let go, giving her every bit of violation she seems to crave.

For two, maybe three thrusts, I'm in control. Then something shifts somewhere during the fourth plunge inside her. She grinds her teeth together, her hands clenching more of the sheets. *More. More. More.* Then she grabs my thigh, sinking her nails in deep and drawing out a groan I can't silence. Her own gasp mingles with it, breathy and vulnerable. Stacatto's whore likes it rough, apparently. Before I can find a rhythm, she arches up, deepening every thrust and hastening the burning, savage need humming through my blood.

I grab her by the waist and pin her down, but she twists and writhes, forcing her own ragged pace. When I don't comply fast enough, her nails rake downward, ripping bits of skin away.

"Shit!" My vision shoots red—but it's a different shade from before. No matter how many men I've beaten with my fists or faces I've smashed into a wall, I've never breathed this violent shade of ruby before. It drenches everything, and then...there's clarity. It's brief and lasts only for as long as I thrust inside her, grunting with the effort. *Faster. Faster. Harder.*

As if from far away, I hear her moan. I see black. My ears pop with the violent disruption in gravity. I feel electricity crackle all the way to my fucking toes. I'm alive with the sensation of her—her heat, her silky, fucking wet...

Then, too soon, it's over. I'm tumbling back down with only seconds to pull out before I come so hard that my teeth chatter. I don't notice that she hasn't climaxed until I hear her gasp and feel her shift underneath me. Her nails return, catching the left side of my ass, and I rise up onto my knees and snatch her hand away, pinning it above her head.

"No." My voice is too jagged to hold any true anger, and she's too far gone to hear me anyway. With a hiss, I flip her over and then shove my fingers inside her, thrusting them in and out.

Her breath catches. She whines when I grind against her clit with my thumb, and words tumble out into the sheets, broken, hoarse, and definitely not English.

"*Filho da puta! Merda. Merda. Merda*—" She breaks off. Her spine curls, and then she comes hard, riding my fingers so violently that my knuckles pop.

When I pull my hand away, I swipe it against the sheets to erase her, but something makes me pop my thumb into my mouth for a second, swallowing her taste down. I shouldn't feel hard again already, watching her. I shouldn't wonder what the hell she said. I *should* kick her out of the fucking bed. Make her sleep in the tub.

I shouldn't collapse down beside her, high on the aftermath of the sex. But what the fuck. She can't seem to move, either, so I decide to chalk it up as a victory. I let my eyes drift shut, and I nearly convince myself that she isn't here.

"Who hurt you? Was it a man or a woman?" There's no hint of fear or restraint in her voice. Just plain, shameless curiosity. "Who made you carve those marks into your skin?" she adds when I don't respond.

My eyes open, and I can't stop my hand from sliding down my left thigh, sensing the tiny nicks and scars left there. Irritation gives way to suspicion. "How do you know I made them myself?"

She sighs and the mattress shifts beneath her. Suddenly, her forearm juts across my vision, but she makes no attempt to attack me with it. For a moment, my eyes trace the pale skin until I notice the near-invisible flaws that catch the glow from the alarm clock: ten thin, delicate scars that form a neat row right before the juncture of her elbow.

"The first days," she says. Exhaustion thickens her accent, and I try to remember where she said she was from. *Brazil.* "The worst days. I needed to remind myself that I was still real..."

It's a morbid topic for pillow talk. I close my eyes again and ignore her, unwilling to take part in her post-sex game of tit for tat. But the joke's on me. I close my eyes and I see his face. I hear his voice trickle into my ear while my face is pressed into the pillow. *"God forgive me..."*

I bolt upright and rise to my feet. She's watching me, her eyes tracing my own row of scars, openly curious about the story behind each jagged line. *Fuck her.*

"I needed to remind myself that I was still real," she said. I needed to remind myself that I was still human. That I could bleed. That I still had control over some part of my skin. An injured beast caught within a trap will chew its own limb off to escape, after all.

I grit my teeth and try to smother the emotions by shoving my legs into my jeans and dragging them up. It doesn't help. Thanks to Stacatto's nosy bitch, I will need to find some asshole to punch to drive the fucking buzzing from my skull. I let the anger push me to the door, and I slam it shut behind me.

But, somewhere between the front door and the couch, the buzzing dies down, and I slump onto the cushions instead.

I don't sleep.

I breathe. I feel. I count every surging beat of my heart, and I tally up all the ways I'm still—biologically, at least—somewhat human.

Daniela

Lucifer is breaking me.

In three days, he's cast five years' worth of Vinny's hard work down the drain. Lynn wouldn't ask questions. Lynn wouldn't defy. Lynn wouldn't crave the fiery hell only the devil could deliver...

I would give anything in the world to be that cold shell of a woman again, if only for a second—it would certainly make it easier to drive a blade through my chest.

Lucifer has his own demons, it seems. Secrets he just won't spill. Vinny loved to spin the tale of the poor immigrant boy who—with *"fucking hard work and determination"*—grew up to be one of the most feared crime lords at the ripe age of twenty-nine. He saw himself as an inspiration, I think. He saw himself as a warning sign. The little, meek, poor boy most men picked on could one day grab a gun of his own. His heart, hardened by years of neglect and bitter jealousy, could easily pull the trigger.

Monsters are never born—not the evilest and most demented, at least. They are made, forged within the fires of rage and pain.

Vinny and Lucifer have been cut from the same cloth, but they aren't entirely similar—a bit like steel and silver. Both nearly identical at first glance but made from different materials at their core. One is meant mainly to adorn and be adorned. The other is for cutting. Carving. Slicing. Killing.

Which one was which?

Silver, I thought, picturing Vinny. Lucifer's ice-blue eyes were pure *steel.*

He doesn't like me. He doesn't like that he has to tolerate me. It is so strange to be around someone so open in their hatred—someone who calls it what it is and doesn't try to describe it as something else. In Lynn's world, violence was always garnished by love. *I love you, Daniela. I've done it all for you. I would bleed the world for you.*

How ironic is it that Lucifer can't even seem to hit me? Oh, he's wanted to. Some moments, he's even come close to it. I learned to steel myself around men when their shoulders tense or their eyes get mean. Vinny rarely showed restraint, and the warning signs were almost always followed by a blow.

Lucifer displays his anger in nearly the same way. Sometimes I'd swear he is about to lash out. But he still has yet to hit me.

Even when I've prodded him to.

You never ask a man—a beast—about his scars. Even Vinny, for all of his bravado and "success," got touchy if someone remarked on his limp or stared too long at his unsteady gait. *Touchy*, as in he'd break their jaw—or, even worse, he'd give them a scar of their own to ogle.

Lucifer has thirty-three marks on his hips, each one carefully cut into the skin. Not too deep. Not too light. Just enough to bleed, but not enough to draw attention. It's a careful method I taught myself. Poor Vinny learned within a week of moving me in that it was better if he stripped my room of razors and scissors. One cut per day—just one—

like a morbid trail of breadcrumbs left behind for a woman in danger of going insane.

Daniela was still there somewhere, screaming through pale skin. She wasn't dead yet.

Vinny chalked the mutilation up to grief at first, but it wasn't long before he realized that every cut on Lynn's pure flesh was an insult to him. They were my way of saying that I wasn't his, not really. Not back then.

I bite the memory back and drag myself upright, pulling on the gray boxers with my knife still inside the pocket. Gray light streams in through the windows, fighting back the shadows that still linger stubbornly in the corners. Shadows linger over me as well—dark marks over my hips and thighs and most likely my throat, left by groping fingers and brutal strength.

I wince when I stagger upright and make my way to the bathroom. I brush my teeth. Wet my hair. I go through the motions of cleaning myself with a filthy washrag. When I finally creep into the living room, I don't expect to find Lucifer there, lounging lengthwise on the couch the same way a panther might lurk within a tree. He's asleep. His chest rises and falls in a steady but fast rhythm. Without those eyes to give them harsh definition, the planes of his face softly catch the light. He's entirely angelic, the devil right before his tumultuous fall. His bare chest ripples with tension, however, even in his sleep. Muscles flex and twitch beneath tanned skin, constantly on edge. If I go to touch him, he'll spring away before my fingers even make contact.

I tiptoe around the outer edge of the room instead and make my way into the kitchen. I find the box of Chunky Bites in a high cupboard, pour myself a bowl of it, and eat it dry with my fingers, watching Lucifer all the while. Tattoos dot his skin, more deliberately etched than mine. Letters span his neck, though I haven't bothered to read the word they spell. There's also a six-pointed star over his left breast and a plain cross inked high onto his left hip. More scars form subtler designs, spanning across his rib cage and his arms, but they aren't neat like the ones I know he made himself.

It's a strange sensation to watch him like this. In a matter of days, I've learned his body more intimately than I know Vinny's, and I can't help this greedy part of myself that feels compelled to memorize him. Every inch. Every strand of black hair. Every indigo hue of his eyes...

I claw each part of him away to horde somewhere inside myself, where no one will find him.

He doesn't wake by the time I'm nearly finished with my dry cereal. I toy with the idea of taking a shower and sneaking on some of the deodorant the boy gave me—his borrowed clothing carefully hidden underneath the sink. I begin to shift toward it, keeping my gaze on Lucifer the whole while...

Then the door opens, flooding the room with the scent of alcohol and stale body odor more potent than my own.

"You." Green eyes bore into mine, and I don't even have the time to react before the red-haired man has crossed over to me and seized a handful of my hair. Using his grip like a leash, he drags my head down to hiss into my ear. "You stupid little bitch."

He shoves me hard and I go flying. *Wham!*

I taste pain—wet, coppery, and vibrant—as my head ricochets off something and my shoulder strikes an even harder surface.

"Arno? What the hell?"

The growl taints the edges of my periphery, but before I can pinpoint the direction it's coming from, someone seizes my shoulder and drags me forward. The air changes. We're in the hallway where there is no scent of lust or stale sweat or sugary cereal. I tense up, instinctively trying to feel for the stairs, but the grip on my arm is insistent, and I'm dragged down every last one, stubbing my toe on the landing.

I stagger to keep my balance, still held by my hair. The red-haired man nearly wrenches part of it out by the root as he hauls me across a room that smells like cigarette smoke. I hear a door open, and I recognize this section of the flooring as it gives way to the rickety basement steps.

He doesn't bother to drag me this time—he shoves, and I land on my knees two steps down. A foot being rammed into my side kicks me down another four. When the world finally stops spinning, I see flashes of light mingle with the otherwise dreary backdrop of the basement interior. Standing before me, the red-haired man glowers, his eyes bloodshot.

"Tell me," he demands. "Tell me again what your little plan was supposed to achieve?"

I don't know what he means, but I recognize the murderous tension in his left arm. I brace myself for the blow, and he doesn't disappoint, slapping me hard across my already bruised cheek.

"Read." He reaches for me again, pulling me by the arm to the table, where a cell phone lies upturned on the surface, its screen displaying a single text message.

My eyes stream. I have to blink twice to clear my vision enough to make out the words that speckle the screen.

No deal. Tell Lynn that I've remembered my purpose.

"I don't see him rolling over to get you back," the red-haired man growls. He says something else, the words dying down to nothing more than burning embers crushed beneath the inferno of terror that consumes me whole.

Vinny. Vinny. Vinny.

How could I have been so stupid?

I see nothing but the flickering light bulb dangling from the ceiling as my hand slips into the boxers and encloses around the knife. I pull it out, feeling its weight against my palm. The next second, it's on my neck, pressing, tearing, sawing...

"No." The voice that stops me doesn't belong to the red-haired man. His hand isn't the one that snatches the knife away and leaves me slumped and breathless against the edge of the table.

I'm laughing. The sound trickles out, high-pitched and hysterical, mingling with the tears that fall unchallenged. *I've remembered my purpose...*

His purpose.

My demise.

All of us—these stupid, brutal, reckless men—were nothing more than playthings at the mercy of their puppet master.

"Keep laughing," someone snarls. "I'll fucking show you funny when I send him a new video and string you up by your—"

"Are you really that stupid?" I don't recognize the woman who speaks. Her voice is a whip.

Even the red-haired man flinches beneath the bitter sting. "What the hell did you just—"

"Don't you get it?" I slam my fist against the table, hammering the sick, twisted mindset of Vinny into my bones. "Don't you realize by now? You were never in control, not really. You were just part of..." I snicker and have to clutch at my stomach with one hand just to find the breath to speak. "You were just part of my *punishment*."

———

THE FIRST GAME WE EVER PLAYED WAS HIDE-AND-SEEK. He started it, sneaking up behind me on my way home from school and yanking my notebook right from my hands. I gave chase with all the gusto of an energetic eight-year-old already hardened from a few months of starting school in America, where the kids snickered and the teachers cordoned me off into my own section of the class. *Integration,* they called it.

I was angry when I finally caught up to the grinning boy with brown eyes. "*Vai te foder,*" I told him, using the same words my father would shout at the vendors in the market who dared to overcharge him. Part of the fun came from the childish knowledge that he, like the other American children, couldn't understand me.

But he laughed. "Say it in English," he challenged, holding my notebook high above his head, where no amount of jumping would ever allow me to reach.

I licked my lips, already well aware of what the words translated to in English. "G-go...go fuck yourself."

He chuckled again and nodded. Sunlight glanced off his chestnut-brown hair and reflected in his eyes. "It sounds stronger in English," he said. "And I've done you a favor." He shook my notebook once.

I flexed my fingers, eager to run them over the glossy image of a unicorn on the front, speckled with glitter. At that moment, it was my most prized possession, and as if knowing that, the boy waited nearly five extra minutes before finally lowering it within my reach.

"You should thank me," he said.

At the time, I was able to pick out only pieces of what he'd said, still learning English, but I used the strange syllables and strangled vowels almost as a guide to drive my suddenly fervent desire to learn the language of my new country. Eventually, I was able to decipher every word, and I tucked them away within myself like a hard-fought trophy.

"I've given you back your purpose," he told me. "Just minutes ago, you were pouting and defeated because those kids made fun of you and made you feel bad. I made you remember why you went there in the first place."

"Your name?" I demanded afterward, clutching my notebook to my chest.

"Vincent," he said, "but you can call me Vinny. Okay?"

I nodded, only catching the gist of the request. Pride blossomed in my chest and seared through my skin. An older boy was willing to let me call him something that I suspected only a few people were allowed to.

"My name is Danny," I said, testing out one of the few English phrases I had known before immigrating.

The boy frowned. "Danny? That's a man's name."

I flinched, stung by his rejection of my own precious nickname. "Daniela," I clarified, trying again, but he didn't seem to like a name that even my American teachers told me was "beautiful," using the opportunity to teach me a new word.

"You deserve a prettier name."

"Pretty?" I perked up at the mention of another word I knew. *Bonita.* "Like...Lyndsay?" I wrinkled my nose, mentioning the name of one of the girls who tormented me.

The boy nodded. "Yeah. Lynn. That's cute. Can I call you that?"

I glanced down at my navy jumper, feeling my cheeks flush. An older boy thought I was *cute*. He wanted to give me a pretty name to match what he saw on the outside.

"O-okay," I told him, tasting yet another new word on my tongue. "Lynn."

It's funny how hindsight can taint the most treasured memories with the harsh truth of knowledge gained since then. Fifteen years ago, I was nothing more than a stupid child falling beneath the subtle manipulation of a boy who —even I could admit—wasn't entirely evil then. In one instant, I gave up my name, with little idea that I would eventually be forced to give up so much more.

It's a pain that cuts deep—and never truly stops cutting.

"Look at me." The voice slices through the memories and drags me back to the present. Lucifer's eyes pin me in place, keeping me here when all I want to do is just surrender already. Vinny already won. "Look at me." He waits until my eyes focus on his lips before speaking again. "What do you mean?"

He isn't skeptical like the red-haired man. Lucifer is worried. He doesn't underestimate the cunning of another devil.

I shake my head. "It was too easy." Maybe, underneath the pain and the torture, I'd known all along. These men plucked me from Vinny's car, on the way to meet him. Of all places. Or all times. I was dressed "pretty," anxious by his days of silence.

Nothing good ever followed when Vinny had the chance to brood. Just like when he'd goaded me into chasing him all those years ago, Vincent Stacatto did nothing without motive—only, this time, I was the unicorn notebook dangled for his benefit.

"He let you take me," I say, smiling while the devious nature of his own sick plan unfurls inside my head.

I dared to hesitate when accepting his ring, and like a true teacher, Vinny aimed to show me the folly of my decision. He let me be taken by men who hated him. He wanted me to be used and abused. He wanted me to remember my *purpose*. It seemed too twisted, even for a madman.

But hell, he'd planned similar lessons before.

"What do you mean?" Lucifer asks. He speaks every word crisply while the red-haired man rants and raves behind him.

"Stupid bitch. I nearly lost two of my men trying to grab her—"

"How did you know where I would be?" I ask. The car was late that night by nearly fifteen minutes. Even in his madness, Vinny was always punctual. Someone else must have orchestrated this little plot on his behalf. "You had a man on the inside," I guess, thinking out loud. "Someone who gave you the intel...only you merely thought he was working for you. He was really Vinny's all along."

I rack my mind and frown as the answer becomes clear. There's only one man with that kind of clout. Only one man Vinny would trust to spin a web around his naughty, disobedient Lynn.

"Gino." I glance up, scanning both men's faces for recognition. "Big man. Polish accent. Blond. Maybe he approached one of your men. Maybe you approached him. For a hefty price, he'd tell you what time Vincent Stacatto's fiancée would be leaving the hotel and where you could intercept."

No one tries to disagree with what I've said, so I keep talking.

"You thought it was too good to be true, but you needed your revenge. How could you pass it up? Little did you realize that Vinny had men following you, seeking out every bit of intel he could use to wipe you out."

It's a plan Vinny himself gloated over to one of the men he was torturing—how he'd let a rival drug dealer steal from him once, just to watch him "scurry right back to his doghouse. It's like catching a fucking rat in a trap."

Lucifer's face reveals nothing, but the red-haired man's face hardens. "How did you—"

I laugh again. I can't help it. "Too easy," I say. "Vinny doesn't make sloppy mistakes."

Such as hiring a man who arrives late or allowing his fiancée to travel unguarded. I was such a fool not to realize it until now. The fun part of his game is that I knew without a doubt that Arno Mackenzie wasn't even his true target. The man may have tried to have him killed, but there was no insult greater than rejecting Vincent Stacatto's hard-earned name.

"He *wanted* you to hurt me." Not merely to cause me pain —oh, no. To serve as a reminder. A lesson delivered every bit as well-intentioned as when he first taught me those words of English I'd guarded in my heart for so long. "You might as well kill me now... We're already dead."

"She's a psycho little—"

"What next?" Lucifer asks. His hands grip my shoulders on either side, forcing me to face him. "What will happen next?"

My tongue flicks out to wet my lips. The next part of the game? He won. Checkmate. The naughty pawn would be brought back to her master, and another one of his opponents would be swept off the board. There is only one way I can save myself and at least take some of his fun away. I slide my hand along the floor, scanning the room in search of the knife.

"No." Lucifer catches my chin in the flat of his hand, wrenching my head around to face him again. "*Think.*"

My gaze drifts over to the cell phone and I read the time. 7:49—I know without even having to check that the message arrived at seven on the dot. "You...you have ten minutes," I tell him. Even when he plotted murder and revenge, Vinny liked to run a tight schedule. "By eight. They'll be here, though he probably already has men watching all of the doors—"

"Do you have any way out of this shithole that doesn't open directly onto the streets?" Lucifer demands of the red-haired man.

Arno blinks. Then he snaps his fingers and jerks his chin toward the walls. "Yeah. There's an old tunnel that leads into an abandoned warehouse across the street. I'm not stupid enough to box myself in. I learned my lesson after the last time, eh, Dante?"

The two men share a nod, referring to some event in their past. Fools. I shift onto my knees and spot something gleaming from the corner of my eye. My fingers tremble when I reach for it only to have them batted away seconds before brushing the handle of the knife.

A sharp sting flares through the uninjured side of my face. It's nothing like the brutality contained in the hands of the red-haired man. A single slap. Confused, I glance up and find Lucifer standing over me, his hand outstretched. So he does have the potential to hit me after all.

"You have a choice," he tells me, his voice inspiring shivers that threaten to shatter my body into a million pieces. "Give up now. Kill yourself." He kicks the knife over to me, and I have to dig my nails into my palm to stop from reaching for it. "Or you can do something the bastard *wouldn't* expect."

"Like what?" I croak. I'm too tired for this; there's a war raging within myself. Lynn is quivering with fear, while Daniela is resigned and exhausted.

He doesn't even get the point—Vinny *wouldn't* expect me to kill myself, not his precious, scared little Lynn. But I'm curious as to what knowledge of my beloved fiancé he's already gleaned. His dark eyes brim with countless horrors I can only pray that I never have to fully experience.

"You fight back," he says as if it were that simple.

Maybe it is. My little stunt with the camera pushed Vinny beyond his limit, just enough to make him tip his hand so that I'd feel him coming for me. His arrogance has bought us ten minutes. During the childhood games we used to play, I could turn one of his inevitable wins around in ten seconds.

Numb, I reach for the knife, curling my fingers around the dull blade. Lucifer watches as I carefully shove it into the pocket of my borrowed shorts. "You'll need guns," I say. "Not that it will matter."

"Arno," Lucifer snaps, but the red-haired man already seems to be thinking along the same lines.

He reaches into his waistband and withdraws a pistol, which he slams onto Lucifer's outstretched palm. "I have more upstairs."

"Good. Get everyone out. Then pick your best men and find positions on the outside." The smile the devil's lips form is as beautiful as it is chilling. He looks at me, his gaze full of an expectation that makes me shudder in anticipation. "It's time to play a little game. Pick one."

CHAPTER TWENTY

Dante

ONE MINUTE BEFORE HER OWN DEADLINE AND THE girl gets antsy again. Her breath scratches my shoulder, heavy and unsteady. The scent of her blood taints the air, dripping from the cuts in her throat, which she doesn't even seem to notice. She managed not to sever anything vital, apparently, but she'll have a nice set of brand-new scars to remember her fiancé's sadistic "punishment" by.

Stacatto isn't the only sick fuck on the game board though. Arno certainly learned a few lessons when it came to planning the layout of his hideout—even I have to give the asshole credit. The tunnel opens into the basement of the warehouse. The upper level is a cavernous interior filled with dust, and most of the massive windows are boarded shut. If Stacatto has gotten wind of this little route, it would make for the perfect slaughterhouse.

Luckily, Arno learned how to keep his fucking mouth shut in the five years I've been gone. There's no one patrolling the main level at least. Positioned near one of the windows, I have a clear view of the front of the pub through a gap in the plywood. At first glance, it appears just like any other sleepy street at the ass crack of dawn. About half a block down, a man is lounging on a bench, reading a newspaper, a stroller nearby. A few cars drift past, but none look like the type I'd imagine Stacatto's men driving. I almost believe that the bitch got her information wrong, at least until I hear her gasp.

I flinch at the sensation of her finger trailing down the length of my forearm. She's cold. Her breath paints the air white, and I can hear her teeth chattering as she brings her hand over the one of mine holding Arno's pistol.

"What are you doing?" I should shrug her off. I don't know why the hell I don't.

She shuffles closer, and I imagine her straining on tiptoe to bring her mouth close enough to my ear for her to whisper, "There."

I don't resist the gentle pull of her fingers. She steers my hand up, aiming it directly at the man on the bench. I scoff and lower the weapon. She's paranoid. She's insane. She's...

With a sigh, I raise the pistol. It's nearing eight. If this little scenario has any chance of being turned around on its head, now is the time to act. I pull the trigger and deliberately miss, striking the dirt at the man's feet.

Instantly, he bolts upright, tossing the paper aside. What would seem like a normal, panicked reaction from anyone else is just a little too smooth when enacted by him—honed reflex. He takes no time to get his bearings before reaching into his coat and drawing a gun.

"Get down!" I shove the girl aside and aim again.

It takes two more shots before the fucker falls to his knees, but his friends have finally arrived at the party. One of those "harmless" cars slows, and even more men climb out. There are five of them at least. At a glance, I take stock of their muscled builds and stoic expressions. They're professional. Hardened. True killers.

Stacatto wasted no chance on not getting his pretty little fiancée back. Caught unaware, Arno and his merry band of idiots wouldn't have stood a chance. My eyes stray to her before I can help it. Does it even register that she saved my life?

Does it really fucking matter if we're all still dead within ten minutes if I can't clear a good enough route?

I grit my teeth and peer through the window. Shit. The bastard I shot is still alive, pointing frantically in the direction he thinks the shot came from. It's just my luck that he's right. The men split up, three heading toward the pub and two heading straight for me.

"Shit. We need to move." I grab the girl's arm and pull her toward a battered exit I scoped out earlier. The alley beyond it seems clear at a glance, and I drag her forward, pressing my back against the brick wall of the building, listening hard with every cautious step.

The men are still at the front of the warehouse. I hear a thud and realize they decided to forgo knocking and kicked the fucking door in. Perfect. I raise the cell phone in my free hand and bring it to my mouth.

"Arno, go. Go *now*!"

A grunt of acknowledgment comes from the other end, leaving the girl and me with about five seconds to get clear before all hell breaks loose. Breaking cover, I run like hell toward the nearest alley, all but dragging her behind me.

Two.

Three.

Four.

Five.

Gunfire erupts from the warehouse—courtesy of Arno's arsenal turned on two hired thugs. Defeat is still a risk, and a part of me wants to double back and fight. As if sensing the direction my thoughts take, Arno's voice crackles through the cell phone.

"Got it covered, Kitty. Meet you at the rendezvous spot."

Seconds later, I'm about two blocks down from the pub. The gunfire's gone silent, but I'm not stupid enough to chalk it up as a victory yet. Only God knows what else Vinny Stacatto might have lurking up his sleeve by way of backup. Though maybe God and *one* other soul. She's watching me with vacant, hazel eyes that don't register anything until I snap my fingers beneath her nose.

"It worked."

Worked. She mouths the word, seemingly confused. Her gaze trails down over her hands, and she flexes them, satisfied with their movement. When she glances up, the manic, slightly unsteady gleam in her gaze should make me uneasy.

"I always beat him at tic-tac-toe."

The bitch planned her strategy on a children's game. It's as impressive a thought as it is terrifying.

"Now what?" I demand, though the question isn't directed at her or at the cell phone I toss to the ground and quickly stomp beneath my boot. *What fucking now?*

Stacatto's woman watches me, unwilling to put forth an answer. She's shivering in nothing but my shirt and bare feet. Wearing only jeans and my boots, I'm not dressed any warmer. Arno set a rendezvous point, but even I'm not stupid to head there now without knowing just who the fuck might be on my trail.

Tucking the pistol into my waistband, I look over at the girl. "Come on."

It's a bad decision to travel the main street. We draw eyes wherever we go, her most of all. Even cutting through alleys doesn't seem to soothe the paranoid itch that we're being followed gnawing through my skull. We cover nearly a mile before I finally scope out a familiar block of territory—far from both Stacatto's and Arno's playpens. It's still clear—for now—but we won't last long without catching the notice of someone.

I find a bus station and make a calculated risk. The few security cameras face away from the terminals, and I don't see any near the bathrooms where I shove the girl inside the one marked *women's*. A quick scan reveals that there's no one else inside.

"Give me my shirt," I tell her, pushing her toward the nearest open stall.

She staggers inside, clutching at the toilet seat.

"Now."

She does so without question, curling up naked against the wall of the stall while I slip it on. She flinches when I hand her the gun, and I have to press it against her palm when she doesn't take it for herself.

"Stay here," I tell her while slamming the stall door shut to hide her from sight. "If anyone who isn't me tries to get in, shoot them."

I head for the door without giving her the chance to answer, but when I glance back over my shoulder, I see her dirty feet slowly lift one by one to disappear into the stall as if she's climbed onto the toilet and tucked her heels on the rim and her knees beneath her chin.

When I exit the station, I head south and go down another block before coming to a boutique already opening its doors. One quick glance around reveals that there are no other options within the block, and I don't have the time to seek one out. With a sigh, I reach into my pocket, withdrawing the money I got from that punk Andre.

When I step through the doors, the saleswoman behind the counter freezes, a charming grin stuck on her face. "Can I help you?"

"Yeah." I shove the money in her direction and her entire body language shifts at the sight of nearly a grand in cash. "I need an outfit for a woman. Shoes too." I glance around at the sequin dresses on display, frowning. "Something *practical.*"

"Practical." The sales girl licks her lips and gives her earnest smile another go. With her eyes on the cash, she prances over to a section of hangers and runs her fingers along the collection of colored clothes. "I can work with that. Leather or lace?"

Daniela

Three people enter the bathroom after he leaves. I jump every time, holding my breath as they march into an empty stall, imagining Vinny all the while. I tell myself that I could use the gun, even as my fingers hesitate to find the trigger.

I know instantly when Lucifer returns, however. The floors tremble with his presence. I'm already scrambling to my feet before he even knocks on the door to the stall, though when I try to push it open, it won't budge as if he's braced one hand against it.

"Gun."

My hand shakes as I bend down to hold the pistol out underneath the stall. He takes it and then shoves something else into my grip. The handle of a shopping bag, I see when I carefully pull it into the stall. It's black with the name of a boutique written in silver script. *Cassandra's.* Inside, I find a black sweater and a pair of dark-wash jeans. While simple, they're both high quality. There's a pair of boots too: black leather with a low heel. And a matching jacket.

Reeking faintly of perfume, they remind me too much of the carefully chosen outfits I left behind. I almost prefer wearing his clothes. "W-why—"

"Put them on," Lucifer commands.

I do so cautiously. The bastard guessed my size. Vinny's personal tailor couldn't have done much better. The shoes, however, are a little big. They clatter against the floor when I finally ease the stall door open and join Lucifer at the sink.

He found a coat as well: a black one that hangs down over his waist, hiding the shape of the gun tucked into his pocket. My clothes don't do much to dispel the hollow creature staring back at me. I'm the demon to Lucifer's imposing devil.

"Wash up," he snarls, wrenching the faucet on and cupping his hands beneath the spray.

I watch as he splashes a handful onto his face, scrubbing at the grit hidden within his stubble. Stepping up to the next sink over, I turn the water to the hottest setting and just let it run, watching my section of the mirror fog beneath the heat. My hands sting and burn when I finally wet them, marred with a million tiny scrapes and cuts. There's one on my forehead, dripping blood down my jawline. My bruised eye looks worse in the fluorescent lighting. Splotches of green and yellow mingle with the darker purple. My split lip is scabbed over, and my ear...

I grimace when I peel the duct tape off and toss it into the trash. The wound is no longer bleeding, but the surrounding skin is red and hot to the touch. It hurts, I realize when I prod the flesh an inch away and still wince. For all I know, the wound could be infected. I dab at it anyway with clean water and cover the worst of the injury with my hair—which is a disaster I simply don't have the time to manage. I do what I can with my fingers, smoothing the strands down around my shoulders.

Satisfied, Lucifer meets my gaze over the mirror's surface. "Come on."

I follow him out into the hallway and then out of the station itself. It's raining. My jacket doesn't have a hood, but Lucifer draws his low over his face and then steers me along by my forearm. We walk for what feels like blocks before he finally stops and pulls me toward a small café.

I dig my heels in. "N-no."

We may have escaped Vinny once, but there is no way in hell I'll sit and wait for him to find me.

"Come on." Lucifer yanks me forward so hard that I nearly stagger into his chest. Before I can, he shifts, steering me sideways. "They expect us to run," he says.

I can't argue with that. We were nothing more than mice let loose for the cat's amusement.

"They won't expect to find us here. It's safe."

Safe. I scoff at his use of the word, but I don't resist when he opens the door to the café and drags me inside. Our struggle out front must have caused a scene. What few patrons there are have paused—some mid-sips of their coffee—to watch as we creep over the threshold. So much for Lucifer's plan of going unnoticed. He grits his teeth, but he still muscles me into a booth near the back of the small dining room.

It doesn't look like a place Vinny would frequent, at least. The walls are an inviting shade of lime green, and the floors are linoleum. A smiling waitress approaches us, her notepad at the ready, but I don't miss the way her warm expression falters when she sees my face.

"H-hi," she stammers, licking her lips. "W-what can I—"

"Eggs," Lucifer says curtly. He doesn't even glance at the menu. "Scramble them. And coffee—make it black."

"Okay." The waitress jots his order down, and then both she and Lucifer turn expectantly to me.

Seconds pass. *Oh.*

Vinny isn't here to plan my meal down to the very last calorie.

My fingers flutter over my placemat, and I reach for the menu Lucifer ignored. I find the very first option and read it out loud. "The breakfast special, please."

Smiling her strained grin, our waitress nods and takes off.

Left alone, Lucifer and I don't waste time on small talk. He watches the door while I stare down at my hands. They shake, though I don't know if it's from adrenaline or shock, as my eyes drift over the devil seated across from me. It may have been my idea that kept us from being pinned like rats in a trap, but he was the one who listened to me. *He* didn't question the paranoid delusions of a madwoman but staked his life on them instead.

I can't understand why. Answers don't present themselves when our waitress returns with his coffee and gives me a glass of ice water. I sip at it, careful of my sore lip, and merely watch.

There is something about my devil that makes the women gathered at the table across the room turn to stare. They draw their gazes down from his face to the rest of his body, stripping him naked in their minds to see the man hidden underneath. A man I've met more than once.

It feels so strange to acknowledge that without the threat of Vinny's video hanging over my head. I know what Lucifer looks like with his pants off. I know what he feels like inside me. I know the sounds he makes when he climaxes. I know the hue of blue on which his eyes can touch right before he throws his head back and bellows his release out.

"Let me know if it's too hot for you, darling."

I jump when the waitress sets a plate of steaming food down in front of me. She scrambles back while I sniff at two sunny-side eggs and two links of sausage. I poke at the meat with a fork fished from the table, but I can't bring myself to eat until Lucifer piles a mound of scrambled eggs onto his own fork and shovels the lot into his mouth. He chews. I nibble. In silence, we both clear our plates and head out after he's paid the bill.

Through the rain, we trudge up two more blocks to a bus stop, and then we spend hours riding the same three routes. He doesn't explain why, but I suspect that it's to confuse anyone who might be following our trail. My head is spinning by the time he finally steers us toward a new direction. We're in a more distant part of the city now, closer to the outskirts. In the storm, there are only a few people out on the streets, but I feel eyes on us wherever we go.

With every step, my feet chafe within their new boots. By the time Lucifer pulls me to a stop, pain is a constant throb shooting through my calves.

"Wait here."

For the first time, I glance around and take serious stock of our surroundings. We're on a partially deserted lane in a neighborhood that has definitely seen better days. Dogs bark in the distance, and up ahead looms a shadowy dwelling with a long driveway reaching back into a section of woods. The whole property is cordoned off by a chain-link fence with a security panel affixed to the front of it, like the kind you might find outside of a high-rise. Leaving me at the curb, Lucifer starts forward, his shoulders tensed and head bowed low.

So, this is their rendezvous point. It's far enough from Vinny's kingdom to avoid notice—that is if the red-haired man was half as cautious as Lucifer in making sure he wasn't followed.

When he reaches the security panel, Lucifer grumbles something into the speaker. A minute later, I hear a door open somewhere on the property, and a shadowed figure breaks away from the main structure to approach the gate. I try to observe them carefully, but Lucifer takes precedence when his gaze seeks mine out. He jerks his head for me to come closer, and I do, every step cautious.

For the very first time, I consider running. He has to have expected it by now. I wonder if that's why he's kept such a close watch on the gun. He's willing to use it if he has to. On Vinny's men. On me.

When I approach him, I look up, ignoring the drops of rain that dribble down my forehead. "When we go in there, I'm not his captive anymore." I don't have to mention the red-haired man by name.

Lucifer clenches his jaw in understanding.

"I enter this place of my own free will," I tell him. "I'll help you take down Vinny, but only on my terms."

Lucifer frowns. He doesn't like being commanded, least of all by me. "And if I refuse?" he wonders, his voice deep enough to rival the thunder echoing over the horizon.

I shrug. "You trusted me already." I inhale sharply and play the only card I have in my arsenal. "I saved your life—"

"You saved your own ass."

"*Exactly*," I agree. "If I wanted to go back to him, I would already be begging for mercy while your head adorns the wall of his study. I won't run."

Lucifer doesn't seem so sure of that. He's suspicious, my devil. I suppose that's why he's still alive. *Stupid*, evil men didn't tend to live too long. Vinny's brutality taught me that.

"He's taken *everything* from me." My voice tastes bitter with the five years of pain I've had to suppress. Memories threaten to spill out from the dark corners of my mind, and I fight to swallow them back. "I want to take something from him."

Lucifer still doesn't give me an answer. I'm a slave to the scrutiny of those blue eyes, frozen in place until he finally nods—just once, so quickly that I may have missed it.

"You coming in?" A figure wearing a gray sweatshirt with the hood drawn low stands at the gate, holding it open.

I don't answer, but Lucifer speaks for the both of us by stepping forward through the gap presented by the gate-opener. I follow him, my gaze on the dwelling up ahead. Apart from being secluded and well-guarded—which I sense from the human-shaped shadows lurking on the edges of the property—it doesn't look like anything that would attract the interest of either Vinny or the red-haired man. Dogs bark somewhere nearby, and with every step we take, the stench of cigarettes and stale cologne gets stronger.

Up close, I realize that the property doesn't contain just one house, but a collection of buildings. At the front of the property sits a main square one formed out of brick. A matching detached garage rests a few yards behind it, and then another building looms slightly over the rest, perched on a small hill at the mouth of the woods. Neon decals flash from the square windows built into the lower level of the main building. *Mack's* is written in red script on a sign hanging above a blue door. The man who came to the gate pulls it open, and pulsing music eagerly rushes out.

"After you."

Lucifer enters first, his shoulders squared, his stance open and wary. Almost immediately, however, he relaxes, and I see why when I finally creep forward in his shadow.

The red-haired man is sitting on a stool on the other side of a narrow, packed barroom. When he sees Lucifer, he beckons him closer with a wave of his hand. "You made it." He has to shout over the music—an angry pulse of hammering percussion and guitar riffs I can feel in my bones.

Lucifer grits his teeth and seems to have to physically keep his hands from slapping over his ears. Jerking his chin, he indicates for me to follow him through a crowd of men and women wearing an array of ragged clothing Vinny certainly wouldn't approve of. Skirts more revealing than my "video costume," ripped jeans, and dark leather clad this ragtag bunch. They eye us warily, and the moment Lucifer reaches the bar, the music shuts off.

"Dante." The greeting comes from a tall man with dark, closely cut hair who muscles his way through the crowd to approach Lucifer from his left side. He's wearing a leather vest, which hangs open to reveal a heavily muscled chest decorated in what seems to be an even mixture of scars and tattoos. "Long time no see." The man extends a hand. There's no hostility in his gaze, but Lucifer eyes his palm for a few seconds before slapping his own against it.

"Mack," he says gruffly. His eyes cut over to the red-haired man as he speaks, and they share a silent look that I'm sure doesn't go unnoticed by everyone else in the crowded room. Lucifer isn't pleased by what I assume is a tense reunion.

The moment Mack draws his hand away, Lucifer steps toward the bar and jerks his shoulder in a subtle invitation for me to follow. I do, less out of obedience and more out of unease at the way the eyes of this stranger graze over my skin. Mistrustful. Hateful. Cold.

A choked sound catches in my throat as I bite back an irrational urge to snicker. Is this how Vinny felt in the few unguarded moments I looked at him and was too exhausted to tailor my expression?

No wonder he hit me.

"This her?" Mack inclines his chin toward me. His brown eyes linger over the V-neckline of my sweater, and he licks his lips. "Not bad."

He takes a step toward me and nearly runs right into Lucifer's chest. The devil says nothing, but I feel his presence all the way down to my bones. *Possession.* Is that what this is? His claim has a different flavor than Vinny's. My skin prickles with his nearness. He may have already chewed me to pieces, but he isn't quite willing to share me.

Yet.

"You've certainly done a number on her," Mack ascertains. "Hey, Sammy!" He looks back at someone in the crowd and draws them out with a jerk of his chin. "Get over here."

Lucifer doesn't move, but suddenly, he seems taller. The shadows lingering around the periphery of the bar converge on him, deepening the definition of the muscles evident even beneath the leather of his coat.

"Relax." Mack laughs, but the carefree emotion isn't shared by the others gathered around us. They tense and their eyes flicker from Dante to Mack and then Arno in the corner; it's a silent tennis match. "Sammy here's a doctor of sorts." Grinning, Mack places his hand on the shoulder of the considerably shorter figure who appears at his side.

Sammy is an older man, but he's clean-shaven and seems nice enough—though his camouflage-print slacks and gray wifebeater certainly don't scream "doctor."

"Damn." He whistles, his bloodshot eyes on my face. "You'll definitely want to get that ear looked at. Unless you want it to turn gangrene and fall off!" He chuckles at what was apparently a joke, but it seems lost on everyone else.

"Let Sammy check her out," Mack suggests. "While she's gone...we can have a little chat." His smile widens, but Lucifer doesn't bother to return it.

There's something he isn't saying. Something that lurks beneath his skin and turns him to stone. Finally, he nods just once.

"Um...g-great." Sammy takes a step toward me, reaching for my wrist.

Once again, Lucifer manages to dissuade anyone from touching me without even having to say a word. He merely inhales and poor Sammy shrinks beneath his gaze and quickly hastens two steps back.

I'm not stupid enough to mistake his actions for protection. He's merely guarding his investment. I'm a pretty little toy he doesn't want tarnished too badly. Vinny wouldn't want me *too* broken after all.

The thought gives me the strength to step around Lucifer, implying that I'll follow without having to be forced. Sammy audibly sighs while Mack simply...watches. His smile never wavers, but there's no ounce of joy in it. The man simply likes flexing his teeth, the same way a wolf does in the face of an opponent. He doesn't take Lucifer's lack of reaction as an insult.

He accepts it as a challenge.

For whatever reason, he doesn't follow me when I head toward the back of the bar with Sammy leading the way. Whether he's welcome to or not, Lucifer falls into step behind me, and I hate this part of me that feeds off his presence.

Alone, Lynn would shrink inside herself, trapped with all of these unfamiliar men. She'd hate where their eyes leered as she crept past them, unsteady in her boots. Her heart would race, and she'd entertain—for a minute—that returning to Vinny wasn't the worst possible fate a woman could face.

Arno and his brutes were drunk on revenge. These men are driven by another thought that makes my skin crawl once I identify it. *Greed.*

I keep my gaze trained on Sammy's brown curls, but I can smell the others. I hear them.

"Pretty little bitch."

"Looks like she can take a hit. I wonder how many."

"Hot piece of ass."

It's only when Lucifer takes a step closer to me that they fall silent. His heat burns through my back. His breath rustles the hair at the nape of my neck. It's like he's breathing his scent onto my skin—marking me in a way that even these animals are forced to respect. Does he do it out of duty to our private bargain?

Or merely because he likes exerting his authority over men who would be foolish to challenge him?

It's an amusing thought to consider as Sammy finally comes to a stop before a wooden door decorated with strips of police caution tape.

"Ladies first," he says while opening the door, revealing the small room beyond it.

I'm surprised to find that it's organized like a makeshift clinic. There's a black recliner in the center and a row of counters against the wall, cluttered with trays of syringes and vials. So maybe less of a clinic and more like...a druggie's paradise.

"I can t-take it from here," Sammy says when Lucifer starts to follow me inside the room.

"Yeah, he's got it," another man seconds. Tall and imposing, he comes from nowhere to guard the door, conveniently inserting a foot in between me and Lucifer.

"Come on, Dante," Mack playfully scolds from across the room. "Leave the women to their business."

He's outnumbered. I can sense his frustration in a single grunt that sends loose strands of my hair flying, but I suspect I'm the only one who notices. The next second, he's gone, heading toward Mack and Arno. The lack of his presence is like a Band-Aid being forcefully ripped from a wound. I don't know if I miss it or if I'm relieved by its loss.

At least, now, I can bleed in peace.

"Step right up," Sammy says with a nervous laugh.

I tear my gaze from Lucifer's retreating form and cross over the threshold. He gestures toward the recliner, and I settle onto the edge of it while the door shuts with the one thug on the other side of it.

Sammy eyes me carefully, clicking his tongue. "Let's get a look at that ear." He reaches for the hair on my right side and then hesitates as if silently asking for permission. I nod, and he withdraws the strands, groaning when he sees the wound up close. "Jesus! Did they let a fucking butcher take it off with a hacksaw?" He shakes his head at such a poor method of torture. "Sloppy. Just fucking sloppy."

Muttering under his breath, he turns to the counter. There's a long mirror hanging on the wall above it, and I studiously observe his hands as they flit over the scattered materials.

"It's a bit too old to do much, I'm afraid," he says. "Otherwise, I'd attempt stitches. I can clean it for you, at least." He glances over at me and winks. "I wasn't kidding about the gangrene."

From behind him, my reflection stares back. The haunted shell seems a little more animated now. There's a harder line to her jaw that wasn't there before. She's on edge. She's anxious. The man before her keeps sneaking glances at a vial of liquid when he thinks she isn't looking.

"I should clean it with some peroxide, I guess." He approaches me with only a bottle of alcohol in his hand and a wad of gauze.

Gritting my teeth, I force myself not to react as he methodically cleans what's left of my ear. The burning sting goads my eyes into watering, and I can't suppress a wince when he presses too hard.

"Oops!" He drops a bloodied bit of gauze to the floor, and I automatically lean down to grab it—but he expects the motion. His fingers are already waiting to seize my wrist, holding tight while he jabs a needle fished from his pocket into my vein.

"Shhh." His free hand traps my mouth as a searing heat shoots through my wrist.

A drug. Whatever it is works fast. Already, my body feels heavy. It takes twice as much effort than it should to stick the fingers of my left hand into the pocket and find my knife.

After several tries, I clench it in my fist and jab it straight back, striking whatever is in reach.

"Son of a bitch!"

Sammy's hand slips from my mouth, and I lunge from the chair, aiming for the door...but my legs move too slowly. I land on my side, my feet still tangled in the armrest of the chair. The fall knocks the air from my lungs. God, I feel so heavy.

"Fuck! Fuck!"

I can hear Sammy scrambling behind me before a crushing weight slams into my lower back. Grasping fingers graze the side of my jaw, seeking out my mouth again while I gather the strength to suck in one last gulp of air and release it on a single scream.

"*Dante!*"

CHAPTER TWENTY-ONE

Dante

Of all people, the bastard came to fucking Mack for help.

Mack, whose sole definition of the term "friend" only extended to how far up someone else's ass he could shove his foot out of pure amusement. *Mack*, who would have easily chopped Arno into pieces and sold him for scrap back in the day if the parts would have brought him some easy cash. *Mack*, who liked to shoot Parish up with dope and fuck her for kicks.

Mack, who looked at Stacatto's woman like...

I inhale, my eyes narrowing at the way his gaze traced her body. He looked at her like he was already imagining her riding his cock. Willing or not, the bastard didn't give a damn.

"Don't give me that look," Arno mutters while the fucker is

still out of earshot. "While you were in prison—ignoring phone calls and visitors, I might add. Fuck, I even sent you a letter once." He scoffs, shaking his head. "Anyway. Things aren't the same. CJ. Kade. Trolito. Benji. Alex." He holds his hand up and ticks the fingers off one by one. "Dead. Dead. Prison. Dead. *Accountant*." He shakes his head. "Don't ask me how the fuck that happened—"

"Why *him*?" I growl, dragging him back to the question at hand.

"He's the only one fucking left," Arno argues. "At least the only one with enough infrastructure to take on someone like Stacatto. Take a look around, Dante." He gestures with a wave of his hand. "This is what's left of the Saints. But trust and believe that I don't like this any more than you do." His eyes narrow, and I know he hasn't forgotten how the bastard treated his sister in the past.

"I don't like it," I say—not that it fucking matters. This is Arno's battle, after all. The woman isn't my responsibility, and I don't owe her a damn thing—least of all the need to plead her case.

"I want to take something from him."

"If you want to hit Stacatto, you need a plan," I heard myself admit through gritted teeth. "She's the only one who knows how his fucked-up mind works."

Arno scowls, and I don't have to remind him that she already outsmarted Stacatto once. Who knows what she learned while tucked away in his gilded cage?

"*She* is all we need. We could regroup somewhere else. We could—"

"Now, don't be stingy, Dante." Mack grins as he approaches the bar.

The asshole's done well for himself, it seems. I count at least thirty men in this room alone, and there are even more stationed outside, monitoring the property's perimeter. What Mack lacks in charming personality he's certainly made up for with brutality and paranoia to help win him some new friends.

"I want to help. It's the least I could do for Parish." The bastard has the nerve to actually pretend to care. He bows his head for Arno's benefit, but I'm not impressed.

"Then let Arno handle this *his* way."

Mack flashes another cocky grin, erasing all traces of mock concern. "Now, where's the fun in that, Dante?" he asks. "Vinny Stacatto's no average fuck. I want a piece of him too."

Not out of revenge, I suspect. Mack merely wants a piece of the pie. He wants the girl. He wants to use Arno's fuck-up for his own gain.

Some shit never changes.

"The pub is gone," Arno says, explaining the reason why he's already lurking around the nearest stash of liquor. "Everyone got out, but the fuckers set it on fire—"

"Espi." I'm already on my feet, but Arno places a hand on my shoulder and shoves me back down.

"You think I wouldn't make sure he's okay?" He scoffs. "He was already out running *errands* for me, but I made sure that he knew what's up. When he's ready, he'll join us here."

When he's ready. I grit my teeth and somehow manage not to wrap my hands around Arno's neck until he tells me where I can find the kid. Instead, I cut my gaze to the back of the room, where one of Mack's punks is still guarding the door to the "clinic." Unease is a useless emotion. I don't like to feel it, and I clench my hands into fists, craving the vicious surge of anger in my blood to replace it. *Anger,* I understand. Men like Mack react to it better than any other fucking language, written or spoken, anyway.

"Dante." Arno's watching me, uncharacteristically tense.

We're no longer in his domain. This is Mack's territory. His property. His rules. *My* quickly thinning patience. It doesn't take this long to simply bandage a wound. My gaze returns to the door and I scan the stoic expression of the man standing beside it.

"Dante thinks the woman could be of use. If she's on our side," Arno says to Mack, picking up the thread of conversation.

That's right. Apparently, the three of us are supposed to be planning something. Bullshit. Dogs don't plan. They steal. They scheme. They react on pure instinct.

"We... Dante?" Arno reaches for me when I stand up, but his fingers graze off my shoulder as I start across the bar.

My eyes are on the door while I shove past asshole after asshole, not caring who the fuck I have to jar out of my way. The man by the door perks up when I get close. He glances over my shoulder to where I know Mack to be and nods once.

"I can't let you—" he starts to say, his posture tensing and stance turning hostile. His lips move, and words keep churning from his mouth, but the buzzing blaring through my skull drowns them out.

It's like my brain separates from my body for a second. I'm merely a machine, cold and empty. My footsteps slow before I enter the man's personal space though. Maybe I even mean to turn back.

Then I hear it. I hear *her*, even above the buzzing. Faint. Desperate. Pleading.

"*Dante!*"

All I know is that I laugh first. The dumb bitch is calling for me. She thinks I actually give a damn. That I'll come to her rescue. She thinks I'd care. She thinks. She *thinks*.

I don't think; I react. My fists go flying, striking flesh, bone, and wood. I register nothing but pain surging through my knuckles. I see red. I taste it. When I blink, I'm standing inside a narrow room with a black chair in the middle and a row of counters lined with vials of drugs. I spot her instantly; she's sprawled over the floor, crawling for the door.

Her eyes widen when she sees me. Then she sticks one hand out, the fingers shaking. "He...he drugged me."

The fuck he did. Her words are already running together.

When I take her hand and pull her upright, her entire body jerks like a kite on a loose bit of string. I let her stagger against me, her hands pawing for purchase over my chest. Behind her, the man named Sammy cringes back against the wall, clutching at his left shoulder.

"She stabbed me! The fucking little cunt stabbed me—"

"Now, Dante." The voice gnaws on my thickening rage, injecting clarity back into my brain. "This is no way to make new friends." Mack stands just beyond the doorway, shaking his head while *tsk-tsk-tsking* through his teeth. "We're all family here."

Ignoring him, I focus my attention on the man huddling in the corner. "What the hell did you give her?"

Sammy jumps. One of his hands starts to claw at his wrist, the nails raking the skin. "J-just a little something to take the edge off—"

"Heroin," Mack says without a fucking ounce of shame. "Nothing lethal. Just enough to make her docile."

Docile. I force a dark chuckle from the back of my throat as I skim my gaze over Stacatto's battered and now *high* woman. Her eyelids flicker, the hazel irises swirling. She'll be docile, all right. I have to press my hand against the small of her back when her knees buckle.

I swallow hard, shaking my head to hear above the fucking buzzing. "Why?"

Mack shrugs. "To make it easier to send her back to Stacatto in a body bag."

I laugh. It's only when I see Sammy cringe into his corner that I realize the sound comes out more like a growl. Trust Mack not to have read the fucking CliffsNotes.

"Arno tried that."

Mack's expression flickers, and suddenly, the bastard's harder to read. "*Arno* did," he admits. "But I'm not above using other methods of persuasion."

"Other methods?"

Chuckling, he runs a hand over the stubble along his jaw. He's sizing up the details of his plan, picking out just how much information he's willing to share. He was always a sneaky little fucker. "Let's just say I already have a buyer lined up."

"A buyer?" It takes two seconds before the words click and his genius plan unfurls in my mind.

He wants to sell her. Whore out Vinny Stacatto's girl, getting off on the man's humiliation. It's sadistic. It's lucrative.

It's fucking stupid.

"If you want to take down a fucker like Stacatto, then you go for the head," I say. "You cut it off the fucking snake. She"—I jerk my chin toward the woman—"knows the inner workings of his organization. His habits. His weaknesses. We use her to take him down, and you stick to whoring out your women on street corners."

Mack rubs his chin. "Who's to say she can't speak while she's riding my buyer's cock?"

Red. It's only when Stacatto's woman whimpers that I realize my fingers tensed, threatening to crush her spine beneath them. "She'll help us take him down on her own."

"Funny." Mack rocks his head from side to side, stretching out the muscles in his neck. "I've heard about the little tape you made with her. If she's that good of a fuck to get Dandy Dante on her side, then maybe I should double my asking price?"

"No." The hoarse command weasels through my eardrums before I even register stepping forward, jarring the woman clutching my shoulders.

Her head falls back, those unfocused eyes seeking mine out. "No...only...you." She utters the words softly enough that only I can hear them, not that they make any fucking sense.

Only you.

"Arno's already agreed to it," Mack adds with a casual jerk of his thumb toward the ginger bastard in question. "Look at her. She took the high quickly. The little princess won't feel a fucking thing—"

"No."

Mack knows business the way a mutt has inner workings of the stock market. He prefers to snarl over scraps to make a quick buck. It's why Dino overlooked him as a successor; the bastard never thinks with his head.

"You string her out and trade her for cash. Then what? What next when Stacatto comes knocking with an army at his heels? You didn't see the men he sent to Arno's. They were machines. Professional." I can't help a flicker of appreciation. A monster can respect the skill of another predator, after all. "Who's to say that your buyer isn't already cutting a deal right now to sell you out to Stacatto himself?"

Mack lets another gruff laugh loose. "Dandy little Dante," he says, shaking his head. "Always Dino's favorite. You still love putting that unfinished high school education of yours to the test, I see." For a split second, he drops the act. True hatred lurks in his gaze, unfinished despite the years I spent in prison. Now that's more fucking like it.

"And you're still nothing more than a mutt, I see. Still running with the dogs."

He doesn't react to the insult, but even five years ago, the fucker had quick reflexes, known to have a knife drawn and a man gutted before the poor bastard even knew what had hit him. Arno may have had the temper, but they didn't call Mack the "Mad Dog" for nothing.

He watches me coldly, tallying up the differences he finds in me. I do the same to him. He's leaner, and despite the lazy swagger, there's something careful about everything from the set of his shoulders to the open position of his hands.

"This isn't quite the reunion I imagined, Dante," he admits, his tone harder than before. "But what the hell. Let's do Dino proud. Two methods. Two good ideas. Let's settle this in the old way and give the boss a show he can enjoy from hell."

The old way. My fingers throb, recognizing the implications of the words before my brain even does.

"No." Arno finally steps forward, shaking his head. "No. Dante, just let the bitch go. This isn't your problem."

Let her go. I do, and she falls to her knees. One of her hands flutters against my thigh, braced against it for balance, but she doesn't try to stand. She doesn't move. She merely tilts her head back to look up at me. There is no fear or hatred in her eyes. Just grim acceptance that's quickly swallowed up by the haze of the drug flooding her system. She's too high to speak out loud, but I can almost hear her voice echoing through my head. *Just remember to kill me first, before you send me back to him.*

I step away from her and seek out Mack. "If I win..."

"What the fuck?" Arno tries to muscle his way into the room. "Dante—"

"The woman's yours," Mack says, placing one hand on Arno's shoulder to hold him back. "We use your plan. But, if I win, we do things my way. *And.*" He stresses the word, and I bark out a laugh, unsurprised. And there it is—with Mack, there is always a fucking catch.

"What?" I demand.

"I win and you come to work for me. Prison's probably taught you a few new tricks, Kitty," he adds with a malicious tilt to his mouth. "I could make a lot of money off you."

"You've kept up with the cage," I surmise, once again un-fucking-surprised.

Arno may have left Dino's meal ticket behind, but Mack seems to be living large off the methods of our old master.

"Cage?" he echoes on a deadly soft chuckle. "Dante, I run the *Kennel.*" He turns and jerks his head for me to follow.

I step forward. I know that my expression reveals nothing when I stoop on one knee and toss the woman over my shoulder first. It's an action that goes unmissed by no one, but with as light as she is, I can almost forget.

Almost. Her scent floods my skin, equally as potent as the drug seeping through hers. It's not out of any kindness that I intervene in Mack's plans for her. It is simple retribution. A man owned by no one had to keep his fucking promises, after all.

Regardless, the simple act of shouldering her body makes her a target. A pretty little bone caught in the jaws of a rival dog. No man can ignore her scent. Mack won't ignore my claim.

I should have stayed in fucking prison. At least the invisible lines we bastards drew in the figurative sand were somewhat clear. In this domain, anything goes. It's a familiar, if hostile, territory as I follow Mack across the barroom and through a door that opens onto a fenced-in yard. A few paces ahead is a small, level building that appears to be a shack at first glance. A man is guarding a metal door, chained with a padlock, for show of course. The real security comes in the form of at least twenty pit bulls all herded into individual pens just on the inside of the building. They bark and snarl, gnawing at the chain-link pinning them in.

Mack expanded cage-fighting to dogfighting, it seems. He doesn't comment on the animals as he leads the way past the kennels and into an open space with concrete walls and two other men posted on either side of a pair of heavy metal doors.

"Welcome to the Playhouse," he says, flashing his teeth. "Ladies first."

Ignoring the insult, I stalk forward with one hand pinning the girl in place. The other I brace against one of the doors and push it open. For a second, I'm almost glad I took the challenge and went first just so the bastard wouldn't be able to see my face.

He's emulated Dino down to the very last detail. It's a setup almost comparable to the dog kennels in the other room but larger. A giant chain-link cage, shaped like an octagon, is in the center of the room. The floor is cement, coated with gray sand in the pit, making it easier to clean the gore and bloodstains after each fight. Around the cage is a rectangular placement of bleachers, at least twenty deep in every direction. On second thought, this isn't like one of the old gambling dens Dino used to run out of a garage with maybe a few hundred spectators a fight at fifty bucks a head. The bastard's built himself an arena.

"It's nice, right?" he wonders, appearing at my left side. "Reminds you of the old days."

I certainly don't need a reminder of the "old days." I still wear the scars. On the nights I feel like it, I still have the nightmares. More often than not…I still wish I could live them again.

"When?" I ask, my voice hard. Being here brings back the old, steady pulse I used to feel in my core right before a fight. Only then would the buzzing die off, like a wild animal that knew it would be sated soon. "When do we get this over with?"

"When?" Mack steps forward, raising his hands toward the gray ceiling—a gladiator in his colosseum. It's only when he looks back at me that I see the true beast lurking underneath the human exterior. This man isn't a gladiator. He's the fucking lion sent in to crush the hopes of a mere mortal slave. "We do this *now*."

He snaps his fingers and one of the men guarding the door appears, his posture erect like a soldier called to war in jeans and leather.

"Well, go rile up the masses," Mack commands with a wave of his hand and a wink. He's cocky again, the swagger returning in full force.

It's not bravado that swells him this time though. It's confidence. While I've been in prison, he's been sharpening his claws and honing his skills. I have no doubt who the star attraction of this cage is.

If there is one thing Mack loves more than money, it's the spotlight.

Within minutes, people start to trickle in, men and women, their expressions wary. At first, I assume that they must have followed us from the bar, but it seems there are more than that. They fill the seats, streaming past Mack and me; I can already sense bets being laid and stakes being raised. Whether he gets Stacatto's woman or not, Mack will make a tidy profit from this event.

I intend to make him work for every goddamn penny.

After nearly ten minutes of waiting, I glance around at the corners of the room, anxious. Doors lead off at random intervals throughout the main arena—most likely to rooms where each fighter can warm up in private. My muscles tense, aching to do just that. I almost start to approach one, eager to find out for myself where they lead, when a voice rings out. Soft. Honeyed. A woman's.

"Dan...Dante?"

I turn and don't have time to catch the figure who throws her arms around what little of me she can.

"Oh my God! I thought you were in prison!" She pulls back, beaming. Five years did little to the petite blonde, who's still sporting the same fiery smile that's equal parts seductive and charming.

I wonder if she's still "working" her old profession. The shit she's wearing now supports that theory: tiny black shorts and a tight red top.

"Darcy."

She looks good. Almost like the girl I left behind. Almost. But there's a maturity in her gaze that wasn't there before. She holds her head high, with a confidence that comes only with a position of power. Then I catch Mack staring at her ass and realize why.

"You're with him," I say. There's no emotion in the observation. It's just fact.

Darcy doesn't answer. Her gray eyes flit up to the woman slung over my shoulder instead. Whatever questions she has, she knows better than to ask.

She sighs instead and forces her smile wider. "So, when did you get out?"

I shrug and trail my gaze from her over to Arno, who's watching me with an expression even I can't decipher. "About a week ago."

That timespan triggers something; Van Hallen owes me money, the fucker—and I intend to collect in full.

"A whole week?" Darcy shakes her head in disbelief. "And you couldn't even come say hi?" She's still smiling, but I don't want to dissect the look that distorts her features for merely a second. I don't have the time.

Apparently, neither does Mack. "Baby." He jerks his head as if calling a trained pet.

But, to her credit, Darcy takes her sweet time turning to face him, her hands on her hips. "Yes?"

Mack grins. "Show Dante's...*friend* to the best seats in the house." He points to a bench at the highest point in the arena with the clearest view of the cage below. "It's gonna be quite the show. The little Kitten returns to the cage."

"Show?" Darcy frowns. Apparently, she wasn't around for the excitement, but I don't fill her in, and neither does Mack or Arno. She's left to suspect the obvious from my stance and Mack's excitement. Eventually, her gaze turns to the woman slung over my shoulder. "She okay?"

"She's high," I grunt, shifting so that the girl's feet hit the ground, but she can't even hold herself upright.

Darcy has to slip an arm around her shoulders just to keep her from falling, but she murmurs something, her gaze focused in my general direction.

"Don't. No," she slurs, the words running together. "Don't. Don't. Igobackto—"

I turn on my heel, cutting her off. Irritation runs down my spine when I realize that Arno is within earshot, watching me, his expression still unreadable for once. Mack, the fucker, is already strolling down the center of the arena, toward the cage.

"Twenty minutes per warm-up, Kitty?" he suggests without turning around. "Just like old times." He wiggles his fingers toward a door that's directly parallel to the center of the arena.

"Fine." Already, I can hear murmuring about how quick of a fight it should be.

Mack the Mad Dog. Mack who fights dirty. Mack who has never lost a match since he opened his own cage.

I shrug hard, as if that might brush the doubt off. Some of it even trickles from the back of my own mind. Prison games were a little different from the fights in the cage. There was no entertainment factor. No money on the line. When some upstart punk came at you with a shiv, there was no boss waiting to step in and pull the match. I was a show dog who'd been thrown from the stage and into the bowels of the pound, where a battle became less about glory and more about survival.

I flex my fingers, feeling them sting. The truth is that the "Kitty's" claws were worn off from scratching at the concrete walls of a prison cell. He was forced to shove new weapons into the gaps—whatever tricks and skills he could learn from men with more body counts to their name than the people standing in the cafeteria line every day. How well would those makeshift weapons stack up against a well-fed, regularly trained mad dog?

Well, we would just have to fucking find out. I head for the door while Mack approaches another on the opposite side. I barely make it a step before a voice, low and mangled, calls me back.

"Wait." Stacatto's girl is watching me when I look over my shoulder. Her eyes drift up and down my body as if she's trying to decide which end is which. "Tic-tac-toe," she says finally, her tongue wrestling with the words.

I can barely understand her through her accent, and Darcy shoots me a worried look.

"Don't worry. I'll take care of her—"

"Tic-tac-toe," the woman insists, stressing every word as best she can. She's fighting the high, trying to resist the pull of the wave sweeping her under.

I know from experience that she doesn't stand a fucking chance.

I jerk my head in a nod and turn on my heel without responding out loud. *Tic-tac-toe.* She certainly loves her old games—the strategy she laid out was simple but effective: split the board. Allow your opponent to set the first piece and then draw them into opposite corners of the grid while you skillfully lay your trap. By the time you finally spring it, you've taken the center of the board before they know what hit them.

The little bitch thinks that one lucky round with a batch of hired guns makes her an expert on battle plans. I laugh darkly to myself as I skirt the end of the cage and pull the door open to a small room that contains only a row of blue training mats lined up lengthwise against the wall, a set of weights, and a flickering light bulb. After closing the door behind me, I strip my coat and my shirt off and then approach a mirror hanging near the back corner of the pen. I don't recognize the man staring back at me compared to the boy who first cut his teeth on the cage at the age of sixteen. The Kitty's grown up. He's lost his love of chasing the bloody ball of yarn for scraps. He's honed his skill in the alleys, and he doesn't like to play with his food as much anymore.

Nowadays, he prefers to grind it down into a pulp to make it easier to swallow.

CHAPTER TWENTY-TWO

Daniela

So this is hell: a cage of gleaming metal, built high upon a sea of ash. Countless demons spectate from the shadows, their growls and roars proclaiming their hunger for fresh blood.

It all creates an intoxicating atmosphere in this playpen for the damned. *The Kennel,* according to a row of black paint depicting the letters against a concrete wall. I'm on a perch high above the pit down below, seated on a long bench beside a woman who smells like the pies *Mamãe* used to make. A metal bar sits in front of me, meant to pin the spectators this high up in place, lest they plunge down the long row of seats that lead like steps to the bottom level.

Splat!

The world drifts in and out of focus while faceless men dart to and fro, preparing the ring for battle. I'm not sure how much time has passed before Lucifer himself appears at the mouth of the ring, stripped naked save for a gray pair of boxer shorts that hug his domineering frame. Scars and ink mar his body—the shackles of the humanity he's left behind. His eyes remain the only divine part of him now, possessing a single sliver of his soul. They, more than anything, strike the most fear, those eyes. They prove that, at some point, this beast was once human.

He's joined by another devil who appears at the opposite end of the cage, only he's entirely naked. The muscles rippling beneath his skin catch the light from nearly every angle; the hard strips form the bulk of his shoulders and the curves of his ass. He's stone, through and through, except for his cock. It hangs between his legs, semi-hard like a snake, but I don't snicker at the comparison. Even Vinny's knife never seemed like a more terrifying weapon.

"Jesus Christ, Mack," I hear the woman beside me scoff, her voice a cadence of a million different sounds and syllables. "Show-off."

Shooowwww-offfff. I mouth the word. There's a show taking place, all right. Two fallen angels fighting over scraps, it seems. Some poor, demented soul is the prize of this battle —but glory is the true cost. Neither demon wants to lose this fight. They eye each other, prodding their opponent's invisible armor for weaknesses—even before a man marches to the center of the pit, a pistol in hand. He mouths words that barely nibble above the din of bloodthirsty howls. *Get ready!* Grinning wildly, he raises the gun, pulls the trigger, and fires off one shot into the ceiling.

Bang! Just like that, the angels become monsters. Shadows feed on their corpses, corrupting their broken wings while the ashen ground they stand on streaks their skin, betraying the evidence of sweat.

My Lucifer is no match for the devil with dark eyes who paces like a true caged animal as the man who sounded the gun quickly exits the pit. If Lucifer is still clinging to a shred of his humanity, then *this* other man has already gleefully ripped his out.

The moment the doors of the cage slam shut, they're threaded with metal chains and then padlocked. For show, of course. Neither monster will leave without proving his point. The dark-eyed one wants power. Glory. His cock stiffens beneath the shouts and chants bellowing from the stands. He feeds off it, his body rippling as he flexes his fingers and considers when to strike.

My Lucifer...

Well, I don't know what he wants. His motives are a mystery. His eyes reveal nothing—not even pain when the dark-eyed devil lunges and catches him unguarded with one punch to the chest. The crowd explodes in howls, but my devil lands his own blows in the blink of an eye. Two quick jabs to either shoulder.

They part. Then lunge toward each other again, but they're too fast. My eyes struggle to catch up with the motion, and I only see colors. *Black* when the darker devil lands his carefully placed strikes. A dash of *red* for Lucifer, a punch to the gut and another blow to the hip.

Black. Red. Black. Red.

Black, black, black.

The walls bleed in celebration of the violence. It drips down, washing over the hungry demons avidly watching the events in the cage and lapping at the ashen island encased in twisted veins of metal. Lucifer spits out droplets of it after taking a punch to the face. He starts to feint to the left, but the darker devil is already upon him.

Black. Ebony. Gray. Grunting, Lucifer lands on his knees amid a cloud of ash. It rises up to claim him while the darker devil plants his foot against the center of his chest.

No! I think I shout it out loud, my voice echoing brokenly amid the cheerful jeers. All of a sudden, I'm weightless, falling forward against a hard bar of metal my fingers struggle to grasp. My body melts, dribbling over the top of the railing, my arms dangling over it. I'd fly down to him if I could. Slap him. Say things to him that I could never say to Vinny. *Get up. Fight. I need you to...*

As if he can sense my thoughts, his head cocks and his eyes seek mine out. I don't know what I expect to find in them when I pick them apart and probe the blue irises. Defeat? Pain? Certainly not anger. It sparkles between us, a hot, molten amber. He's furious, in fact, insulted by my lack of faith. After all, he's using my very own strategy...

The cage takes on a new shape as blood paints the corners of the cage like a makeshift grid. When the opposing devil attempts to deliver his finishing blow, my Lucifer bucks out of reach and counters the blow with one of his own: a fist to the ankle and then a deliberate hook with his right knee to bring the other man to his knees. It's a dirty, vicious, brutal tactic, and the crowd roars their approval. With yet another punch, Lucifer has him flattened, and before the man can even muster up a counterattack, Lucifer's foot is on his throat.

Just like that, the final X' is placed. Three in a row. *Tic-tac-toe.*

The other devil is cold in defeat, his eyes like coals. However, Lucifer is almost bored in his triumph. He holds his dominant position just long enough to make his victory clear. Then he steps back, swiping the blood from his chin with the back of his hand.

He doesn't bask in the shocked murmurs and grudging glares of respect from the unsatisfied demons. His gaze finds me again, and he hammers home just what his victory means, driving every implication into my skull. *I've done this for you.* Vinny would utter those same words gleefully, expecting my gratitude. This man hates the lengths he's been forced to go to on my behalf.

Because of me. In spite of me.

Vinny would expect me to be grateful for his supposed gift. For this man, I will bear the burden of his sacrifice. It's a mark I wear deeper than any tattoo. It's engraved onto my soul, somewhere Vinny's taint doesn't reach.

The devil went into hell for me. Like lingering smoke, I taste his presence over my skin. His possession. I'll wear it only temporarily—he won't own me for long...

But, for the moment, his heat fuels my blood, gathering between my legs until I have to writhe to smother the ache. That blue-fire gaze lays me bare, his for the taking. Piece by piece. He strips me of everything even before he stalks toward the gate and waits until it's opened. Sweat drips down his body as he surges into the crowd, his eyes on me, hunting me.

I'm ready and willing as he mounts the steps of the bleachers—one, two, three, four, ten—and stands before me. He seizes my wrist and easily hauls me over his shoulder so that no one can attempt to claim his prize. Then he turns to descend the steps, returning toward that little sliver of hell...claiming my soul in the process.

Dante

I drew it out for too fucking long—Mack will make me pay for every fucking second I let him believe he'd already won. If I want to be gracious, I'll claim that I'd merely gotten sloppy.

If I want to be honest, I'll admit...

That I knew she was watching. How would Vinny Stacatto's whore react once exposed to violence? Not the steady drips and dribbles Arno had fed her, either. How would she react when her nose was rubbed in it? Brutal, no-holds-barred violence for glory. For entertainment. For her fucking benefit.

If her reaction to Arno's torture has taught me anything, it should have been to never fucking underestimate her. I expected the little bitch to be disgusted, even high as fuck. I wanted her to stick her pert little nose into the air and avoid eye contact with the big, bad monster who'd been forced to save her ass—literally. Mack's buyer certainly paid for the privilege to violate Stacatto's woman in more ways than one.

I wanted her to shrink from the grim horrors of bloodshed. She stared on instead. She watched my every move in the ring. She didn't take her eyes off the match once. I could feel her. Every blow I took carried the impact of her fear. Her doubt.

The little bitch should have known better than to doubt me. I expected her to flinch in disgust when I finally won, proving that she thought she was entirely above this little shitshow. She met my gaze instead. She didn't cringe at the display of dominance—she accepted my win and everything it meant.

She welcomed it. Even down in the pit, I could smell her. I could see the challenge in her gaze. *Claim me. Own me. Fuck me.* When I left the cage, she shivered, half drugged out of her skull, as if expecting me to do it right there in front of Mack and his men. In spite of Stacatto. In spite of everyone. Just stake my claim on her right there for the world to see.

Maybe I should have. Maybe I should throw her against the wall of the training room and take her pressed up against the mats. Maybe I should make her regret that she accepted Dante Vialle so easily.

Maybe...if she weren't too busy riding out a high, too far gone to remember her own name. Her head lolls as I set her down on the floor, her back propped against the wall. Her eyes stare, vacant and distant, chasing imaginary figures around the corners of the room.

Mack may be a son of a bitch, but I know he packs good dope. The little princess is on cloud fucking ten. She doesn't react when I prod her leg with my foot before pulling my jeans back on. I shove my feet into my boots, but I don't bother with the shirt.

Already, I hear murmurs from the main room swelling to a hum that mimics the buzzing taking residence at the back of my skull. Confusion seems to be the overriding emotion. Their Mad Dog has never lost a fight—as far as they know. Mack most likely didn't keep any history books lying around, but the tally of scars on both of our bodies reveal the true score. Mack has only beaten me *once* during the entire length of our storied "careers." Coincidentally, it was the same night I turned myself in for first-degree murder. How was that for fucking irony?

As far as our track records go, this was just another match among many where the Kitty has beaten the mad pup— but, in the years since, the dog grew an army of fleas. If he changes his mind and decides to change the rules of the game, I'm not stupid enough to believe I could fight my way out. The girl would be his, and I would be locked in a Kennel for his amusement.

It should be a sobering thought. Not a tempting one. My body shouldn't hum with excitement as I swipe a streak of blood from my lip before dragging the girl upright and letting her slump against me. My body craves another fight —the result of an addiction that goes deeper than dope or the love of the spotlight. My head is only clear when my fist is pummeling something. Crushing. Bruising. Hurting.

But Mack, while still a sore loser, apparently hasn't grown stupid.

"We'll do things your way, Kitty," he tells me, leaning against the door of the cage when I finally exit the training room. The bastard put his pants back on. His gaze drifts over to the girl at my hip, but they don't linger, toeing the boundary I just reinforced with my fists. "Darcy will show you where you can sleep. We've gotta make our guests welcome, now don't we?"

Only now do I realize that we might really be forced to stay *here*, on the bastard's property. With Arno's pub blown to shit, it isn't like there are any other options.

"It's a nice place," Darcy pipes up from across the nearly empty arena, still seated in the high viewing box. "And your friend, she can stay with—"

"She stays with me."

She's limp enough for me to throw her over my shoulder again, and I wince as pain surges through my right arm. The bastard must have bruised something, but I grit my teeth and spit at my feet. It's tinged red.

Mack notices the blood and smiles, but his hand doesn't quite leave his throat. I made sure not to cause any lasting damage, but my finishing move was no love tap, either.

"Fine," he concedes with a grisly chuckle. He's bleeding from his nose but doesn't bother to wipe the mess away. It bubbles up around his lips when he speaks, giving every word an acidic edge. "I'm sure the bed is big enough. So, when do we get to hear this enticing master plan the little princess has devised?"

I tear my gaze away from him, eyeing the now empty row of bleachers. "She's not revealing shit until whatever the fuck you gave her is out of her system."

Going off the fact that she's still conscious, I can only suspect that he gave her less than a full gram but a little more than the average starting "happy" dose. He wanted her hooked fast and quickly conditioned to accept her fix with a new john. The exact same method he used on Parish.

I don't see Arno when I look for him, but at the moment, I'm not sure I even want to. Stacatto may have filmed his humiliation and given Parish the lethal shot, but it was no different from what Mack had done to her—only the bastard had done it slowly, spreading out his torture over years rather than two hours. Back then, I think he called it "love."

My gaze flits over to the blonde slowly picking her way down the bleachers. She keeps her head held high above the carnage, her gray eyes cool and unaffected by the blood staining the sand a few feet ahead of her. I didn't watch her during the fight, but now, I wonder just who she was rooting for.

"I'll give you a day," Mack says, though I suspect that the fucker never really stopped talking. The corner of his mouth quirks when he realizes just who my gaze went to. "Until then, you have the full run of the compound. Darcy will show you around." He jerks his head just as the woman approaches me, trailed by a light, sweet scent. *Strawberries?*

She seems taller than she did before, though her head still comes to the same spot, right at the top of my left shoulder.

"You...you okay, Dante?" she asks, reaching up to trail a thumb along my jaw, inches away from the budding bruise. It doesn't seem to matter to her that Mack is still within earshot, but I shrug her off and head for the door.

"Fine." It's a fucking lie, but oddly enough, there are no physical reactions to contradict it. My hands aren't shaking. My head feels clear. My nostrils flare, catching a spicy hint above the dust and blood and Darcy's artificial shampoo. It's...more real than all three—an earthy scent emanating from the strands of black hair that fan out behind me with every step. Suddenly, my body does betray me; the front of my jeans tightens.

"Wait."

I grit my teeth but force myself to glance over my shoulder at Mack . There's a knife in his hand—a slender kitchen one with a blade too dull to cut the palm of the hand he's tapping against it.

"Don't let the princess forget her knife," he warns, holding the blade out in my direction. "You wouldn't want to leave her without protection."

I say nothing when I cross the arena and snatch the knife from him. Then I shove it into my pocket. There's blood on the blade—she must have cut that fucker Sammy good. I head for the door and clench my jaw against admiration before it even rises up.

"It's this way," Darcy murmurs.

Without even realizing it, I was already barreling my way out of the arena. The night air is a slap against my sweat-soaked skin, and I relish the hit like a jolt of my own electric heroin. Goose bumps prickle along my arms. My senses are on hyperalert. I can sense every prick Mack has stationed in the woods, watching me. I hear their unsteady footsteps and jagged breathing. Stupid fuckers. I dare any one of them to...

"Hey."

I flinch when a warm hand settles over my forearm, and it takes everything I have not to grasp the slender wrist it's attached to and break it.

"It's just up ahead," Darcy says. Her face gives nothing away, but she quickly removes her hand from me and uses it to point to what appears to be a detached garage a few feet away. "There's an apartment upstairs. Mack calls it the guesthouse—"

I come to a stop, jarring the woman dangling over my shoulder. Narrowed, my eyes trail from the building's single door up to the windows along the upper level.

"It's safe," Darcy insists. "Trust me. He makes the people he *doesn't* like sleep in the Kennel." Shuddering, she glances over her shoulder at the building that houses the arena. "Come on. I'll show you inside."

I don't attempt to follow when she prances forward, her hips swinging, her blond hair bouncing over her shoulders. Her fingers grasp the knob of the door, but she hesitates before pulling it open.

"It's been five years, Dante..." She tilts her head, watching me through her lashes. "Don't tell me you've stopped trusting me already."

There's a bitter challenge hidden in her soft tone. I don't know how to classify what we had before. Friendship? Emotions other than hate rarely make a mark on my psyche, but I can't resist the part of me that grudgingly steps forward when she finally opens the door, and I follow her inside.

The bottom level sports a few motorcycles and crates of tools and equipment. A rickety staircase along the wall leads to an upper level where a battered door separates a narrow apartment from the rest of the structure.

The small place reeks of stale cigarette smoke and booze. There's a narrow kitchen across from a stained couch I'd consider using as a toilet before I ever sat on it. Down a short hallway is a cramped bathroom and then a room barely large enough to fit the king-sized bed shoved inside it. Slipping past me, Darcy perches herself on the end of the mattress, running her hands along the plain, black comforter.

"It almost feels like old times," she says softly. "You kicking Mack's ass in front of a packed house. He was vicious, even back then...but the skanks who'd hunt you down after were worse." She laughs and eyes me with a playful shrug. "You rarely went off with one of them though. Back then, you used to only fight for money."

I don't bother to answer the question in her tone. I approach the bed instead and toss Stacatto's woman down onto it. Her fingers fly out in search of stability. The pale skin of her stomach is bared; her sweater rode up far enough to reveal the jagged edges of an N and T. After shoving her onto her back, I wrench the hem down.

"She's pretty," Darcy says, propping her hand beneath her chin. "She's foreign, too. She wasn't speakin' English the whole time. Was it Spanish?"

I shrug without giving her an answer, but I can't help the part of me that wonders just what the little bitch said. She isn't talking now. She's staring straight up at the ceiling, her pupils pinpricks, her breathing heavy and slowed. There's sweat glistening over her forehead, and her lips are slightly parted. She looks dead.

I know that look. As Mack suspected, the little princess is liking the high. Only God knows if Stacatto drugged her at all, but I doubt it. She's swept away on the burning wave of dope, locked inside her own private cocoon, safe from the pain. For now. The first high is always the sweetest—the cruel benchmark addicts spend every high after that attempting to chase. You can never reach that bar again. It's why Mack chose his initial dose carefully, knowing just how much of the hook to bait. He could have sold her out to ten men tonight and it wouldn't have mattered. She'd still crave the next fix.

"I need to sleep." I grit the words out while staring down at my hands, which are covered in Mack's blood and my own. Adrenaline's still flooding my system—I'm too fucking wired to sleep, but Darcy takes the hint.

"It was good to see you, Dante," she says, rising to her feet. Then she surprises me by stepping forward, placing her hand once again along my swelling cheek. "I know I'm not... I know I'm not someone like Arno. But I was your friend too. And Parish..." She breaks off and stares at the floor, pulling her hand away.

A good man might let her wallow, but I can't help but state the obvious. "If she was your friend, then why are you fucking the man who *really* killed her?"

Stacatto may have been the lethal bullet, but Mack's the one who loaded that gun six years ago when he coaxed a seventeen-year-old Rish into getting high that very first time.

Darcy doesn't appreciate the reminder. Her eyes flash, and I see the hint of the woman Mack has turned her into. She may shiver at the thought of the Kennel, but screwing the alpha means she can't ignore what puts food on her table.

"Don't attack *me*, Dante," she says. "The last time I checked, I wasn't sleeping with some guy named Vincent Stacatto."

She leaves, her lips pursed, her eyes blazing, bitter and angry. But I don't miss the way her hand flies out to gently brush my shoulder on her way past.

"Night."

"Night," I force myself to reply. Seconds later, I hear the door open and then quietly click shut, but the sound has the impact of a gunshot.

Exhaling, I take up the spot Darcy left, keeping my back turned to Stacatto's woman. Her breathing taints the air, a slow, raspy melody. I shouldn't give a damn about what thoughts might cross her mind in the morning when she comes down from the high. I shouldn't give a damn as to what might happen if she craves it again—and she *will* crave it again. A life of cruelty leaves an almost irresistible itch for something to take the edge off the pain.

Cocking my head, I turn to look at her and snap my fingers once. It takes a second for her eyes to focus and crawl in the direction of my hand.

"Hey." I snap again and reach for her when her eyes start to turn vacant.

She ignores me though, and no one's home when I snatch her knife from my pocket and wipe that asshole Sammy's blood off on my jeans. Then I jab the edge of it into the flat of her palm, pressing deep enough to break the skin. Blood wells up when I start to cut, sawing a single jagged line about an inch long in the center of her hand. The pain barely wakes her up, but she's back again, watching me with hollow eyes.

"It feels good now," I tell her, knowing she can probably process only about half of the words I say. "But it won't last. It never does."

A low sound buzzes from her throat. Words? A tattered laugh? I can't tell. Whatever it is trails off when I stand and reach for the buckle of my jeans. I tug them down while I circle the bed to stand directly beside her, my hips positioned above her head so that she can't miss a single fucking detail. I shed my boxers next, feeling what Mack must have felt when he stepped into the ring, prepared to face an old foe with newly learned tricks up his sleeve.

I wait until she focuses on me. My cock is already stiff when I reach for her hand and place it on my hip, positioning her fingers so that she can feel every jagged variation in the skin. Then I watch her, my eyes narrowed, and issue one single command.

Daniela

"Count," the devil tells me, pressing my fingertips into the ridge of scars that turn the top of his thigh into one of those

"Touch and Feel" books they would give me in school to help me connect common sensations with the English words. *Soft. Fur. Feathers.*

Lucifer feels...*raw.* A million stories lurk within his skin. A million new words and sensations to learn. I drag my thumb along his thigh, straining to see the irregular, silvery edges of the cuts. It's too dark, however. Touch is the only sensation I can employ to study him, and I'm greedy to learn.

"Count," he told me. His scars, I assume. But I already have, though the number is somewhere...deep...down...away. I have to start over.

My head swims around the room while I crawl to the edge of the bed and use him like an anchor to hold myself upright. Naughty, naughty Daniela. I pretend that I don't notice his cock as I cling to him. My head comes too close, the tip of him grazing my hair. Lucifer growls, but like a good teacher, he won't let himself forget the task at hand. His grip is a vise clamped down over my throbbing fingers as he steers them to the top of his row of scars.

Count. I do, carefully stringing the numbers together like popcorn on the Christmas garlands my mother and I used to make. *Um, dois, três, quarto.* I take my time, learning him with every degree of dedication it took to learn English. Dante is a tougher, more archaic code to crack. I'm on the fourteenth dash when he finally decides to speak.

"I made the first one the night I swore...that I wouldn't let it happen again. He wouldn't come into my room again. I'd stop him."

A darkness taints his words. I can see it dripping out of his beautiful mouth and speckling the air like spray paint. I keep counting, however, using my grip on his leg to keep myself tethered. *Fifteen. Sixteen.*

"The fucker liked to wait until he thought I was asleep," he says, his gaze on the far wall, his jaw clenched. "Sometimes he knew that I'd raid his liquor cabinet and drink whatever I could find just to make it easier to pass out..." He breaks off, inhaling and exhaling hate like a dragon. His body ripples with emotions that spill into my waiting hands. More *hate. Hate. Hate. Fear. Regret...*

"I cut myself that night," he tells me, brushing his hands alongside mine to prod the remnants of that very first shallow wound. "As a reminder. This was the last time... There was a knife under my bed. I was ready for the fucker. Then he came in and I just...lay there while he fucked me like an animal." His voice breaks, but I have never heard such a dangerous sound pass the devil's lips. He's a creature formed entirely of rage.

My fingers tremble against his white-hot skin, and I've lost count. I start over, but this time, I let my hands fall and bring my face in close, brushing my lips against his uneven flesh. His story is too complex to be felt. It needs to be inhaled. Swallowed. Consumed. *Sixteen. Seventeen. Eighteen.*

"I did the same thing the next night," he continues by the time I finally reach the twenty-eighth mark. "And the next. And the next—" He inhales sharply when my tongue grazes his skin.

My lips go dry at his taste. Sweat and musk, way more potent than whatever's in my veins. He travels deep down inside me to where no one else has ever been. A place that Vinny doesn't even know exists. It swells with the presence of him, and I'm infested with the devil himself.

"Thirty-four days," he says, his voice catching over the words. It's more than a number. It's the price of his soul. Thirty-four days before he finally managed to fight his way out of hell. "I didn't use the knife, either. I hit him...with my fists. I kicked him. I couldn't stop. The bastard wasn't even hurt. He didn't try to stop me when I ran out of the house, half fucking naked, screaming that I'd tell the police. Maybe he wanted me to..." He laughs; it's a twisted hollow sound that drips down over his chest like falling blood. "I was twelve."

My head throbs beneath the weight of his confession. It wants to sink back down into the warmth...the nothingness. My brain doesn't want to feel, for once. It wants to sleep. The drug makes it so very easy to sleep.

But the devil's taste is on my tongue. I wince as I sink forward and fall to my knees. My mouth is on him, still pressed against the shrine of his body, and I breathe in each word of his morbid sermon. I memorize every cut, and he lets me clumsily attempt to trace every one. His bitter truth is enough to counter the opposing rush of the heroin.

But it's a bittersweet cure—he's ruined one high and given me another. The substance he wields takes me impossibly higher than anything else, but he's stingy. He won't ever give me another taste, and my teeth sink into his flesh in punishment, though my jaw feels too heavy to truly bite down.

He flinches back with a hiss, raking his fingers through my hair to latch onto the back of my skull. He forces me to look up, holding my gaze. Then he hauls me upright and shoves me back onto the bed, leaving me there while he stands against the wall.

He watches as my tongue shoots out and seeks all traces of his taste from my lips. He watches me swallow every last bit. He watches...and he knows exactly which budding addiction will win out when I finally come down from the high.

CHAPTER TWENTY-THREE

Daniela

Morning descends with all the intensity of a freight train slamming into my chest at full speed. My lips part beneath a groan first, cracked and painfully dry. Next, my eyes blink themselves open to a stained, grimy ceiling illuminated by a swath of gray daylight.

My brain is mush, my skull composed of a million bricks that clatter together when I try to sit up. I barely lift my head clear of whatever lies beneath it only for it to fall right back down. It takes three attempts before I can roll over onto my hands and knees. I'm shaking, forced to rock back and forth to stay upright. The world is spinning when I finally manage to lift my head and focus on the shadowy figure watching me from across the room.

"Get up," Lucifer commands. His tone is clipped with impatience.

How long has he been waiting? How long has he been wondering whether or not I'd survive my little brush with a powerful opiate? His eyes reveal nothing as I scramble to remember how to control my limbs. It hurts when the muscles in my legs contract in order for me to stand. They shake too badly, and I flop back onto the mattress, clinging to handfuls of the comforter for balance.

Panting, I glance at him through the wild, tangled mess of my hair. "Help... Help me." I hold my hand out, gauging his reaction to the request.

His eyes narrow, but before I can even guess whether or not he'll move, he approaches me and snatches my wrist.

I cry out when he pulls me to my feet. The bastard isn't gentle. I stagger forward and have to clutch at the wall for balance. Clinging to it, I tremble, every nerve loose and unstable.

"Look at me." He's at my shoulder and grabs for my chin himself when I don't obey quickly enough.

The breath catches in my throat as he manipulates my body against the wall and presses me back while he steps in closer. His scent sneaks into my lungs: sweat and blood. He hasn't washed yet. Bruises paint his jaw and discolor the center of his chest. Battle scars.

I can't stop myself from reaching out to trace the mark just above his right pec. He stiffens at the contact, but I doubt that it's out of pain. His grip over my chin tightens, craning my neck back so that my eyes return to his. They peer deep down, searching me. At first, I think he's checking to see if I'm fully free of the aftereffects of the drug. Then he steps closer, pinning me against the wall with his bulk, and I realize his true intention.

Do I remember? If so, how much? How much of Lucifer's dark, dirty secrets still taint my skin?

I school my expression into revealing nothing, and he grunts in frustration, his nails digging in. He won't break me though. Vinny taught me well how to wear a mask—but, beneath it, I peer over what snippets I do recall. Just who hurt him as a child? His father?

The devil gives me no answers when he finally lets me go. It's only as he jerks out of my reach that I realize my fingers never left his skin, stroking absent patterns against his bruised flesh. Letters. *D A N N Y...*

Lucifer knew my own dark secret. Now, I have one of his.

But there are no winners in his game. Just bitter round after bitter, brutal round. Which one of us will finally leave the cage as the victor? Will we ever leave at all?

Lucifer gives away nothing of his battle plan as he retreats down a narrow hall. He doesn't command me to follow, but I do anyway, bracing one hand against the wall.

This apartment is even smaller than the last one. In just two steps Lucifer enters a tiny kitchen. There's a bathroom to my left, and to creep inside it, I would simply have to shuffle two inches sideways.

"Here." Lucifer snatches a plastic cup from a cupboard above a metal sink built into one of the countertops. He runs the faucet and fills it with water from the tap. "Drink," he commands, slamming it down on the counter closest to me.

I reach for it only to flinch as pain sears through the center of my palm. It's a shock to find blood pooling there, seeping from a gash I don't remember causing. Then, like the scattered fragments of a nightmare, I remember—him. My eyes seek him out, and I realize I left blood over his chest, the real reason he pulled away.

"You cut me."

He doesn't appear ashamed, but then I realize I'm not exactly angry. I *remember*. The words he said drip through my ears in a distorted melody. "It feels good now," he told me while I was swept under the heroin. "But it won't last. It never does." I wonder if he spoke from experience. His face reveals nothing, and I don't ask.

Instead, I lift the cup and drain it dry. My head is swimming when I set it back down and swipe at my mouth with the back of my uninjured hand.

Lucifer's searing eyes miss nothing. "If you haven't thought of a plan for taking down Stacatto," he starts, "now is the time."

"P-plan?" Still dizzy, I shift so that my back is resting against the wall, and I brace my good hand against it.

"To take him down," Lucifer clarifies, his voice hard and unnerving.

I'm going to "take down" Vincent Stacatto. When it's said out loud—by such a serious man—I can't help but laugh just once. Lynn might have been able to entertain the notion in her head, but putting it into practice?

I shake my head. "I...I can't—"

"You don't have a fucking choice." Lucifer steps out from around the counter, and within seconds, he closes in on me. "Think."

I jump when one of his hands finds the center of my chest, the thick fingers pointing toward my throat.

He makes a show of pinning me flat against the wall and leaning in, his breath hot on my skin. "What are his weaknesses? His businesses? Who are his allies?"

I'm still shaking my head. "He didn't tell me—"

"Bullshit." His fingers flex hard enough to send tiny jolts of pain exploding throughout my rib cage. "You've dreamt about it. Don't tell me that you haven't spent every waking moment fantasizing as to how to bring the bastard down..." His voice rumbles through my ears and resonates down my spine.

I shiver, and my tongue shoots out to wet my lips, tasting blood. "He...he deals drugs—heroin and cocaine," I say, racking my brain for the snippets of conversations I wasn't meant to hear, the words I used to drown out whenever he'd force me to play during a torture session, the little bits and pieces of information I gleaned on my own. "He owns a taxi company—Sunshine—and uses the drivers to distribute the supply throughout the city."

Lucifer nods, accepting the information without comment. The pattern of his breathing changes, striking the side of my neck at a slower pace, but he still isn't satisfied, and a silent command is conveyed when his hand presses a little harder against my chest. *Go on.*

"He...he deals in women." I cringe, picturing the girls he gave to me as "gifts." Anger mingles with the heat of Lucifer on my skin. I shrivel and burn beneath both, and it's easier to get the words out. "They have accents. He must get them from overseas. I don't know where he keeps them." Apart from my maids, I only knew of the women from the scattered conversations his men would have in the suite when they thought I wasn't listening. *Do good tonight and we might stop by and see the new girls. Sate your cock for once.* "And as for allies..." My recent thoughts hold nothing. I have to dig deeper, into an older store of memories that make me almost grateful for Lucifer's brutal strength to hold me up. "I just know one. A detective."

Lucifer perks up. I don't know if it's because of the hatred in my voice or the mere irony that a crime lord cavorts with an officer of the law.

"His name?"

"Detective Andrew Sosa."

"Sosa." He frowns. Apparently, the name doesn't ring a bell. Regardless, he's satisfied by the information, and he steps back, pulling his hand away, my chest expanding greedily. "I'll look into it."

"It would have to be quick," I say, "whatever we do. Vinny will—"

"Vinny." Lucifer scoffs and then releases a full chuckle that drips out through his teeth. "No matter what. You still call him that."

"W-what?" I'm thrown off by his line of attack.

"Vinny," the devil snarls. "You have yet to call the fucker by his full name."

His full name. *Vincent.* It strikes me that the devil thinks I am weak for still calling my tormentor by a nickname. I see it in the way he shakes his head and laughs, his eyes narrowed over my body like the barrel of a gun, but I don't shy away.

If only the bastard knew.

I'm the one to enter his personal space this time. Just a single step that takes me no farther from the wall than where I can still cling to it. Lucifer stiffens regardless, his mouth caught mid-chuckle.

"His...his name..." I have to lick my lips to find enough traction to speak. I'm too tired to rein my accent in, and it takes over, mangling each word. Lynn's crisp voice is dead. For the first time in fifteen years, Daniela fully rears her head. "His name is the only bit of power I've ever held over him," I admit. "I call him *Vinny,* and I never forget everything else. Ever."

Lucifer holds my gaze for so long that I lose track. The disgust lurking over the irises gives way to something else, though I'm not sure I can name it. Describing him requires an arsenal of words I have yet to master. *Guilt? Respect? Acknowledgement?* I can't decide which is which before he finally nods once in a grim apology.

Without another word, I turn and stagger toward the bathroom. There's only a sliding wooden door to fasten shut with a metal latch. Then, in private, I reassemble myself the only way I know how. I wash my face with my hands and scrub at my teeth with my thumb and a streak of bar soap. Using my wet fingers, I comb through my hair. When I finish, I eye my reflection and try to find some semblance of my old self lurking beneath this stranger's gaunt features.

I'm still not sure who this new Daniela is when I finally turn to the door, my fingers fumbling with the latch. By the time I get it open, I am too distracted to notice the heat wafting from the other end. One tug on the sliding door and Lucifer's presence fills the narrow gap. I stagger back instinctively, and just as my back strikes the glass surface of a tiny shower stall, he's already wrenched the door fully open. One of his hands goes to the buckle on his jeans, wrenching on the fly and revealing the shape of his cock through his boxers.

I swallow hard, my fingers catching against the frosted glass behind me. I should look away when he steps up to the toilet and blocks the doorway in the process. I should force my way past him. I definitely shouldn't stare as he tugs his boxers down his hips, revealing his semi-hard cock and...blood. Sloppy streaks of it paint his hips, obscuring the row of his scars. Some drugged worshipper left her scarlet fingerprints all over the priceless statue in the church garden. Gritting my teeth, I start forward and snatch a wad of toilet paper from the roll. Before I can even touch him, Lucifer catches my wrist with his free hand, still guiding a stream of piss with the other. He shakes out the few last drops but doesn't let me go while he shifts over to the sink.

He wets that one hand beneath the faucet and then shuts it off. His pants are still down around his ankles while he eyes his reflection. The devil isn't alarmed by the bruises earned during his battle. He wears victory like just another scar, and my stomach twists while I trail my gaze over him. The places where I touched him during the night glow more vibrantly than the bruises or cuts left over from his fight with Mack. They adorn him like the medals on a general, but my blood... It clashes with his olive skin. My fingers twitch, aching to wipe it off, but his grip tightens, and he turns, steering me back against the shower stall with every step he takes. When I have nowhere left to go, he herds me inside it, watching as I press myself beneath the showerhead.

Once he's just inches away, he lifts my hand by my captive wrist, his eyes on mine. "Drop it."

His tone is jagged glass. I obey, and the wad of toilet paper strikes the tile with barely a sound to its name. Lucifer doesn't release me, however. He merely shifts his weight to block me in, his gaze unreadable. I don't know what to think when he reaches down, pulling my hand along with him, and rummages through the puddle of his jeans, eventually withdrawing a knife. It's the dull kitchen one he let me keep.

Rising fully, he waits until he's sure I'm watching—so that I don't miss a single detail when he holds the flat of his hand out and starts to cut. With barely a wince to show for it, he gouges out a single line similar to the mark he made on me. Once finished, he lets the knife fall, its blade gleaming beneath my blood and his. I don't react when he reaches for my hand and presses our bloody palms together. Clasping our fingers, he raises them both above my head, his expression penetrating me deeper than any knife ever could.

"You wanted me to promise," he says gutturally.

Apparently, this is how unowned men cement said promises. Not with handshakes or simple words...but this. Blood against blood. *Eternal.*

The muscles in my arm burn as I force my grip to tighten, grinding my open wound against his despite the sharp throb of pain it triggers. Droplets of red escape, striking the cracked tile beneath my bare toes. A drop lands on my ankle, and I shiver, but not out of disgust. Only Lucifer could turn blood into a weapon. The tiny droplets sizzle, searing his claim into my skin. My veins hum, surging with the hazy memories of violence—him down in the arena, fighting for me. Punching, kicking, striking for *me.*

My body is a fool, still thrumming on the edge of the high. I haven't fully come down when I feel searing heat creep between my legs or when my nipples tighten against the coarse fabric of my sweater. I blame the heroin for the need that makes me shudder and clench my thighs together. I blame...everything and anything but *him*. Those eyes don't affect me. Not the way they narrow over my throat as if he can sense every reaction sparking beneath my skin.

When he finally releases me, I can't silence a sigh of relief. I want him to leave. I need him to drag the wooden door shut. I need to shove my own hand between my legs and ignore the things my fingers will have to do in order to ease this ache. I wait, shame a painful ball at the back of my throat, eager to be swallowed down. Lucifer *makes* me wait.

Then he takes a step back, and air trickles into my lungs in one greedy breath only to escape just as quickly when he raises his uninjured hand and...he palms his cock. *No.* My head falls back against the stall, hard enough to make sparks appear before my eyes. I squeeze them shut. I don't look. I don't listen to the slick, wet sounds as his own fingers glide up and down the ridge of his shaft. I don't let myself dwell on the fact that he's pleasing himself right in front of me, completely unashamed by the act. He's a beast, after all, merely giving in to a beastly, primal urge. The devil is selfish and bold in fulfilling his own needs, and I need... I *need*...

I shove my blood-stained fingers into my mouth and bite down while my other hand bolts to the front of my jeans. I attempt to suck in my stomach and shove them beneath the waistband, but in the end, I have to undo the clasp one-handed and kick them down, leaning against the glass behind me for leverage. Any embarrassment flies out the window as I take two fingers and...*yes*. My gasp nearly drowns out the sound he makes: part inhale, part growl. It reverberates off the glass, adding a delicate chime to the harsh slick of his stroking hand. *He's moving faster*, I think. Tightening his grip, getting off on watching me listen to every sordid little sound...

And then even that isn't enough. My eyes open, boldly drinking him in. His cock is thickened steel. His eyes are an inferno; I swear I can even see sparks of orange mingling with the bright-blue flames now. Less than a foot apart, we watch each other. We touch ourselves. Daring. Taunting. Drips of silvery fluid weep from the tip of his cock when I finally crook a thumb and force it inside me.

My bloody fingers aren't enough to smother a cry. I have to bite the inside of my cheek and choke down a gasp while my hips buck, unsatisfied by the partial fullness. With a terrible sense of desperation, I know I'd have to use my whole hand to mimic the fullness of his cock—and even that would be a poor imitation. It's like the bastard reads my mind. He grits out a broken sound and gives up, his hands falling open at his sides, his stance predatory. I'm still stroking sensitive bundles of flesh when he approaches and gathers up the material of my sweater in both hands. One harsh yank and the wool parts, revealing my breasts, which are already swelling, aching for his touch.

Lucifer is a cruel tormentor. He stands there and merely waits for me to arch my spine and present myself to him.

He doesn't touch me until I do, and only then it's to drag a thumb over one nipple while he clenches his jaw at the sharpness. My fingers cease their maddening circles—it's oddly more satisfying to watch him. To see him devour my body through his vision alone. He shows me no mercy, the same demonic creature he was in the ring, searching out every weakness to exploit. He finds one in the letters of Vinny's brand, and he vandalizes the mark with a single bloodied handprint that presses me back against the wall of the stall.

His finger returns to my nipple, teasing it into a throbbing point before he turns to the other and gives it the same brutal, lavish attention. Then he tugs on my hips, spinning me around until I have no choice but to brace both palms against the frosted glass while he muscles in behind me.

He doesn't bother to be gentle with the first thrust. He slams into me, forcing my hands to inch higher and higher above my head, leaving a bloody streak that dribbles down while he pulls back and enters me again. Again. *More*. He doesn't stop until he's in to the hilt, his balls slapping the backs of my thighs with the final harsh jerk of his hips.

Then the devil switches tactics, and he goes slow, consuming me in tendrils of hellfire that lick at my spine. Back and forth. Harsher. Slower. Like a true sadist, he takes time to build up friction I can taste as each carnal sensation ricochets through me, drawing out whimpers from my lips. *Heat. Hot. Fire.* My nails rake the glass, my breasts swaying with the steady rhythm, my body at his mercy.

He counters every hit he took in the cage by grinding

himself into me, making sure I feel every ridge, every ribbed curve of his cock. *I did this for you.* I shift, sore and greedy. I'll remember every inch of him no matter what happens the moment we leave this stall. I let him fuck his victory into me. I wait until he grits out curses and increases his pace. Then I move, letting myself fall back, forcing him deeper. Harder. Faster.

My mind drifts. I'm higher than I could ever reach with only a narcotic. I'm in the heaven that kicked him out, floating high above the hell Vinny made of my life. Every harsh, brutal thrust takes me even higher...higher still.

But the stall is too small. He's too big. His body is forced to bend over mine to find the right leverage, and he slips out so suddenly that I can't silence a whine. Panting with lust, he's clumsy when he palms his cock and tries to dive back in. The head of his cock bats between my legs, but when he starts to thrust, it's against the wrong opening, and my body clenches against him.

I cling to the stall, panting. Even Vinny never touched me there. It's the one part of me he never seemed interested in claiming—not even on the women he forced me to watch him violate. Lucifer's presence inspires an entirely new fear. And I want him to vanquish it.

"N-no," I choke out when he starts to head lower instead. "Here." I take one hand from the wall and reach back, dragging his hand back up...

He stiffens. "F-fuck...fuck no!" He jerks back, horror flashing through his eyes. He's disgusted. He's...terrified, but it's a fear I know well.

My fingers shake when I reach for him and grasp the tip of his softening cock. He doesn't resist when I ease him closer, stroking the head with sloppy, unsteady motions of my thumb.

"Please." My voice rings stronger than I've ever heard it—at least not since I was a girl of eight, telling a cruel bully to go fuck himself. "Please. I need... I need you..."

It's too sick of a request to put into words. Too selfish. I need him to claim me in a way even Vinny wouldn't. I need him to rip me open and leave his mark on the ruined flesh. I *need*.

But it's only when the fear clouds his eyes that I remember what he told me when he thought I'd be too disoriented to remember. *"He fucked me like an animal."* Something inside me breaks. My heart? Scarred and battered, it cracks open, and something slithers out, directed at him. Understanding? A fallen angel can only relate to another cast-down creature, after all. I may not be an angel—merely a lost soul—but the fires of Hell have burned us both.

"Please..."

While Lucifer stares down at my stroking fingers, his gaze darkens, fire and brimstone spilling out. "No lube," he grits out, but apparently, he's already thought of another makeshift substitute. Batting my touch away, he grips himself with his bloodied palm, painting himself with the result of the promise he swore he'd never make. His eyes meet mine, devoid of any compassion. He won't make this easy. *This will hurt.*

But I don't look away from him. I don't grit my teeth and brace myself. I'm panting even before he finally eases the head of himself against me, testing the give of my body. One thrust and he can only ease the tip of himself inside, but he groans, his head shooting back against his shoulders. Pleasure thickens each beautiful sound that spills from his throat, enticing the heat building within me to burn even hotter. Two more thrusts and he's forced an inch. Then he bucks, sinking deeper, thrusting harder. My body resists, fights...spreads...surrenders.

"Oh, God." I rock into the invasion, blinking back the tears that blur my vision. "F-fuck. Jesus. Fuck!" My voice breaks, echoing off the walls, and then I can only moan when he sinks in fully. My body is on fire with the aftermath of every searing thrust. It's too tight a fit. Too much. He's too deep. Too big. Too hard. Too *perfect.*

I lose my voice when he starts to thrust in earnest. Bitter...burning...electric. The vicious friction makes it too hard to watch him. I have to brace both hands against the wall and press my cheek against the glass instead. His gaze burns the back of my neck. His blood paints my skin. His groans form a melody more haunting than Bach. I could never recreate it on my cello no matter how many combinations of strings I played. I'll have to rely on memory...

SoI struggle to remember everything about the way he feels inside me and consumes me from the inside out. It's too hard. My thoughts scatter as my head lolls—I'm drunk on him. It's only when he thrusts deep one last time that I realize the words leaving my throat are more than just inane nonsense. It's a name.

"Dante. Dante..."

His growl drowns me out, and then I'm flooded with his release. I feel it drip down my legs when he finally eases himself out of me, panting. He almost seems drunk as he staggers back against the wall of the stall, rattling the glass in its frame.

Boneless, I sink to my knees, my body aching, throbbing, burning and my heart bleeding and gaping. I'm not sure which feels more assaulted. More violated. I'm even less sure which pain frightens me the most.

I wait for him to leave me here, but when I finally hear him move, I'm not expecting the grip on my forearm that yanks me upright. My strength is no match for his, and he pins me easily against the wall. Murder is written in his eyes, and I can't fight when he lowers his head, his mouth crushing mine. He shoves his tongue inside me, forcing me to react and push him back with my own. Within seconds...I don't know what's happening. Vinny only ever kissed me on the cheek or with a closed mouth. Never like this. I never wanted him to kiss me like this. Hungry, violent, brutal—even harsher than the sex. He bites my lower lip until it bleeds. Then he steals the droplets away and swallows them down.

I'm dizzy when he finally does pull away. Then he drags his pants up and storms out of the shower and then the bathroom...eventually the small apartment altogether. The building trembles with the force when he slams the door shut.

Left alone, I can only trace my lips with my fingers and wonder why the hell the assault of his mouth pierces me deeper than the sensation of his cock. A beast could fuck anyone.

But not just anyone could get close enough to wound one...

Dante

Fuck her.

Rain glances off my back as I circle the garage and head straight for the perimeter. Mack's guard dogs must still be asleep this early; there's no one to block my path when I reach the woods surrounding the property. There's no one here to get in my fucking way, either. No one to punch.

When my vision bleeds red, I improvise and pick a tree, punching until the bark rips at my knuckles. Splinters of wood chip off and go flying, but I don't let up until I'm shouting with every goddamn blow. "Fuck! Fuck! Fuck-fuck!" I slam my fist against the tree one last time and hear something crack. A bone? A branch? My fucking sanity?

Whatever it is, I don't give a shit. The loss of it doesn't erase the memory of her. Her skin. Her heat. Her fucking wet cunt. The tighter feel of her channel...

It's not enough to just punch. I tear until my fucking nails are shredded and all I see is goddamn *red*. The buzzing roars through my ears, but even it isn't loud enough to drown her voice out.

"I need you. Please. I need you."

How fucking cute; she *needed* to be fucked in the ass. The little princess loved having a dirty, naughty criminal violate her in ways even her crime lord of a fiancé wouldn't—because, of course, that fucker had to be the reason why she wanted it.

I could have stomached being used if she'd sobbed like a little bitch the way I had—but not with how she looked at me...hungry, full, desperate, needy. *Fuck her.* I could have, too. I could have draped the little bitch in my cum and sent her to Stacatto just like that...

But the bastard wasn't on her mind when I sank into her to the hilt. I saw her eyes. Saw into her. His name didn't come from her lips...and I will make her pay for that.

"Fuck her..." My voice isn't hard enough. Angry enough. I *need* to feel the anger. I need to erase her taste from my mouth, and I spit her out, grinding the evidence into the earth with my bare fucking foot.

It's still not enough. My cock still drips with her—throbs for her—and it's a good thing I left the knife behind, because nothing would stop me from sawing the fucker off. Now, more than ever, I crave the violence of the cage. I should find Mack and demand a rematch. I need to crush, tear, and bite. I need to...

Fuck her.

Yes, a sick fucking part of me agrees. *Fuck her. Taste her. Claim her. Mount her. Take her again. Make her scream...*

"Dante?"

The voice sinks through the scarlet haze like a hook. *Shit.* I blink until the forest regains its natural hues of brown and green, but one splotch of color doesn't belong. Darcy is standing only a few yards away from me, pale and slender between two trees.

In the distance, I can make out the garage. I haven't gone far.

"Dante?"

Irritated, I drag my gaze back to Darcy. Her eyes widen as they trail over my chest, taking in the bruises and blood.

"Stay away from me," I tell her before she can even take a step closer.

"Dante, your hands—"

They're shredded, but I curl them into fists, ignoring the pain. "What do you want?"

Darcy flinches at my tone, and I finally notice the gray duffel she's carrying, slung over one shoulder.

"I...I brought her some clothes. You too."

Clothes. With a harsh sigh, I run a hand through my hair, feeling the raw skin protest. "Give them to me." I stalk forward and snatch for the straps. The bag feels light when I swing it against my back and head for the garage.

Darcy follows, but I don't send her away—her silent questions pelt my skin though.

I don't offer any explanation as I wrench the door to the garage open. I need to be numb. I need to be *smart*. Mack's original plan is sounding more plausible by the second; the sooner the bitch goes back to Stacatto in pieces, the better. I picture it as I mount the stairs and barrel straight for the bathroom. The little bitch beat me to the punch, however. While I was gone, she managed to wrestle the sliding door in place. When I pull on the handle, it rattles but won't budge. She locked it.

The simple act drains me of rage, and I wind up laughing while Darcy watches. I hear the shower running, and I can almost taste the steam as Stacatto's whore washes all traces of me away. Knowing that I'm standing here must make her scrub a little harder, curled up in the corner of the stall.

I laugh again, and then I toss the duffel against the wall so hard that something inside it cracks.

"There was... I packed some d-deodorant," Darcy says, her eyes wide, but she doesn't move to pick it up. She keeps her distance, and there's less shock in her gaze than I originally thought. Living with Mack must have made her immune to a bastard's temper by now. "I...I'm going to make you some breakfast."

Before I can protest, she wiggles her way past me and rummages through the cupboards in the kitchen. She must spend enough time in the place to keep it stocked with food. There are eggs and a carton of milk in the fridge. In the cupboards, she finds a box of pancake mix and sets to work with an ease that betrays a mothering instinct she had even five years ago.

She may have changed the man in her bed, but underneath, she was still the same Darcy. I don't like how much comfort a twisted part of me takes from that. In the end, I approach the couch and sit down, eyeing my torn, bleeding hands. I've even tracked blood across the tan carpet with scarlet-tinged footprints.

"I can bandage you up when I finish," Darcy offers without glancing up from her work at the stove. "Mack keeps first aid kits under the sink."

I don't answer. It doesn't seem to matter whether I bleed now or later. Arno wants a war, and well, he is about to get one, courtesy of the bitch scurrying from the bathroom and wearing the jeans I bought her and a ripped sweater held together by two pale hands.

Darcy swallows hard when she sees her; a shower only erased some of the blood. Her lip is still bleeding, painting her chin in fresh droplets of it, but her princess mask is firmly in place again. She doesn't look at me once, not even when she has to face in my direction to see the duffel Darcy's pointing out to her.

"I...I brought you some clothes."

Clothes. The word takes a minute to register. Once it does, she nods and stoops for the bag before scurrying into the bedroom. The door slams shut behind her, and I hear the lock engage once again.

"Look..." Darcy pauses, an egg in one hand and a spatula in the other. She doesn't look up right away, but I know that her eyes are the color of steel. "I may know about Mack's...*business*, but there are rules. I don't allow it. Not around me." She's implying something. Hinting at it. "I don't know who that woman is, but if you're hurting her..."

"I'm not."

She glances up and holds my gaze for a second longer than necessary. Then she nods just once. "Okay, then."

I say nothing else while she scrapes food from the pan and eventually hands me a plate of scrambled eggs and pancakes. I eat with my hands, ignoring the gritty taste of dirt and salt. When I'm done, I stand and reach past Darcy to dump my plate into the sink just as the bedroom door opens and Stacatto's woman finally tiptoes out of it.

Darcy must have given her the plain, white shirt with long sleeves that reach her fingertips and hide the cut in her palm. She's wearing the jeans I gave her, but there are socks on her feet and a pair of baby-blue sneakers that fit her better than the boots did. She's pulled her hair back as well, but the style only serves to reveal the mess of her ear. I don't miss the way Darcy's eyes cut over to me when she notices.

I ignore her as I push my way past the woman scrambling against the doorjamb to enter the bedroom. Inside the duffel, I find a few men's T-shirts and jeans. I grab one of each and enter the bathroom, where I take my turn washing the bitch off my skin.

Twenty minutes later, I return to the main room of the apartment and find her and Darcy watching each other. If they spoke at all, they apparently didn't have much to say. Neither woman's gaze reveals anything when they turn to watch me shove my feet into my boots and head for the door. Before descending the stairs, I glance back at Darcy, my voice cold, my temper honed and ready.

"Take me to Mack."

———

THE BASTARD IS IN THE BAR AGAIN. LIKE ARNO, HE seems to enjoy rising before the ass crack of dawn, but he apparently isn't as fond of sampling his own merchandise. He's nursing a glass of water instead and a handful of what I assume is beef jerky, the package on the bar in front of him. Arno sits on the stool closest to the wall. He may have come crawling to Mack, but he has enough sense to always guard his back, at least.

Mack always has liked sticking his knives there, after all.

"Eh, Kitty!" The bastard tears off a chunk of meat with his teeth and noisily washes it down with a chug of the water. "Out of your litter box so soon? I gave you a day." His eyes narrow in suspicion even as he flashes a grin. "I expected you to let me sweat it out down to the last fucking hour."

And, any other time, I would have. "I want this over," I admit through clenched teeth. I know without even having to turn and see for myself that Darcy and the woman followed me inside. I raise my fist and force it to open to jab my thumb toward the bar. "Sit."

I don't expect her to comply so easily, but she shuffles past me, her head down, and takes the stool as far away from Mack as physically possible. If I'm surprised by the obedient little show, Mack isn't. He merely watches, taking another sip of water; it's the perfect display of captor and captive.

Once he swallows, however, he rubs at his chin. "I've been thinking..."

I cut my gaze over to him and feel my stance automatically open up. "About what?"

"Now now, Kitty. Don't look so grumpy. I won't renege on our bargain. But, if she's really willing to play dirty, then I need to see it for myself." He fishes into the pocket of his jeans and pulls a cell phone out. "Call him," he says to her, shoving the phone in her direction. "If you're so willing to turn on your master, then I want to see it—and hear it—for myself." He looks at me, and his expression isn't mocking for once. "After all, it's easy to claim that you'd bite at your own leash but a bit harder to put into practice. You know that better than anyone, eh, Kitty?"

I don't answer. Instead, I mull the request over. It makes sense in theory—but Mack doesn't do shit without some other motive. Not that I really give a damn. The itch to just get this over with is too irritating to resist. "How do we know that he can't fucking trace the call?"

Mack actually seems pissed off by the question. "As if I'd be that fucking stupid. Sammy programmed this baby himself. It's a burner. Jesus fucking Christ wouldn't be able to trace it."

"Okay, then." My eyes home in on the girl. "Do it."

She keeps her face blank when she reaches for the cell phone—though I'm sure I'm the only one who notices how her fingers shake, and now, it makes fucking sense. Mack *wants* to see her break. He wants to see how she holds up when forced to confront Stacatto directly. Hell, maybe I do too.

Things rarely end well when a wild dog confronts its owner while off its leash. One or the other has to assert their dominance: either the leash is wrapped back around the dog's neck or the owner gets bitten. Stacatto's girl wrestles with her choice, her eyes wide, her soul hovering on the edge of flying away or staying to face her old master.

Before she can decide, I take a step toward her, coming just within the line of her peripheral vision. "Do it," I grunt. "Call him."

Her fingers tremble even more, but she curls them into fists. Just when I think she'll refuse, she finally lets her thumb strike the call button on the contact Mack already pulled up.

The phone must be rigged to automatically turn the speaker on, because the sound of the dial tone echoes throughout the room and she doesn't even need to lift the receiver to her ear. When a man's gruff voice finally answers, he sounds crystal clear.

"Hello?"

The woman inhales. "G-Gino." There's a smattering of static from the other end as if the person holding the phone is adjusting it. "Can...can I talk to Vinny?" Her voice wavers slightly, but there's a hardness to her expression. She doesn't let it flicker, not even when the man, Gino, replies.

"Just one moment, Miss Manzano."

All noise from the other end suddenly cuts off as if someone has placed their hand over the receiver right before they go to fetch the recipient of the call. Stacatto's woman waits patiently, her hands neatly folded. Only her feet give her away; they aren't primly crossed at the ankles now. She's grinding her toes into the bottom rung of her stool, balancing on the edge of control and terror.

"Lynn." The newer voice carries an edge that makes even Arno and Mack sit straighter.

"Vinny," the woman says softly.

"I've missed you..." *Possession.* It all but drips through the speakers and forms a noose around the woman's neck, tightening with every octave the voice lowers. "Tell me that this call means that those...monsters will let you come home." He's taunting her; the fucker knows damn well who the real monster is.

"No." Hazel eyes home in on mine and never look away.

I know that expression. As long as she can't picture his face, she's fine—it's the same tactic a child uses to ignore the monster under the bed.

"I don't think I'll be coming back any time soon, Vinny."

Stacatto chuckles into the phone. "I received your present, Lynn." The bittersweet tone suddenly gives way to a harsher growl. "That was my *mother's* ring."

The woman swallows hard, and her feet leave the rung of the stool to kick at the air. "I...I just gave you what you wanted, Vinny," she croaks. "My humiliation. Isn't that right?"

He barks another harsh bit of laughter, but it's colder than before. "I've only ever wanted your loyalty, Lynn. Your respect. Your fidelity. But do not fear... One day, I will *earn* those things from you."

"Never," she says, and just like for the camera, the woman flips her switch. Her eyes still won't leave mine, but I don't recognize the creature staring out from them anymore. "I'm never coming back. You will never own me again. *Never.*"

"Is that so?" Stacatto seems to mull her declaration over the same way one might a silly request from a naughty child who doesn't know any better. "I've sent you a present of my own," he adds, changing the subject. "Have they given it to you yet?"

I glance over at Mack, who shrugs.

"They haven't," Stacatto murmurs, and if his voice could hold anything resembling a human emotion, it might be...glee. "Show it to her, you motherfuckers. I know you're listening in. And, Lynn..." The sound from the other end changes. He's holding the receiver closer. I wouldn't be surprised if his fingers were stroking the back of it and he were imagining them caressing the fragile line of her throat. "I love you, *Mi Bella*. This has changed nothing between us, and when I find you...I will make you understand."

He cuts off his end, and the sound makes the woman slump against the counter. Her face never changes though. Her mask remains firmly in place, but it's cracking at the edges. When she looks at Mack, I can already see the dread she's struggling to hide underneath it.

"What did he send?"

Mack rubs his chin thoughtfully. If his opinion of her has changed after the little telephone conference, he doesn't reveal it. "A rather entertaining video," he says. "But it's not exactly...suitable for a lady."

"Show me it." Her haughty tone cracks like a whip, but Mack doesn't seem to mind the sting.

He grins, licking his lips. Then he stands and crosses over to her, reaching for the phone. "I'm merely obeying the lady's request, Dante," he snaps, his shoulders tensing just enough to warn anyone stupid enough to creep up on him that he's ready to fight.

Only now do I realize that I'm already standing between him and the girl, forcing him to reach around me to fiddle with the phone's screen. I don't look back at her, but I can sense her stiffen; she's uneasy by how close I am. The little bitch can only tolerate me when she's being fucked, I guess.

"It's in rather poor taste," Mack admits as he slides the phone in her direction again and steps back. "I would have chosen better lighting."

My eyes travel to the screen at the same time she sits forward, her bound hair falling over one shoulder. The grainy display of a video appears. As Mack said, the lighting sucks. Through the shadows of what appears to be a small room, it's only possible to make out a woman braced against a floor on her hands and knees. Red hair spills down her shoulders, but the rest of her face is too dark to make out.

"Say your name." The commanding voice contains the same accent as Vincent Stacatto's. He must be the one positioning the camera, because the lens begins to focus in on the woman—just enough to see the tears streaming down her face and the outline of a small nose.

"M-Maria," she whispers.

When I hear the woman seated beside me gasp, I know she recognizes her.

"Open your mouth," Stacatto commands the girl on camera. The shot is too tight to show his face, but I suspect that his hand is the one that appears, holding a glinting diamond ring.

The woman inhales sharply, but hell, even I recognize it. He must have fished it from Arno's place before he set it on fire.

Maria starts to sob. "P-please—" Her plea is silenced when he shoves the ring through the part in her lips, sealing her mouth shut with his palm.

"You will watch this, Lynn," Stacatto murmurs toward the camera. "All of it."

The lens pans out, just enough to reveal the woman choking on a fourteen-karat ring while a larger man shoves her down and starts to tear at her clothes. "You will watch..."

"No!"

Mack's phone goes flying off the bar and lands on the floor, batted away by a pale hand. The fall isn't enough to cut the video off, however. Shrill screams erupt from the speaker but are drowned out by the sound of a stool toppling over and rolling across the floor. A streak of black hair is my only warning to lunge, and I seize a handful of white cotton— but I'm not expecting the ferocity she fights me off with, and she claws at my fingers until they let go.

"I've got it," I grit out to Mack and Arno before they can even move as Stacatto's woman barrels through the doors of the bar.

She's faster than I thought for someone so damn poised. She runs wild. Reckless. Fuck, she seems about ready to jump the fence when I finally catch up to her near the perimeter. My hand flies out, but I don't have to touch her.

She stops in her tracks just as I come within reach. For nearly a minute, she just stands there, her back to me, her shoulders heaving...and then she screams.

The piercing sound travels through me like a bullet, ripping apart flesh and bone. It's the primal howl of a wounded animal. Still screaming, she falls to her knees, clenching her fingers in the dirt until her voice starts to break. When it does, her hands form fists and hammer at the ground with the same rage I attacked the trees with. She shrieks and hits, and I don't know if I mean to stop her when my hand falls over her shoulder or if I simply want to feel her breaking. If that's the case, I'm not fucking disappointed. Cracking into pieces beneath porcelain skin, she whirls on me with a shout.

Whatever she calls me isn't in English, but she accompanies the insult with a clumsy punch to my jaw. When I grab her by the wrist, she slaps me with her free hand. Then she hits me again, forcing me to take a step back. Growling, she strikes *again*, her nails raking my skin this time, but I don't try to stop her.

On the tenth swing at me, she finally misses, and as if someone suddenly cut the strings holding her together, she breaks. Before I can move out of range, her arms go around my shoulders. She's sobbing wordlessly into my chest, her tears seeping through the cotton of my shirt. I *feel* the fight drain from her. The loss of it weakens her knees, and she nearly pulls me down with her. I have to stagger forward and brace both hands against the top of the fence while her fingers paw at my hips and her face connects with my left knee. When she finally speaks, her voice is a whisper that somehow has no trouble rising above the distant sound of barking dogs.

"He...he killed my entire family." She sounds so detached that she could be talking about the rain.

It pelts us in scattered drops that glance off my body before they can reach her, but I don't feel the need to move. Yet. I grit my teeth and eye the row of trees in front of me instead.

"I know he did," she insists. "My parents... They knew that all I wanted in the world was to be able to play the *violoncelo*." Whatever language she natively speaks seeps into her words, tainting some of them.

In fact, I wonder if he's part of the reason for how she struggles to hide her accent; it's only when she's angry that it creeps out in full force.

"They let me practice whenever I wanted, and even though I couldn't afford one of my own, my father made deals with the theater he worked at to let me use their instruments as long as he cleaned... It was my dream to play in a symphony when I graduated. I wanted so badly to get into a performance school...but I knew that we couldn't afford it."

She breaks off, and I can hear the violent click of her teeth clenching together. She doesn't want to go this far, and I tell myself that my impatient grunt isn't what makes her keep talking in the end.

"When I was seventeen, they surprised me with a bus ticket upstate so that I could audition for a scholarship... My father worked hours of overtime. My mother gave up her weekends for extra shifts. They sacrificed so much. I... It was the happiest day of my life. They...they even rented a cello for me to play at home. I got there early. I practiced until my fingers ached. I played...and I made it to the final round of auditions." Two tears slip from her eyes and roll down her cheeks, the only sign of life behind her fractured mask. "My parents were so proud of me. My brother even helped me practice, tapping out the beat with his pencils."

I stiffen when her palms flatten against my lower back, but for some reason, I don't shove her off.

"I hadn't thought to tell Vinny until the night before the final auditions," she says. "I'd never seen him so angry. *'You're leaving me,'* he said. *'You think music is more fucking important than loyalty? I love you, Mi Bella."* She gives the words Stacatto's guttural pronunciation, and her nails bite even deeper into my flesh. "My father tried to warn me. He didn't like how possessive such an older man had become of his daughter. Vinny intimidated the other boys my age. He interfered when I tried to date. My father said he was too jealous. *'Brincando com fogo,'* he used to say. His temper is like playing with fire...but he was my *friend.*"

Her eyes shut against the word, and more tears fall down her cheeks. "He knew how important music was to me. He knew how much I'd staked my future on joining an orchestra. He knew. He *knew*...and later that night, he invited me out to dinner to apologize. We went to his favorite place, owned by his boss. Capellas. He ordered the chicken marinara and even bought enough for my entire family."

Her voice starts to lose its coldness—pain makes it shake, and the words crack, straining against her tongue. "I-I felt so s-sleepy when I got home. I went straight to bed. Vinny had to walk me inside—I could barely see straight." She swallows hard. Her eyes open again and her hands slide down my hips, landing on either side of her in the mud. "When I woke up...everything was so quiet. *Mamãe* wasn't humming in the kitchen as she cooked breakfast. My father wasn't cursing at the news. Christoph wasn't ramming his toy trucks against my door. So f-fucking quiet. I thought that...that maybe they were planning a surprise."

She giggles, her gaze wide and unsteady. "It...it was my birthday, after all. But, when I went into the living room...all I saw was Vinny. *'It was an accident,'* he told me. *'A terrible accident, Mi Bella.'* Someone had tried to rob us, apparently. They took my mother's golden bracelet. My father's watch. They ransacked the house, and they slit my parents' throats while they slept. They never woke up, not even as they drew their last breath. It was so strange... They hadn't even changed yet. My father had even taken a plate of food to bed, so excited to try Italian cuisine. My brother, however..."

She inhales sharply and shakes her head as if her protest alone can keep the memory at bay—but fate's a cruel fucker, and I know that, when her eyes widen, she's seeing every single detail etched into her brain forever.

"They...they found him in the hall. He had woken up when the attacker crept into his room. He tried to fight him off, and th-they had to stab him fifteen times. He'd been heading toward my room. His eyes were on my d-door. I know he was screaming for me. I still hear him." She's silent, and the storm begins to build in earnest as if feeding off the morbid picture her words paint. "Vinny had a detective there. *Sosa*," she spits out. "He corroborated his story despite the fact that there was no sign of forced entry. Burglars did it. My parents were *lucky* to be asleep while they were butchered. And...I almost believed it. I almost let myself fall for his lies..."

She frowns as if wondering whether or not that would have been easier to swallow than the truth. "But Christoph didn't like saucy foods. He didn't touch the meal Vinny brought. He was awake when my best friend and protector returned in the middle of the night with a knife. Christoph fought back. That's why Vinny made him suffer."

I don't say anything. I steel my shoulders against the rain, and I squash the fucking emotion that flickers through my chest too quickly to name. When I finally start to move, she touches my knee.

"I want him dead."

I have to glance down to make sure the icy voice came from her, but she's already looking up, staring dead into my eyes without flinching.

"I want Vinny *dead*," she insists, and there's a hint of wonder in her tone, as if she finally had the nerve to voice some deep, dark secret out loud. Her eyes flicker—a part of her doesn't like giving in to the violence, but she blinks, and it's gone. "I want...I want to watch him burn." When she tilts her head back, her forehead leaves the shelter of my chest and raindrops slide down to her lips. She licks at them, tasting Stacatto's blood in the rain. The flavor must be her own potent narcotic, because for just a brief second, her body goes limp. "I want...I want to set the fire myself."

I don't know what the hell she finds in my eyes that makes her tug one of her sleeves down to her wrist, revealing the bloody gash in her palm. I don't know what the hell makes her raise that hand toward me while thunder rumbles in the distance. I don't know what gives her the fucking nerve to make a demand out loud.

"Promise me?"

And I don't know why the fuck I take her bloodied hand with one of my own, sealing yet another oath in blood.

CHAPTER TWENTY-FIVE

Daniela

VINNY PREFERRED TO DISCUSS MURDER DURING mealtimes. He'd sip glasses of Chardonnay and tally up the bodies of rivals he wanted killed that week. The men themselves typically received the usual treatment: a bullet or two to the brain. *Bada bing.* The real fun for him came when their families and loved ones were thrown into the mix.

How many ways can you make a bastard suffer? Vinny liked to ponder that question aloud while he cut into his steak and dabbed the blood from his lips.

He especially enjoyed using women to cause a man pain. Their daughters. Their wives. If they were lucky, he'd merely slit their throat while the unlucky "motherfucker" was forced to watch. If he was in a mood, he might sell them off to the highest bidder and send the man photographic evidence as a little reminder never to fuck with Vincent Stacatto.

I was used to the splendor that came with plotting destruction—but Lucifer and his fallen brethren apparently chose to discuss such matters in a dimly lit bar, their faces grim, their voices clipped. Forsaking the bar counter, they stand huddled around an empty pool table, treating it like a makeshift battlefield.

The blond woman left the moment Lucifer returned with me in tow. "Go and make me some fucking lunch, baby," Mack had told her, slapping her ass on her way out. But I saw her eyes as she scurried for the door; she wanted no part in this.

"I say we hit the fucker where it hurts," Arno proposes, slamming his palm down against the green felt. "All-out, full-frontal assault." His eyes gleam at the thought of taking Vinny on, guns blazing.

I want to laugh, but Lucifer beats me to the punch.

"No." His guttural tone takes all the "fun" out of our lethal game. The devil isn't playing, he's strategizing. "Taking him out in the open would be suicide—"

"So says the Kitty," Mack counters with a glittering smile. "Prison's made you even more skittish than before."

If the insult breaks through his skin, Lucifer's expression doesn't reveal it. He merely glares down at the surface of the pool table, his mouth thoughtful. Pensive. He's a scholar of war, planning his every move with the thoughtful care of a general. Arno and Mack scoff and sneer at his silence, but even I know that they're waiting until he finally glances up, his eyes alight with manic fire.

"We take him apart piece by piece," he says. He jerks his head in my direction and cuts me into slivers beneath the intensity of his gaze. "*She's* going to tell us how."

"Bullshit," Arno scoffs.

Mack is less dismissive. "Unless it's while she's spreading her legs for my clients, I don't follow."

Lucifer merely smiles, and...in all the times I've watched Vinny relish in the thought of bloodshed, I've never seen him look so...*desperate* for it. "Tell them what you told me," he commands.

I stiffen. I told him lies—snatches of conversation and rumors. I told him what little I was able to remember in the few moments when fear hadn't clouded my thoughts. I told him whatever Vinny allowed me to hear.

But Lucifer's gaze is steel, reinforced with something vague that makes my chest tighten. Is that trust? I study it and try to match the word to the definition of the term I learned in school. *Faith* was a synonym for it—that same emotion he seemed to want me to feel in the arena. My faith that he would win his battle somehow translates into his trust that only I can "take down" Vinny.

"He...he has three things," I start to say. My throat feels dry. Swallowing hard, I try to combat it, and I wind up scanning the length of the pool table until I find the shelf built into the side of it containing the small colored balls used to play on it. My fingers slip into the crevice, and I pull out three to juggle them in my hands. I pick a yellow one, marked with the number 1, and allow it to drop onto the table first. "His 'palace,' the hotel." I drop another ball, a blue one this time. "His money." The red ball I save for last, twisting my fingers around it. When it finally falls, it rolls into the other two, sending them darting toward opposite ends of the table. "His name."

As Vinny would say, *Bada Bing;* those are the three prized possessions of any self-appointed king.

"You use his name to destroy the other two," I say. "That's what matters most to him."

"How do we do that?" Lucifer demands, but he isn't curious, merely prompting—it's like the man is already aware of the thoughts circling my brain. I can feel him inside my skull, creeping through the darkness, at home in the decay of my sanity.

"My video," I say. "Put it everywhere. The internet. *Everywhere.* C-caption it...Lynn Stacatto, Vinny's soon-to-be fiancée." The move would make him angry, but it wouldn't be enough. Anger was his favorite weapon of all the ones in his arsenal, and that alone would be enough to fuel his hunt for me...but impatience would make him reckless. "While he's...distracted, we launch a true attack on *this.*" I follow the edge of the table and pick up the blue ball again, eyeing it carefully, as though it really did contain all of Vinny's millions inside it.

"His money?" Arno asks from somewhere behind me.

"His *business*," I correct, watching the ball rock back and forth on the flat of my palm. "He deals in drugs, but...I want to hit the women. He traffics them from overseas. We strike him there, and the rest will crumble."

"Hmph," Mack grunts thoughtfully. "Interesting proposal, princess. How exactly does one bring down the multimillion-dollar prostitution ring of a crime boss? Do tell."

I shake my head. It's simple, really. Lucifer must have already seen the memories lurking inside my head, decoding them with all the cunning of a wolf while I was too afraid to. *Think,* he told me. *You've fantasized about this.*

"My last maid. Maria... She was too...too fresh. She talked too much. The first day, she mentioned something about a b-bridge and hearing the ships come in at night."

"The harbor?" Lucifer guesses. "Somewhere near the marina, or maybe the port if she heard them at night."

"The shipping docks," Mack admits—reluctantly if his narrowed gaze is anything to go by. "I've been scoping out the competition for a while now, but you haven't seen security until you've seen the setup he guards his merchandise with, princess. There's no way we could even get close to them without a tank. Trust me. I've tried."

"*We* don't have to get close," Dante says. "Not if we use a proxy..."

"The police." I know I'm right when I see him nod, though grudgingly, as if in shock. It's like my thoughts connect with the pieces he lays out, assembling them as easily as if they'd originated inside my own head. "We use the police to—"

"No." Mack stands fully upright, flexing his massive fingers into even more intimidating fists. "No fucking police. That's your true game, isn't it?" He lashes out from across the table, seizing me by my chin so harshly that my jaws snap together.

Just like that, all of the air leaves the room. Gasoline replaces it. One tiny spark is all that's needed to blow everything from the pool table to the people gathered around it sky high.

Lucifer says nothing, though his eyes go to Mack with the intensity of a wolf gnashing its fangs. He pauses when my bloody hand meets the sliver of the table in front of him though. Slowly, his gaze settles over the bloodied fingers, and I face Mack alone, staring deep into his eyes. His gaze isn't a mystery to me like Lucifer's. I can read each violent emotion clearly—greed and jealousy are a universal language Vinny educated me in so well.

"Why not?" I ask.

He laughs, and his grip tightens hard enough to grind new bruises onto my already battered jaw. "Little girl, you don't even know the half of it. Not even fucking half. Your beloved fiancé owns the goddamn police. We go to them and I might as well just give that fucker the keys to my own little kingdom."

I attempt to shake my head, but I can only jerk my chin, trapped by the force of his grip. "He owns half the police," I admit. "But...the rest..."

"They answer to the public," Lucifer says softly. He frowns and rakes one of his bloodied, bruised hands through his hair—something that I notice he does when he's thinking. "Nobody gives a damn about a drug scandal. But women...girls. A story like that would trigger a larger investigation that even Stacatto couldn't shut down even with every judge in the city in his pocket. It would start a fire that the city couldn't contain..."

"Hmph, and how the fuck do you propose we do that?" Mack demands as his fingers relinquish their hold on me.

"We bait the trap," Dante says as if it's obvious. "We find a way to lure him out of his hiding spot, and then we hit him where it hurts."

"Those are pretty words and all, Dante," Mack counters. "But I'm gonna need something a little more concrete."

"We tip off the police about the girls. When they go to warn Stacatto—"

"He won't give a shit because the police are in his fucking pocket, like I've said," Mack interjects.

Lucifer merely smiles. "Not all of them. You get *one* nosy pig on his trail and that'll force him to at least try to cover his tracks. When he does, we'll be waiting...to steal a little bit of his merchandise."

"Hmm." Mack takes his time drinking in the plan. There's a rough cruelty even in the way he thinks to himself, rubbing absently at his chin. "I get the girls when we're done—"

"No." My fingers release the blue ball, and it bounces twice across the table's surface. "*I* get them."

Mack laughs. Even Arno has to snort. Such a silly idea, the princess wanting to claim a bunch of whores. Lucifer doesn't snicker, however. Maybe he knows my plan already. Maybe he doesn't really care.

"*I* get the girls," I repeat, staring Mack dead in the eye.

"Is that so?"

"Yes," I say. "Because I'm going to use them to hit Vinny right where it hurts."

"Oh, really?" The corner of his mouth quirks, revealing a sharpened canine. "And just how do you plan to do that?"

I shrug. Then...I smile, going against the neat expressions Vinny preferred me to display. He hated when I smiled for anyone but him. He hated when I laughed out of his earshot. It seems only fitting that, with him being the topic at hand, I do both.

"I'm going to let them go—"

"Bullshit." This time, Mack really does come for me, swinging his massive form around the pool table to grab me by the throat. He presses hard, just enough to make it a struggle to breathe, and I feel the curve of every finger, down to the ridge of each nail gouging my skin. "I've had just about enough of this little bitch," he snarls, his breath hot on my face, his mouth still curved into a mocking smile. "Say one more stupid fucking word and I'll find a good use for that smart little mouth of yours."

"Let her go." The command comes from Arno, but his eyes are focused somewhere behind me, where another man lurks, his shadow swallowing mine. "M-Mack, let her fucking go!"

"Should I, Dante?" Mack wonders, directing the question beyond my shoulder. He drags me forward until I have to strain on tiptoe to keep him from crushing my throat. "Should I let the little whore go? Or maybe I should give her a little taste of my cock first?"

He shifts one of his hands and tries to jab the pad of his thumb between my lips. I choke when he goes too far, and my teeth clamp down. Hissing in pain, he draws his hand back, and then *pain*. I see silver. I taste blood. Agony plays a deafening melody through my skull, and when I finally regain my senses, I'm on the ground, both hands braced against the floor in front of me. It trembles. There has to be an earthquake taking place...

Or a body being thrown against the wall.

"Dante, stop!"

There's a beast attacking Mack. Arno does his best to rein the monster in, but nothing can stop a devil unleashed. If I'd been stupid enough to believe that Lucifer's skill in battle extended only to the show within the cage, I would have been sorely mistaken. That fight was child's play. *This* is the true devil off his leash.

He snarls, his muscles rippling with every punch he lands before Mack can even form a proper defense. Blood flies with each blow, after blow, after *blow*... Arno has to throw himself forward to get enough leverage to wrap both arms around Lucifer's waist. He tugs, but the man doesn't move. He doesn't flinch. He doesn't comprehend anything but the violence.

"Eh... Enough," Mack snarls, his voice garbled by the hammering thud of repeated punches. "Enough! Enough!"

When Arno finally manages to haul Lucifer backward, Mack staggers away from them, spitting out blood. His bottom lip is split, but he's laughing, clinging to the wall with one hand.

"And there he is, ladies and gentlemen—the *real* fucking Kitten." He swipes at his mouth while chuckling maniacally. When his gaze meets Lucifer's, there isn't any rage in his eyes. Just glee. Insanity. Hatred. "*This* is the bastard I wanted to face in the cage. We'll have our rematch soon, eh, Dante? And next time...we'll play for keeps." He winks, but Lucifer stares right past him. Through him.

For a terrible second, he's not human anymore, and a monster stands in his place, searching for the nearest prey to bite, gnaw at, and kill. When I start to move, he spots me and takes a step forward, his hand flying out.

I should flinch back like I've been trained to do. I should run—but, when I finally react, it's only to catch his hand before it can even touch me, pressing my palm to his. Only with this does Dante return, glaring out through hooded eyes.

He grips me in turn and hauls me to my feet, but I can't keep up when he starts for the door, pulling me along after him while Mack still cackles. Outside, a steady rain continues to fall, and with every step he takes, I'm forced to stagger forward three. He doesn't care when I trip as he hauls me inside the detached garage and heads for the stairs, dragging me up every single one. After wrenching the door to the apartment open, he shoves me through it, barring the only escape.

I shiver even before he wrestles the door shut—slamming it fiercely—and shoves me back against the counter. I gasp out when the edge juts against my spine, but Dante continues to stalk forward. His face is expressionless, his gaze dark. I wish to every angel in heaven that I could feel fear. God, I *need* to be afraid. I try to force the terror, digging my nails into my palms so hard that I wince. Even that pain isn't enough.

I hold my breath, feeling my pulse race as his body towers over mine, his eyes hovering over my throat. When he opens his mouth, I think he really means to tear into it, but he inhales, and I don't resist when he tugs on my hips, positioning his bloodied, mangled hands on either side to pivot me around so that my back faces him.

He's too close. His chest presses against my shoulders,

forcing me down onto the counter. I think I could be truly afraid now if it weren't for the way my own wide-eyed reflection watches me from the polished surface of the sink. What a greedy little bitch. She's hungry. Her tongue trails her parting lips while she starts to pant, her back arched toward the man standing behind her.

He catches my chin on the palm of his hand, his thumb prodding my split lip. He smears each drop of blood and doesn't seem satisfied until I lick all traces of it away. The heat in his eyes grazes my skin, erasing whatever evidence Mack may have left behind. Vincent Stacatto doesn't exist at this moment, either. To prove it, the devil strips me naked himself, wrenching the white shirt over my head, growling when he realizes I'm wearing nothing underneath. The jeans, too. I'm already bare for him.

And, God, I should be terrified by the possession rolling off him in waves—but I'm spineless for another reason. My skin sears beneath the hand he rakes down my back. He scratches me, and the sharp lines of pain make me clench my teeth and squeeze my eyes shut.

Scream, I tell myself. *Fight. Run. Resist.* Only Vinny had eyes like that. Ravenous. Vicious. Hungry. Starving eyes. His lust should be poison. I shouldn't crave... I shouldn't...

I nearly trip over my own two feet when he yanks me from the counter by my shoulder and manually steers me down the hallway, I see as my eyes open again. He forces me into that narrow, darkened room. He makes me crawl onto the center of the bed, and he positions me on my hands and knees. The mattress protests when he mounts it after me, his body a heavy, solid weight against mine.

Searching fingers trace the back of my skull and find the hair tie I got from the duffel bag the blonde had sent. He tugs it down, freeing my hair to spill over my shoulders. The sound he makes—it's part growl, part groan. His lips graze the nape of my neck, and I half expect him to bite there, holding me in place like a true wolf while he thrusts deep.

His fingers tangle in my hair instead, wrenching my head back. My gaze is on the ceiling when he slides a hand down my backside and nudges my legs farther apart. *This is it*, some part of me murmurs. Vinny may have claimed my soul, but Lucifer...he breaks it, grinding himself into me so hard that I see double. From far, far away, I hear a woman scream, sharp and piercing—he doesn't enter me in the usual place, and without the preparation from before, it hurts. It burns. I'm on fire, and I don't know what creature is reborn in the ashes when the flames finally die down and he starts to move.

He's slower than before, grinding into my inner walls and testing the give of my body. It tenses, every inch of me unsure whether to shut him out or let him in deeper. My body wants him out. My head—it lets him in, overriding the instinctive clenching of my muscles until his thrusts become easier while my vision clears again.

When I blink, I see his shadow thrown over the wall in front of me, tense and endlessly black. He stiffens up, and I make out the shape of his hand as it falls against my lower back for leverage—did he even realize where he chose to thrust? Before he can change his mind, I flex my hips, urging him deeper, conveying what I can't with words. *I want this. I need this...*

Grunting, he starts to move again, and I don't force his pace this time. I dig my nails into the comforter, arch my back, and I...I just let him fuck me.

I don't think. I don't feel. I breathe him in. I taste his scent on my tongue. I let his thudding heartbeat set the pace of mine. I let him own me and take whatever the hell he wants. I don't resist.

And, this time, he doesn't hold back.

The mattress sways with every harsh, violent motion of our bodies. Somewhere in the chaos, he starts to increase his pace, finding a pleasure that makes him grit out curses that set my cheeks on fire.

"Fuck. So fucking tight. Fuck. Fuck."

I'm half mindless when he finally slows, his body heavy against my back. I don't react when he pulls out and comes against me. I just lie here, relishing the heat he gives off in the otherwise cold room. He doesn't shift his weight from me when I slump facedown against the mattress. He braces a hand against my spine instead, once again rubbing his release into my skin, using his thumb to meticulously paint me with every single drop. Once finished, he hits the mattress beside me, his breathing harsh and unsteady.

"Lynn," he grits out. "Is that your name?"

I flinch and shake my head, though I'm not brave enough to lift my face from the pillow. I inhale the dust that's embedded in the cotton along with the sweat from my own skin and his particular brand of musk. Seconds pass before I realize I never gave him the correct answer. All this time and he hasn't cared to ask my name. Maybe he still doesn't; the devil is as curious as he is volatile.

In the end, I lift my head just enough to free my mouth and whisper, "Danny. My name is Danny."

He grunts in acknowledgment, but I can't tell what he thinks of it. Did he expect something different? Something prettier? I nearly laugh out loud at the fact that his approval actually seems to matter to me.

"Only Vinny calls me Lynn," I add, though I'm not sure why. "My real name is Daniela. He thought it wasn't good enough for me."

It's strange how detached I sound, as if the silly matter of a name didn't bother me in the slightest when, for fifteen years, it's been one of the shackles Vinny has used to keep me under his control. He's turned me into three different women. Only now can I start to somewhat reconcile those broken parts into one cohesive person again—though I don't seem to be the only one with a nickname hovering above my head.

I wait for nearly a minute before I gather up the nerve to ask him. "Why do they call you Kitty?" By "they," I mean Mack, who wielded the moniker like a weapon.

He's inches away, but I still feel him stiffen. Lucifer can make a natural silence seem eternal. Even the steady huff of his breathing quiets. It's not fair. Music has always been my refuge, and he takes every sound from me until the frantic beat of my pulse is all I have to count the rhythm of my sanity to. Finally, he shifts, the mattress creaking under his weight.

"My first time in the cage, I tried to climb out," he admits. "I was sixteen, and I was the bait before the real fight. A warm-up," he explains. "The man was nearly twice my size, but all I had to do was last ten minutes and I'd earn three percent of the cut—but I didn't last five before I chickened out and tried to scale the fence. One of the men running the cage waited until I nearly cleared the top before he stuck a knife through one of the gaps and stabbed me in my side —" His hand moves to his thigh, hovering over a particularly nasty scar. "When I fell back in, he shouted that 'scared little kittens' didn't belong in the cage. Only mad dogs could survive in this world." He inhales and then exhales on a sigh. "I broke three ribs and didn't earn a fucking dime. But I came back, and they never forgot the scared little Kitty who couldn't run with the pack. Until I started to win, that is..."

I picture him down in the arena, cold and calculating. Then I imagine the way he went after Mack. Those two creatures don't even seem to be one and the same. A calculating devil and an out-of-control monster.

"Whatever they call me, it doesn't fucking matter," Lucifer adds. "It still wouldn't change a damn thing."

Part of his words resonate deep down inside me and linger long after the high from the sex has worn off. I didn't even orgasm this time, and I don't know why it doesn't seem to matter. He used me the same way Vinny's men did their "prize" whores, sating himself and leaving nothing behind.

But his breathing sounds easier. The mattress dips deeply beneath him as he spreads out on his back, and for one brief, dangerous second, Lucifer is completely relaxed—as much as a devil ever could be. How easy would it be to fish my knife from my pocket and jab it into his throat? Maybe it's the fact that he tore my pants off in the other room that makes it easier to lie there and accept this. Accept *him*.

The thought alone is a sadistic game to play. He *is* Russian roulette, only the gun is fully loaded with bullets. His eyes are a barrel to the chest. The rasp of his voice against my aching skin is like being pistol-whipped with the body of the gun itself. But, when his fingers come to trail the length of my shoulder blades, he's mercilessly putting the gun to my head and pulling the trigger. *Bang.*

There's no real warmth in the scarred, callused hands, but my flesh is so sensitive that I can feel every wet, open inch of his. His blood paints me too, mingling with his sweat and his seed. I should feel disgusted, I suppose, but my corrupted pores open wider, eager to absorb every last, twisted drop.

Suddenly, it isn't just enough to lie here. I have to draw my legs together and arch my back to find enough leverage to relieve the pressure building there. His hands are still on me, and Lucifer doesn't miss the movement.

"Does it hurt?" He doesn't sound concerned. Just curious. He really is like a cat, always prodding a new mystery with his claws.

I wince and draw myself upright farther, propping my knees against the mattress and my hands against the pillow. "*Yesss,*" I admit, my voice tight. It hurts. The pain of the first time was easier to ignore in the tense moments that came after. I'd turn the water in the shower to scalding and worked until my shoulders throbbed, scrubbing away at every trace of himself Lucifer had stained me with. This time, I'm left gaping open. Misused muscles scream out in torment, having been ripped apart during his invasion. I try my damn hardest to sink into that pain. I gnash my teeth and clench my thighs until tears spill from my eyes and sink into the cotton sheets. *It hurts, it hurts, it hurts,* I chant to myself.

But even the agony he delivers is a bitter poison. My body prefers to focus on the heat he gives off instead and the pulsing ache between my legs that I won't be able to ease with the pathetic friction caused by rubbing my thighs together. I know pain, fluent in every nuance of it both mental and physical.

But whatever he gives me is foreign, and I want *more*. Admitting that stings worse than any blow Vinny's ever inflicted. I need him to leave. I need him to take what he wants and ignore the mess he leaves behind. When the mattress shifts, betraying the moment he stands, I assume he's of the same mindset. *Let's make this clean.*

I hear him pad into the hallway, and it's only when I'm sure he's gone that I lean against one elbow and slide the opposite hand down along my belly. Carefully...slowly... When my fingers finally make contact with sore, vandalized flesh, I can almost pretend that they aren't my own. The lie feeds the flames, and they rise up into an inferno. At first, I only move my fingers in rapid circles where my body craves friction the most. I don't think.

But the needle's in the other room, and like the world's most pathetic addict, I can't stop myself from prodding the tip of it. Drip by precious drip, my mind floods with lethal doses of him. I picture him down in the cage. The way he looked at me... I see him in the bar, fighting Mack. *Him. Him. Him.*

I gasp when my body finally begins to ride the high, but it's just an echo of the pleasure only he can bring. This is that tasteless nicotine gum Vinny used to quit smoking; there's no real satisfaction, and deep down, some part of me registers a terror I refuse to let myself dwell on now. Whatever happens within the next few days...gum is all I'll ever have—my own fingers struggle to imitate the fire only he can set. He was so worried about the heroin, I think, choking out a bitter laugh while my fingers swirl and twist.

Lucifer was *worried* about me. He used his own pain as a bitter antidote to counteract the drug—only I was the fool who got addicted to that new sting. Vincent Stacatto couldn't have devised a crueler form of torture.

My eyelids drift shut. My head thrashes, tethered to my body when all it really wants to do is break off and float away. I'm panting with the effort it takes to drive myself toward the edge of sanity, but right when I'm just about to tip over it, I'm back inside my skin. My fingers stiffen and pull away before I realize why. Then I hear him, his footsteps heavy as he crosses over the threshold of the room and finds me there, hunched over and red with shame.

"Turn over."

I flinch at the command. *No*, my body tells me. *No. Hide. Ignore. Hide.* I should curl in on myself the way I used to when Vinny would come into my room at night to "show" me how just he loved and needed me, stroking his cock while I was forced to watch.

Only God knows Lucifer's intentions—an ironic twist.

But it's that mystery that makes me finally move, twisting around to flop onto my back. I keep my eyes shut though. I wait until the anticipation practically boils me alive before I finally allow myself to look at him. He's holding a rag in one hand and a plastic case in the other. A first aid kit? I don't have long to guess before he sets it on the end of the mattress and braces one knee between my parted legs.

No. I make a noise somewhere between a protest and a whine. *No.* I want him to hit me with the cloth he's brandishing in his free hand. *Hit me with it. Hit me. Don't...*

He drags it along my hip, and my breath catches; he wet it.

"N-no," I choke out when he starts to stroke across my belly. "You don't... You don't have to."

The devil doesn't give a damn about my protests. He cleans me up with soap and water. He wipes his blood from the surface of my skin and grinds something else into me in the process. I can't stop the heat that floods the farther up my body he travels. I can't stop myself from watching him, and his eyes trace my skin the same way I'd observe my cello right before I played, imagining just where to place my fingers and how to arrange my bow for the best sound.

The devil plays me expertly. I gasp out in tune, and he draws out the melody, forcing me onto my stomach when he's done with my front.

It's harder for him to wipe away the sticky mess on my back with just the cloth. He has to use his strength, rubbing my flesh raw in the process. When he's finished, he tosses the cloth aside, and I crane my neck to find him wrestling with the case. He gets it open and pulls out a roll of white gauze.

"Give me your hand," he says without looking at me.

Which one? I wonder. Then I flex my fingers and remember the wound he made. I twist around, hold the injured limb out flat, and watch in shock as he proceeds to wrap a length of gauze around the cut. It's not much of a neat job considering that his bloody hands taint the ivory bandage. He tries to rip it from the roll and winds up leaving darker splotches of red in the process.

"S-stop." I lean over and flick my fingers through the objects in the case. They find a pair of scissors, and I manipulate them one-handed to snip at the gauze before he can do more damage to his hands.

I shouldn't touch him. I should let the beast lick his wounds in peace—something tells me that that scenario wouldn't be far from the truth. I grasp the devil by his wrist instead, and I ease the gauze from his grip. There are antiseptic wipes in the first aid kit, and I use all twelve on his open wounds. It looks like he shoved his hands into a meat grinder, but he doesn't even flinch when I dig into his scrapes to swipe away as much mud and grime as I do blood. He only protests—a deep, low growl—when I aim for the ones on his face next, using a clean bit of gauze and some clear antibacterial gel I found in a tube.

Maybe, if he were any other demon, I'd let him win this one battle and cower from the danger promised in his gaze. It's *his* fault I resist.

When I actually do try to wipe at the scratch on his chin, he bats my hand away and jerks out of reach. "Don't."

"You're bleeding," I counter. I don't feel any ounce of fear when I lean forward, the gauze in my hand, and dab at his chin.

He clenches his jaw against me, and I know he doesn't move only because he refuses to back down from the challenge.

"Hold still," I add, my voice hoarse.

An insane comparison is back when Christoph would skin his knees while playing outside and *Mamãe* would bandage him up with antiseptic. He'd scowl, trying his best to remain stoic while she cleansed his cuts, but she would always have to encourage him to sit still through the worst of it. *You can do it, my big man.*

Lucifer can only stomach the attention for a little over thirty seconds before he knocks my hand away again. Then he snatches the gauze from me and starts bandaging his wounds himself, wrapping it lengthwise around the hand that's worse off. He bites the gauze off with his teeth and doesn't bother to treat the other open areas. He would rather bleed all over the bedspread than appear weak.

It's a strange choice of action to take. Vinny guarded his health almost jealously. Every scrape or wound would have been seen to by a trusted doctor kept at his beck and call. Once, he lost control beating a man half to death and bruised the knuckles of his right hand. He wore a brace on it for a week afterward. "To protect my investment," he claimed. Violence and bloodshed were his cultivated traits, after all. Every punch he threw himself was an investment into the foundation of his very kingdom.

I wonder what legacy a man like Lucifer might invest in with those hands. So far, he seemed indiscriminately reckless with the tools of his trade; he's spilled more of his own blood than he's drawn, a fact Vinny would scoff at.

Lucifer wasn't as careful in cultivating his empire. He was a wayward wolf, striking down a kill out of necessity rather than for personal gain.

I don't know which method I find harder to stomach. Vinny never let me patch him up, not even partially. It's almost as if he knew I'd pray that infection would seep into every single scratch he would force me to bathe and bandage. *Gangrene,* Sammy said—I'd have wished for that, for every limb to rot and fall off.

Confused, I stare down at my hands, and I watch my fingers flex, bandaged with gauze stained with the devil's blood. I should feel disgusted, I suppose. Instead, I don't feel anything. No pain. Just...hunger. It gnaws away at some place far beyond my stomach—and it's a cruel ache that somehow knows that it will never be satisfied.

I don't look up when the bed dips as Lucifer stands once again. He snatches up the remains of the first aid kit and moves to place them in some distant corner of the room. When he returns to the foot of the mattress, I expect him to issue some kind of command. *Sit up. Get up. Clean yourself up.* Anything to reattach the invisible collar of captive and master. The muscles in my legs tense, almost eager to obey. I'll roll over. Fetch. Beg. Anything to remember the need to survive above all else.

But he doesn't say a damn thing. He watches me. Something sick and weak within me makes me look up and find his eyes boldly staring between my legs. They're parted. I'm still throbbing. God...I'm on fire.

And Lucifer, the devil, doesn't look away. He doesn't have the decency to even appear ashamed. He boldly takes me in, his hand falling over my hip when I start to bring my knees together, branding his lust into my skin. I should push him off the same way he did when I tried to cleanse his wounds. He's a bitter salve against lacerations that I didn't even know are still open. His heat sinks into my skin, his fingers mending the rent and ruined pieces. When my head falls back, however, it's the universal sign of surrender: a doe presenting its neck for the killing blow. And he *kills* me, sinking to his knees with a guttural sound that rattles me inside and out.

He swipes a hand between my legs, making me part them myself rather than force them open. It's a chilling sense of helplessness. He sees into me, admiring the fire his very presence stokes—particularly the way the flames lurch against the harshness of his fingertips, aching to be fed. He uses a thumb first, sinking it deep...

A whine tears from my throat. My back arches, my throat dry, my eyes squeezing shut. The devil doesn't like that.

"Look at me," he commands, his voice gruff.

I do, and then I drown in the blue of his gaze and the dark tumult of emotions swirling inside it. He's a confusing mixture of darkness and light, my Lucifer. I can taste every bitter dose of rage and hatred he carries. The other flavors are harder to decipher. Lust...maybe. And something else, something more potent than the rest—the very thing that drives him to rear back onto his knees, his eyes finding mine and boring deep.

"Touch yourself...like before." His voice is so gritty that a part of me chafes against it.

But, like a good puppet, my hand's already twitching to obey. He watches my trembling fingers creep down my belly. He waits...and then he observes the way my fingers ease against the flesh dominated by his still penetrating thumb. I'm not brave enough to join him there and expand the burning fullness. I find that tender piece of me instead and I rub...swirl...twist. My body knows what it wants, and my hips arch violently, jarring my hand against his. Whether as a result of the jolting contact or of his own volition, he's pressing harder. Deeper.

"Fuck." My teeth clip over the curse. It's the language he taught me the same way Vinny forced me to learn English: through example. Maybe my pronunciation is off, because Lucifer's eyes narrow further.

He jerks his wrist, increasing the pressure...

Fuck. Fuck. Fuck.

My own fingers are pathetic emulators. The things he does. The way he moves. You can't learn that kind of predatory domination. He makes me try, however, and when my hand slows, he stops generating any friction.

"Touch," he growls, and he doesn't touch me again until I do.

It's a slow, agonizing climb. Slow because he wants it to be. Agonizing because it's not my pleasure he's after. It's merely his own curiosity he seeks to fulfill. How far can he push the "little bitch" before her spine jerks against the bed and her hips twist, seeking out the brutal contact only his fingers can deliver? How long before she starts to moan despite the way she attempts to seal her mouth shut by digging her teeth into her lower lip? How long before she stops suffering his half-assed thrusting and makes him give it to her...

Hot, fierce, brutal, violent things. *Everything.*

He grits out something unintelligible, shoving another finger alongside his thumb, and thrusts them both so hard the motion pushes me toward the middle of the bed. His knuckles pop when he twists them inside me and makes my vision flood with sparks of blue and white. I go limp beneath the assault. I stop breathing. I stop thinking. I stop fighting.

My injured hand flies down to slam into his shoulder while my lips move of their own accord, issuing insane demands no woman in her right mind would ever ask of a beast.

"More... Mouth... *M-more.*"

His tongue shoots out, wetting his lips as they contort into something gruesome that might be a smile on a human man. On him, it's the snarl of a wolf. That last savoring glance of a beast before it sinks its teeth into his prey and rips it apart.

There's already a scream rising up my throat before he even breaks my grip over his wrist and lowers his head. I feel heat. Wet. Fire. Pain. Friction. Need. A million different sensations clash through my system, overloading my senses and crashing through what little defenses remained during Vinny's cruel reign. He fucks me harder with his mouth than he ever could with his cock. This is his true weapon of choice: gnashing teeth and raking fingernails; the harsh, flat surface of his tongue; the pistoning force only broad shoulders and a thick neck can deliver.

I never stop crying out. Long after my voice breaks and my throat is rubbed raw, moans still trickle out of me, wrung out with every searching thrust and ravenous suck. *Eat out.* I heard one of Vinny's men use that phrase once when he described all the demeaning things he'd never do to please a woman. "I won't eat a bitch out," he declared. It's almost hilarious how that term comes to me now.

Lucifer *devours* me, swallowing down every last aching, desolate drop. He takes me to that hazy, dark, quiet place where nothing else matters, and he holds me there, forcing a single malicious realization into my skin and ensuring that I feel the sting. This is what true pleasure is: an after-bite of pain. I won't ever feel it again delivered by anyone else but him. He makes sure I know it. Understand it. Admit it to myself. He holds me down by my waist and forces eye contact from over the ridge of my heaving belly until I do. Until the exact moment his name tears from my lips like the answer to the riddle even he isn't hateful enough to ask out loud.

Who do you really belong to, Daniela?

Who fought for you?

Bled for you?

Say it. Fucking say it.

"Dan...Dante!"

Only then does he draw his lips back against his gums and let me fall. The force of the release barrels into me and rips me to shreds. I lose minutes, and when I can see again, he's standing beside the mattress, stroking himself with the wadded-up rag he washed me with. His eyes scan my swollen, throbbing flesh, satisfied by the ravaged ruins of me he left behind. The sight finishes him off, and he comes again, grunting, into the washcloth.

I should feel degraded...I think as he drops the rag and shakes what little bit of his seed it didn't catch from his fingers. He's a predator leaving his mark near the carcass of the meal he's not quite finished consuming yet. When he leaves, walking into the hallway, I glance down, my gaze drifting over my damp curls and spread legs, then down to the floor where his lust taints the carpet and sets the air on fire.

I stare. I can't take my eyes off that pathetic piece of cloth. I can't stop myself from running my tongue over my sore, cracked lips and tasting him.

CHAPTER TWENTY-SIX

Dante

When I kill her, I'll make it slow. I'll grind my fingers into her windpipe and feel her vocal cords strain. Maybe I'll fuck her when I do it, wrapping my hands around her throat right when she begins to come. I'll cut off that high-pitched whine mid-song. I'll choke her out before she can say my name.

After all, I have a promise to keep.

The vicious method is one I make to myself as I rinse her taste from my mouth with handfuls of water from the bathroom sink. To completely erase it, I have to use the bar of soap on the counter, grinding the substance into my teeth. I spit her out only to breathe her back in; her scent fucking clings to my skin.

When I meet the gaze of my reflection, I can almost see her there, those hazel eyes wide and demanding. She's so hungry for the violence she believes only a man like me can give her. Violation. Destruction. Mutilation. She relishes every single mark carved or beaten into her skin; she'll wear the scars like medals for the benefit of her fiancé. Hell, she'd string herself up in the middle of the fucking city, bloodied and broken, just to get a rise out of him. Make him suffer. Pay.

The fucker has driven the soul out of her. Even when she cries out my name while being fucked...I'm not the one she's imagining. My cock isn't what gets her off. It's the simple fact that she's giving away what the bastard can't have.

And that shouldn't fucking matter. Mack. His plans. Avenging Parish. Arno and his fucking imaginary gang war. *That* is the shit that matters. I splash a handful of water onto my face as if the sting can drill it into my fucking brain and erase everything else.

And it does. I'm blank. Cold. It's the same icy cool I used to feel right before I stepped into the cage. I am an animal, entitled to nothing and owned by no one—certainly not some little bitch who got off on another man's humiliation.

"Focus," I growl and slam a fist onto the counter hard enough to jar the sore bones and shredded skin. The creature staring back at me from the mirror narrows his eyes in determination. He is done beating around the fucking bush.

The steely mindset steers me back into that room, where I ignore the woman still slumped on the bed, and I reach for the duffel bag Darcy sent. She picked out two shirts for me, but they don't feel like Mack's. I don't sense his stench tainting the cotton, either. They're worn. Familiar. I finger the frayed edges of one of the sleeves, and the truth hits me like a punch to the stomach.

She saved them—those old clothes worn by a punk who spent most of his free time shooting up or fighting over scraps in the cage. Dino had given him a room above the pit. Even on his nights off, he could still hear the men beating the shit out of each other down below. Five years ago, when everything went to shit, Darcy must have snuck into that little room and rummaged through what little shit the poor bastard had, salvaging three T-shirts.

I slip one over my head, refusing to give in to the rush of fucking nostalgia. The shit still fits, though it's tight, stretched taut over the muscles I've built up in prison. Gritting my teeth, I find my jeans and wrench them on.

"Get dressed," I tell her, making my voice hard. I enter the living room and wait for her, unsurprised when, five minutes later, she appears, creeping into the kitchen to fish her jeans from the floor, and...

She decided against the now bloodstained white blouse, She's wearing one of my shirts instead. It's a gray one, tethered to a few old memories that surge forward like the images of a slideshow. It's *the* shirt. I don't know how Darcy got ahold of it—she must have tried washing it, but even bleach couldn't get out the bloodstains near the bottom hem; they cling to the weathered cotton, shades darker than the rest of the fabric.

I try blinking to erase them and wind up seeing red. "Take it off. Now!"

The woman flinches at the harshness of my tone, but she obeys without question, stripping the shirt over her head and leaving her breasts bare. Vincent Stacatto's name shields her just as well as any shirt though. The indigo letters form a crystal-fucking-clear reminder: She's untouchable. *His.*

A part of me wonders if I should just leave her like this. Arno or Mack wouldn't dare fucking challenge her motives then. Loyalty isn't something that can be driven into flesh. To prove it, she holds her head high while I eye the edges of her mark and doesn't flinch. She doesn't try to hide the damage done to her. Her armor may be different from mine, but she wears it all the same.

Without a word, I pull the black shirt off and toss it in her direction. She tries to catch it, but it lands at her feet, and she has to stoop for it.

"Put it on."

She does and watches while I shove my feet into my boots and jerk my chin toward the blue tennis shoes Darcy gave her. She's silent as she follows me out of the apartment and down to the lower level of the garage.

Speak of the devil, Mack's already waiting down below. He's standing with his hand resting on the handles of a parked motorcycle. Darcy's leaning against the wall, coincidentally a few feet between us. She eyes me carefully, scanning my bare chest and the scars that cross it. Then she spots the woman behind Mack and he speaks up before I can analyze her expression.

"I've thought it over, Kitty," he says. He hasn't changed—blood still covers his gray shirt—but he's schooled his face into an expression I recognize from the old days. It's the same one he wore in the cage: a warrior ready for battle, ignoring everything else for the sake of the fight. For now. "We'll do things your way...but with *my* expertise."

I glance at the woman. She's standing near the stairs, her hair hanging limp and wild down to her waist. Her eyes are downcast, but I'm not fooled by the demure act. She's listening to every word Mack's saying. In her pocket, I make out the shape of that knife—she must have grabbed it on her way out. Not only that, but she keeps her hands at her sides, and she's positioned herself closest to the nearest exit, just in case Mack comes for her again. The little lamb's learning fast.

"How?" I demand, turning to Mack.

He watches me carefully. There's that foxy gleam in his eye that I hate. He's scheming. He's plotting. "Your plan is fine in theory, Kitty," he explains. "But there's one small problem. Vinny keeps his girls in at least ten enclaves all over the city. To really hit him where it hurts...you'd have to find a way to target every single enclave at once. Or at least make a threat large enough that he's forced to move as many of the women as he can. Then we make our mark and pick them up, hand-delivered." He smiles coldly. "The only problem is that no one knows the specific locations of *said* enclaves..."

"But I'm guessing that you have an idea," I say, taking a shot in the fucking dark.

Mack smiles wider. "I know a guy. He'll tell us the locations. For a price."

"And what is that?" Somehow, I know the answer even before he jerks his chin toward Stacatto's woman.

"Her." He beckons her forward with a crook of his finger and a malicious expression.

She's cautious, but she steps closer, wincing. My mind immediately goes beneath her jeans to the raw skin of her cunt underneath. She feels me with every move she makes. I've left my mark in bruised, sore flesh, far away from that fucking tattoo.

"This...associate wants to make another video staring Stacatto's little bitch. He'll need insurance, you see, for when Vinny's kingdom crumbles right out from underneath the bastard. If you agree, we can do it tonight."

"No." The word tears from my throat at the same moment Stacatto's whore steps forward even more, her chin pointed to the ceiling.

"I'll do it."

Black. It's a more jarring change to my vision than the red. I can't see anything. I can only hear: my heartbeat, the blood rushing through my veins, and the distant hum of Mack's satisfied chuckle. I can even hear her standing there, her movements stiff due to her sore, abused pussy. For five seconds, my sense of hearing is the only thing that tethers me to the present before my vision returns in bits and pieces. I see Mack first, his eyes gleaming. Then I see Darcy, her gray eyes narrowed as they flit from me to Mack and back again. And *her*, Vinny Stacatto's pretty little whore. She's watching me, her expression unreadable.

"No." I turn to Mack, who's still sporting that cocky-ass grin. It widens, and suddenly, the smile is more of a wolf's snarl than anything remotely human. "You whore her out on the off chance of what? That your 'associate' might gather enough balls to take on Vincent Stacatto?"

"I'll do it." She makes her voice loud enough to counter mine.

The black returns, creeping along the edges of the room, covering Darcy in shadow and swallowing Mack. All I can fucking see is her, those hazel eyes gleaming as she pictures yet another way to screw over her beloved "Vinny."

"I'll get the information."

"You'll spread your legs," Mack clarifies, just to hammer the point home, but he isn't satisfied by her blank expression. He'd prefer that she squirm, but she merely stands there, a pitiful excuse for a sacrifice.

"I said *no*." For the first time, the protest actually seems to fucking resonate.

The girl stiffens, and Mack... The bastard practically chuckles with glee.

"Not your call, Dante," he says. "You're outnumbered."

Outnumbered. Vinny's whore is the deciding vote in her own goddamn fate, and I shouldn't care. I don't...

"No," I spit through clenched teeth. "We find a different way. How the fuck do I know that you won't have your 'client' disappear with her afterward?"

It's a prospect that even Mack can't deny with a straight face. I'm sure he's thought about it. Money and benefit are all he sees when he looks at her—and maybe a hot piece of ass, not that he'd admit as much around Darcy.

I know fuckers like him inside and out. Hell, I *am* one. A mad dog always plays both sides of the fence.

"Fine," he concedes, eyes narrowed. "You could send one of Arno's men with her—"

"No. Him." Once again, the woman breaks her role by speaking up. She's suddenly at my shoulder, her scent teasing the air, her hair swishing against her lower back. "*He* comes with me." She even points one slender finger in my direction.

I can't smother a laugh. I'm her guard dog, apparently. The convenient mutt she fucks whenever she needs a fresh dose of pain to reinforce the fact that she's away from a man she seems to fear more than death itself. The cut on her palm is a leash, and she flexes the wounded hand as if subconsciously giving that tether a little tug. *Heel, Dante.*

I turn on that fucking heel and head for the door. "Send her alone." I don't give a fuck if Mack strings her up for his own gain. I don't care if she's fucked on camera by a million sweaty businessmen with bones to pick with Stacatto. Let the little junkie get her fix.

She's high off the danger, apparently, and I was such a fucking fool for thinking that the heroin could even faze her. When revenge was your drug of choice, nothing was more addictive than the steady drip of your own self-destruction.

But she doesn't like that course of action, and her gasp stops me in my tracks. There's confusion in that damn sound. Even more amusing, there's *fear* in it. For all of her bravado, she can't jump into hell by herself, apparently. She needs an escort. She needs *me.*

"I'm fine with that plan," Mack says. "We'll leave now. This guy gets antsy after sundown. Pissing off Stacatto has left him with very few...friends, if you catch my drift."

Through a window straight ahead, I can see that the sky is already gray, the sun sinking below the horizon is a fiery kiss-off. It'll be a new moon tonight; there's no sign of it waiting in the wings to take the sun's place. It's a perfect setting to pick the kingdom of a mob boss apart. Some sick bastard might even deem it "poetic."

And Stacatto's beloved little whore is ready and willing to drive the final nail into his coffin. She even wants me to hold her hand while she does it.

"I'll take good care of her," Mack promises, and I can sense the smirk he's wearing without even having to turn and see it for myself. "I'll even give her another taste of the good stuff to make sure she's a happy camper."

I don't know why I look over my shoulder at her. Her back is turned to me, her posture perfectly erect. You could balance a book on her head—she's that stiff. Does it faze her at all that she's signing her freedom and sanity over to Mack as easily as most people decide what to wear in the morning? There's no care in it. No finesse. Hell, to a criminal, her lack of tact is fucking insulting.

"Wait." I turn, and in two steps, I have a good grip on her shoulder. She can't fight it when I drag her two steps back merely to throw her off-balance and watch her stagger to regain her poise. "I go with her. We get the information, and then what? You gladly march in and lead an assault on Stacatto's enclaves?"

Mack reaches up to flick something imaginary from his chin. "Don't be hasty, Dante," he says. "All in good time. First things first."

First things first. I glance at the woman from the corner of my eye. *Danny,* she said her name was. I'd expected something complicated or foreign in the few seconds I felt bored enough to wonder. *Felecia. Anastasia. Dolores.*

Danny is too fucking simple. It's a crown of weeds and thorns for this prissy, stolen queen.

"Fine," I say. Then I shove her toward the door and leave Mack to follow. "Let's go."

CHAPTER TWENTY-SEVEN

Daniela

THEY TAKE ME TO A HOTEL, AND IT'S THE IRONY TO end all ironies; for five years, my prison was hidden inside of a hotel. To find my freedom, I have to delve into another —with a monster at my side—all while wearing a black corset hidden underneath a long coat.

"Look pretty," Mack snarled before pressing the clothes into my hands and shoving me into the back of a van while Dante rode shotgun.

Pretty. It was Vinny's favorite word, but would he apply it to me now? The concierge who pretends not to notice me entering the lobby doesn't seem liable to. He averts his gaze with a practice that I figure this particular establishment has trained its employees to perfect.

Lavish wealth drapes everything from the polished marble floors to the shining oak-paneled walls with gold filigree.

Once you take the elevator up to floor thirty-seven, however, that extravagant atmosphere gives way to a simpler layout of black carpeting and forest-green walls. It's dark. Discreet. It's the perfect place for a man to have a half-naked woman delivered to his door just as easily as he might order a bottle of wine.

I inhale sharply as we turn the corner in search of suite number eighty-eight. Dante's silent beside me, and I know without even having to look at his face that he doesn't appreciate my bold little sacrifice. In the same breath, it doesn't faze him. He'll stand by the door and wait patiently while I fuck another man for coveted information. He'll let someone else leave their mark on my ruined flesh, and he won't give a damn.

It's a dizzying thought. I have to brace one hand against my chest to keep my heart there, neatly in place. Something firm nudges my fingers, and I pretend that it's one of the ribs of my corset so that my face gives nothing away.

These men treat heroin like candy. They dole it out in prefilled syringes with neat, clear caps and seem almost too eager to jab the poison into your veins to send you off to Neverland. The moment the van pulled up to the hotel, Mack couldn't wait to yank a syringe from his pocket and free the needle.

"Now be a good girl and hold still," he warned before reaching for me from the driver's seat while Lucifer watched.

Like a patient lamb, I waited until right before he could jab the tip into my vein. "Not there," I protested.

After all, we wouldn't want the buyer to know that his little bit of collateral wasn't fully present, now would we? How could he make her scream for Vinny's benefit? I knew of other discreet places. My legs maybe? When Mack seemed more than willing to jab his needle there as well, I asked to do it myself. Rolling his eyes, he gaze me the syringe, and I brought it to my thigh, hissing on cue at the burning pinch.

Only God knows why he didn't asked for the syringe back —maybe, for the first time in five years, Lucifer's vengeful maker was finally on my side? He's gotten me this far, after all—a room at the very end of a long hallway, where a balding man in a two-sizes-too-small three-piece suit opens the door with a grin.

Mack's buyer is at least fifty, with a bulging gut and graying black hair styled carefully around that crowning bald spot. "You wait outside," he tells Dante before ushering me inside with a hearty chuckle.

Shock nearly roots me to the floor, and I have to swallow it down before I can move. I expected some faceless monster. Some stranger. But...I *know* this man. I met him just once before at a dinner Vinny hosted in a lavish restaurant downtown. It was one of the few times he brought me along to his business meetings, and I was suffocating in a red dress with a collar that choked my throat and reinforced his possession.

There were two other men there, and they all spoke in code about "kittens" that needed "new homes" and were eager and willing to be placed for "adoption." One of the men had a funny-sounding name. Don something. *Donahugh.* He spent most of the night looking at me with long, searching glances that barely disguised the lust lurking within them. Vinny punished me brutally for that. How dare I catch another man's gaze—was I a lady or a whore?

The current turn of events is enough to make me snicker as I stagger into a wide suite decorated with elegant, sleek furniture. A few leather couches frame a breathtaking view of the bay. It's a cozy yet secluded atmosphere that seems the perfect backdrop to be captured by the camera set on a tripod in the corner of the room.

"Mack said no directors," Donahugh scoffs as he waddles over to the camera and flips a switch that I assume turns it on. "But he promised that you'll be a good little girl. Isn't that right?"

He returns to me and runs a meaty finger along my chin while I, like "a good little girl," obediently shed my coat, revealing the outfit underneath.

Beady eyes home in on my cleavage, and his cock practically bulges against his already constricting pants. He's so different in his lust than Lucifer or even Vinny. He's greedy and eager to fuck his pretty little toy. It doesn't matter to him if her eyes are dead and she's already battered; he's too damn busy trying to pull his pants down one-handed while he steers her to a leather chaise with the other.

"Lean down," he tells me, his breath heavy on the back of my neck.

I obey, bracing both hands flat against the leather while he tugs at the back of my corset and unhooks the clasps within seconds. My hands fly to my chest once the garment comes undone as if to preserve what little modesty I have left.

Donahugh is not impressed. "Don't be shy now, you little slut," he growls into my good ear. "I saw the video you made. We'll make a better one, eh? I'll let you ride me too—"

It's hard to manipulate a syringe with one hand. The movies make it look so easy, but once you turn and jab the needle into a man's shoulder, it takes more pressure to apply to the plunger than you'd expect. The muscles resist the poison; it won't go in.

"What the fuck?" Donahugh bats my hand away, leaving the needle sticking out of his skin, the syringe still filled with heroin.

I have to throw myself at him and brace one hand against his meaty neck, but it still isn't enough. He shoves me off, the needle comes free, and I only have seconds to aim for a new spot and jab my thumb on the end of the syringe. His hand flies to his neck, trying to snatch the needle out, but this part of him accepts the liquid easier. He's already losing his balance as he starts to chase me across the room. I hit my hip off a leather sofa and collapse on top of it just as he manages to wrestle a cell phone from his pocket.

"You fucking little cunt..." He fiddles with the screen, but his fingers are too sloppy. He can't even get past the lock screen. He comes for me instead but hits the floor on his knees just feet away.

I watch him, panting. Shaking. Shocked. The success of this mad plan is a variable I can't bother to assess right now.

Mack wanted information. He'll get it someway. Somehow.

On my terms.

I try to hammer that point in. *My* terms. I agreed to his plan for me: to prove something to that insane hole in my chest Lucifer has rubbed open and ground salt inside. I wouldn't let him own me unwillingly. I won't become his burden.

So I lied. I took initiative. I dragged him along with me without so much as a solid plan. I was reckless. I am *insane.*

Donahugh seems to agree as he looks up at me with glassy, marble eyes. He can't quite get them to focus, and maybe now I understand why Dante fought so hard to keep me anchored to *something* while I was high—even to him. Donahugh's far gone, at war with his own body. The hate alone isn't strong enough. His fat lips are already fighting a stupefied smile as the heat consumes every bit of him in hungry little bites.

He doesn't react when I slip my foot from the edge of the couch and kick him with it, but it's not a very hard blow, to be fair—so I try again. This time, when my toes connect with his bulging stomach, he groans.

The poor man managed to get his pants halfway down, revealing the hairy tops of his legs and the part of him straining against a pair of white underwear.

Now what, Daniela? My fingers shake when I brace them on either side of me and dig into the leather. *Vinny. Girls. Locations.* I let those three things rise up and dissolve the revulsion at what I'll have to do. I'm going to do it. I can. I will. I...

I feel heavy when I stand and stagger toward my discarded corset. Fear, pain, and anger are their own potent opiate. They take me away to some dark inner place inside my fractured soul as I carefully extract the small kitchen knife I managed to hide within the lacy lining.

It's a familiar weight against my palm, heavy and already primed with the taste of blood. Sammy's. Mine. Lucifer's. I can use it to draw more. I'm ready. I'm able to look past the demented insanity of what I've done...and of what I *will* do.

I can.

The world begins to sway when I turn back to Donahugh. My vision blurs and tears slip down when I try to blink. I don't know if it's fear of Vinny, of Mack, or of *myself* that drives them to escape.

Donahugh tries to talk when I take a step toward him. His head lolls and a stream of drool dribbles down his lip, speckling his cleanly shaven chin. I keep walking. I size him up the way Lucifer scrutinized me, deciding within a second which place to strike in order to cause the most damage.

Lucifer chose my heart, driving himself into the fragile organ like a nail. I choose Donahugh's meaty left fist when I stoop down and drag the blade of my knife across the tops of his outstretched fingers. It's not hard enough to break the skin, merely a little taste to make him flinch.

The next cut does the trick, however: a tiny nick in the flesh that draws forth a ruby smear of fresh blood. At the sight of it, memories flood back, hemorrhaging beneath my skull.

Play, Vinny told me once as he crept into my room at night. He woke me up and made me sit groggily on the edge of my bed, with my cello between my legs and my bow in hand. Then he stripped down to nothing but his boxers and stuck his hand inside them. *Play.*

He watched me while I performed, stroking himself—but it wasn't the cadence of the music or the quick, precise movements of my fingers that made his pleasure creep higher. Oh, no. It was my mistakes. With every one, his eyes would flash an alarming shade of amber that always made me tighten up in anticipation of a blow.

The worst part came once he took the boxers off, freeing his cock. I made the most mistakes then, and he would count each one out loud as they occurred. Classical music was always one of his passions, but he studied it to the point of obsession once I moved in. For *me,* he claimed. He knew the exact note of every concerto, solo, or suite I played. He memorized every variation of the tune down to the last detail if only to know when and how I made a mistake.

At the end of my little performance, he would tally up my flaws and recite them like a spoken-word poem to accompany my song. *Wrong key. Too short. Very sloppy, Daniela. Sloppy.*

After that, he'd finish himself off, grunting into his palm, and stain my floor with the evidence. Once he left, I'd crawl back into bed more worn-down than I felt after his beatings.

It was the one punishment he didn't feel the need to explain fully, but I eventually figured out its purpose. He relished watching me cling to the only outlet I had from him. The one thing that rivaled my fear and loyalty to my dearest "friend." The one thing that had almost taken me away from him.

He could make me play, and he could force me to relive everything he'd done to my life over and over...and make sure I suffered for daring to choose anything over him.

If he were here, he'd find a new game to take pleasure in. A new way to watch me struggle to keep my head above the insanity. *Play, Daniela*, he'd tell me while I scan Donahugh's arms and legs. *Play. Cut. Put on a good show, Mi Bella.*

"Where are the girls?" My own voice, bitter and husky, is enough to counter Vinny for now. I can still sense him lingering within the corners of the room, but as long as I focus, he can't quite reach me. "Where?"

I try to make my tone slow and soft, like honey. In a way, I think I'm trying to imitate the same way Lucifer spoke to me while I was high—dribbling each word into my ear like carefully dosed medication.

Donahugh doesn't appreciate the tact. "Stupid...bitch... String you up...little cunt."

He breaks off when my knife connects with the back of his hand and more blood bubbles up. I don't remember flicking my wrist—making a sawing motion with the blade—but the wound is deeper this time. I think it actually hurts and pain overpowers the pleasure delivered by the heroin. Donahugh cries out.

"The girls," I insist, making my voice a little louder. It's a stupid mistake considering that I don't know if he has thugs lurking nearby. Though, if he really did manage to get on the wrong side of Vinny, then there are bound to be at least some bodyguards waiting to help him from the shadows.

I should be more careful. I definitely shouldn't cut him *again*, badly enough that he howls. His hand is painted by a steady stream of red now, but he still won't talk.

And I am a fool. I laugh at the depth of my own insanity while I rock back onto my heels and balance my weight on my knees. Silly little Lynn. In four days, she's become a whore, a captive, and now a torturer. She's not even sure which hat she likes wearing more. For so long, Vinny's designed her wardrobe, deciding with sole authority which woman she was allowed to be that day.

My knife is a cherished new accessory, more beautiful than any designer shawl or priceless ring. I wield it inexpertly—

I'm not used to owning my own things, after all. Maybe it's this newfound freedom that makes me feel so strange when I start to cut the man again, earning myself yet another anguished grunt and a stream of disjointed curses. It's madness...this heady rush of emotion that floods my head and makes it detach from my body. Maybe this is why Vinny loves playing with his toys so much, using them to carve and rip pieces out of his victims.

Madness is catching.

I'm not just hurting Donahugh when I form a fist and slam it down against his chest. I'm hurting Vinny. My fist carries the weight of all of those girls trapped under his thumb. "Where are they? Tell me."

Donahugh tries to shake his head, but he can only manage to roll to one cheek, his eyes mocking. "Dumb...bitch," he chuckles at me. "Fuck yourself."

During moments like this, Vinny could show the most restraint as he toyed with his victims. He relished in their insults, drawing out the worst bits of his plan until the moment the poor fool believed they still had control. He certainly wouldn't slap Donahugh with the flat side of his knife, leaving a dark bruise across his perfectly groomed face.

"Where?"

He grunts at the pain, his eyes narrowed in hatred, but he brushes me off. I'm nothing more than a foolish little whore. He'll bide his time until the drug wears off and he can call for backup. Then he'll string me up, as promised, and fuck me "pretty" for the camera. If I'm lucky, he'll send me back to Mack in pieces.

It's like I can read the bastard's mind, and I snicker at what I find there. Maybe he's correct. I don't have the guts to butcher him the way Vinny would. I don't have the strength. Lynn needs to discover her own method of attack. She needs... She needs *help*.

I stumble when I stand upright and head for the door to the suite. It's only when cool air tickles my bare breasts that I realize I'm only wearing the lacy, black bottoms that match the corset.

Dante's face, once I get the door open and stick my head through the gap, is uncharacteristically stoic. Lucifer always displays one emotion, even if it's rage. Now, his eyes are blank, his jaw is stone, and there's no hint of recognition when he sees me. It's only when his eyes sweep over my breasts and Vinny's brand that some hint of life flickers across his expression. His gaze is on fire again, smoldering for merely a second. His fingers flex as if aching to cover me —how dare I display myself to anyone but him. Then again, he might be merely reacting to the fingerprints he left around my neck. Lucifer may have a different idea of modesty than Vinny with his high collars and delicate satins —this beast displays his ownership in the bold confidence it takes to let her walk around with nothing but the knowledge that he owns her hidden beneath her skin.

He *owns* me. That simple fact snaps me back from the brink, and the knife falls from my fingers to clatter across the floor. It's only now that he seems to finally notice the man in the process of crawling across the floor behind me.

"Shit." He utters the curse quietly as he forces his way inside and manages to get the door shut with only one hand. He grabs for me with the other, using the contact to steer me forward.

"He won't talk," I croak by way of explanation. I sound so disappointed. My messy little experiment failed. Donahugh isn't quite so willing to divulge the information on my terms. "I *need* him to talk."

Lucifer looks at me, and if someone were to give me every single shade of blue in existence, I still wouldn't be able to recreate the color of his eyes. They flicker with a million nuanced shades as his gaze travels slowly from me to poor Donahugh, whose pants have bunched up around his ankles, and he spends more time than I would expect eyeing the man's partially bared ass. His grip tightens. Electricity prickles from him, and with one gruffly uttered statement, my devil sets the entire room on fire.

"Did...did you fuck him?"

I blink, confused. He asks a million questions at once with those four words. *Did you fuck him? How? Did you like it? Would you do it again? Did you fuck? Fuck, did you FUCK?*

Once again, I'm struck by the differences his web of possession holds from Vinny's. When the former accused me, even with his eyes, of being a whore, I accepted the assessment without question. If a man could find pleasure in my form even when I was wearing a turtleneck, then it *was* my fault. Vinny's shackles were a constant restraint I always needed to adjust. Sometimes, inside my head, I might forget him. I might play the cello for a minute too long, and while the tune still lingered, I could pretend. Vinny never truly owned me; therefore, his paranoia was expected. Endured, even.

Lucifer is different. His possession is something I don't have to think about in order to *feel*. He fought for me. He owns me—whether he wants to or not.

"Did you *want* me to?"

He doesn't seem to understand the question. His jaw clenches. His nails dig into the flesh of my arm, though he doesn't even seem to realize it. Slowly, he maneuvers me to stand in front of him, forcing direct eye contact. I can feel the heat of his breath all the way to my toes when he leans in, our noses brushing, every word carefully clipped and uttered with control.

"Did. You. Fuck. Him?"

"Did...did you want me to?"

I'm unprepared for the brutality with which he shoves me backward. I wind up sprawled on the couch, slouching down, my toes braced against the polished wood floor.

Lucifer advances on me like a wolf, primal and cold. There's a predatory grace in how he leans over me, his eyes on my throat, his hands braced against the back of the couch on either side of me, caging me in. But he's an odd predator,

I'm starting to realize. He always asks for permission from his prey before sinking his teeth into their flesh. It's been that way throughout, I think, as one of his hands shifts away from the leather upholstery and then drifts down to my throat. He hovers there, the fingers twitching...but it's only when I tilt my head back that he finally curls them around my neck. I don't even think he notices that brief moment of hesitation. Maybe it's something that only matters to me. Vinny never asked for permission to enter the cage he built around me.

"Did you?" The question comes softer this time, directed solely at the lacy, black panties that shield me from his gaze. His hand lowers, the stained gauze wrapped around his wounds clashing against the ebony fabric. Once again, he waits until my legs part for him before seizing the waistband and sliding his fingers underneath.

My reply rides a jagged gasp as he trails his touch over aching flesh. "Did...d-did you *want* me to?"

He frowns, sliding a finger inside me, but if he finds me wet and gaping...it's from him. I'm still suffering from this morning. I didn't wash. I didn't erase his scent from my skin. I can feel his teeth if I walk too fast. I still feel the broadness of his tongue.

Lucifer tests me carefully anyway, easing his thumb through those inner parts of me only he knows how to navigate. He takes his time, seeking out any sign of another predator in his den. Any bite marks he didn't make. Any scent apart from his own.

When he doesn't find it, he slowly withdraws, though he can't seem to stop himself from bringing his hand to his mouth, snatching my taste from his fingers with his tongue, just to be sure. A pitiful whine breaks loose from between my lips. He thinks it's out of pain and he recoils, dragging his hand from his lips, his eyes dark.

My own mouth twitches, aching to throw out more questions than I have the energy to ask. Did he *want* me to go along with Mack's plans and "fuck" someone like Donahugh? Did he expect me to? While Lucifer differs from Vinny in some ways, I would have thought that all monsters were united in the terms of their possession. They didn't like to share their toys. Is Lucifer a different breed?

Looking at him, I can't be sure. He's tasted my answer, but he's not benevolent enough to reveal whether it satisfies him or not. And, suddenly, I need to know. Curiosity burns a trail through my body and makes me bold in a way I never could have been around Vinny.

"Did you *want* me to fuck him?"

Lucifer flinches. His gaze drifts down to his hand, the fingers glistening. He makes me wait for forty-four seconds before finally giving me an answer. "No." His frown deepens as he removes his free hand from my neck and catches the bottom of my chin with the pads of his fingers. He tilts my head back, forcing my gaze to meet his again.

I can't read the emotion I find lurking there. A part of me really doesn't want to. Mystery and Lucifer go hand in hand anyway.

"No," he says. "I didn't."

I should leave it at that. He didn't want me to be used by Donahugh, not even to further his own plan. A good captive might take some kind of comfort in that. I think, deep down...I'm insulted.

Lucifer doesn't react when I reach for his hand with one of my own—but it's a trained sort of stillness. He's the cautious wolf who learned not to pounce at the slightest movement, but he watches me warily, his fangs at the ready. One wrong move and he won't hesitate to kill me.

I'm careful as I grip his wrist and raise his hand to my lips. I smell hell on his fingers. Blood and violence and sex and need and...*me*. He watches me with a question in his eyes as I use my other hand to ease his thumb away from the rest. I aim it toward my mouth like a bull's-eye and let my tongue shoot out to lick the damp tip. He stiffens, but if I'm not mistaken, his thumb jerks, and suddenly, more of it is between my lips, seeking my tongue out. We're a sordid, acquired taste—his blood and my essence mingled together.

Maintaining eye contact, I swipe my tongue along his thumb again, a little bit more greedily than the first time. A man owned by no one makes his promises in blood. A woman devoid of any possessions makes hers with *this*: sweat and liquid lust. It's all I have left to offer him...

But my loyalty is a gift not even Vinny could possess—at least not since the morning he made me wake up an orphan. Lucifer accepts it without any hint of acknowledgment. He merely pulls his hand away. The moment is broken when he turns, spotting Donahugh, who's cackling on the floor. He watched our entire little exchange. Grinning, he winks at me.

"I tried to make him talk," I say, my voice rough. "He wouldn't."

Only now does Lucifer seem to comprehend what I mean. His gaze slowly roves over to the empty syringe resting a few feet away, and I can almost hear him putting the pieces together in his mind. Once they click, the grin he flashes is wicked. All teeth and curled lips.

"You volunteered to *get* the information," he says as if he only now understands the literal interpretation of those words: I never told Mack I'd sleep with the man. Lucifer's amusement is gradually replaced by something else that makes his eyes gleam. He holds his hand out, flexing the fingers expectantly. "Get the knife."

I hasten to obey, crossing the room and bending down to fish my weapon from the floor. Donahugh finally has the nerve to look afraid when I approach Dante and place the blade on his empty palm.

"Make sure the doors are locked," Dante tells me, his voice cold.

Once again, I do so without question. I test the latch on the door to the suite and tug once just to make sure.

"It's locked," I call back.

"Good." He jerks his head and waits until I appear dutifully at his shoulder. He stands tall, holding the knife loosely within the fingers of his left hand—the same one that sports my cut. He makes sure Donahugh sees him clearly—the darkness in his eyes—but he doesn't react when I take a step forward and sink down into a crouch, allowing the poor man to make eye contact with me instead. This is *my* game, and like any good participant, the devil is willing to let me go first.

"Where are the girls?" I ask while my hands reach for the buttons of his shirt. I undo them swiftly, freeing a chest covered in greasy, graying black hair. Biting back disgust, I run my finger along his sternum as if imagining the perfect place to cut and I dig my nail in hard enough to make him flinch. Then I glance back at Dante and attempt to mimic the devil's low, steady tone. "Tell us where they are. Every last one."

CHAPTER TWENTY-EIGHT

Dante

Stacatto's bitch is still a thrill-seeker, touching pointy objects with no idea as to what damage they might cause. It's easier if I believe that—easier if I ignore the practiced confidence she wields that knife with. Her beloved "Vinny" has molded her well. I don't think she even realizes just how much she enjoys the tendrils of fear she inspires in the prick lying beside her.

"Dante."

I clench my jaw at the way her accent caresses the syllables of my name; I liked it better when she didn't call me a damn thing.

"Would it hurt much if someone cut a man's cock off?"

Her tone counters the shock of hearing those words come out of that prissy little mouth. She doesn't sound like she's bluffing. She's thinking. She's curious. *Would it hurt?*

"Yeah," I grunt. "It might." Standing above her, I see the way she seizes her lower lip between her teeth, those hazel eyes thoughtful.

"Would it hurt more if you used a butter knife?" One of her hands slides down the man's beer gut, and two slim fingers dance over the hem of his tighty whities.

Even I have to flinch in sympathy. "Damn right, that would hurt." I flex the hand holding the knife. "It will be messy," I admit, though even I hear the excitement dripping through my tone.

The girl shrugs, her bare shoulders flashing like ivory in the light of a chandelier dangling from the ceiling. "I could find a towel." She starts to rise as if she's eager to do just that, and the man moans out a stream of words.

"Fuck...little bitch... Kill me... He'll kill..."

I frown, taking a step closer. I tower over him now, and he has to make himself cross-eyed just to avoid looking at me. "*He'll* kill you," I repeat, stressing that single word while I nudge his side with the toe of my boot. "You wouldn't mean Stacatto, now would you?"

The girl flinches, withdrawing her hand as if stung, and the bastard seems to realize that he said too much.

He shakes his head while sweat beads over his brow. "No...no..."

"And this little video," I add, making my voice as level as I can. "You wouldn't have been planning to take the girl for yourself after you were done...'directing' it, now were you?"

The sharp jerk of his chin gives me my answer. *Bingo*. Trust fucking Mack to walk right into a trap...and trust Vinny Stacatto's little princess to spring it. I don't know if it's admiration I feel when I glance over at her or just plain irritation; a wolf doesn't like to be out-foxed by his own prey. Though I was the one who voted against the damn plan in the first place. For all I knew, Stacatto could have had a legion waiting to rush in if this fucker didn't check in *with* the girl in tow. For a second, I inhale shadow and see red. I almost don't recognize the cool sensation that falls over my fingers until I glance down and see her hand there, gingerly brushing the one holding the knife.

Clarity comes back, but it's almost too sharp. Colors are brighter when she touches me. Her eyes are green and gold, swirling around two black holes. I shake my head, jerking my hand away. Then I raise the knife and eye the dull edge.

"Come here," I tell the girl, and she rises to her feet, taking a step toward me.

She doesn't fight when I pull her closer. Her bare back hits my chest, and my hands cage her in. I slip the one holding the knife beneath her arm and raise it, allowing her to clasp the back of it. Then I snatch up the fingers of her other hand, manipulating them one by one.

"Hold the knife like this," I tell her, showing her the proper grip—at least if she was going to enter the cage.

She copies me like an eager student, her fingers flying to the proper positions as I guide them there. Only then do I remember what she said about playing an instrument. *Cello.* I don't know too many musicians, but she has the hands of a dagger-thrower I met once, quick and slim. They're not fit for pounding and smashing the way mine are. She's a fluid little assassin, and I'm the animal.

"Hold it tight," I explain, showing her how. When I yank on the blade, she doesn't slack her grip and something that might be a smile tugs at my mouth. Once again, she proves to be a fast learner. "Now *when* you cut him—" I glance over and find that the bastard is watching every bit of this little lesson. "When you cut him, he'll fight a little, but once the blood loss sets in...well, it will be like carving a slice of birthday cake."

"Okay," she breathes out, but there's no ounce of disgust in her voice. She's memorizing every word, watching my fingers move with hers. "Cake."

"The first cut will be the trickiest," I explain, shifting closer so that I have a clear view over her shoulder. I flick my wrist sharply, slashing the blade through the air. "You need to get it in as deep as you can."

She nods and deftly pries the knife from my hand. She wields it just as well as any cage-fighter, pointing the blade at the sky. Then she jabs, ripping into her enemy. "Like that?" She sounds breathless. Eager. Ready.

I take a step back and steer her so that she's facing the man on the floor. "Like that," I tell her, my mouth near her ear. "But it will be messy."

I can't see the motion fully, but I...know she licks her lips. I can *feel* the wet slick of her tongue. I hear her throat work as she swallows. I sense her smile.

"That's okay."

My hands move to her shoulders, guiding her like a coach leading a boxer to the ring. We only manage to take a step closer before the man begins to thrash.

"All right! All rrright!" He practically bucks in an attempt to get away, and a stream of words and letters shoot from between his lips. It takes my brain a second to process what they are: addresses.

"Pen," I snap, scanning around for one.

The girl's already on it. She lunges across the room, grabs a customary pad and a pen from a desk, and scribbles until the man finally goes silent.

"Is he waiting for you?" I demand while the girl tears a page from the pad and crumples it in her fist. "Stacatto?"

The man grunts, shaking his head. "No... Gonna sell her."

"Ah, I see." I rub my chin as the fucker's plan becomes clear. "You were going to use her to try and weasel your way back into Stacatto's good graces. The video was your insurance."

The man says nothing as his eyes struggle to focus. The girl gave him Mack's best; he won't come off cloud nine for a long, long while. The true extent of his fuck-up won't even sink in until then.

I rove my gaze over to the camera. A red light's flashing. It's still recording. I don't take my eyes off it when I reach for her and jerk my chin toward the lens. "Say hello," I tell her. "Your fiancé is watching."

She stiffens. Her eyes delve into the camera, and I doubt that her entire soul fully comes back out. She takes a step forward without seeming to realize it as she processes my taunt. *Say hello.* She turns to me, and I see the knife slash through the air. I don't know why the hell I don't fight. Why I don't even flinch when the blade grazes my cheek as she hooks that same hand around the back of my head and draws me in. Her lips meet mine—that's what I know. Warm. Wet. Soft. I move against them solely out of fucking instinct.

Before my teeth come into play, that is.

Whatever this is…it's solely for *his* benefit. I tell myself that while I lash at her lips with my tongue. Pry them open. Shove my way inside. Bite her. Claim her. *Kiss-the-living-fuck* out of her.

It's for his benefit, but that doesn't mean I can't put on a damn good show. That I can't draw on her lower lip until she moans. Crush her to my chest with one hand against her spine and cradle her ass with the other.

Stacatto may be watching.

But that. Doesn't. Mean. Shit.

For five seconds, she's mine. I taste her. I own her. I make her bleed.

It's five fucking seconds I know she never gave to him.

And it's only five fucking seconds I have to save myself the same way I starved my veins of heroin and spent those first weeks writhing in agony while in the Pen. Withdrawing from her brings its own irritation, but I ignore it when I shove her back and wipe at my mouth with the back of my hand.

"You won't say a fucking thing." I direct the threat at the man on the floor and wait until he nods. "You say a word to Stacatto and I won't only show him this video"—I gesture to the camera with a wave of my hand—"but I'll find you. I'll bring her with me. And next time...I'll teach her how to cut a man's dick off using nail clippers. It's not very efficient, but I'm sure it's doable."

"Though messy," the girl pitches in, shaking her head. She sounds so deadpan that she could be serious—though, fuck it, maybe I am as well.

I'd take her with me to hunt the fucker down. I'd show her a brand-new way to inflict pain and watch her get off on yet another way to get back at Stacatto. It's more tempting a thought than I'd like to admit. I grit my teeth and curl my hands into fists, willing back the heat that creeps up them.

"Understand?" I demand of the man.

He nods again, and ignoring him, I spot the girl's clothes—or what little she wore in—across the room.

"Get dressed," I tell her. While she does, I head for the camera and rip it from the tripod. "How many men do you have?" I ask the man as the girl heads for the door.

A rich businessman with a hard-on for Stacatto, planning to kidnap the man's fiancé from an asshole like Mack on his own? *Bullshit.* No man would form a plan that fucking stupid without sufficient firepower.

When he doesn't answer, I take a step closer. Then I lift my boot and slam the sole of it down on his chest, applying just enough pressure to make him wheeze. "How many?"

Rather than speak, his beady eyes roll in the direction of a cell phone lying a few feet away. I reach for it and swipe my thumb across the home screen. Three text messages pop up, unopened and from a blocked number.

In the wings, says the first message.

Say the word, reads the second.

It's all shit code—the hallmark of a cheap mercenary, but the last message is a little more specific. *No answer, we come in. Ten minutes.* The time stamp says the message was sent eight minutes ago.

"Shit." I look at the girl and cut my eyes to the door. "We need to go."

But not without taking the trash out first. I grab the bastard by the sleeve of his suit and drag him to the first closet I find, barring the door with a chair.

Tucking his phone into my pocket, I brush past the woman and peer out into the hallway through the peephole. With one minute left, I open the door, dragging her out after me. I only have a split second to think before I throw my arm around her shoulders and pull her close. For appearances, a woman wearing a black trench coat and a man who might have a gun in his pocket may seem less threatening if they walk down the hall like two patrons of the hotel rather than criminals. In *theory.*

She wobbles on the heels Mack made her wear and has to hold her arm awkwardly against her chest to hide the knife in her hand. Somehow, we manage to make it to the lobby using the stairs. I don't catch sight of any mercenaries rushing past on our way out, either, not that we stick around to get a good fucking look.

Mack's still waiting in the van out front—at least the fucker hasn't run.

"How'd it go?" he asks without even craning his neck to look at the woman I'm shoving onto the back seat of the van.

The front seat is still open—his men chose to sit in the very next row, hunched over and tense—but I don't know what makes me climb in after her, pressing her slender body against the opposite door. I don't miss how the act takes her out of Mack's line of sight. He doesn't, either.

"Dante?" There's a hard note in his tone. The Mad Dog's used to barking out his own orders these days. He doesn't seem to remember when he and "Kitty" fought and clawed over the exact same scraps. "Did she go through with it?"

"No." I slam the door shut and the overhead light clicks off.

Mack's men perk up instantly, feeding off the hostility that laces the air. It's a bitter, cheap drug, *hatred*. I let them get high off it and rise to action, readying for the moment Mack says jump. Then I replace it with a harsh dose of reality.

"It was like I said: You walked right into a fucking trap." I palm the camera and throw it between the heads of the two punks in front of me, leaving Mack to catch it.

He does with one hand, his face expressionless. "A trap?" he wonders coldly.

"He planned to make his little video and then take the girl. The fucker even hired a few mercenaries to help him nab her right out from under your nose." I point through the windshield as if one of the bastards in question might suddenly appear on the hood of the van. "I suggest you move."

Gritting his teeth, Mack glances at one of the men seated behind him and inclines his head once. "You drive. Go!"

The man climbs into the front seat, and the van takes off, careening down alleys and side streets. We're maybe a block away from the hotel when Mack finally lifts the camera; the glow of a nearby taillight makes the lens glow red.

"What the fuck is this, then?"

My mouth twitches into something that could be another goddamn smile—or maybe it's a snarl? Whatever it is, I wear it while I stare the fucker down until he turns his attention to the dashboard instead.

"We made our own video," I say. "Send that to Stacatto."

Mack laughs—it's a harsh sound punctuated by the growl of the mutt I know well. He's bitter, snarling for his missing bone. "And what about the information? Did you forget about that while you were too busy making sure that no one else fucked your little toy?"

Anger flares...but with the scent of spice in my nose, it's easier to fight it down. My vision stays clear, but my lungs expand, instinctively rebelling against the substance they breathe in. *Her.*

"Watch the tape," I tell him. "I'd hate to spoil the ending...but we got the locations."

"And?" Mack prompts, his tone sharp.

"And *she* has them." I jab my thumb at the girl. "Locked away in her pretty little head."

Mack goes silent, allowing the words to sink in. It's a dangerous game to play tug-of-war with a pit bull. Years in the pit have honed Mack's baser instincts. He can't resist a challenge. I sense the girl stiffen, damn well aware of the fact that I've just made her the shiny bit of rope in this game—but prison has taught me a few tricks of my own.

I know just how far to push my newfound bit of leverage. And I know, even before he clenches his jaw in defeat, that Mack won't be able to resist taking a bite.

"And I thought prison had made you soft, Kitten," he murmurs loudly enough for me to hear. It's not a compliment—oh, no. It's a threat. "Just tell me what you plan to do with the locations of the girls but no manpower to go and get them? And please, Dante, don't insult my intelligence by claiming to go to the cops. You were always the *smart* one, remember?"

I know I grin again, but as usual, it doesn't feel right; I show too many teeth. "You're going to help, of course," I say. As much as it fucking stings to admit, Mack is the only one in the position to spring that kind of operation—for now. "But you won't keep the girls. You'll get the drugs."

"Drugs?" He tilts his head without seeming to realize it— I've got his interest.

"When we hit up the enclaves for the women, we launch a simultaneous attack on his distribution channels. We get the girls, you get the drugs." From a monetary standpoint, it's the short end of the stick: a stash of hot dope could net only a single net profit if sold to the right buyer. A stash of women, however, could promise a steady flow of cash for a very long time.

Logistically, though, the drugs were less risky and much easier to stash than a hoard of scared, traumatized women with mouths to feed and screams to smother. While a greedy son of a bitch, Mack wasn't completely stupid.

"Let's say I bite," he says, still stroking the base of the camera in his hand. "What's to stop me from watching your little video and discovering the locations of the enclaves all on my own?"

I don't bother to smother my laugh. While he watches, I reach into my pocket and trap a small square of plastic between two of my fingers. I hold it up and a slash of orange light cast by a nearby streetlamp lights it up just long enough for Mack's cocky smirk to disappear.

"You didn't really think I left the memory card in, did you?"

He chuckles darkly, shrugs, and then tosses the camera to one of his thugs, who barely manages to catch it. "Fair enough, Dante. Let's get home and discuss this around the table like big boys. My woman's making dinner."

CHAPTER TWENTY-NINE

Daniela

DANTE WEARS TENSION THE WAY MOST MEN WEAR clothing. He draws it tight around his chest, and it cloaks him all the way down to his toes. When the van comes to a stop in a section of woods that I assume is near Mack's fenced-in compound, it ratchets up until I can taste it, barreling off him in waves.

Vinny rarely got nervous, but he didn't handle it well. It made him antsy and more liable to lash out at anyone who so much as looked at him wrong. Lucifer, on the other hand, shoulders his nerves with pride. Calm, the man is untouchable, uneasy; he is a creature one might find only in the pits of hell itself. Some beast who would thrive in the relentless heat of the fire.

I don't know what to make of it as Mack climbs out of the van first, quickly followed by his two men. I expect Lucifer to exit as well, but he lingers and pins me here right beside him, his hand gripping my wrist. His free hand pries my fist open and prods the crumbled piece of paper hidden inside it.

"Read it," he tells me, his voice a harsh rasp. "Memorize it. Swallow it."

I know in an instant what he means—the weapon he's just given me—and a part of me wants to ask why. Why make *me* such a central piece in his plan? He told Mack that only I knew the locations: a lie. He made sure to maintain control of the only other object that might ruin his hand, and he positioned the pieces on this twisted game of chess to get me exactly what I wanted.

So, *why*? His broad face, guarded by the shadows of the van, offers no answers. I'm not stupid enough to risk tempting him, so I nod once and crush the paper against my palm. The next second, Lucifer has the van door open, and he pulls me along by the wrist, coincidentally keeping me close. Mack's men can't muscle in to separate us, and Lucifer makes sure of that by wrenching me even closer when they try.

Like hound dogs, Mack and his men sniff at the air instead, so eager for a little taste of the treats Lucifer's holding over their heads. But he's a good master, and he wields the figurative whip well. Without waiting for the others, he hauls me forward and starts up what I realize is a driveway paved in loose gravel. I have to cling to him more than I like—more than he likes. My nails clutch at his coat, and I sense the bulk of the man underneath. His heat is a flare in the darkness, guiding my way until the vague outline of a structure comes into view, illuminated by the light spilling out of sparse windows. It's the building that houses the pit, I realize as we pass it and my ears pick up the howl of barking dogs. Up ahead lies the garage and then the bar.

"Food's in the Chain," Mack says, referring to the bar, I suppose. His voice tickles the lobe of my good ear, a fact that doesn't go unnoticed by Dante.

Suddenly, I'm wrenched to stand on his other side. I turn my head just in time to catch Mack's trickle of laughter. His eyes gleam in the faint light as he jerks his head toward the bar.

"See you inside, Kitty. Though, if you do decide that you aren't hungry, I'll have Darcy send you a little doggy bag."

He breaks away, and his men fall into step behind him. Dante slows, waiting until the moment they nearly reach the one-story structure. Then he turns and marshals me toward the garage. When he reaches the door, he opens it first and peeks inside, every bit the cautious cat Mack teases him to be. Whoever he finds there makes him stiffen, but he steps inside anyway, allowing me to follow him in on my own.

"Dante..."

I glance over Dante's shoulder to make out Arno leaning against the base of the steps, his arms crossed. When he sees me, his eyes narrow.

"You might want to get her out of here—"

"That him?"

The door to the apartment opens, and someone else appears at the top of the stairs. A man, tall and slender. The moment those blue eyes meet mine—so similar to Lucifer's—I sense everything in the entire room stiffen. Unease rides the atmosphere. Lucifer doesn't know whether to take Arno's advice and shove me from the door, and the artist—Espi—can't seem to decide what to make of my outfit or the new bruise shaping up over my chin, courtesy of Donahugh.

There are only seconds to react. Seconds to break the tension on my own before it spills over. In Vinny's world, I would go with the first option and obediently hide out of sight. This time, I step free of Dante's shadow.

Looking past the red-haired man, I face the artist directly. "H-hey…"

He sighs, and some of the tension that crept into his posture eases up. "You're okay."

I force a nod, though Dante's gaze is like a knife that cuts through me. He hides his shock well, however. His fingers twitch to reach for me, but he doesn't. He eyes the artist—his brother—instead, and I can almost taste the amount of control it takes him to keep his voice steady.

"Espi. Where the hell have you been—"

"That's none of your damn business," Espi counters. There's a duffel hanging from his shoulder, and he wrenches it higher while descending the steps two at a time. He shoulders past Arno and then approaches the door, his narrowed gaze focused solely on Dante.

The two brothers eye each other, one fallen and one still above reproach. All you'd need is a sheet of glass between them and you would have a twisted mirror. I eye the artist's wiry frame and the lack of shadows lurking within his blue irises. Was this how Lucifer looked before his tumultuous fall from grace? The thought tugs at something inside my chest, and I have to brush it aside.

They communicate in their own silent language, more ancient than any spoken tongue. I can almost see the emotions that spark between them. In the end, Espi has the last word, and Dante shifts his weight ever-so-slightly to the side in defeat.

"I'll see you around, Pyro," he tells me, cocking his head in my direction. "Take this for now. I'll try to bring you something more *girly* next time."

"N-next time?"

Without answering, he shrugs the duffel from his shoulder and presses the straps into my hand. I take them, testing the weight that dangles from them. There are more clothes inside it, I suspect. Maybe another case of deodorant. All in all, it's just one more simple act of kindness I will never be able to repay, but he's gone before I can even get a thank-you out.

Dante watches him head out of the door, his jaw clenched. "Espi..."

Whether the artist doesn't hear him or just ignores him...I can't tell. He disappears into the darkness, and for a moment, my devil almost looks human. Pain softens the intensity of those eyes before even more cold ice replaces it.

"He knew about her," Arno says, starting forward. "Espi. He asked about the little bitch." His eyes cut over to me, blazing with suspicion. "Did you hear what the fuck I've just said? Dan—"

"We'll talk about this later." Lucifer rakes a hand through his hair, displacing the black strands across his forehead. The look only serves to intensify the hard expression bolstering his words. He's a wolf, his hackles raised, and the red-haired man knows when to back off.

He chuckles darkly and then waves a hand through the air before strolling to the door. Over the threshold, he hesitates and glances back at Dante. "Let's say that I want her. Now. Would you give her to me?"

I don't know what terrifies me more—the thought of truly being at Arno's mercy or the look in Lucifer's eyes when he stares the man he called his brother down. It's completely unreadable. Stone. Once again, Lucifer proves to be a code I'm not adept enough to crack. Arno, however, has no trouble.

He shakes his head suddenly, choking out a scoff. "I thought so."

He's gone in an instant, and in his absence, Lucifer switches from stone to...lightning. His gaze is piercing when it finds mine. His fingers flex at his sides, hungry. I know I have a second to save myself, and for some reason, I take it rather than do the smart thing, which would be to let him flatten me beneath his rage.

"I knew him," I choke out, taking a step backward until the railing of the staircase juts into my spine. "Espi. I m-met him once...before."

"How?" It's a simple question made dangerous by the harsh undercurrent of anger it carries.

"A few days before...before I was taken," I admit. "He was painting in the alley near Vinny's hotel. When we were at the apartment, I met him again. He made me answer the door for him—"

I hear a sound like something striking wood and the world sways—my foot, I realize when I glance down. I've mounted the first step of the staircase without even realizing it. Unconcerned, the devil continues his slow advance toward me, and I find myself climbing yet another step.

"He told me he'd call the police if I didn't," I say, though for some reason, my voice doesn't hold an ounce of fear, even as my heart threatens to pound its way right out of my chest. "I let him think—"

"What did you tell him?" Lucifer's demand rivals the insistent howl of the barking dogs I can hear even from here. The blistering rage gives way to the tumult of emotions that lurk underneath. Fear. It's the strongest, breaking through before he even seems to realize it. *What did you tell him?*

"I told him..." My tongue shoots out to coat my bottom lip as if that bit of moisture might protect me from the heat he's giving off through those scorching eyes. "I told him that I was a prostitute and that you were helping me escape my pimp."

The devil stops in his tracks. He wasn't expecting that answer, and he frowns as if tasting it against his mouth. Maybe he feels the same why I do: It's uncomfortably close to the truth. The devil is helping me escape my "pimp," but he doesn't particularly seem to relish his newfound shining armor.

I flinch when he takes another step toward me, his posture hunched and loose like a predator's right before it's poised to lunge. His gaze sweeps along my body, but I don't cringe backward this time. I stand still as he mounts the first step, his bulk dominating the narrow stairwell, his heat consuming me in waves.

Tilting my head back, I face my devil head on and allow him to search my expression for any hint of a lie. "I didn't know he was your brother," I say. "Not until he told me."

"So, you talked to him?" The words hiss from him like sparks from a blaze. Wherever they land, my flesh burns.

"Yes."

Suddenly, he mounts my step, bracing his feet on either side of mine. His size forces me to lean backward and cling to the railing for balance.

"He told me not to tell you."

The devil's mouth quirks into the twisted semblance of a smile. My breasts graze his chest as he reaches for my chin and traps it between his fingers. There's no real strength in his grip—I could break it if I wanted to. His gaze holds me in place, however.

"Don't...don't keep shit from me," he tells me in a voice that grapples to maintain control over its low, raspy baritone. In some places, it slips, and the hint of a growl licks through. "Ever. You tell me everything...or I'll—" He breaks off and glances down at his hands. They flex, and when he glances back up to meet my gaze, Lucifer doesn't bother to hide the murderous impulse he literally has to swallow down. "I'll fulfill my end of our bargain on a much quicker timeline."

He pushes past me and lopes up the staircase. When he reaches the door to the apartment, he jerks his chin in my direction. "Did you fucking read it yet?"

I feel my hand clench tighter over the page containing the addresses. Carefully, I pry my fingers open one by one and scan the words scribbled there in the dim lighting of the garage. There are ten addresses. I don't recognize the numbers or even the street names, but I read them. I burn every single letter into my skull. While Lucifer opens the door and barges his way inside, I read the addresses again. Again. Again. Only when the letters mingle through my thoughts as if branded there do I finally tear it down the middle and crumple both halves into a ball.

Lucifer is waiting for me when I mount the top of the stairs and swallow the last bit of evidence down whole. His eyes go automatically to my hip and the bag I'm carrying. The memory of his brother makes the devil uneasy. He turns and barges into the bathroom before slamming the sliding door shut so fiercely that it nearly jumps off its track.

After closing the door behind me, I set the duffel onto the couch and pull on the zipper. Inside, I find more clothes—a few sweatpants and some plain, gray hoodies—yet another package of deodorant, and my very own toothbrush and a tube of toothpaste. I run my fingers through the gifts while the shower kicks on down the hall and Lucifer sets about erasing the night from his skin. While I'm alone, Donahugh's touch is harder to bear. After making sure the windows are covered by blinds, I strip the coat and the lingerie off right here next to the small kitchen, and I pull Espi's clothing on. His stuff fits me much better than Dante's; I don't feel like I'm swimming in cotton, at least. Once dressed, I wrestle the soiled clothing into the duffel and zip it up.

I wait there on the couch for only God knows how long. Watching. Listening. Dante is taking his sweet time. I can almost hear him from here, grinding his teeth to erase my taste and scrubbing away the topmost layer of his skin. I'm not sure if only an hour has passed or even longer when the door to the bathroom finally opens again and he reappears wearing the same jeans and shirt. His hair is slick, dripping moisture down his back as he enters the kitchen and wrenches the faucet on. He drinks mouthfuls from his cupped hands and then shuts the tap off with a sigh.

"Stay away from Arno," he tells me, looking over his shoulder. Strands of black hair obscure his eyes. I can't tell if he's threatening me or *warning* me instead. "From Espi too."

"Why are you helping me?" I blurt out, crossing my arms over my chest. "When your brother asked me the first time, I didn't know what to say. I should have a better answer for if he asks me again."

Lucifer frowns, but there's no aggression in his posture when he turns to face me. He's thoughtful. He's hostile. He's confused by his own fucking motives.

"Stay away from—"

"Why *are* you helping me?" I ask again, making my voice just loud enough to overpower his. It doesn't take much effort; the shower repaired his control, and his baritone is a low, steady hum once again.

"Why the fuck does it matter?" he counters, flexing the hand that I know bears his mark. "You're getting your 'revenge.'"

"I am," I admit.

Prodding him is a reckless game I can't seem to quit playing. His taunt haunts me. *I'll fulfill my end of our bargain on a much quicker timeline.* He meant it to be a threat, but it's more like a tempting suggestion. Maybe it would be better if he did kill me now and end this sick game before the rules changed. A devil needs to remain a devil. A dangerous man is meant to be feared. I know that best after having lived with Vinny, but I don't know what would happen if those lines started to blur. Evil shouldn't be...craved.

"Are you helping me because of what happened to you?" I ask in a desperate bid to vanquish that fear. "Because of what that...man did? I know that's why you gave me the alcohol."

Anger. On him, it has a smell. It permeates the air like smoke, and before the flames can even touch your skin, you've already suffocated. Rage paints his eyes an unnatural shade of blue, and for a moment, it's the only thing I see. I'm sure it will be the very last thing I see...

Then the devil surprises us both.

"I got my own revenge," he says coldly, though his mouth frowns as if he's unsure why the words are tumbling out of it. "So you can write off that little theory."

"How?" I draw my knees up to my chin and stare at him from between them.

"The cage," he says finally, each word harshly clipped. "You remember it?"

A shiver runs through me, and I force myself to nod. I remember it. I can't forget it. I will always picture him inside it. I squeeze my eyes shut and pray with every cell I possess that Lucifer will make good on his promise. Kill me now with that image in my head for the last time. *Kill me now...*

"I was sixteen the first time I fought in one," he says. There's a steady edge to his voice; he doesn't like to mention the past, but the violence that lurks in those memories comforts him at the same time. "I told you that...that I tried to climb out. But it was good money, so I kept coming back. Running drugs was easier but riskier—no one could fuck with you while you were in the cage." His voice lingers over that statement. The chain-link fencing and gritty sand of the pit were home to him. He missed it. "Apart from the bastard paid to beat the living shit out of you, that is. But it was better. As a runner...there are only so many places in the human body you can hide a stash."

I cringe at the imagery. Then I envision a certain place on the human body...paired with his own traumatic memories. My heart aches. I hate this part of me that feels for him— aches for him—more than I do the part of me that cringes at the thought of Vinny. The devil isn't mine to hurt for. He isn't mine for me to wonder just how many awful things he's been forced to do to survive. He isn't *mine,* and I shouldn't feel this gross, morbid satisfaction that he claims to have gotten his revenge, at least.

"Dino preferred his fighters anyway, and even as bait, I made enough to keep my spot in the ring and keep my head down—"

"Dino?"

The devil falls silent. I can almost hear his teeth click together in irritation, but he humors my questioning and throws me another bone of his past to taste.

"Dino Mulligan. A man who ran a gang called the Saints. Heroin distribution. Illegal gambling. You name it, he ran it, but his favorite was the pit. Cage fighting. He could make up to ten grand a night with the right fighter and the right crowd."

"You admired him." I lift my head and peel my eyelids open just enough to see such an emotion on him for myself. The devil displays his respect in gnashing teeth and eyes that flash like gems.

"I respected him," he admits. "The man took me in when I was fourteen in a way. People called him 'Oliver Twist' because he had a habit of taking in boys off the street to use as runners or bait. He was a cold son of a bitch, but he ran his territory well."

"Fourteen?" It's a two-year gap from twelve. I'm not sure if I want to know what dark secrets fill in those missing months. Thankfully, the devil doesn't seem willing to tell me.

"I lived on the streets for a while," he says, leaving it at that. "If I wasn't bouncing in and out of a group home, I was stealing. With Dino, though, I at least had a roof over my head and food in my mouth."

I don't dare to judge him. It's a sad story he weaves: A criminal sheltered him when no one else would.

"So you fought in the cage."

He nods and drags a hand through his hair, leaving it buried within the dark strands. "I did. It wasn't bad. I got my ass kicked, but I would rather eat with a busted rib than not at all. I did okay as bait for a while. But, one day, they threw me in with a different fighter than the street punks I was used to. They called him The Machete. A sadistic son of a bitch who liked to put on a 'good show' in more ways than one for the sick fucks who watched him fight. He requested his bait specifically...liked them young and 'pretty.'"

His voice breaks and the guttural rumble melds into a snarl. He has to clench his fists at his sides as if fighting back the memory before it's even descended. "He chose me, but it wasn't a normal match. The rate was ten percent when the normal cut for bait was only three or less. The cage was different, too. And The Machete... He was a huge son of a bitch." His eyes widen. For a moment, he's there again. The past consumes him, and I feel something crawl painfully through my chest when his breathing gets heavier and his eyes narrow into slits. "It was only right before the match when one of the handlers started muttering about 'rumors.' 'It'll hurt less if you don't fight, kid,' he told me. 'Just let him rile the crowd. For the love of fucking god don't...don't be a little bitch and cry.'"

Each word is a deadly rasp, burning coals over my flesh. I've never seen him look so cold. So hard. So soulless.

"The cage was run by another man. Some punk Dino hated who let his fighters do whatever twisted shit they wanted to fuel the crowd. Death matches. Torture. Whatever. As long as the money was good, he let it fly, and Dino gave him a few fighters for a hefty price. But business is business." He grits his teeth, grinding his hatred between them. "The Machete liked young boys. He beat the shit out of his bait and liked to strip them naked afterward and make them scream for kicks. I didn't know that until he'd already broken one of my fingers and cracked my eye socket. It was the point when I usually would have been dragged from the ring, but he...he started to tear at my shorts, murmuring about how much he loved 'fresh meat' and 'new little piggies to make scream.'"

He shakes—no, Lucifer *sways*. His hip careens into the counter, but he doesn't even seem to notice the pain. "I remember looking at him," he says hoarsely. "I remember staring dead into the bastard's eyes. I remember trying to fight him off while he laughed. I remember..." He shakes his head, and his hand falls, relinquishing its grip on his hair. "The next thing I knew, Dino was dragging me off the fucker. I couldn't...I couldn't see. I couldn't hear. All I could taste was blood."

He glances down and eyes his hands in the dim, artificial light. There's a careful, practiced way that he extends each finger, the same way a knight might draw his sword from its sheath or the way Vinny palmed his precious knives. Bone, nails, and sinew were his weapons of choice, and he wields them as well as any other warrior.

"I put the bastard in a coma for six weeks," he says. "Dino was pissed. I cost him a lot of money... He made sure I paid for that. But, not even a month later, before what would have been my next match as bait, he pulled me out of the lineup. Told me to pick a 'real' name for myself. If I could fight the way I did against The Machete, then he would make sure I earned him 'every fucking dime' he'd lost." The sound that trickles from his throat is coarse, but it might even be a real laugh. He raises a hand and points to his neck.

I strain my eyes and lean forward to make out the script of the tattoo there: *Kitten.*

"I chose the name he gave me himself. I earned him his fucking money back and then some. Being a fighter was a different world from being bait. It was darker. Colder. You looked at a man and you trained yourself to see him as only a piece of meat, nothing more. You sized up his weaknesses in two seconds, and you bet your life that you made the correct assessment. I...I fucking *loved* it." He didn't mean to admit that out loud, not to me. He frowns, but it's too late to take the words back.

I know how I could sound when I spoke of the cello. How my tone could verge into the territory of a sigh and how people would sometimes shift uncomfortably if I droned on and on about the complexities of Bach. Lucifer applies the same joy I find in music to the ferocity of beating the shit out of other men in the cage.

Do I think of him any less for admitting as much? It makes my head hurt that I can't tell. Admiration. Disgust. Where does one end and the other begin?

"That was the first time that Dino saved my life," Lucifer states. "The bastard would never admit it, but he paid off The Machete—once the fucker healed—to keep him from coming after me. He trained me hard. Trained me well. He made sure I didn't lose a fight that was in my favor, even if the payoff would have been greater if I did. He was a cold son of a bitch...but I trusted him with my life. Up until then, I had never told him about what it had been like before he took me in, though. All he knew was that I came from the streets and never looked back. But right before I turned eighteen..." He falls silent for so long that I almost assume story time is over.

Maybe I want it to be. *Need* it to. The spot in my chest he's already scraped raw won't survive another beating. I will break, and only God knows what will happen if that part of me gives way. For five years of torture, my heart managed to survive—in five minutes, Lucifer has it splintering.

"I kept tabs on the fucker," he snarls. "My mom, she had another kid after me, but when she died, they sent him to live with our grandparents rather than with *him*. 'Couldn't raise a baby,' he said, and they couldn't manage two kids, let alone a toddler. But, when he turned eight, they couldn't handle Espi anymore, either. 'He needed to be with his father.'" He spits the words out. "I don't know what lie he told them about me. That I was a runaway. I was on drugs. I was fucked up. But I was there the day they brought Espi to him. I watched from an alley across the street. Poor kid. He had no clue." His voice breaks, and for a second, the devil is little more than an angel caught mid-freefall.

There's an ageless pain in his eyes that I recognize. Some days, I saw it in the people Vinny tortured. Some days, I even see it in myself. It's a helplessness that goes deeper than mortal constraints. You feel it in your soul, and there is no way to ease the sting.

"He had no clue...and I couldn't. I couldn't do a fucking thing." He forms a fist and smashes it against the counter so hard that I hear something pop. Crack. *Break.* If it's bone, his face reveals nothing. He's too busy glaring into the past to give a damn about the present. "I was an animal that night in the cage. I went too far and nearly killed the man I fought. Dino almost beat my ass himself...but I told him. I told him about Espi. I told him about that fucker. I told him *everything*. He didn't say a damn thing. I think he already knew. He made me get dressed. He drove me to the house. He walked me to the front door. The fucker tried to close it in our faces, but Dino forced our way in. Espi was in the living room, watching television. It...it was an hour until bedtime."

He inhales sharply, and I expect him to attack the counter again. He looks at me instead. I don't know what he finds in my gaze to make his breathing a little easier and his posture less tense. Maybe it's the fact that I'm shying away from the horror he's spilling out. I listen. I wait. I watch.

"Dino introduced himself as a 'long-lost uncle' and made me take the kid upstairs while he had a chat with our father. I didn't know what Espi would think, but...they must have told him about me, because he knew who I was. 'You're Dante.' 'You're my big brother.' 'Want to play trucks?' I

knew then and there that if...if anything...if that bastard—"
He inhales. Exhales. Tries again to speak. "I would kill him
myself. I would. But I knew without even having to ask that
we had made it in time. Espi was okay. So we played trucks
while Dino made our father have a little 'accident' that
broke his arm in four places. I went there every day after
that. I made the fucker move into the basement. I took Espi
to school. I cooked his meals. I tucked him in at night...
The only thing that fucker did for him was give him health
insurance and a roof—the only shit I couldn't get him with
what I earned in the cage. That's it. I did everything but
sleep there. I couldn't... Never again, but he never touched
Espi. I made fucking sure of that. I slept during the day
while he was at school, and I watched over him at night in
his room."

My feet throb when they hit the floor, but I don't even
register standing until he stiffens and eyes me warily from
across the room. Each breath I take scrapes the insides of
my lungs as I take another step forward and lift the edge of
my borrowed sweatshirt with both hands to reveal Vinny's
mark.

"I told him I hated him," I say, the words sticking in my
throat. It takes four more raspy breaths before I find the
strength to continue, rewarding his dark foray into the past
with one of my own. "It was after he'd tortured the third
maid in front of me and made me listen to her s-scream. I
told him that I hated him. I shouted it at him...and then he
hit me so hard I saw blood." I tasted it as well. He'd struck
me in my chest, and it was only three days later that his
doctor deduced I had fractured three ribs.

The memory makes me sway. I'm not strong like him. I have to cling to the counter just to find my balance again.

"He pinned me to my bed and told me about a Russian slaver he knew who tattooed his 'whores' to keep them from running. He'd mark his name on their faces or their backs so everyone would know who they belonged to. Vinny caressed my cheek and told me that he could never ruin my beauty that way. So he stripped me naked and strapped me down while he tattooed his name on my chest the way the slaver had taught him."

Stick and Poke, the technique is called, or so I learned afterward. He used only a needle jammed into a stick of wood, a bit of thread, and ink. It took him three hours to carefully cement the letters in ink, stab by vicious stab.

"He told me that it was so that...so that I would never forget who really loved me."

Lucifer doesn't react to my dark secret. I've obeyed him this far, at least; there is nothing else I've kept from him now. He knows it all. He owns me in that way, too. I don't know if he means to exert that ownership when he reaches out to me just as the door opens and a soft voice warily calls out.

"Dante?"

I wrench the hem of my sweatshirt down while Lucifer muscles past me, his gaze on the door.

"Darcy," he states when a slender, blond figure creeps inside.

She smiles when she sees him, but the expression flickers when she notices me. In her hands is a single plate carefully wrapped in tinfoil. "I brought you some food. I didn't let Mack anywhere near it before you give me that look." Her tone is playful, but there's a hint of truth lurking in it before Lucifer can shoot the food a wary glance.

He watches her set the plate onto the counter, but then she lingers, her fingers toying with the foil. I don't miss the second look she shoots at me, two parts confusion mixed with a tiny bit of uncertainty. She wants to talk to Lucifer alone, and I don't miss the familiarity that taints the air between them. They know each other, and I hate this part of me that wonders how. Who is she to him? Who was he to her? Where do they stand now?

It's harder than I'd like to admit to swallow the nosy questions down and stoop for the artist's duffel. I sling it quietly over my shoulder and enter the bedroom, closing the door behind me. Then...

I should crawl into bed. Put the sheets over my head. Play pretend like I'm not straining my ear to catch every softly spoken word. I *should*.

But, in the devil's lair, the rules of etiquette no longer apply.

CHAPTER THIRTY

Dante

I LIFT THE TINFOIL FROM THE PLATE JUST ENOUGH TO make out two pieces of fried chicken, a hunk of mashed potatoes, and some macaroni and cheese. It's not enough to share with the woman in the bedroom—a fact I can't ignore. Darcy was never rude, so the only other explanation is that she, for whatever reason, didn't think there would be another mouth left to feed.

I drag my gaze along her face, searching the smooth planes of it for any hint of what Mack could possibly be planning. I know she's aware of the suspicion, but she just smiles and pushes the plate toward me.

"Eat up. I don't think Mack brought along any snacks on your little 'boys' outing—"

"Not hungry." I cut my gaze over to the door and wonder if the little bitch would stick her nose up at it over fucking

Thai though—that is, if Darcy were being honest about Mack's having been nowhere near it.

"I thought Arno would have taken her back by now," Darcy admits, swirling the edge of her thumb along the rim of the plate.

"Why?" The question comes out more harshly than I mean it to, and Darcy flinches. After all, the bitch is Arno's problem. His responsibility. His prize. *His...*

And he can fucking try to take her if he wants to. My fingers flex at the thought of it, burning hot. He can *try*.

"He said that was why she was here." Darcy nods to the bedroom, but I'm already scanning the scarred wood as if I can see her leaning against the other side of it. Hell, I can smell her, the nosy little cunt. "He said that she was part of his plan for getting revenge for Parish—"

"You can tell Arno that he can have her...when I'm done *fucking* her." I make my voice loud enough for her to hear and hate that I can only picture her reaction.

How would the little princess react to being referred to as my whore? If she lets out a haughty little gasp in disgust, I don't hear it above the sound of Darcy choking.

Clutching her throat with one hand, she lunges for the sink while I swipe a plastic cup from the cupboard above her head.

"Here."

She downs two glasses and then sets the cup aside. Her cheeks are red, and I do a double take, my eyebrow raised. If I'm not mistaken, she's blushing, and a woman who—at one point, at least—fucked strangers for a living has some damn nerve blushing at the mention of the word.

If she notices the look I give her, she doesn't let it show. Instead, she wipes her mouth off with the back of her hand and then tucks a blond curl behind her ear. Mack must like her to dress like a bar bunny, even in the middle of October. The jean shorts and the pink, low-cut top leave little to the imagination, but the tattoo above her right breast proves without a doubt just who owns her. *Mack.* I try to remember how she dressed before, as one of the girls Dino kept on his payroll to please the men riled by the violence of a cage fight. Apart from a hazy image of her lurking around the outskirts of the ring, I don't recall much.

"It's been a while," she says softly, as if sensing the thoughts circling my head. "Oh! I brought you something." She reaches into her pocket and withdraws something clasped in her fist. "Do you remember when I first gave this to you?"

She opens her hand and lying on her palm is a silver necklace—the cheap kind women like her seem to love trading the money they've earned on their backs and knees for. Hanging from a silver chain is a line of script that forms a single name: *Dante.*

"I remember," I admit.

Birthday present, she claimed, though seeing as how she didn't know the exact date of mine, I assumed the gift was more or less a "so you didn't die during your first round in the cage" present. She gave it to me right after I'd gotten my tattoo. Maybe it was her way of reminding me that, at some point, I used to be this person named *Dante*—though she didn't know just how eager I was to shed that weak, pathetic bastard.

"You left it behind," Darcy says, dangling the chain from her finger. "When... I want you to have it." She curls it gently within her fingers and presses it against my palm.

I snatch for it and tuck it, chain and all, into my pocket. "Thanks."

She shrugs, but an odd expression tugs at her mouth. A smile? She can look back at the old days and smile. I look back...and I find nothing worth grinning about.

"See you around, Dante." Darcy slips past me and leaves, wiggling her fingers in a parting wave.

I wait until the door shuts behind her and I hear her descend the stairs. Then I turn to the bedroom and swipe the plate closer to me with an outstretched hand. "You hungry?" My voice could be heard from the pit, but the bitch doesn't answer.

So the little princess wants to play pretend.

Scoffing, I snatch the plate up with one hand and head for the bedroom door. When I wrench it open, she isn't there lurking on the other side of it. Instead, she's watching me from the bed, sitting cross-legged on the bedspread. Her head is cocked, but she meets my gaze almost as if daring me to challenge her coy little act. She could have fooled me —almost. But her chest is heaving beneath her sweatshirt. Not only that, but the comforter is slightly off-center as if someone had leaped onto it.

I consider calling her out. Instead, I step forward and drop the plate onto the bed, spraying a glob of macaroni and cheese onto the mattress. "Eat."

She reaches for a leg of chicken without hesitation, and I catch myself staring. So many women are odd when it comes to food, but she doesn't seem to care that I watch her rip into the meat with her teeth and swallow down chunks whole. She moans. Her free hand comes to pick a bit of macaroni between two fingers, and she samples that too. There's something wild about the little lamb when she thinks the wolf isn't watching.

I wonder what she's like when she's with him, the bastard who stabbed his name into her chest. Does she lick her fingers when she's finished and carefully strip every bone of flesh like she's doing now? I try to compare this woman to the one Arno kidnapped: the bitch who could watch another being abused and laugh.

I'm not sure which woman is staring back, pushing the now licked-clean plate toward me. I take it and leave to toss it into the sink. When I return, she's still sitting, watching me, waiting.

Ignoring her, I scan the wall, prepared to pick a corner to sleep in—maybe within those hours of silence, I'll finally figure out a way to deal with Vinny Stacatto's whore. I head for one near the window, but the girl surprises me by leaping from the mattress before I can even take a step.

"You sleep." She jerks her head toward the bed. However, when I don't move, she staggers backward until she occupies my corner herself. "*You* sleep." She sinks down to her knees, stretching her legs out in front of her.

I should snatch her from the floor and strap her to the fucking bed. I close the door and sink down onto the mattress instead, my back facing her. "Suit yourself."

She makes a soft sound in response. Part acknowledgment and part satisfaction. *Okay, I will.*

I can't understand why the sound irritates me so fucking much as I close my eyes and pretend to sleep.

———

PRISON CAN TEACH THE DEEPEST OF FUCKING SLEEPERS how to jolt awake at the slightest noise. Sleep becomes as steady as blinking—you take it in little fucking snatches at a time, always on alert. For hours, I've listened to her shift against the floor. I knew the exact moment when she rose to her feet, trying and failing not to make a sound.

I felt the bed shift with her weight. I smelled her. Felt the heat of her skin with every careful move she made toward me. I kept still even as she straddled me, balancing her weight across my stomach, inches away from my already hardening cock.

It's only when she presses her knife against my throat that I finally let my eyes open.

She doesn't so much as blink. Her eyes gleam in the grayish light of dawn filtering in through the window. It paints her skin, making her glow. She's a ghost on my chest, threatening me with a dull-ass blade.

"Do you think I won't do it?" she asks, jerking her chin at the weapon.

"You won't." There isn't a shred of doubt in my voice. No fear.

Vinny's whore may have entertained the idea of hacking a man's dick off, but she can't drive her knife through my throat—even though it would probably be in her best interest to.

"You would have done it already."

She doesn't challenge that. Instead, she tilts her wrist, digging the blade in just a fraction deeper. "If you were Vinny, I would." As if she's not quite sure of that, the knife digs in even deeper. "I *would*."

She's not ready when I shift my weight and throw her off. Within seconds, I have her pinned beneath me with the hand holding the knife trapped against the headboard. When my gaze meets hers, she lets the knife go, and it bounces across the pillow.

"Are you going to give me back to him?" she demands in that haughty little tone of hers, proving once and for all that she really was listening in last night. "To Arno?"

I choke out something that might be a laugh, but it's too damn cold. "Do you want me to?"

I expect her to cringe and shake her head no. I expect her eyes to widen at the thought of spreading her legs for Arno or his men. Instead, her frown deepens. She's thinking.

"I guess...Vinny wouldn't care how many men I've fucked when he gets me back."

Red flashes across my vision, painting her. I don't know if it's anger at the blatant way she assumes I won't fulfill my promise to kill her or the fact that she's so fucking cavalier about the possibility of being...fucked.

"Do you want me to give you to him?" My voice is hard. Hard with rage. Hard with a promise. All she has to do is say the fucking word and he can have her. "Do you?"

She holds my gaze, her chin pointed toward the ceiling, her eyes unreadable. Then...she breaks. "N-no." Real, cold fear spills out of her, and I jerk back, rising up on my knees. "I don't want to go to him."

"Then don't fucking ask me about it." I climb from the bed and snatch a fresh shirt from the pile Darcy brought. After ripping the old one off, I pull the new one on, but it's not enough to erase the bitter sting clinging to my skin.

Trust Vinny's whore to be a good damn liar on top of everything else. Sometimes I can almost believe the little act she puts on: the stuck-up mob bitch too hardened by pain to truly fear what might come her way next.

Seeing her stripped of that illusion isn't any better than watching her hide behind it. It isn't until I hear the mattress shift behind me that I realize I'm standing here, glaring at the wall. My head hums. My fingers flex, on fire. My jaw aches. I want to punch something. I want to fucking pummel.

But it's not that little bitch I want to destroy. Trust the fact that only the threat of her precious, beloved Vinny is enough to make *Danny* rip her pretty little mask off. *"I want him dead,"* she's said. For just a second, I join in on her little fantasy; I'll kill the prick myself if only to see how she'll react without being haunted by her quest for revenge.

After Arno, and Dino, and Mack...

I've had enough of fucking revenge.

"No! Wait!"

Her voice stops me dead in my tracks before I even register heading for the door. My hand is on the knob, already in the process of wrenching it open, and when I glance over my shoulder, she's on her knees.

"N-no." She shakes her head, sending that black hair flying. "No one else... I don't want to go to anyone else."

She's telling the truth this time. It's too damn bad that what she wants doesn't really fucking matter.

I enter the hallway and slam the door behind me. In five minutes, I'm out of the garage, marching toward the bar up ahead. Inside, I find Arno sitting on a stool at the bar, but he's not drinking for once. He glances over his shoulder as I cross the room but doesn't greet me. Overnight, he's reverted to the shitty little punk I met in the streets, cursed with the stigma of being Dino Mulligan's bastard.

"Where's your little toy?" he wonders nastily when I take the stool beside his.

I feel my eyes narrow. "Fuck her."

"I'm sure you have, more than once," Arno sighs, but before I can react, he lifts his free hand above the counter, revealing the bottle he had hidden on his lap. He shoves it in my direction, and I rip the cap off and take a sip without even looking at the label.

It burns. It's shitty, cheap vodka, but it washes the taste of her from my mouth.

"Feels like old times," Arno says, glancing around the bar, his jaw set. "You and Mack fighting each other for scraps. The cage. All we need is Dino dangling the meat over your heads and it could be the good old days again." There's a hard note in his tone that I don't miss.

The "good old" days weren't very good to Arno. His father may have been a stone-cold criminal, but he didn't do the fathering too well to the kid who actually carried his blood.

Scrawny and weak, Arno wouldn't have lasted a day in the cage. It was only after Dino died that he grew claws of his own and honed his own bite.

"Something's up," I suspect, noticing the way Arno curls his hands into fists. He isn't one to dwell on nostalgia for the hell of it. The puppy only brings up the past when he's itching to beat out a new future in pain and blood. "What is it?"

"Mack." Arno snatches the bottle from my grip and downs a fourth of it in one go. "The bastard... He'll take it all. Stacatto's empire. What remains of the Saints. Everything. And I...I fucking handed it to him."

I grab the bottle before he can take another swig, but I don't drink from it myself. I stare down into the dark liquid instead, watching it swirl within the glass. In this lighting, it's the same color as her eyes. Those fucking eyes. All that's missing are the hints of green and specks of gold.

"It's not too late," I say, but I don't elaborate.

Arno can build his own damn kingdom. "Scared little kitties" don't do well in groups once they get released from the pound. After this is all over, I'll find some place to lie low. Some way to carve out a new name for myself, away from the cage or the violence—and I try not to give a damn as to where Stacatto's little whore might factor into that.

"It's not too late," I repeat, slamming the bottle down in front of Arno—and, this time, he doesn't reach for it. "Mack's not the only one with 'friends.'"

Arno chuckles. "You make some connections in prison?"

"Something like that."

Arno doesn't react when I stand. It's only when I hold my hand out that he has the nerve to look interested.

"Got a phone on you?" I ask.

Shooting me a wary look, he reaches into his pocket and pulls a cell phone out. "Yeah. Why?"

I don't answer, and he slaps the phone onto my palm anyway. I toy with the keypad as I cross over to an empty section of the bar, just out of Arno's earshot. It must be busy at the police station this early. I sense that the dial tone is about to cut over to voicemail when a tired voice finally answers.

"Fourth Precinct."

"Can I talk to..." I inhale sharply and spit the name out. "Dick—*Richard*—Van Hallen?"

There's a slight pause from the other end, and I can hear papers being shuffled.

"May I ask who's calling?"

"Tell him it's his long-lost nephew."

"Just a minute."

Nearly three pass before a new voice answers the line. "Van Hallen."

"Hello, Detective," I say coldly. "This is how we're going to play this game. I'm going to speak. You listen, and only if you have something worth saying do you talk back. Understood?"

"Vialle?" The detective sounds gruff, pre-coffee. "What the hell are you playing at—"

"Vincent Stacatto," I say, cutting each word short. "That name ring a bell?"

Van Hallen grunts. After almost a minute of silence, he finally spits a reply out. "Go on."

"What if I were to tell you that his human-trafficking operation is about to take a nasty hit. Tonight. Would your men be able to stop tailing me to be around to catch the fireworks?"

He's silent, wondering whether or not I'm yanking his chain. "Stacatto runs a *multimillion*-dollar operation, Vialle. That wouldn't be fireworks we're talking about. It would be an explosion."

"I want to see him burn." Well, the little thrill-seeker will get her fucking wish.

"That doesn't answer my question, Detective."

"Ah...yes—all right. I could spare a few men if your tip was fucking credible."

"Next question. Stacatto kept a woman around him. Young. Foreign—"

"You've just described just about every missing adolescent girl in the international database," Van Hallen snarls.

"Not this girl. Speaks English. Her name is Danny...Daniela—"

"Manzano?"

I assume it's a last name. Daniela Manzano, Vinny's pretty whore.

"He's kept her close," Van Hallen says, but now, he's even more cautious than he was before.

"What do you know about her?"

"Humph... Stacatto barely lets her out of his sight. She was his neighbor, they say, growing up. They lived in the same building. She's young, like you said. About twenty-two...twenty-three. Family came from Brazil, I think."

I don't like how quickly Van Hallen settled on the right woman. He wasn't lying about having a hard-on for Stacatto, at least. "Do you know anything about a murder case connected to her?"

"Terrible, terrible crime," Van Hallen says softly. "Poor kid lost her whole family. The photos of the crime scene haunted the precinct for weeks."

"Next question. Detective Andrew Sosa. Know him?"

"No," Van Hallen says carefully. "But I do know of a *Chief* Andrew Sosa."

Chief. Apparently, being a prick in Stacatto's pocket could make a man rise through the ranks within the course of five years.

"What do you know about him?"

Van Hallen hesitates. "I know that he writes my departmental performance reviews."

"Well, I'm going to go out on a limb and tell you that I know for a fact that he's working for Stacatto."

"That's a very stupid accusation to make, Vialle," Van Hallen warns, but he doesn't trash the notion outright. Smart bastard.

"He worked on the Manzano case, right?"

This time, Van Hallen takes almost a full minute to answer. "Yes..."

"Then take some words of advice, Detective. He's Stacatto's man—but that's your problem. Last question: If...*if* I could get you someone like this Daniela Manzano...could you smuggle her out of the city? *You.* Not your fucking corrupt police chief. Not any one of your little rookie cops. You." I know that it's a stupid plan before the words leave my mouth. Fuck, I don't know *why* they leave my mouth. My neck itches and I have to reach up to scratch at it while Van Hallen takes his sweet time digesting what I've said.

"Vialle, if you could get me someone like Daniela Manzano, the only place I'd be able to put her is on the witness stand. She could sink Stacatto's entire operation with her testimony alone. Or at least turn the public against him.”

“Well, that answers that question.” I rip the phone from my ear, prepared to hang up.

“Wait!” Van Hallen breathes heavily into the receiver. “You... This is all just *hypothetical,* right? You don’t really have her? Because, if you did...well, then that makes what I’m about to tell you a little clearer: Stacatto’s put out a hit on a man who sounds an awful lot like you. Half a million dollars for a bastard with blue eyes, dark hair, and a tattoo that says ‘Kitten’ across the left side of his neck.”

Half a million dollars. I have to chuckle at the amount. It’s the biggest pot put on my head, though definitely not the first. I have a feeling that it won’t be the last.

“You’re right, Detective. Sounds an awful lot like me.”

“I knew you had an interesting rap sheet, Vialle,” Van Hallen admits, “but getting on Stacatto’s shit list within a week is quite the feat to manage.”

“I’ll expect my award in the mail,” I toss back.

This time, Van Hallen doesn’t parry with a jab of his own. “Look...if your information is credible, it’s probably best if you contact me again through my direct number. If what you’re saying is true about the girls...then I think any prosecutor worth the paper his license is printed on would overlook a few murky details if a rogue detective launched his own counter investigation.”

I don't say anything. It's his neck on the line, but the bastard seems eager to put it there just to nail Stacatto to the wall. *Heroes.* Or maybe it's just plain, old stupidity.

"Memorize this number," he says before spouting off a round of digits. "Call it only when you have something tangible I can work with."

He hangs up, and I return to the bar counter and toss the phone to Arno. He catches it with a wary look—though, if he overheard anything, he's smart enough not to admit it out loud.

"Mack won't be up for a while," he says, tucking the phone into his pocket. "The fucker went heavy on the drink..." He cracks a tired smile that almost reaches his eyes. "You must have shown him up good."

I feel a matching grin tug on the corners of my mouth for a second. "Just like old times."

I leave him there and head for the garage. I don't know why I take my time mounting each step, my gaze on the door to the apartment. I can almost taste her beyond it. Nervous. Anxious. The little bitch probably thinks Arno is right at my damn heels, and a part of me takes pleasure in that. If thunder weren't choosing this moment to rumble in the distance, I would go back to the bar and get the bastard just to prove...

What? That her little pleas don't matter? That *she* doesn't matter? I could turn her over in a second and still fucking sleep at night.

When I finally get the front door open, I don't find her in the living room or the kitchen. For a second, I entertain the notion that the little bitch wised up and ran, but I catch her scent lingering just beyond the doorway to the bedroom, and I find her seated on the edge of the mattress.

Blank. Her expression registers nothing. She's the same creature she was the night Arno's man first brought her in. Empty. Distant. She's ready for whatever I'll throw at her—and it won't fucking faze her.

"Arno's waiting downstairs," I tell her as I enter the room. With one hand, I reach for her wrist, gripping her so tightly that I feel the bone underneath. "Come—"

She waits until I drag her to her feet before she lashes out: Nails. Teeth. Hands. Feet. The little bitch comes to life kicking and screaming. "No!" Her wounded hand lands a blow across my cheek, and I taste her blood. She ripped the cut open again, but the pain doesn't even seem to faze her.

When I drag her closer, pinning her arms to her sides, I find terror in her eyes, but the fear isn't directed at me. Oh, no. The little bitch is afraid of *herself*. She doesn't know why she's fighting. Why she's angry at the thought of me turning her over like a piece of meat. She would have never fought *him* like this, and it's that realization that makes me shove her back so hard that she lands faceup on the mattress.

"Stop."

She lies there, her teeth bared, her hair streaking the dark comforter like a shadow. Her face stands out in stark contrast, displaying a real, true emotion for once. Hatred—only the dumb bitch isn't smart enough to direct it at me.

She hates herself.

"I'm not going to give you to him," I say, flinging the words at her like punches.

Her chest heaves. She sighs. She's...relieved. Her eyes shut against the admission, but not before I catch sight of it. Stacatto's little whore only has enough room in her bed for one monster, apparently. Realizing that pisses her off—as much as a little princess can be pissed off. Her teeth sink into her lower lip, and she bites down until it turns red.

"Unless you want me to change my mind?" I add, but it's a vicious taunt, and she winces as if I'd slapped her.

Her mouth twitches anyway. *Yes.* She wants to say it. She wants to don her emotionless armor and take every evil thing dished out at her like a good, caged songbird. But she can't. Her newfound will is too damn strong, even for her to resist.

"N-no," she croaks, wrenching her eyes open to stare me down. "No one else." She drags herself upright, raising her freshly bloody palm as if she's not quite sure why. "No one else..."

I don't move. That's a promise that I won't make—not to a bitch with another man's name on her chest. Not to her.

Her fingers flutter, dripping blood onto the bedspread, but she can't seem to pull the hand back. Maybe she can't bear to be used, even to piss off Stacatto. Deep down, maybe the little bitch doesn't want to die, either. It's a grim realization she can't force herself to face, and I'm not sure what course of action she'll take when a knock rattles the front door.

My eyes cut to her. Cut through her. "Stay here."

She stiffens when I enter the hall again. I move slowly. Cautiously. My fingers flex, and I almost wish I'd taken her knife. My hands have taken enough of a beating over the past few days.

"Who is it?"

The only response is another quiet knock. I shift my stance as I pull the door open, prepared to shove anyone right down the fucking staircase before they can make a move. I see a shadow. A hulking figure. Blue eyes.

"Shit." I pull back at the last second and brace my open palm against the nearest wall. "Espi?"

The kid doesn't acknowledge me with more than a flick of his eyes and a grunt. "She here?"

She? Something tugs at the back of my mind. Her. She's spoken to him, and who knows what the fuck she really told him.

"She isn't—"

"Is she here or not?" Espi pushes his way past me, muscling through the door, dragging something behind him. It's a case, oddly shaped.

My mind is slow to place it as he pulls it into the living room and scans the corners for Stacatto's woman.

"Danny? Danny, are you here?"

When there's no answer right away, Espi glares at me and seems about ready to hit me with whatever the fuck he has when she finally creeps to the doorway.

"H-hey." She smiles, but her bruised lips undermine the expression. She does her best to move without wincing as she enters the hallway, and I know why. She's suppressing every ounce of pain, humiliation, and abuse...for him.

I can't tell if Espi can see through the bullshit or if he chooses to believe the illusion instead.

"I brought you something," he grunts, manipulating the case so that she can see it.

When she does, she stops moving. Her eyes widen. They fill —flood. Whatever has been done to her, Espi's magic case is enough to erase it long enough for her to stagger forward and brush the length of it with a trembling finger. Without a word, he sets the case onto the floor and undoes the latches before flicking it open.

I don't know what I expect to find inside it. Gold? Money? Dope? Besides pussy, those are the things that seem to matter wherever you look. Most men—let alone most people—wouldn't be brought to tears by the sight of a wooden instrument, and her own words haunt me. *Cello.*

She glances up at Espi, shaking her head. "How...how? Why—"

"I got it from a friend," he says, gently cutting over her.

Speechless, she caresses the body of the instrument like it's glass. Like it's the motherfucking holy grail. For a second, I know she's forgotten all about Vincent Stacatto, Arno, Mack...Dante Vialle. We're just dust on her periphery, swept away by her one true passion. Right now, I understand why her precious Vinny was willing to kill her family as punishment for pursuing her dreams. Why he made her play while he killed. Why he held her captive for five years and forced her to bear his ring.

He knew what I know now: Nothing in the world will ever matter to her as much as this.

She will never look at another man the way she looks at a fucking piece of wood.

It's the kind of knowledge that would drive some jealous fuck stupid enough to fall in love with her insane.

CHAPTER THIRTY-ONE

Daniela

THE FIRST TIME I EVER SAW A CELLO BEING PLAYED, I froze in my tracks and stared. What an ugly instrument. It wasn't beautiful and elegant like a harp or shiny like a flute. It was huge and ungainly, manipulated with a stick held at an awkward angle. When the cellist began to saw at the strings, I'd expected some harsh sound, like the kind made when you tug on a taut rubber band.

Instead…music poured out, more beautiful than anything I had ever heard. *Bach* read the title of the booklet the player read from. I knew then that I would do whatever it took to master that big, hulking piece of wood. I would make it sing for me.

The one Espi has brought me is old. Scratches scar the body of the frame, and the bow is made of cheap fiberglass and plastic rather than the one of Pernambuco wood Vinny gave me. Touching them both, however, is like reconnecting with an old friend. I can't stop myself from easing it from the case, holding the familiar weight of it balanced between both hands. Before I know it, I'm sitting on the end of the couch, the bow is in my hand, and...

I play. I breathe. I feel. I'm Daniela again, and for as long as I manipulate the strings, fear cannot touch me. The room fades. The pain dissipates.

I'm whole again.

The notes come before I can even register the song being played, not that it really matters. I let myself play, and I know deep in my heart that it could be for the last time.

And...

It isn't enough. For the first time, the motion of my hands and the sweet melody they create doesn't take me away— something keeps me tethered to *this* couch and *this* floor. Someone. I open my eyes and find him watching me, only the devil isn't impressed by my song. He watches me try to fly, and he yanks me back down by my already broken wings. I'm anchored to him, no matter how hard I try to resist.

My fingers move faster in defiance. My movements are stronger. I can barely hear the song, but I know I'm playing better than I ever have in my life—and on an inferior instrument than the many Vinny supplied me with— but...it still isn't enough.

Lucifer keeps me here. He won't let me go. Tears spill from my eyes, sliding down my cheeks and mingling with the feel of the tuning pegs against my neck, but the devil doesn't give a damn. He watches me drown. He waits for the very moment I realize I'm stuck, and then he storms out of the room and slams the door to the apartment in his wake.

"Damn." The artist's voice fills the space the final note of music leaves behind, and I glance over and find him crouched beside me, shaking his head. "Damn, Pyro. You definitely weren't kidding about being one hell of a musician."

"I'm nothing," I insist, gently tilting the cello back in its case.

Vinny, for all of his cruelty, was correct in his assessment of my talent, at least. I was raw. Rough. Untrained. Untested. It was the same assessment every judge at every audition I performed would give. *You are good now, but with some work, you could be...*

The term always varied, but the sentiment was the same. With training, I could be a true cellist, but at the moment, I am nothing more than a finger painter compared to a serious musician.

"I dunno," Espi says, shaking his head. "That sounded damn good to me."

"Thank you." I let myself smile while I wrestle the case shut. Only then can I think again.

Vinny, Lucifer, his plan... Those are the only things that matter now. Music is just one of the many things I'll have to leave behind.

But the thought hurts less than I thought it would. When I run my fingers along the side of the case...all I can see are piercing blue eyes daring me to fight him—and I hate him so much that it burns.

"I've gotta jet." Espi rises to his feet again, swiping a hand through his hair. "I'll try to stop in to see you later. Stay strong, Pyro Girl."

He heads for the door, but before he can even get it open, Lucifer returns.

"We need to talk," he starts, pushing his way in, and a part of me suspects that he never truly left, but waited near the door, listening in.

Espi looks past him. As slender as he is, he has no trouble slipping past the devil and darting down the stairs. "Bye, *Danny*," he calls over his shoulder.

I hear the door on the lower level slam shut, and I can't help the question that trickles from my throat before I can reel it back in. "What happened between you two?"

The devil whirls on his heel to stare me down with hellfire in his eyes. "Wouldn't you like to fucking know?"

His tone is a lashing whip, but some sick part of me relishes the sting.

"I would." I'm too tired to lie or cower from his rage the way I did around Vinny.

He's poisoned me with the truth, and even now, he can't resist stabbing me with another taste of it. I can see it in his eyes—but, this time, he holds back. "That's none of your damn business."

I settle my hands on my lap and tilt my head to observe him carefully. Drawing this secret out of him will require another one of mine, I suspect. Our little game of tit for tat knows no end.

"Do you want to know when I really hated Vinny? Truly hated him?"

The devil remains motionless near the open doorway. He's curious, but he won't admit it out loud.

"It wasn't when he killed my family," I add, though the words hurt to leave my throat. "It wasn't even when he tortured my first few maids or kept me prisoner. I truly didn't start to really hate him until nearly a year in, around the first anniversary of their d-deaths..." The memory tugs at my consciousness and it's harder to speak. I try to. I *need* to...but it's only when the devil shifts to face me fully that words actually leave my lips again. "He signed me up for an audition. For *fun*, he said. Fun." I shake my head at that.

I can still remember the elegant theater. He took me himself that time, and he sat in the audience, watching from beyond the judges. I still remember his smile.

"I played, but when I was accepted into the next round, Vinny said nothing. Then the next, and he was silent. It was only when they offered me a job in the orchestra that he made me..." For a split second, the room disappears. I see the interior of the theater and the rich backdrop of the ruby curtains that shielded the stage. I see the face of the director who praised my talent and offered me a spot.

And I see Vinny, his gaze malicious as he made me turn them down.

"I knew then," I hear myself say as if Lucifer were there with me, watching four years into the past. "I could see it in his eyes, what he was. What he had become. A monster."

It feels so strange to admit it all out loud. Vinny could torture me for weeks and I could still love him. I still recited that stupid list in my head: *He likes to read, he likes the color green, he loves classical music.* Only then did I see what lurked within the shell of the man I'd once called my best friend.

"He made me turn...turn them d-down. Every year after that, around the same time, he forced me to audition again —a different theater every time. Sometimes he watched me, sometimes he wouldn't. This time..." My throat aches. I have to stop talking and gulp at the air just to keep from being swept under again.

Pain has a different flavor here than it did with Vinny. It's a potent, powerful drug, and once it hits...all I feel is rage. I can only see fire, hot and burning, licking at Vincent

Stacatto's skin. In Lucifer's realm, pain is nothing more than hate, and I won't survive the reckless high it brings.

"This time, I knew the theater. I had only been there once, five years previously...but I knew the general layout of the area. Vinny couldn't accuse me of lying if I said that I wanted to take a walk home from the subway station. A week before that, I had sold one of the pieces of clothing he gave me—a designer shawl. I used the money to pay off some thug I met on a street corner to have men waiting in an alley for a 'young woman who looks like me' that night. They...they could do whatever they wanted to her, just as long as they killed her. Slow. Quick. It didn't matter. She merely needed to d-die." My voice cracks.

The room starts spinning. The shadows distort and become the two men whose death warrants I signed the moment I just lay there and let them try to get their bit of fun in before killing me. Maybe...I even felt like I deserved it—the pain, the humiliation, the brutality. Maybe I'd needed to feel it all just to erase the harsher ache of flirting with the only future I had ever envisioned for myself and having to walk away.

Maybe...maybe.

It's only when a hand falls on my shoulder that I realize I've said all of that out loud. The fingers clench, gripping me down to the bone, but not because of what I've said. I'm choking. Tears spill down, blurring my vision, and I can't keep up with whatever sound is leaving my mouth now. My ears cringe from it. At some points, it sounds like laughter. At others, it sounds like sobs.

The devil waits until I catch my breath and smother the sound, but for some reason, he doesn't pull away.

When I gather the nerve to look up, I catch the tail end of a searching look. It's confusing that I don't find the things in his eyes that I expect to or should—no hate, no disgust, no pity. I look into his gaze and I see myself staring back, my eyes wide, my hair a mess.

"I never hated him," he tells me, his voice so gruff that I could have imagined it—but even my dark fantasies were never so twisted. "I never hated...him. You can't hate an animal. You pity it. You fear it. You want to put a bullet in its brain to end its fucking misery, but hate? No..." He backs away, shaking his head, and my shoulder burns with the loss of his touch. "You don't waste an emotion like hate on a creature that can't even feel." He flexes his fingers, and I think I understand what he means.

A man who makes his living off violence can't afford to be reckless with the tools of his trade: hate, pain, rage. They fuel him, making it easier for him to envision himself as merely another worthless animal fighting its way out of a cage.

"Espi hates me because...no matter what I fucking did, I could never protect him. It was *never* enough." His voice carries a wave of pain even someone like me—scarred and abused and tormented—can only dream of.

It's the ache I feel whenever I think of Christoph, only magnified by every year and every day he had to build the shadow of an illusion around the only person he seems to love.

What was it like for him? Having to enter that house every day to shield Espi from the monstrous "animal" lurking in the basement? What was it like, waiting to kill his own father the moment he heard footsteps on the stairs at night?

There's nothing I can say. I can only sit and watch as the devil retreats and storms into the bedroom, slamming the door shut behind him.

I can only breathe and reach down to finger the length of the cello. I can only pray that, if I play long enough or hard enough, I can escape this hold he has over me.

I won't let the devil destroy the one thing Vinny never could.

———

I play for hours. My fingers ache. My arms are on fire. My mind is still *here*. I'm still painfully aware when the door to the apartment opens and a new presence slinks his way inside. He watches me with a scowl, his green eyes blazing. Apparently, he isn't a fan of Bach's cello suites.

"Can someone shut her the fuck up?" Arno takes a step toward me only to freeze in his tracks. A quick glance over my shoulder reveals why.

Lucifer's guarding the doorway to the bedroom, his arms crossed like a true beast from Hades. I don't know how long he's been standing there, but with one look, he pins Arno in place. With one look, he steals away every semblance of peace I have ever found while playing. In defeat, my bow-wielding hand falls, and the song dies on a harsh, broken note.

"Mack's waiting for you," Arno says. "Wanted to come get you himself, but I 'volunteered.'" He's implying something. Something that makes Lucifer perk up from the top of his head down to the tip of his toes until he prickles with energy, electric.

"He can fucking wait." His tone leaves no room for challenge.

Chuckling to himself, Arno doesn't even try. There's a hint of admiration in his gaze. Despite the anger that sometimes burns hot between them, I sense that—though I don't think by blood—these two really do harbor the bonds of brotherhood between them. There's respect in the way Lucifer lets him off with only a visual warning when Arno takes another step toward me.

But there's a challenge between them too. A dare. Maybe even a game. I'm the ball, but Lucifer won't give me up so easily.

"Anything else?" he wonders, his tone steady and cold—but I don't miss the way he shifts, bringing his bulk just a fraction of an inch closer.

"Nothing," Arno concedes, taking a step back. "Just that Mack seems to want to do this shit tonight. Be ready."

"Am I ever not?"

Arno doesn't reply when he turns and leaves, closing the door behind him. The tension doesn't leave Lucifer's muscles until the door on the lower level slams shut as well, the sound faint through the walls. Even after that, he merely shrugs.

"Get up."

I obey, setting my bow aside and propping my cello against the couch.

The devil approaches me with slow, measured strides. My breath hitches and something inside my chest tightens when he enters the shadow of my personal space and reaches out to trap my chin against his palm. With one scorching look, he stares at me, into me, *through* me.

"About what you said... Do you hate him now?"

"Yes." I don't even have to think. The rage will always be there, festering in the pit of my soul. I hate Vincent Stacatto with every fiber of my being. Maybe that makes me weaker than him, the devil able to reserve his hatred for only those creatures he deems worthy of it.

Lucifer frowns and his fingers tighten. I feel the ridge of every one pressing into my jaw, tilting it so that I'm forced up on tiptoe, and his face is closer.

"Do you hate me?"

I flinch away from his touch, but he doesn't let go.

"Do you?" he asks, but his voice holds a dark confidence as if he already knows my answer. *Yes.* "I hurt you." His thumb drifts up to graze my ruined ear, and I can't silence a whine. "I don't give a shit about you. I would have let Arno and his men rape you on camera. I'm going to kill you..."

Yes, yes, yes, a part of me murmurs, seconding all of those things. I should hate him. I need to. God, I even want to. Hatred is one of my safe, familiar emotions. Hell, these days, it's one of the few things that drives me through each waking moment, apart from fear.

It would be so damn easy to hate Lucifer, my devil in the flesh.

Fuck him for taking that choice from me.

"You can't..." I clear my throat, and when I meet his gaze again, something sparks in the air, dangerous and hot. I see deep into those cold, lifeless eyes—and he lets me in. He lets me boldly prod and pick over the remains of humanity so that I can see for myself. He is truly evil. There is no warmth in him. No compassion. No soul. "You can't...you can't hate an *animal*."

I don't know what makes me touch him, bringing a hint of life to those blue eyes as my fingers trail the front of his chest. Anger? Rage? His own twisted bit of hatred for me? He lets me drag my touch all the way down to the hem of his shirt. He lets me slide the tips of my fingers underneath. He lets me feel his hard, warm skin.

My devil has a pulse. He can bleed. He can feel—he likes to feel my fingers along his waistband especially. He liked fucking me. He liked to taste me. My devil didn't really want to own me...but I suppose that is the twisted irony of hell. Every soul gets shackled to something.

"You can't hate an animal," I croak, my voice breaking as that realization sinks in with the same brutality with which my nails dig into the flesh of his stomach.

Lucifer growls, invading my tiny section of carpet and forcing me back against the couch. I retreat until my backside hits the top of it rather than sink onto the cushions at his mercy. He's ready for me anyway, forcing himself between my legs and bringing his mouth in close. I hear his teeth click together, hungry for flesh with every bit of the instinct of a wolf. Rather than bite, his tongue swipes my ruined ear, raising a wave of pain amid a shockingly wet heat.

"Animal," he grumbles, tasting the word. "And you...you're just a little bitch." His hands brace against the wall on either side of me, trapping me between both surfaces. "I could fuck you," he tells me in a guttural rasp. "I could make your cunt bleed. You still wouldn't mean shit to me."

I nod along with every dark promise as the space between my legs throbs—hell, maybe I even want him to follow through on it.

"You can't hate an animal," I repeat, gasping the words out. It's a curse—some horrible truth that tethers me to this monster I can't even bring myself to hate. At least Vinny taught me well enough how to see someone else as an animal. "Animals are meant to be owned," I tell Lucifer, but my fingers have a will of their own, and they start to hike his shirt up, revealing the chiseled planes of his chest and a dusky covering of fine, black hair. "Animals...animals are branded."

He grunts, rolling his hips against my thigh. He's hard; I know that fact without even having to look or feel. His lust taints the air, unashamed—he's merely a beast surrendering to a natural impulse, and for some sick reason, it only grows when I reach into the pocket of my sweatpants and withdraw my knife.

The devil laughs, the sound ripped from a corded neck. He watches me drag my thumb along the dull edge. He waits until I raise it against his skin. He waits until I dig the tip of the knife into him, but not hard enough to draw blood.

Suddenly, the room dissipates. We're both on fire, drowning in hell. I should throw my knife away. Beg for mercy. Plead. The violence promised in the devil's blue gaze will swallow me whole.

And it's about damn time.

I flick my wrist, digging my knife in even deeper, and he grits out a sound between a curse and a groan. His hand finds my wrist, gripping it tightly enough to hurt. Break. Then he applies more pressure, forcing the blade in...

The world shifts. Lucifer is lying on the couch while I straddle him. My free hand paws at his shirt, but he's the one who tears it off in the end, baring his chest to me, and I can't help an appreciative groan. Hell didn't spit out too many monsters like him these days. All chiseled, hard anger and rage melded against a human form. Fixated, I drag my thumb along his abdomen, enthralled by the vibrant trail of blood that bleeds from a wound no longer than my fingernail.

Animals are meant to be branded. I'm possessed by insanity when I dig my knife in again, lengthening the cut into a longer, straighter line.

"Fuck!" Lucifer bucks underneath me, straining my grip on the blade—but he isn't in pain. His head lolls, his eyes searing. *Do it,* they tell me.

So I cut him again. It's a careful series of delicate little marks to form the letter D. I won't maim him the way Vinny did me. I'll make my brand carefully, cementing my ownership in the devil's skin. He won't ever forget what he is: an animal. Untamed. Wild. Mine...

I shiver beneath that thought, but before I can process it fully, the devil takes my hand and jabs it against his flesh again, guiding the carving of an A. We take our time, making sure to sharpen the edges. The Y takes the longest; I curve the end of it back to underline the other letters.

Danny. The devil bears my mark much in the same way I bear his. It's a grim realization that doesn't empower me the way I thought it would. Ownership of Lucifer is a heavy cross to carry. His pain is mine. His anger is mine. His rage...

Those emotions meld together in the splotches of blood gleaming against the edge of my blade. Vinny never shared anything with me but his obsession. Lucifer holds back nothing. He weighs me down with him, and I struggle beneath the stress of it all. A beast like him isn't meant to be owned, and therein lies the danger—because he owns me too.

I see the possession in his eyes when I finally draw the blade from his skin and glance down at the marks on his chest. Something feral rumbles through his throat as deceptively harmless as a roll of thunder right before the paralyzing flash of lightning.

I've never owned many things. Curiosity to know what it feels like draws me to lower my head, bringing my mouth inches over my bloody brand. I inhale, tasting his scent on the air, and I can't stop myself from dragging a thumb along the angry, red letters. *Mine.*

Lucifer growls in acknowledgment. *His.* He flinches, jerking his hips when my lips brush the flesh of his stomach. The front of his jeans bulge, and he throbs against my chest, molten and hungry. I don't feel anything but an answering pulse in my core as I drag my fingers down to the latch of his jeans.

Within an instant, I'm on the floor, lying on my back, as Lucifer hovers over me. He fists his hands in my sweatpants, but he doesn't wrench them down my legs until I arch my back. He waits for me to moan before he slides a hand beneath my sweatshirt and palms my left breast. He waits...for me to thrash, groan, whimper—any reaction that can be construed as permission.

When I'm finally stripped naked, though, he doesn't touch me. His hand flies down to the clasp of his jeans, but he takes his sweet time, watching me grind my thighs together to ease my own ache. My name glows red, etched forever into his skin. The sight of it alone is enough to make my breathing hitch and my vision blur around the edges. Then the devil takes control and nudges my knees apart with one of his own.

"Look at me."

I do, trailing my gaze up to his. The monster inhales me, and slowly, he begins to tug his jeans down his hips, freeing his cock. He springs forward, lethally hard. Beads of white weep from the head of him, and he's already pulsing for me.

He yanks his pants down to his knees, but when he starts to crouch forward, he rears back. Frowning, he swipes at something jutting from his pocket; it must have stabbed in his thigh when he moved. It's a chain, I see as it dangles helplessly from his fingers. A necklace. I snatch for it before he can toss it aside and observe the pendant with shaking hands.

It says his name. *Dante.* So simple. So powerful. I glance down and scan the letters of the name etched onto me, but I don't feel the same thrill. And, suddenly, I need to. I want to. The devil can't erase Vinny's mark—but he can make his own.

"Wait—" Lucifer bites his protest back when I shift out from underneath him and rise, shaking to my feet. He won't beg for me. He watches instead while I cling to the counter on legs that can barely support my weight.

When I reach the stove, I flick one of the burners on with one hand and brandish the necklace in the other.

He must realize what I intend to do, because suddenly, he's beside me, wrenching the necklace from my grip. "Fuck." His eyes are on the newborn flames that match the hue of his eyes.

I can't tell if he's disgusted or...tempted as his gaze roves over to the chain.

After a second, he shakes his head as if trying to clear it. "No—"

"Please." I don't recognize the plaintive little voice that tears from my throat. Lynn has returned, this time begging the devil himself to set her free—exorcise her out of my skin with the power of his name alone.

Lucifer frowns again. Then he reaches beyond me and tugs at drawers and swipes open cupboards. Somewhere, he manages to find a bottle of vodka. I don't know what he means to do with it when he wrenches the cap and off wets a rag snatched from the counter with it.

"Where?" he grits out, scanning my naked torso. His eyes linger around Vinny's name, but I shake my head and point to my collarbone.

"Here."

He says nothing as he swipes at the area with the rag, cleansing it with the alcohol. "Hold it above the flame," he tells me, jerking his head to the stove.

I obey, dangling the necklace by the chain so that the pendant hovers directly above the flames.

"Lower," Lucifer directs. "And don't bring it up until I say so. This shit will catch fire."

Alcohol is *flammable,* I remember as the insanity of what we're doing rushes to my head. Heat shoots up the slender chain, biting into my fingers, but I don't let go. Not until the devil finally wrestles the necklace from me himself and raises the heated metal. He scans my chest carefully, searching for any bead of volatile alcohol that might linger. To make sure, he presses me against the counter and exhales once over my skin, making my nipples tighten at the contact.

"You...you sure?" He doesn't make it sound like a question, but a dare.

Are you sure, Daniela?

I nod and press both hands against the counter on either side of me, arching my back to present him with the flattest surface possible. "Yes."

With only a nod, the devil agrees, and he hefts the chain with his bare hand. Using my knife, he slams the heated metal against my skin and...

Pain. I see black as Vinny's evil is driven out of me like a nail. Agony and blood and gaping flesh are all that's left behind, and the devil makes sure to brand his mark over every shuddering inch. I'm not sure how long he holds the hot metal there. When my vision clears, the necklace is smoldering somewhere on the floor and Lucifer's eyes are on mine.

"You okay?"

"Yes..." My throat aches and my voice is a rasp. The echo that reaches my ears tells me why; I must have screamed. I stare down at the mark he made. I feel it deeper than I've ever felt anything in my life, pulsing and volatile. "I'm fine."

His brand is an angry red against my skin, bleeding in some places. The mark will scar. Once again, another man's name stains me, but this time, I put it there. I don't know if Lucifer's surprised when I lunge forward, sealing my mouth against his. If he is, he hides it well by lashing his tongue against my lips to pry them apart.

We kiss in hungry, violent, greedy snatches. Impatient, Lucifer tugs me into the narrow hallway and flattens me against the wall. He's panting, his cock practically thrumming with the need to be inside me. I reach down and palm it, stroking until he grits out curses with every breath. Guiding him closer, I stare dead into his eyes as he muscles his way between my legs and enters me in one hard thrust. My heels dig into the backs of his thighs, my legs holding him tight with every hungry, fierce roll of his hips.

He's rough. Brutal. I'll feel him inside me for weeks after. Months. It's still not enough. My nails bite into his shoulders, goading him on until he's grunting with each thrust. *More. More. Harder.* He slams into me, crushing me into the wall, and an icy splash of pain in my core tells me that the devil stayed true to his promise. *"I could make your cunt bleed."* He stiffens when he realizes and tries to pull out, but I sink my teeth into his shoulder before he can. I bite down hard until he stiffens, becoming steel inside me. *Mine.*

Grunting, he rides me without a shred of mercy, driving himself into me and wrenching himself back out—only to plunge in even deeper. Harder. Faster. I hover on the edge of pain and sanity until, with one last thrust, he breaks me open.

I wail against his skin, memorizing every growl and groan he smothers into the side of my throat. It's a more potent tune than any I could caress out with my bow or any complex suite. This is a melody I could never play with my cello or any other instrument—only my soul. Only like this, bare flesh against bare flesh, with nothing but blood and pain to eke each brutal, violent note out. The devil makes his music in screams, burning flesh, and rent, ruined skin.

And I'm drunk on it.

"Say it," I gasp out. My hand shakes as it finds his punishingly gripping my waist, and I urge it up to brush the stinging flesh of his brand. "Say it," I beg him, my saliva mingling with the blood I managed to draw with my teeth. "Say it...please."

You are mine. Those words Vinny loved to boast for my benefit. They'll make for the crescendo of this twisted melody. I need to hear him say it. I *need* to. I bite him again when he doesn't comply quickly enough and the devil howls, twitching inside me.

"You," he growls, ramming into me so hard that I see stars. "You... *Yours.*"

Yours. I can only moan in confusion. It isn't the right thing for him to say.

I'm yours.

Mine. Fire burns white-hot, scalding my spine and reducing my body to ash. I can only cling to him and scream as an orgasm rips me into pieces. Lucifer is careless with the ruined parts of me. He fucks his release into me and then goes limp with the final thrust, pinning me to the wall with his weight alone.

I don't know how long we stay like this. Minutes? Hours? The only thing I'm aware of when he finally withdraws from me is an agony that cuts me deeper than any pain I've ever experienced before and has me sinking down to my knees. It has nothing to do with the throbbing in my bleeding, abused core or the callous way Lucifer shoves himself off me and then staggers in search of his pants.

One single realization obliterates what's left of my heart, leaving scorch marks on my soul: As long as Vinny is alive, none of this fucking matters.

Not one damn bit.

CHAPTER THIRTY-TWO

Dante

THERE'S TOO MUCH OF HER BLOOD TO JUST WIPE OFF on the sides of my jeans. I need a shower. I need to scour the bitch from my skin. I need...I need to fucking kill her. *Now.*

I find her slumped against the floor, her eyes vacant and distant. No one's home. She doesn't even react when I pick her knife up from the floor and come toward her with it drawn. The little bitch has flown off again, terrified by whatever she saw even as she rode out her climax and drenched my cock in her release. She looked at me...and she saw *his* face.

I don't know whether to strangle her or let her fucking suffer. Let her see the fucking bastard who truly owns her. Let her get high off the fact that he can't touch her here. Let her fuck her way through the rest of her life while she tries to pretend that he doesn't haunt her every step.

Or maybe I should put the little bitch out of her misery now? I am an *animal* after all... Baring my teeth, I trail my gaze over the rest of her, ignoring the way my cock lurches, still fucking semi-hard. I reach for her with one hand while adjusting the knife on the palm of the other. I don't think before I cut. One hard jerk of my wrist...and there is no blood. No screaming. No death. There's only a lock of ebony hair in my fingers, still warm with the heat of her. It even fucking smells like her. Growling at the realization, I tuck the shit into my pocket and aim for her again. This time, it's her arm I grab, but for some reason, I don't cut. I drag her upright instead, watching her head loll against the wall and her vacant body grasp for anything within reach to help her find her balance.

I consider dropping her when the little bitch starts to clutch at my forearm. Her nails scrape my skin and every little pinprick sensation bolts down directly to my cock. She turns my entire body into her little plaything, stoking a lust I learned in childhood to suppress and control. Lust makes men stupid. It makes them fucking weak.

Fucking her makes *me* weak.

My hand drops the knife, and the fingers find her throat. Those hazel eyes watch me, flickering with only a hint of life, as I press hard, sealing her windpipe off. Five minutes, I decide. She'd likely be dead in one, but five would make it slower. Five would make her suffer. For five fucking minutes —her very last—she'll see my face instead of his. I press harder, and the pain makes her fly back into her body. Slowly, her eyes register me, and she realizes what I'm doing.

How I'll do it. That her death will be drawn out painfully over every last fucking second. She understands it...and if she could, she'd fucking sigh.

It's about damn time.

I let her go to gasp and wheeze on the air, and while she sways, I throw her over one shoulder. When I reach the bedroom, I pitch her onto the mattress and leave again. In the narrow bathroom, I find a washcloth and wet it beneath the sink. The creature glowering into the mirror is a stranger. Some sick, stupid fuck with some bitch's name carved into his chest. He doesn't even have the nerve to seem ashamed by it. Hell...I think the son of a bitch even got off on the pain of those five little letters being etched into his skin. Thirteen years ago, Dino tattooed my "new" name on me himself. Kitten, the scared little fuck who one day grew claws.

"You don't just let any bastard with a needle touch your skin," he told me. "I'd rather let a bastard kill me than ever ink me without my goddamn permission. This." He pointed to his throat, where his own name inked the flesh. "This is your armor. Whatever you put on it should adorn your fucking soul. Those dumbasses who get pussies or birdies tattooed on their arms? Deep down, that's all they really are. Cartoons and fucking scared little birdies. Every scar and mark you wear with fucking pride, or you don't let the shit touch you at all."

I let that little bitch cut me. I let her draw her mark onto my skin. I *let* her.

Damn her if she thinks I'll let her get off that fucking easily. When I return to the bedroom, she's lying limp in the center of the mattress. She doesn't react when I grab her by the ankle and drag her closer. With one knee propped against the end of the bed, I lean over and drag the rag between her legs. She's bleeding, but it's just a streak across the end of the rag. My seed drips from her more steadily than anything else.

The more of her I touch with the rag, the more of her that creeps back into those eyes, which watch me warily. She doesn't like being cleaned. She doesn't like when the monster of the story wipes his mess from her skin. She likes it even less when that same beast goes to grab a bottle of vodka from the kitchen and carefully pours it onto the brand he made on her skin.

She tries to fight me off then. "No...no."

I fight back, pinning her down by her arm until she whines. My name will leave a nasty scar. She'll never be able to erase it. And him... He'd have to cut her fucking shoulder out to override my claim. The little bitch is mine, for however long I say so.

Vincent Stacatto can go fuck himself; he won't *ever* fuck her.

"Look at me."

She does, still trying to bat my hand away. I set the vodka aside without even drinking from it, which would be the smart thing to do—erase the lust that flares up when she looks up at me with fire in her eyes. Danny...the little bitch who sold her soul to a man who never really had one of his own. Does the thought of that frighten her? *Something* has her spooked, because she tries to stare beyond me. She tries to fly off, but the moment I seal my mouth over hers, she's trapped. She's still fighting though, even as she slams her tongue against mine. The cloth in my hand is a whip, and she flinches with every inch of her I claim with it, bathing the blood from her skin. She's a rebellious little bitch—she fights me harder than I know she ever did against him, but it's no use.

With a groan, she surrenders, her hands fisting in my hair and her hip arching into my touch.

For the next five minutes, she'll forget about him and die in another way—with every kiss I take and the climax I'll wring out of her with my fingers. For the next five minutes, she's mine alone. I'll make sure of that.

I'll crush the bastard from her skull if I have to.

———

MACK'S WAITING BY THE MOUTH OF THE KENNEL FOR me when I finally leave the garage just after sunset with the taste of blood in my mouth and cunt on my tongue. Three of his men surround him, keeping just enough distance to show that Mack isn't afraid to face me alone—he just wants to reinforce just how much power he has here. All hail the fucking *king*.

"Enjoying the guest house?" he wonders, cocking an

eyebrow once I come within a yard of him. "You must have broken in the bed, at least. I can smell her on you."

I say nothing, giving him no ounce of emotion to bite into. I simply stare the bastard down until he remembers the business at hand.

"Tonight," he grunts out, crossing his arms over his chest. "We do this quickly. Do you have the addresses?"

I jerk my head toward the garage. "She has them."

Mack chuckles. "Well, then it's a good thing that I've made sure *she* attends this little party..."

Something in his tone makes me glance over my shoulder just in time to catch a man leaving the garage with a slender woman in tow.

Red. It paints everything beneath a roar so deafening that my ears pop. Even knowing that Mack is watching can't stop me from taking a step toward them. My fingers are on fire in a way I have never felt, not even in the cage.

The fucker doesn't dare touch her, at least. He makes her walk in front of him instead, her head held high, her chin pointed to the sky, those haughty eyes on fire. However, there's a noticeable limp she can't hide. Her ravaged cunt aches with my possession—she won't feel right again for a week, at least.

"Relax, Dante," Mack croons behind me. "I made sure that she's in safe hands."

It's only now that the hair of the man herding her forward catches a flicker of light—copper.

"I'll have her stay with Arno during our little adventure," Mack clarifies. "Safe and sound."

Arno watches me as they come closer. He makes sure to keep enough distance from her, and he doesn't reach for her, even when she staggers over the uneven ground. He stares me dead in the eye the entire fucking time.

"Now," Mack starts, and I drag my gaze back to him. "Give me the addresses and we can get this little party started."

"No." I clip the word so it's clear enough for the bastard to understand. "I handle the girls on my own with Arno's boys. You take the drug ring."

Mack chuckles, shaking his head. "Now that wouldn't be very fun, now would it, Dante?" His expression hardens, and I know without a doubt that he's already formulated his own plan. "We split up. You take half of Arno's men, half of mine, and I'll do the same. You hit the enclaves first. When and only *when* you give me the signal that you're all clear, I'll move on the drug ring—but you play this your way, Dante. You bust open the enclaves without backup, and you get out of there on your own. Any losses you take are on your fucking head, understood?"

I force myself to nod once. The rules were simple: no holds barred, no easy outs—the same ones we played by whenever we fought in the cage. "I got it."

"What about me?" Arno pipes up, his voice gruff.

Mack shrugs. "You and the girl will stay out of sight. I'll tag a few of my men along, of course...but we can't have her falling into the wrong hands. Yet."

I don't like it. I don't like Mack's cocky fucking smirk or the way he glances from me to the girl, putting the pieces together with the awkward way she's standing and the blood on my shirt.

"Fine. But, when this is over, you take Stacatto's money, and we get the girls. Understood?"

Mack nods, his eyes narrowed. "A fucking waste, but understood."

"Good," I toss back. "When do we go?"

Mack smiles. "Now."

CHAPTER THIRTY-THREE

Dante

Mack may be an asshole, but he keeps good men in his pocket. They don't make a damn sound as they spread out beside me across the roof of a warehouse overlooking the one containing Stacatto's women. It's back too far to launch an assault from, but it gives us the best vantage point to make a plan. Though tucked behind the docks on the city's Lower East side, the first enclave is as shitty a place as it is secure for a king to stash his merchandise.

Rats scurry out in the open, and the stench blowing off the bay makes the air reek. In the distance, I can hear the ships bellowing as they enter and leave the harbor, just like the girl's maid claimed. That being said, most people wouldn't have their trash stored here—let alone women worth a few grand a head.

Then again, Stacatto did seem to get creative when designing his prisons. According to the addresses the girl stole, there are nine other safe houses, positioned relatively close, all along the waterfront. While the area seems unguarded at first, any man with fucking eyes in his head could catch the telltale signs of professionals patrolling in unmarked vans.

Mack was right. Taking on even one of them alone would be pure suicide. It's a good fucking thing I have a plan B.

"Give me your cell phone," I tell the man crouched closest to me, and he obeys without question, slapping a silver phone onto my outstretched palm.

When I call 911, a tired voice answers. "What's your emergency?"

"Send a car around the edge of the Forrester docks," I say and hang up without waiting for a response. Then I dial a different number, but the person who picks up on the other end is a bit warier than the operator.

"Either this is Vialle or the bastard gave my number to a telemarketer, in which case...I suggest you lose it."

"You have ten minutes to catch the fireworks show, Detective," I tell him. "Don't be late."

I can fucking *hear* the man scowl.

"Where?"

I give him the address. "Now, here comes the fun part," I add. "If you don't want to get your hands dirty yourself, then pick a man—someone you trust with your life, Detective. If you can't think of anyone, then we're both shit out of luck." I wait, but Van Hallen says nothing. I take that as a good sign; the bastard is listening. "Whoever he is, tell him to go to the chief directly—no subordinates. A trusted informant has just warned him of a group of women being held against their will. A girl. Calls herself Danny. Suggest that he send out a patrol."

Van Hallen exhales, and I sense him shift the receiver against his ear. "Pardon me, Vialle, but I thought that's what I was doing by sending my men there in the first place?"

I chuckle. "Oh, Detective. You'll just be catching the show. The real fireworks will come when your chief tips off Stacatto."

I hang up, and then I wait. Exactly ten minutes later, on the dot, a crew of men burst from the enclave. In their wake scurry at least ten women the men herd with guns into a nearby van.

"Bingo."

I shift out of a crouch and rise to my feet, drawing the pistol in my pocket while the men wait for my signal. Never one to disappoint, it comes in the form of a pre-written text message that is delivered the moment I hit send.

"It's showtime."

———

THE MOVIES LIKE TO MAKE THE BATTLES IN A SO-called "gang war" seem violent. Messy. Men shoot each other to death at point-blank range, right there in front of terrified pedestrians. There is no finesse. No stealth involved. Just gunfire and blood.

In reality—like in any true war—the fighting is done mostly from the shadows. Each side moves their men around the board like the pieces in a game of chess. The first fucker to outmaneuver the other wins checkmate. As for the loser...

Most of the games I've ever played employed a "take no prisoners" approach.

"Get into position," I tell the others before leading the way myself.

A rickety fire escape is the only way off the roof, and it opens onto an alley merely a few yards shy of the enclave entrance. Curses muttered in Russian and Italian echo off the brick walls as Stacatto's men try to get the van loaded. Once again, Mack's men manage to impress as they follow me in silence around the block to where Arno's men are waiting in their own van. Once they see me, they jump out, their weapons already drawn.

If Dino were alive, he'd flash a rare smile—hell, the fucker might have even shown teeth. He'd place bets on which man could draw the most blood just to "make things interesting." This current matchup would have had him salivating. Which men would be more lethal? Arno's men still hunger for revenge, but Mack's are just eager for a good fucking time. It makes for an interesting batch when we circle around to confront Stacatto's men before they can drive off. Cats and dogs. Mutts and purebred bulldogs born and raised in the pit.

Professional or not, Stacatto's pricks don't even know what's hitting them when the first round of bullets fly. I let Arno's men take the lead while I head for the van. The driver already has a cell phone to his ear, shouting something in Italian—but he's brutally interrupted when a bullet flies through the windshield and strikes him right between the eyes.

"Clear this place out," I hiss to the man standing beside me, his pistol drawn. "Only the girls leave alive."

"Got it."

By the time we finally reach the van, another thug is dispatched with a bullet to the chest, and the only figures we find inside the vehicle itself are the women, curled up on the seats.

"One down," I hear myself say. "Nine more to go."

CHAPTER THIRTY-FOUR

Daniela

They herd me into the back of a van with Arno and a man who smells like cigarettes and liquor. There are no seats. We crouch on the bare flooring and brace our backs against whatever surface is in reach—I choose the ice-cold siding of the vehicle itself, pressing both hands flat against it for leverage.

Save for the glow of a cell phone the other man's holding in his fist, it's dark. I can just make out a black duffel beside him, and I entertain a morbid curiosity as to what might be inside it—at least I do during the few precious seconds when I'm not dreading what might happen if this entire plan fails.

Lucifer demanded my faith once, but it's harder than I thought to deny it to him now. Who could doubt that cold, predatory calculation of his; he bites with his teeth fully drawn and saves any thoughts of failure for later, after he's done feasting on the belly of his conquest. Years of living on the streets and fighting in the cage have left him immune to fear.

I'm not so lucky. Vinny's possession drips into my sweat. His voice is a constant presence at the back of my head, and I know that, as long as he's alive, I'll never be able to silence him...

I own you, Mi Bella.

"You're jumpy."

I jolt back to the present as Arno makes that assessment while watching me from the other end of the van, his green eyes sharp even in the darkness.

"You're worried your precious fiancé will get you back tonight." He jerks his chin at my throat as if he can see Vinny's possession wrapped around my neck. When I flinch, he laughs. "You don't know Dante. I've seen the way he looks at you."

I raise an eyebrow. "Like how?"

"The same way he looked at the men he wanted to tear apart in the cage," Arno admits. "Like he can't wait to put his fist through your skull, and no one better get in his fucking way... Come to think of it, he's looked at you like that for a while now. But you're still alive." He frowns and rubs his chin as if trying to figure out why. "Either way, he won't let you go until he *decides* you can go—whether or not this stupid plan works. Mark my words on that."

Right when he finishes, the van comes to a stop, and the man Mack sent—a brute with black hair and mean, brown eyes—shifts out of his crouch, settling down on his knees. "Can we cut the fucking chitchat?" he grunts while an overhead light cuts on, which he uses as his cue to tug on the zipper of his duffel.

It's full of weapons: two guns and a roll of black canvas. The man sets the guns on either side of him and unfurls the roll against the floor of the van, revealing three knives sheathed in leather holsters. Freeing one of the blades, he tucks it into the pocket of his pants and inclines his chin to Arno. "You want?"

Arno accepts a blade in silence, but I don't miss the telltale bulge of his own weapons hidden beneath his battered leather jacket. Unsurprisingly, no one offers me a weapon, and the next few moments pass in tense silence while my mind refocuses on unease again. Mack gave Dante an hour. An hour to get into position. An hour to crack Vinny's most cherished organization.

An *hour* to live.

The seconds gnaw at me, though Arno doesn't seem worried. He's...bored. The fingers of his right hand keep twitching, and I try to picture that "look" he claimed that the devil reserves only for me. I think Arno's wearing a similar expression now, longing for the violence of bloodshed to sink into.

And, despite what Mack seems to think, I'm not stupid. Arno doesn't defer to Dante any more than the latter does to him. If Arno came along to babysit Dante's "little bitch," then it was for a reason. Anticipation to learn exactly why spurs my pulse on until I can almost hear it counting the minutes down.

Five.

Four.

Three.

Two...

"Any sign?" Arno finally asks, jerking his chin toward the silent phone.

"Not yet."

"I need to get some fucking air." Shifting toward the end of the van, Arno wrenches the door open and climbs out.

I get only a glimpse of what I assume is an alley before it slams shut again, and the tinted windows don't reveal much. I can't tell how far we are from the enclaves or even from the hotel. It's a strange sort of blindness. For five years, this part of the city has been my prison, but somehow, this feels worse. I don't know what to prepare for. Vinny? Dante?

I copy Arno by watching the phone in the other man's grip, waiting for a noise or a sound—any sign as to what might be happening, but when he catches me staring, his eyes narrow.

"See something you like?"

His tone sends prickles of alarm shooting through my chest.

"N-no." I turn away to stare at the opposite corner, but I see him moving from the corner of my eye.

He rises as much as he can, crouching beneath the roof of the van. In three steps, he's beside me, his repulsive scent filling my nostrils. Without permission, he rakes a meaty hand through my hair, twisting a lock of it between his fingers.

"You're a pretty bitch," he admits as if it's something I should be proud of, but when he reaches for my shoulder, three words spill from my throat.

"Don't touch me."

Vinny would be pleased, I think. His precious Lynn is finally protecting his investment...but, for once, he's not the one I see. His scent doesn't overpower me, even here. His claim isn't burning through my skin.

"Now, don't be shy," the man snarls, muscling in closer. "Word has it that you're hungry for any cock that doesn't belong to Stacatto..."

Run! My muscles barely start to tense before he shoves me down.

The man uses his weight like a battering ram to position himself above me, grunting with the effort. I kick and dig at his face with my nails, but he's too strong and easily parries my attempts. In fact, I think he enjoys my resistance more than anything else. With every failed hit, the excitement in his eyes burns hotter.

"I said don't be shy," he croons against my ear. "Let's see what Stacatto's little bitch has to offer..."

He gets one of his hands beneath my sweatshirt and yanks, revealing everything but the very tops of my breasts. He stiffens when he sees Vinny's mark, and I use the shock to land a kick on his chest that shoves him off me.

There's no use screaming for help—not here. My knife is in my pocket, but when I get it free, the man is already on me again, knocking it out of my hand. It skitters across the floor of the van just as he plants what feels like a knee against the small of my back, causing my chin to smack off the floor. Stars explode through my vision. My head is left spinning as a guttural voice rumbles through my ears.

"Feisty little bitch."

Fear drags me back into my body when a rough hand plunges inside my pants, groping at flesh the devil has already left sore and throbbing.

"I figure we have an hour to kill, so let's play," he tells me while his fingers cup my ass so hard that the nails dig in. "Now, settle down and be a good girl and I can make it go quickly."

Quick. Something about that word paralyzes me, and I don't fight when he peels my sweatpants down to the tops of my thighs. I obey when he nudges me onto my knees. I look at him when he snags my chin in hands that smell like vinegar and wrenches my head around to face him—but every ounce of focus I have left is fixated on an object that I startle him by lunging for.

The moment my fingers curl around the object, I yank it closer while twisting onto my back. The man doesn't even seem to notice when he comes for me, still tugging at the latch of his jeans. It's only when I lurch up and the knife bites into him that he tries to push me back, slamming his hand against my shoulder.

It's in vain. *His* blade is sharp, unlike mine. It turns the own man's momentum against him and sinks deep into his chest. Too deep. I can't lessen the pressure before he grits out something that could be a curse even as his eyes glaze over. Warm, red liquid trickles from his mouth and coats my fingers while he goes limp, crushing me with his full body weight.

Vinny put on enough gruesome shows for me to recognize death when I see it. Back in those days, I would cling to my cello in order to escape the bloodshed, but it's ironic how, now, I can't stop staring into his eyes. I can't let the knife go. I can't stop hearing the devil's voice inside my head.

"Being a fighter was a different world from being bait. It was darker. Colder. You looked at a man, and you trained yourself to see him as only a piece of meat, nothing more. You sized up his weaknesses in two seconds, and you bet your life that you made the correct assessment.

"I fucking loved it..."

My lungs are on fire. Pain seeps into my bones, but I can't move. Not until the barrel of a gun is pressed against the dead man's head and a man's voice coldly warns him to, "Get the fuck off her before I blow your goddamn head off."

I don't think Arno realizes until the man doesn't move or say anything in return that he's already dead.

"Son of a bitch!"

I wheeze for air as the pressure on my chest is suddenly lifted. The man falls sideways, and a thick hand is thrust before my face to help me up.

"Jesus Christ." Arno glances over to the dead man lying a few feet away.

I don't know if it's fear or admiration I see in his eyes when he looks at me again. Maybe it's a bit of both.

He says nothing while I wrestle my sweatpants into place, and for a moment, we just linger here, panting in the tiny, enclosed space while blood forms a puddle on the floor.

In the end, Arno surveys the dead man with a grunt and runs a hand through his red hair. "I guess Dante's not the only one used to fighting his way out of a cage."

"You...you were going to help me," I say, my voice rasping. Not only that, but he wasn't throwing me down, eager to try to "kill an hour" for himself. My fingers tense over the unfamiliar hilt of the knife just in case he changes his mind, and a part of me cackles at the motion.

Anyone should have been easier to bear than Vinny—only a few days ago, I swore that to myself. Am I really willing to fight my way through another man—and possibly even more—just to preserve what little tarnished "virtue" I have left?

One twitch of my hip—which triggers a painful throb in my core—and I know the answer. To protect the deal I made with the devil, I just might…

Rather than make a move for me, Arno grits his teeth. "Yeah," he admits. "But not for you. If I let that fucker touch you, Dante would kill me—and I'm not being funny when I say that. *If I let that man touch you, Dante would kill me.*" He spits out each word so that I don't miss the bitter undertone of truth. "A skinny bit of ass isn't worth my life."

I have to agree with him as I finally let the knife fall.

I'm not worth anyone's life, and when my gaze falls over the dead man again, I feel pity instead of guilt. What a stupid way to die.

———

A rap on the partition separating the back of the van from the front is the only warning before it starts moving again, and I'm not exactly sure which emotion churns my stomach as I scramble to get my bearings. Am I sick with fear? Sick with anticipation? Sick with pain?

All three have their merits, and I'm trembling when the van finally comes to a stop right before the door is opened from the outside.

"Get back." Arno all but shoves me behind him to reach the exit first, and his voice reaches back to me on a low whisper. "We have a problem."

Faint light spills in as Arno climbs out—but I can't make out the figure standing on the other end. Mack is my first guess, but when my vision clears, I make out two piercing blue eyes...

The devil waits until I creep closer before he plunges a hand through the doorway of the van and clasps the one I'm sticking out to meet him, pulling me out onto a narrow street. Relief is such a powerful emotion outside of Vinny's cage. It weighs me down until I can only stand here and observe every inch of my devil. He's not dead, at least, and I don't make out any fresh bruises or cuts forming over his body. But there's a look in his eye... It's familiar for a reason that drenches me in dread. His eyes seem more dead than those of the man I just killed. Speaking of which, I'm jostled aside as an unfamiliar man peeks into the shadow of the van.

"Kayden?" he calls out.

When he doesn't get an answer, he climbs in, and I assume the startled curse he utters next means he noticed the body lying in the corner.

"Kayden? He's dead! What the fuck?" Before the man even fully leaves the van, three men standing behind Dante start to draw their weapons—though they quickly change their minds when Arno pulls his out first.

Two other men automatically step toward him, and invisible lines of loyalty are drawn in the sand.

"Your friend had a little 'accident,'" Arno says coldly. "Had to learn the hard way that 'no' means 'no.'"

"You?" the man who drew the gun demands, his weapon still trained in our direction.

Arno scoffs. "Who else?"

My hands flex, still wet with warm, sticky blood—but no one even looks at me.

Arno wears the suspicion with pride. "You wanna end up like him?"

"We'll settle this later," Dante snaps, drawing the attention to himself. "At the moment, we have about five minutes before the cops home in. I don't know about you fucks, but I'd rather not spend the night in jail."

The men grunt in agreement and follow as Lucifer turns down a narrow alley that smells like fish and into a small, enclosed parking lot currently inhabited by three large vans. I don't understand why we're here until one of the vehicles opens and women—all in various stages of dress —climb out.

Just like that, I stop thinking about murder and death. I forget all about Vinny. The only thing that matters is the emotion shooting through my chest, which robs me of everything, even the will to breathe.

Relief? Triumph? Fear?

The devil came through for me yet again. Because of him, at least one of Vinny's precious businesses has taken a hit. Whatever happens after this moment, there can be no going back—and it's an incredible, paralyzing sort of freedom to know that, somewhere...Vinny is seething because of me.

I'm still paralyzed by the shock, even as Dante explains to Arno how the plan went.

"Police on the way...tipped off..."

I can only start to move when my eyes finally connect with the kohl-lined gaze of one of the women. She's terrified, her pupils massive and her breathing heavy.

"What the fuck do we do now?" I hear someone ask as I start forward.

I make the choice for them, reaching out to trail my bloody hand down the arm of a pale, frightened girl wearing an outfit similar to the one I wore in my video. She flinches, cringing back.

"You're free," I tell her—all of them. "You're free."

"Not so fast."

I turn around just as the devil approaches. He takes his time, his gaze flicking from woman to woman, and I'm not stupid enough not to understand that he's tallying up their worth. Hundreds? Thousands? What will Lucifer find more lucrative? His promise to me or the profit even a handful of these women could net him?

I'm not sure what he decides when he reaches into his pocket and withdraws a wad of money, which he slaps against my palm.

"We found this inside one of the hideouts."

I nod, my throat thick, and the devil says nothing as I turn to the nearest woman and press a handful of bills into her trembling hands.

"Take it," I tell her, raising my voice so that they all can hear me. "Take it and run."

"Spread out," Lucifer adds, coming to stand beside me—my fallen angel lording over the souls he's just saved. "No more than three at a time. Go anywhere—just get out of the city. Run. Hide. None of us will come looking for you. But..." He dangles the word like a juicy piece of bait held over starving dogs newly freed from a life in a cage. "If you want to get back at the bastards that did this to you, then memorize this number. Once you're safe—and *only* then— call it. A man named Van Hallen will answer it. Tell him Dante Vialle told him to take fucking notes, and then you spill whatever you remember."

If anyone answers him, they do so quietly, in murmurs and suppressed whimpers. They're still asleep, I think. Still locked in the throes of the nightmares their lives have become. I doubt that they fully start to wake up until I shove the first girl toward the mouth of the alley where, up ahead, two men are making sure the coast is clear. She staggers, her eyes uncertain while her body pitches sideways. My hand on her arm stops her from falling, but Dante's voice is what finally snaps her awake.

"You all have five minutes," he says. "If you want your freedom, then I suggest you fucking take it."

Just like that, the girl runs, her hair flying out behind her. Then it's a mad dash to shove countless dollars into pale, trembling, grabbing hands before each woman follows suit, obeying the devil's instructions to the letter.

Their faces blur, fearful, young, sometimes with battered features. It's only when one of them presses her cool hand against mine that familiarity freezes me in place. Her blue eyes are more haunted than when I saw them last, caked in mascara that runs in rivulets down her cheeks. Matted, blond hair hangs limp and lifeless down her shoulders, attempting to shield more of her skin than the skimpy, black dress she's wearing does.

Olga says nothing when I press the cash into her palm. Or when I throw one arm around her shoulders in the semblance of something that could have been a hug in a different life. She merely nods when I draw back, and for a second, we are bonded by our scars left by Vincent Stacatto. When I tell her to run, she does so without question, disappearing through the alley like smoke. I only have a few bills left, which I divide evenly between the final few women, and they disappear as well.

I watch them go until the moment Lucifer's hand descends over my shoulder to steer me around to face him.

"We need to go," he says, and I can only nod.

Part of Vinny's empire has just been set on fire, and only God knows what might come out of the ashes.

———

We reach Mack's compound in silence—a strange show of victory for a returning army. Anger licks at the air as the comrades of the dead man toy with what matters to them more: revenge or their lives? They hold off on making a decision until after Lucifer drags me out of the van, at least.

"Mack's inside," someone says, jerking their chin toward the building that houses the bar.

Lucifer doesn't respond, but I sense the tension coiling in his body as he starts forward and pulls me along. Arno falls into step behind us, and the rest of the men trail in our wake while Dante takes the lead, entering the bar first.

"Well done, Kitty," Mack drawls from a stool at the bar counter.

At least forty men pack the room full, watching as the devil hauls me inside. Arno takes up a position near the door, his hands at his sides, open and ready.

"Your plan worked out," Mack admits, though his tone falls flat. He isn't pleased. Not really.

Forty newly freed women are running loose around the city now—each worth at least a grand. Mack doesn't like having his pretty bones snatched away. He snarls in anger even as he counts the money stacked on the counter before him.

"Nabbing the drugs wasn't as easy as you made it seem," he adds, "but we managed to make a dent. Everyone's happy." He forces a smile that seems like a gruesome mockery of the real thing. "Or *almost* everyone." His eyes home in on Arno. "A man named Kayden, to be exact, isn't very happy, now is he, Arnold? A man who is...was...my *friend*."

Arno doesn't flinch beneath the hostility directed his way. In fact...I think he feeds off it. With a wicked grin, he draws himself up to his full height, but there's nothing but ice in his tone when he speaks. "The bastard crossed a line."

"I don't really give a shit," Mack says, his lips still stuck in that impression of a smile. "He could have pinned the little bitch down and forced her to suck him off in the middle of traffic. Unless...you have a problem with that?" His eyes are on Arno, but the question is directed solely at the man tethering me to his side. "Don't tell me that you have a hard-on for Stacatto's whore..."

"It doesn't really fucking matter why," Arno growls, stepping forward. His eyes gleam, and for the first time, I see the family resemblance between Lucifer and him. If Dante is a fallen angel, then Arno is the lost soul he met on his way down to Hell. "I told the fucker to stop. He didn't, and he got what he deserved."

Mack grunts out a chuckle. "A knife to the chest?"

Arno shrugs. "You're right. It should have been my bullet in his brain."

"N-no." I don't realize I've even spoken up until I'm shoved behind Lucifer.

"Shut up," someone growls at me, though I don't know if it's him or Arno.

"Is there a problem?" Dante asks, his voice hard and cold.

Mack is grinning and dangerous in his rage, but Lucifer... He is ice and fire swirling into one unstable inferno. I watch as he cracks his neck while flexing the fingers of his right hand.

"There won't be," Mack admits, "just as long as Dino's bastard pup is willing to accept the punishment for taking the life of his fellow man. I'll think about it, but I hope he's grown some balls since the days he used to beg his daddy not to throw him in the cage."

"Take your time," Arno snarls. "I'll pay your fucking price."

"You *will*," Mack agrees. "But, for now, enjoy the spoils of your war, Kitty. For now."

Before I can blink, Dante already has me outside, and I'm struggling to keep up as he barrels toward the garage with Arno on his heels. A few other men follow, but their wary glances at the bar reveal where their loyalties lie. The devil may not be their king, but he's a hard leader to resist. I can't take my eyes off him, and he wrenches the door to the garage open and shoves me inside.

"What the hell happened?"

"Nothing," Arno grunts.

Bracing my hand against the staircase, I glance over my shoulder at them. "I did it. I killed him. He tried to—"

"I killed him," Arno insists, slapping a hand against his chest. "You challenge that, girlie, and you're calling me a fucking liar." His eyes flash with warning, but Dante steps forward, effectively placing himself between us.

"I have your back," he tells Arno.

"That's all I fucking ask." With one last glare at me, he turns and storms out.

The men still crossing the field fall into step behind him, and it's just me and the devil left watching from the doorway.

"*You* killed him?" Dante asks me, though I can't tell what he thinks. His expression is stone.

I nod. My hand shakes, and I glance down and find it still painted red with blood. Though is it *really* there? I rub my fingers together, but I only feel skin. "I killed him..."

The world sways with the force of that admission. Daniela Manzano is a killer. She stabbed a man in cold blood. She looked into his eyes as the life drained from them. She didn't even feel regret...

Because, if anyone else dared to challenge the promise etched into her flesh, she would probably kill them too.

"Come here." Lucifer grabs my arm and hauls me up the stairs and inside the apartment before locking the door behind us. "Look at me."

He steers me around to face him, his eyes boring deep. I don't know what he finds in mine that makes him draw closer. Or what makes him drag his thumb across my lower lip, raising a fire that sears me down to the core.

He doesn't stop me when I step forward and press my face into his chest. He doesn't hold me, either, or comfort me the way Vinny would—pet names and petting. He lets me breathe him in, however. He lets me brace my fingers against his chest and leech off his heat. He lets me feel his heartbeat.

He lets me break...which I do in bits and pieces. Puppets spend their lives dangling from so many strings that they're unsure of which emotions to feel during certain moments. Most people probably wouldn't snicker from knowing they've killed a man.

Though most people wouldn't be comforted by clinging to a more proficient killer, either.

———

I HAVEN'T SHARED A BED WITH ANYONE SINCE THE DAYS I used to creep into my parents' room as they slept. I still remember how warm the spot between them was, basted by the heat of their love. I had never felt safer than I did at that moment...at least until Lucifer drags me to the bed and climbs in beside me, his arm pinning my waist to his side.

He doesn't acknowledge the act out loud; I'm merely a bone he forgot to unclamp from his jaws. Regardless, it's an awkward exercise to fit his bulk beside mine on the mattress. He has to curve himself against me in order to keep his feet from dangling off the bed. I'm left paralyzed while his heat bathes my body in years of sin, and I know deep down that I'll never be able to erase his scent from my lungs. Or this memory from my head—which is a double-edged sword.

The devil is a drug for which there is no cure. No rehab. No recovery.

Weighed down by the souls he's damned, he's restless in his sleep, mumbling meaningless words into my neck and roughly dragging his fingers through my hair. At some point during the night, he holds me so tightly that I fear my ribs might break.

In the end, they don't...but my heart does. Old fear coats the ruined pieces, and once again, I feel a horrible sense that none of this will last. Vinny will have the last laugh. I'll never have a moment like this again.

The thought makes me hold him tighter. I wish I weren't too sore to take him again. I'd make him fuck the darkness from my skull and chase the fear away. I'd make him own me until I cease to remember anything—or anyone—else before him. My fingers twitch at the prospect, and I glance up, observing the planes of his face through the darkness.

Within a second, I know I don't have the heart to wake him. The devil is as exhausted as he is powerful. I think of those dark days when he huddled on his bed in terror. I wonder if he's ever had a good night's sleep. When I drag my fingers along his chin, he doesn't wake, but his brow furrows, resisting any comfort even while unconscious.

I'm halfway toward caressing a trail to his nose when a sudden sound breaks the quiet. I flinch, bolting upright, but the devil at my side doesn't even stir. My first thought is that one of Mack's men is trying to break in, but the sound is too...musical? It's a sharp, mechanical melody, like that of a ringtone.

Rolling to the edge of the mattress, I scour the room, but the only clue I have is a strange whirring sound that comes from the duffel Espi gave me, tucked against the wall. Faint light of dawn creeps in through the window and guides my way to the corner of the room. I unzip the bag and find something I missed during my first search at the bottom of it. It's a cell phone, small and pink. A yellow sticky note obscures the screen and the note scribbled across it reads *I've got this number programmed into mine. If you need anything, give me a ring, Pyro.*

A tired smile shapes my mouth. When I peel the note away,

the name *Espisido* lights the screen up as an incoming call. After a glance over my shoulder to make sure Dante's still sleeping, I creep into the hallway and into the bathroom. I run the water in the sink at full blast, and then I tentatively bring the receiver to my ear and answer the call.

"Espi?"

"Lynn," a gruff voice replies. "'Pyro Girl.' Somehow, I knew it was you."

My entire world stops spinning. Time is reduced to nothing. Only the sound of rushing water ties my soul to the present as, as if from far away, I hear a strange woman speak. "V-Vinny."

"It's a shame, *Mi Bella*," he croons into my ear, his voice disrupted by static. "I hate to punish you, but it is the only way you seem to learn."

My stomach drops even before he murmurs the next words the same way a caring teacher might announce the day's lesson.

"You are going to listen, *Mi Bella*, while I kill this man. At first, I assumed he was the bastard you fucked, but at least, when I cut his balls off, you will remember your purpose..."

I hear screaming, distinctly male. The sound battles with the running water, piercing my eardrums, and my blood runs cold with recognition. *Espi!*

"No! No! Vinny, no!" I lean forward as my voice comes out as a strangled whisper. In an instant, Daniela dies, and Lynn is resurrected in her place. She knows that the only way to Vincent Stacatto's twisted, black soul is to beg. "Please. Please. Please. Don't hurt him. Please—"

"Give me one reason why," Vinny commands, his accent riding the words more strongly than I have ever heard it. These past few days have strained his control, and when Espi shouts again, I know that Vinny's the reason why.

"You are going to listen, Mi Bella, while I kill this man."

"M-me," I manage to croak. "I'll come back to you. I'm the one you want. Please. Let him go. Please. I love you. Please—"

"You love me," Vinny growls, a laugh tainting the words as if they were some sick joke. "Were you thinking about *me* these past few days, Daniela? Were you thinking about my love when you threw my goddamn ring?"

Espi cries out—no, an animal does, releasing a plaintive, inhuman howl, high-pitched with pain...

"P-please," I beg, but my voice has gone cold. I'm reading from an old script I thought I'd never have to open again. Lynn knows Vinny. She knows how to keep his hand steady when he aches to slap her. She knows how to get on her hands and knees. "I...I d-deserve to be punished," I hear myself say. "I'm so sorry, Vinny, but please don't hurt him. I'll come back. I'll come back."

For a moment, I hear nothing but static, and the only ounce of comfort I have is that the screaming's trailed off. For now.

"You have thirty minutes," Vinny tells me. "If you're a minute late, I'll kill him and drape his body over your bed as a present for when you come home."

"Thirty minutes," I repeat, sounding so damn hollow. "Thank you, Vinny..."

He hangs up, and time begins to tick again with mocking speed. I'm numb as I climb from the toilet with the phone clenched in my fist. I'm a ghost drifting through the air when I reenter the bedroom and spot Lucifer on the bed, still asleep.

My mouth opens...but no sound will come out. Lynn may not be as brave as Daniela, but she isn't stupid. If I bring Dante or his men, Vinny will know... Hell, I think he's expecting it. Espi is a toy—but Dante is the real object of his rage. Only God knows what he would do to him. He'd chop the devil into pieces and make me swallow them.

And Dante... There is no way in hell he wouldn't fight for Espi. He would meet Vinny head on like a true beast, and he would die. He would die...and I would be forced to watch.

And I can't. My soul is a fragile shell, and I know without a doubt that nothing would be left of it if this man dies because of me. My beautiful fallen angel wouldn't miss one less lost soul, but he would never survive without Espi.

And preventing that is worth any sacrifice.

Vinny's timeline is in my head as I grit my teeth and search the duffel for a fresh sweatshirt that isn't covered in blood.

In my search, I find another object I missed—a book of matches with a smiling cartoon moose on the front, and I can't stop myself from tucking it into my pocket.

Espi. I have to bite the pain and guilt back as I stagger into the living room and cram my feet into my borrowed shoes. I leave the shower in the bathroom running and close the door, hoping that the ruse is enough to keep the devil off my trail for even a second.

That's all I need.

When I creep into the main garage, the devil hasn't stirred. It's a silent trek out into the field where Mack's men patrol the perimeter, but they're lax this early, and none of them notice when I reach a section of fence and climb over.

Thirty minutes. Twenty. Ten.

The deadline spurs me onward while I run right back to the hell I knew deep in my soul I could never really escape.

CHAPTER THIRTY-FIVE

Daniela

One minute to spare and it's only the grace of a switching traffic light that allows me to reach the intersection near the hotel while the final seconds count down. *Fifty. Thirty. Ten. Three.* When I finally cross the street, my heart is pounding in my chest—however, the moment my heel strikes the curb, the cell phone in my pocket rings, marking the end of this round of the game.

"Very good, *Mi Bella*," Vinny praises once I've answered it. His voice trembles. He's excited. He's... He's in a mood. "I'm in the car," he tells me just as I spot a familiar vehicle lurking a few blocks ahead. "Walk toward it."

"Wait," I croak, dragging my feet the way a child tries to desperately stave off her punishment. "Let him go first...please. Then I'm yours."

A growl nips at my words. No one ever tells Vinny what to do and lives for the insult—but my old friend is as calculating as he is cold. He may be able to see me, but he can't be certain that I haven't brought along anyone who might be lurking out of sight. At this moment, I hold the power, and I can almost hear him tallying up the pros and cons. Is getting me back really worth losing his leverage so soon?

I don't realize I'm holding my breath until the car door opens and a tall figure finally staggers out. Any fear that he could be Vinny or one of his men is dashed once he hits the ground on his knees. In the end, it takes him five tries to stand upright, and when he turns to me, I see why. Several fingers of his right hand are now just bloody stumps.

My, how that scarlet substance seems so different outside of the devil's domain. It's redder here. Harsher. More violent. Espi leaves a brutal ruby trail behind, and I don't know how I manage to stay standing when he staggers toward me, his eyes widening with recognition.

"N-No." Shaking his head, he tries to turn back, but I'm on him before he can even make it halfway.

Up close, I smell the blood dripping from a cut on his forehead. His left eye is swollen shut, and I can't tell how badly hurt he might be beneath his sweatshirt. When I seize a handful of his collar and shove him past me, he's too weak to resist.

"Run," I tell him without looking back.

"No. Don't do this, Danny." His voice is only a strained whisper, and I hesitate for a single moment.

How easy would it be to run, I wonder as I glance along the deserted street. Though how easy would it be for Vinny to hunt us *both* down?

"Please, Espi. Run for me," I choke out, taking a painful step forward. "And don't stop running until they're gone."

I don't look back to see if he listened. With my gaze on the black car, I keep walking, drawing out every last step to give him enough time. Vinny isn't oblivious to the tactic, and static blares from the phone still in my grip.

"I'm waiting, Daniela," he snaps when I bring the receiver to my ear. "My patience is wearing thin."

I force myself to walk faster, and I pray to God that Espi is already gone by the time I finally reach the black car. As if in slow motion, the door to the back seat opens and a man climbs out, his expression wary—Gino.

"Miss Manzano," he greets, holding the door open for me.

I'm not sure how much time passes before I climb inside. Seconds? Minutes? An eternity?

Freedom doesn't want to loosen its hold on me just yet. It lingers, taunting me with all the new memories I've gained during my time spent outside my cage. Lucifer's words are still in my head. His scent still fills my lungs, and maybe that musk is what gives me the strength to curl my knees and collapse onto a leather seat across from a man I somehow always knew I could never escape.

Vinny watches me without a shred of emotion. He is stone, his eyes darker than coals, as he reaches into the pocket of his crisp, designer suit jacket and withdraws something that glints in the light filtering in through the tinted windows. He makes sure that I recognize it before he slips it on the index finger of his left hand—or at least as far as he can, forcing it just past the bed of the fingernail. It's my ring.

Fixated on the diamond, I almost miss the telltale jerk of his shoulder right before he slaps me and the blow catches me unguarded across my cheek. The icy pain searing across the bridge of my nose warns me that he broke the skin. Unsatisfied, he strikes me again, so hard that my body is flung across the seat and blood floods my mouth. Old habits die hard, and I wipe the droplets away with the back of my hand before they can taint the leather upholstery. Without a word, Vinny waits until my blurring vision clears before he slips the ring off and returns it to his pocket. Then he glances over at the man still holding the car door open and jerks his chin toward the main road.

"Hunt that motherfucker down and put a bullet in his head," he says, ordering Espi's death the same way one might order coffee.

Nodding, Gino takes off, and I can't see anything through the windows when I fling myself against one, bracing both hands flat. I struggle to scream away, hoping that my voice manages to escape. "Espi, run! Espi run—"

Vinny growls, and I *hear* his fist fly through the air before it lands like a missile against the back of my skull. *Black.* Pain explodes behind my temples, but by then, my head was already floating. I'm drifting...weightless. And, for a brief, blissful second, I almost believe that he actually killed me.

But, when I partially regain consciousness on the floor of the car, I feel his hand stroking my throbbing cheek.

As if escape would be that easy.

Dante

I can still smell the bitch. The loss of her heat is what wakes me up, and my fingers are already on fire as my eyes finally open. Red prickles my vision the moment I sense she's not in the room—but I'm more pissed when I realize just who the irritation is directed at. For some reason, it *isn't* at the bitch with the shower running, once again eager to wash me away.

Fuck her...

My cock wants to. It throbs for that stupid cunt, and I scan the room on the off chance I might find my balls somewhere close by. For all I know, she hacked them off in my sleep—it's the only goddamn reason that can explain my lying beside her on this fucking bed. Instead, I find her knife on the mattress, and I grab it, clenching the handle as I consider ending this game now on *my* say-so.

Fuck her.

Keeping her close made sense with Mack hungry for revenge. It had nothing to do with her. Not her heat. Not her smell. Not her...

My fingers burn as if to counter that as I curl a fist and slam it against the mattress so hard that the knuckles pop.

Fuck her.

I should—just force my way into the bathroom and corner her there in the shower before she can scrub me from her skin. I'll mark her again out of spite. Bite her. Come on her. Come in her. Take her. Claim her.

Drag her back to this fucking bed.

Vincent Stacatto may have owned her soul, but I'll take the rest before I kill her. I'll beat his claim out of her with every orgasm and every fuck until her lips forgot how to fucking say "Vinny." Or maybe I'll settle for branding her again until she burns with my name. Until she can only say *my* name.

My mouth aches, stretched into a position it's not used to forming as I shift to the edge of the bed. A smile? A snarl. Whatever it fucking is remains fixed in place when I finally stand and make my way into the hallway. Near the bathroom, my nostrils flare to breathe her in, and a growl rips from my throat as I analyze that scent. Vinny's little whore can't erase me with soap and water this time.

Palming the handle of the sliding door, I picture her on the other side. Would it hurt her to take my cock so soon after the last time?

I'm curious to find out, and I twist the latch.

"Dante!"

The front door trembles with the force of the fist that's I assume rapping on it from the other side. The girl's knife is already in my hand, the blade at the ready—but the voice that shouts over the pounding keeps me from drawing it.

"Dante, open the fuck up."

When I finally do, Arno's already halfway down the stairs, jerking his head for me to follow.

"We need to talk—*away* from your little pet."

"Fine." With one last look down the hall, I slam the door behind me and follow him down to the main level.

Arno doesn't stop moving until he's straddling the threshold of the doorway, glaring out at the gray sky. Sparks practically fly off his hair; the bastard's a live wire, aching to electrocute the fuck out of whoever pissed him off.

"What is it?"

"Mack's decided how I can 'repay' the life I took," he finally growls, his gaze on the storm clouds rolling in over the horizon.

"Oh, really?" I grit my teeth, my hands curled into fists. Whatever this means, it can't be good. "How?"

"A cage match. No holds barred." Arno looks back, staring me dead in the eye as he adds, "It can be a death match at the victor's discretion."

"Bullshit." Only fucking Mack would dangle a rule like that —knowing just who had the advantage. "Fuck that. I'll talk to him—"

"You won't," Arno cuts in.

"The hell I won't. If Mack wants you, he'll go through me." I mean every word—but, for once, the pup doesn't back down, and this time, I'm the one who looks away.

"No, he won't," Arno grunts. "You don't get to fight this battle."

"Arno—"

"Don't fucking *Arno* me, Dante," he snaps. "Don't treat me like a goddamn idiot, either. This is *my* fight." His voice breaks.

I can't even look at him. I don't know what might happen if I do. I might punch him. He might hit back harder.

So I grit my teeth and flex my fists, and I think of Mack. "That bastard's had this coming a long time." I glance over to see Arno nod.

"Damn right he has. He never got over the fact that Dino chose you. Not him. Not even me. *You.* There were men that he'd run with for decades who didn't earn the same honor."

"Don't make it something that it wasn't," I hiss, shaking my head. "Dino didn't do sentimental. He picked me because I was the fucker who shouted back 'how high' when he said 'jump.'" I don't know if I'm ashamed of that though. If

Dino said "jump," there was always a fucking good reason to leap.

"He picked you because he saw himself in you," Arno says. "'*Dante, the little shit with claws.*'" He tries and fails to mimic the man's thick Irish accent. "It's true, ya know. You are the most like him, and it affects the people around you the same as it did him."

"What the hell's that supposed to mean—"

"Don't you ever wonder *why* Espi hates you so much?" he starts, cutting me off. "It's the same fucking reason why I hated Dino."

"Why's that, then?" I can't ignore the unease in my voice.

Arno rarely mentions Dino in any context outside of the past. Hell, even before I went to prison, he rarely referred to the man as his father.

"Espi hates you because he *can't* change you. You are who you are. No matter how hard he tries or whatever reasons he has to, he just can't blame you for being the only way you know how to be, and he hates *himself* more for wanting you to change. He won't admit it, but Espi hates you because it's the only fucking way he can keep from hating himself." Arno takes a deep breath and exhales loudly. "Look, Dino had his own battles. You've had yours. This one is *mine*."

When I turn to face him, the man staring back is the old bastard I remember before grief wore him down and pain left him jagged. Arnold Mackenzie, who was forced to beg for scraps in his father's own gang—and nobody better fucking forget it.

"This is my fight," I say, watching his jaw clench. "*Danny*—she killed that fucker. His blood is on my hands." I still can't believe that. The little lamb grew fangs. She taught herself how to bite back hard—and I saw it in her eyes; the little bitch had relished in it.

But, for whatever reason, Arno's determined to take credit for her kill. "I only came here...I only came to say goodbye," he says over his shoulder, facing the doorway again. "Or...whatever." He starts forward, but I grab his arm before he can take off.

"When?"

"When else?" he snaps, shrugging my hand away. "Mack gave me the 'honor' of choosing the time. I chose now. It's better than drawing it out..." He breaks off once he sees the figure leaning against the door to the pit up ahead.

Mack must have laid off the alcohol last night to be up this fucking early—though I don't think Arno can say the same. He'll have to be twice as fast against a well-rested opponent. Twice as ruthless.

"I've got your back," I say.

Still walking, he looks over his shoulder, and something crosses his expression but disappears before I can name it—and it's a good fucking thing it does. Anything but hate is a liability in Mack's Kennel. Knowing that, Arno remains silent as he leads the way to the entrance, where Mack's already waiting, his cocky grin firmly in place.

"How did I have a feeling that the puppy would go running right to the cat?" he wonders, rubbing his chin.

"Fuck you," Arno says.

But I meet Mack's gaze headon and flash a mocking smile of my own. It's all teeth, and the fucker knows a threat when he senses it. He opens his stance.

"Arno didn't ask me for shit," I admit. "But...if you want to fight anyone, it's going to be me."

"Dante." Arno grinds my name between his teeth. "Stay the fuck out of this—"

"Arno can have the winner," I say over him, my gaze squarely on Mack. "But you fight me first."

If anything, Mack smiles wider as he turns and opens the door to the pit, instantly rousing the dogs inside. "I wouldn't have it any other way."

CHAPTER THIRTY-SIX

Dante

Mack doesn't stack the audience today. Just a carefully chosen few are here to witness his victory. I spot Darcy among them, her gray eyes watching and wary.

The bastard wants to repeat history, apparently. The setup is similar to our last match before I got shipped off to prison—back when Mack challenged me for the crown Dino had shoved onto my head by taking a bullet to the brain and tossing his "kingdom" into turmoil.

Five years later, not much has changed. Mack still has the same cocky swagger, and I'm not much different from the punk I was back then. The biggest difference of all, however, is that this time...

I don't want to lose.

"I say we make this interesting, Kitty." Stalking toward the ring, Mack strips his shirt off—apparently, there won't be a warm-up before this match; we'll fight with whatever energy we already have in reserve. "Winner not only gets to decide what to do with little Arnold over there, but...they also get to keep the *spoils*." He gives the word enough emphasis to make it crystal fucking clear what he means.

I win and I get the Saints. If he wins, he gets *her*.

Being shown up by the little bitch twice hasn't sat well with him, apparently. Chuckling, he watches me process the raised stakes while he opens his stance, baring his teeth. This time, he keeps his jeans on, but he lets his scars do the talking—many of them put there by me.

It's only when I wrench my own shirt off that I remember my brand-new markings, courtesy of a little bitch with eyes like fire and a monster in her head. If I lose this match, I know without a fucking doubt that Mack won't kill me— no, he'll want me alive to watch him fuck her.

"Danny." He smirks, reading the brand while rubbing his chin. "Interesting. Pick your weapon, Kitty." When he enters the pit, the fucker draws his own weapons from both pockets. Two knives honed sharp enough to slice the light reflected off them.

I don't move. Unlike Mack, I don't carry a fucking arsenal in my pockets—though, on second thought... I feel something against my hip, and my fingers settle over a familiar hilt: the girl's silly little knife. The blade won't make a fucking difference in a true fight, but for some reason, I palm it anyway and head forward to join Mack in the center of the cage. One of his men is there to slam the door shut behind me, and there is no gun firing off to mark the start of this battle.

Two seconds. That's how long Mack allows us to circle each other before he lunges and I react purely on instinct. There are no games this time. He jabs at my side with one of the blades and slashes at my throat with the other—apparently, I underestimated the fucker. A death match it is, then.

I can only block one of his blows; I uppercut with my right fist, deflecting the blade from my chin. A quick jab right lessens how deeply his second knife cuts into me, but it's deep enough to fucking sting. My blood speckles the sand when I pull back, and I know I won't be able to draw any of his with only this shitty little knife.

The Mad Dog chose his arena and his weapons well. Without an audience to preen for, he's reverted to the fucking basics: rage, hate, and his bare hands. "Come on, Kitty," he goads, circling my position on the balls of his feet. "Make a fucking move."

A low hum rips through my skull. Every time I blink, Mack turns red, and any other time, I would have taken him up on the challenge—damn how many wounds it might cost me.

All that's holding me back now is...

"Afraid you left your little bitch waiting?" Mack asks. The next second, he's on me, his fists flying, and with every blow he lands, the buzzing in my skull grows louder—deafening —but I still hear his next words. "When I kick your ass, I'll be sure to pay her a visit. My name will look nice on that tight little ass, eh, Dante?"

Black. I go blind. My ears pop, and I can't hear a fucking thing. Vibration is the only sensation that keeps me tethered; bone and flesh reverberating beneath my goddamn fists. Over and over again. Mack could have Dino's playground—but not her.

Stacatto's whore is a little toy I'm not willing to share. Not until I drag every dark, twisted little desire from her head. Not until I make her admit the secrets she won't even spill to herself. Not until I own her fully...

Mack won't have her. No one fucking will.

Searing pain cuts through the haze of bloodlust—Mack won't go down so easily. I grit my teeth beneath a slash to my upper thigh and then an even deeper wound in my left forearm—but even that can't break through the fog in my head for long.

I blink until my vision clears just enough to plant one fucking shot...

There. Mack lunges to the left, leaving his side open, and I take it, ramming the knife into his rib cage—not the blade, but the hilt. The attack catches him off guard. He tries to parry with one of his own, but I'm too quick. One firm kick to the knee and he falls.

Red paints my vision when I slam my heel into the bastard's chest—for Arno. I land another punch against his jaw just to hammer the point in. *Checkmate.*

He's still not down completely when he spits blood out at my feet. "You think this means a goddamn thing, Kitty?" he grits out, laughing. "Want to know a secret? That little bitch is already dead—"

My fist to his jaw shuts him up, but I hear him panting when I approach the door to the cage and snatch the length of chain from the gate.

"Dante!"

I know that Darcy's the one shouting for me when I approach Mack with the length of the chain and loop it around his neck—a collar fit for any animal.

The muscles in my arm pop when I yank, sealing off the bastard's windpipe until his face turns red and no sound comes out of his mouth. Just gurgles. Gasps. Wheezes. I wait until I see the knowledge flash through his eyes, even as his lips form a cocky grin. This is it. *Game. Set. Match.*

When he finally accepts death with one last choked grunt, I let him go, loosening the chain and leaving him gasping for air on his knees.

"Say it," I demand, raising the girl's knife as though it's a legitimate weapon. It bites into his shoulder regardless, tasting a fresh bead of blood. "To Arno. Say it."

I jerk my head toward the man in question, who's watching from the sidelines, unsurprised. He doesn't react, but I know he won't forgive me for taking this moment from him, whether I saved his life or not.

"You...you win, Kitty," Mack grunts, wiping blood from his mouth with the back of his hand. His eyes burn—no pup likes being put in his place, but he won't risk his honor by challenging me. At least not yet. The fucker emulates Dino in every way but the goddamn accent. "You win. Welcome back to the fold—" He chokes out a laugh. "You're alpha now. I hope your little bitch was worth it."

I jerk my hand away and try not to let my irritation show. *Alpha.* It was the title Dino used, demanding it the way most men preferred "boss" or "king." "In a world of mad dogs, the only rules are laid down by the fucking alpha," he would snarl. "A 'king' is a just a piece on a fucking game board—not even the most powerful piece. An alpha is the fucker playing the goddamn game."

For once, I agree with Mack; the little bitch better be worth it.

Gritting my teeth, I look for Arno, but I don't find him by the cage. Or Darcy. The only ones left behind are Mack's men, who glance warily from me to their old master. I almost consider tugging on their leashes and testing out my newfound role, but another issue takes the forefront.

I turn, even before I hear Arno shouting. I smell the blood first—fainter and more potent than Mack's. It rides the air before I see the man Arno is leading inside, practically holding him upright.

I don't think when I plow through the doors of the cage and straight toward Espi. My eyes dart from injury to injury, tallying them up. He has two black eyes brewing. His forehead is cut. His lip is split. His fingers are missing...

I suck in air as the buzzing swells into a deafening hum. Nothing can reach me but the hoarse sound Espi makes when he tries to talk.

"Dan...Danny. Danny." He tilts his head back, just far enough to meet my gaze head on, and suddenly, everything is as sharp as if cut on a razor's edge. "They took her."

CHAPTER THIRTY-SEVEN

Daniela

My head is floating on an ocean of blackness, but pain is like a rudder, steering me back toward my body despite how every part of me just wishes to die. It would be so damn easy to let go.

And maybe I could if the devil weren't whispering in my ear. He calls to me—at least, I think it's him. I swear I can even hear the guttural cadence of his voice, but when I finally regain consciousness, I recognize the fingers running through my hair with terrifying clarity.

"Welcome back, *Mi Bella*," Vinny tells me as he seizes a lock of my hair, tugging hard enough to make me wince.

The brief, searing agony joins the symphony of it playing through my entire body. The lighter notes of pain from my previous injuries meld with the throbbing percussion of the blows Vinny landed. I'm nothing more than a twisted, beautiful melody of pain when I peel my eyes open and face the man who claims to love me above everyone else.

"I've missed you." He runs his fingers along my throbbing cheek, careless of the open wound that burns a fiery trail there. "Look at me."

I blink so that he knows I'm aware. I see him...and no sight has ever terrified me more.

"This...this was not how our reunion was meant to happen," he explains, freeing his hand from my hair and placing it on his knee.

The movement draws my gaze down. I'm naked. He's stripped me to nothing but bruised and bloodied skin against an ivory duvet I recognize as lining the bed of my old cage. With a terrible certainty, I know what he plans to do, even while I struggle to keep my eyes open—one aches badly enough to warn me that, in a few hours, I'll be lucky if I can open it at all.

"Look at me," Vinny commands as he climbs off the bed and stands before me. He starts to undo the latches to his pants, taking his time with every deliberate tug on the zipper. "Apparently, you have no issues with being used as a whore." He sighs at that assessment: twenty-three years of waiting for my "virtue" wasted. "So you shouldn't mind if I *use* you like one."

The words chill me to the core. Desperate for escape, I scan the edges of my room, searching for the familiar shape of my cello, but when I finally find it...the music doesn't come to me like it used to. I can't imagine the stage anymore. The notes of that old, soothing melody don't take me away.

I'm rooted in place as Vinny frees his cock and starts on the buttons of his shirt. My mind spins, hunting for anything to latch onto. I'm a caged bird gnashing her beak against the bars of her cage. The cat is already tugging on the latch...and there is no escape.

Vinny starts to murmur to me, telling me how hard he plans to "fuck" me and which holes he'll soil. I inhale, my heart quickening with fear as my gaze drifts to the ceiling. He's already hard. I can hear him stroking himself, grunting with lust.

It's only when pain flares through my chest that I realize that my fingers are prodding an aching wound there. A burn. Vinny must not have been able to distinguish what it really is amid all of my other bruises and scrapes, but my fingertips tread the path of every single letter. I mouth them all to myself in the end, whispering the devil's name like a prayer.

"...until you scream, and then I'll take my knife and... What did you say?" Vinny's tone cuts me to the bone, awakening an old fear, but with my fingers still prodding my brand, it's easier to ignore him.

It's easier to sink into the cadence of my own heartbeat and replay a song performed on a more archaic set of instruments than a simple cello—bone, sinew, heat, groans. Lucifer taught me how to play him well. I can taste him. I hear him in my head, overpowering even Vinny's shouts.

A stinging slap tilts my face onto my left cheek, and I blink as my vision blurs.

"Daniela." Something sharp sounds near my ear. His snapping fingers. "Look at me."

I do, still tracing the name of the man who owns me in ways this monster can only dream of.

"What did you say?" His eyes rove over to my collarbone and home in on the burn. He observes it more closely, attempting to puzzle out the meaning of the shapes that he first thought were meaningless. His eyes flash; someone new has tainted his toy, and his cock deflates beneath the strength of that rage. That *fear*. "What the hell is that? What does it say?"

I should cringe and keep silent. A part of me merely wants to escape on the cloud my memories of the devil represent. They encase me more strongly than any Bach suite. I could drown in his taste alone. But stroking the part of me he's tainted makes me bolder. Reckless. Stronger.

"Dante."

Vinny draws back—I see him from the corner of my eye, though I'm already staring far beyond him. I don't dream of a stage this time, just a man. One with piercing, blue eyes and rich, black hair and the scorch marks of Hell on his soul.

"What did you say?" When Vinny grabs me by the chin, forcing me to meet his gaze, I don't hesitate to repeat it.

"It says...Dante."

He slaps me so hard that I see double, and I'm left clinging to the side of the mattress. When I right myself, I leave a stream of blood against the white comforter, but I barely feel the pain with my mouth humming beneath the lasting vibrations of the devil's name.

"Dante."

Vinny strikes me again—this time with his fist, I think. The blow knocks me sideways, disrupting the neatly made bed under me. The room is spinning. My lungs ache with every breath I take.

"That's his name? That motherfucker," Vinny asks, and I assume he's referring to the man in the video. "Dante. I will find him, Lynn. I will kill him slowly. I'll have you play something nice while I do it. And then..." He cradles my jaw in his hand, digging his nails in so deeply that I groan. "Then I'll fuck you senseless in a puddle of his blood."

He shoves me down and strolls for the door, wrenching his pants back up as he moves. "Dinner is at seven," he tosses over his shoulder, his voice smooth and suave once again. "I expect you to be dressed and presentable. Don't you fucking dare be late."

———

THERE IS NO MAID IN MY CAGE TO HELP ME DRESS THIS time. I have to force myself to crawl from the bed to the wall and climb upright, clinging to a windowsill for balance. My old wardrobe is a forest of unfamiliar silks and satins, but I settle on a black dress that seems "nice" enough for the occasion.

Dinner. In Vinny's world, meals are a formal affair. Struggling to remember the old routine, I stagger into the bathroom, and I bathe myself without glancing in the mirror. My left arm won't bend the way it should, and I have to wrangle my hair the best I can with only one hand. I brush it flat and settle it against one shoulder—the closest to tying it back as I can manage.

Then, clinging to the countertop, I douse my skin in his favorite perfume. I clean the dirt from my nails. I pinch color into my swelling cheeks and neatly arrange the dress around my broken frame.

The whole while, I imagine the million different ways I could kill Vinny. A steak knife through his chest. A bottle of wine against his skull. The soup dish. The silver cheese platter. A wine goblet. Each fantasy is more gruesome and grisly than the last, but none of them contain the violence someone like Vincent Stacatto deserves.

"Miss?"

I flinch at the sound of knocking on the bathroom door. Gino's accent plays a terrifying melody as it echoes off the marble flooring and elegant cream walls.

"Yes?" I force myself to croak out in response.

"Mr. Stacatto requests that I remind you that dinner will be ready within ten minutes."

I frown. Vinny doesn't send reminders. If I'm late to this meal, it would only serve to give him more incentive to devise the cruelest torture imaginable to punish me. Regardless, I shut the faucet off and tuck a wayward strand of hair behind my ear.

"I'm coming." I stand and limp over to the door on bare feet.

When I open it, Gino's stoic expression is what greets me from the other end. But something isn't right... Maybe it's in the hand he's extending toward me, the palm held toward the floor with his thumb tucked against it. I stare at the appendage for I don't know how long.

Gino knows the rules—unless they have changed so drastically within the course of the few days I've been gone. No one touches me except Vinny. No one.

"Miss," he prods when I don't move. "Mr. Stacatto is waiting."

I consider walking past him—a little over a week ago, I would have. Now, I think it's the thrill of subverting Vinny's wishes that makes me reach for his trusted thug's hand, but before I can touch him, he slides his palm above mine, and I feel something against it that's tougher than skin.

"The toast," Gino says, lowering his voice. "Make sure you offer to pour the glass."

He turns away before I can fully process his words. When I blink, he's already heading across the bedroom and out into the hall. When I follow him, I realize for the first time that we aren't in the hotel suite. The furniture is the same—the layout of this room is nearly identical to my old one—but the hallway curves around a row of closed doors and opens at the mouth of a grand staircase rather than a living area.

A house?

"Mr. Stacatto regrets that he didn't have the time to give you a tour of his wedding gift," Gino explains as we descend the staircase that deposits us into a spacious entryway.

My gaze longingly drifts over to the door, but I'm not stupid enough to move toward it, and Gino doesn't even seem to entertain the thought of me running.

He guides me down an expansive hallway and into a grand dining room, where Vinny is standing at the head of a long table draped in a pure-white tablecloth. Silverware marks exactly two place settings, and a bottle of wine sits between them. I can smell food cooking. Meat. The scent serves as a brutal omen that matches the ferocity in Vinny's charming grin.

"Good evening, Daniela," he croons to me before reaching into his pocket and withdrawing a single object, which he tosses onto the table.

I know in an instant what it is: a woolen cap, like the kind that might hold back a mop of unruly, black curls from brilliant, blue eyes. It's Espi's, and my heart turns to stone in my chest.

"He's dead," Vinny explains, flashing his teeth.

I find Gino standing in the corner of the room, his face expressionless. I eye his hands—the same hands that killed Espi—and my own curl around the object he gave me. I consider throwing it to the floor and crushing whatever it is beneath my bare foot—but, almost as if reading my mind, I swear I see him shake his head once. *No. Wait.* He cuts his gaze over to the bottle of wine. *Make your toast.*

"Come here," Vinny commands.

I take my time approaching him. His gaze drifts appreciatively over my towel-dried hair and the dress I'm wearing. When he sees my bare toes, he frowns, and his fingers flex, aching to deliver a slap for the offense. For now, he contents himself with the obedient way I take my place beside him, my head bowed. Remembering Gino's request, I observe the bottle of wine, but nothing about it seems special. It's imported—Vinny's favorite brand.

"I'd like to propose a toast," he says softly, dragging his finger along the neck of the bottle. "To my love, Daniela. And to Dante...when I find him."

My blood runs cold. The object Gino pressed into my palm is the only thing tying me to the present, and for the first time, I shift my grip on it, trying to suss out the telltale shape. It's square. Small. Familiar...

A goofy, cartoonish image pops into my head—a grinning moose.

"Here," Vinny says, drawing my attention back to him as he lifts a wine goblet.

"W-wait..." I force myself to raise my hand, reaching for the bottle before he can. It's heavy. I have to cradle one hand against the bottom and clutch at the neck with the other. Someone already removed the cap, and I can hear the liquid sloshing within the glass. "I want to make the toast if that's okay."

Vinny says nothing. He merely watches on suspiciously as I tilt the bottle with both hands pressed flat against it.

"To...to our love," I hear myself say while I attempt to pour an amount of liquor into Vinny's glass. But, with my left arm unsteady, I miss. The liquid spreads across the beautiful tablecloth and spills right down the front of Vinny's perfectly tailored, black pants.

"Damn it!" His hand lashes out, and I go flying. The bottle overturns, and liquid careens in every direction, splashing from the table and onto the polished wooden floor. I wind up on my hands and knees, and I finally lift my palm to reveal the object Gino gave me.

A book of matches.

I don't think. I don't even hear Vinny raging above me. Another voice is in my head, taunting me by asking if I enjoy setting fires like a true *pyromaniac*. When I tear free a match and strike it, I do it for Espi. When I spot a puddle of alcohol—which seems way too clear to be wine—I let it fall for Dante. But, when I draw back and watch as fire consumes everything in burning-hot snatches, it's all for Daniela.

The flames are greedier for freedom than I could ever be. They lick at everything in their path, dancing across the floor, climbing up the table. They even try to devour Vinny. He curses when the first embers nudge the heel of his polished loafers. He's able to kick it back, already shouting for Gino to "put this fucking shit out!" He doesn't notice when I throw my arm out within his path until he trips over it, his heel striking bone so hard that I hear a crack. He lands on his knees, already preparing to lurch upright again, but my other hand seizes his pant leg. Then I spot the wine bottle rolling across the floor just a few feet away and reach for it. Surprisingly, there's still liquor sloshing around inside it, and it spills out, eagerly drenching Vinny's thigh when I aim it in his direction. He kicks me off, standing to his feet, his teeth bared, his eyes like midnight.

I don't know how I manage to light another match, striking it against the matchbook with just one hand. Maybe fate is on my side for once, as Vinny doesn't even seem to realize when he takes a step toward me. The "wine" forms a puddle that stretches from my wrist all the way to the heel of his polished loafer. When I let the match fall, it instantly lights with flame. Like a beautiful creature formed of flashing orange light, it lurches across the wood and seeps through the fabric of Vinny's slacks.

He shouts and backs away, fanning at the flames with the back of his hand. Gino. He calls for Gino...but his trusted flunky is nowhere in sight. The door to the dining room is closed. When Vinny tugs, it doesn't open. His shouts grow louder, and curses mingle with the words—someone is on the other side of the doors, watching him through the frosted glass, but they don't lift a finger to help.

"You motherfucker! I'll kill you! I'll kill you—argh!"

Another lit match feeds the flames. I can't seem to stop striking them, even as heat leaches into my body and a sharper, more intense pain joins the melody of it already playing through my system. I strike another, watching the beauty of the fire engulf the tiny wick. When I let it fly, it joins the rest—surging, smoldering, crackling *heat*.

"You stupid bitch!"

Agony flares through my left arm when someone grabs it— a demon. He's on fire, his heat searing my skin and drawing a gasp from my lips. A scream. He won't let go, and I have no choice but to look into his eyes as the fire grows. Spreads. Consumes.

He doesn't seem to realize until it laps at the collar of his shirt. Then he draws back, and the shouting becomes screaming...

A part of me knows what I'm seeing: a man dying. But I don't dare tear my gaze away. I think I vaguely recognize the sound that tears from my lips for what it really is before smoke chokes my lungs—laughter. I'm laughing. I'm crying. I'm watching a man I once called my best friend stagger across a beautiful dining room and crash into the elegant furniture, and I find the sight hilarious for some reason.

A goblet to the head wouldn't do Vinny justice—*this* is the only fitting way for him to die. Consumed by fire. By rage itself. Watched by the creature he molded and shaped into his image.

I laugh because, after five years of terror, I finally embody the twisted, beautiful monster he always wanted me to be.

The thought is a terrifying one. It's freeing. I'm free from the fear and the pain even as the heat sears my skin and my body suffocates on the acrid stench of burning flesh and wood.

I'm free...and when my vision finally goes black, the last thing I see is Vincent Stacatto writhing in agony as the fires of Hell reclaim the black soul they once spit out.

But the harshest of ironies is: The devil isn't here to welcome me.

CHAPTER THIRTY-EIGHT

Dante

WHEN YOU'RE IN THE CAGE, NOTHING ELSE MATTERS. The world becomes a prison and only the bastard locked in with you has the key. To get it, you'll kill, fight, scrap—beat the living fuck out of him—because losing isn't even an option.

But, when a little bitch sticks her fingers through the bars and demands that you set her free...

The rules of the game change—just when you've lived your entire life believing that laws didn't apply. But, even in the most fucked-up end-game strategy, little lambs aren't supposed to make demands of the wolf and then turn around and sacrifice themselves.

"She... He...he took my phone," Espi croaks, sounding a million goddamn miles away, though this is the closest to him I've been since getting released. He doesn't cringe when I touch him and pin him in place by his shoulder while Darcy struggles to staunch the bleeding from his hand. "He called the b-burner I gave her. Ow! Fuck—" The kid breaks off, ripping his hand from Darcy's grip, spraying blood all over the floor in the process.

"Hold still," Darcy coaxes him, still trying to wrap his hand in gauze. When blood soaks through the bandage, she grits her teeth but keeps going. Apparently, living with Mack has made her immune to loss of limbs. "*Please*, Espi, I need to clean them or they'll get infected—"

"You need to *find* her." For the first time in five years, the kid looks at me directly, though I'm not sure just who he sees now. "Dante, you need to find her. He'll...he'll kill her."

"Find her how?" Arno interjects, crossing his arms. "As far as I'm concerned, good fucking riddance. The bitch was as good as dead anyway, but the real question is—how soon before she comes back with Stacatto in tow—"

"Where is he?" The voice of the man speaking doesn't sound like me—and I don't realize that it is until Arno glances in my direction. The calm, collected tone doesn't match what I feel inside.

I'm on fire. These flames are colder than I'm used to, licking through my veins as three thoughts bounce off the inside of my skull: She went back to Stacatto. She went back to him alone. She went to him *alive*.

"Where did he take you?" I hear myself ask again.

"A better question is: How do we know that the bitch didn't plan this all along?" Mack interjects.

"What part of 'she traded herself to that bastard so he wouldn't cut my balls off' did you not understand?" Espi's voice rises in pitch like it used to when he was younger, always whining for shit. Pleading. "I don't *know* where she is."

You need to find her, Dante.

Oh, I'll find her all right, if only to kill the little bitch myself.

"Where?"

Espi shrugs, biting his lower lip as Darcy works on his cuts once again. The hand missing its fingers has been bandaged up tight, but it's still bleeding. He'll need a doctor to check it out. As for his mind? He'll need a hell of a lot more treatment. "I...I don't know. I just ran." He flinches when he admits that out loud, not that I blame him. "One of them caught up to me and shoved me against the wall, but I got away. By the time I found a street that I recognized, she was already..."

Gone. With Stacatto. Willingly.

Those facts jostle in my brain, resonating deeper than any fucking blow Mack could deal with his fists or his fucking knives. The fucker in question watches me, adjusting a bag of frozen peas against his throat. I know that both he and Arno are already plotting a defense against the horde Stacatto will supposedly send our way, but for some reason, I'm not fucking worried.

The little girl didn't go back to talk. On the surface, her actions could have seemed heroic—a better man than me would have even felt gratitude. But Stacatto's precious bitch is as cunning as she is desperate to escape him. She knew I would have gone through hell for Espi, and she turned herself in for no reason other than pity.

She didn't trust me in a head-to-head match against her beloved "Vinny." She didn't trust me to protect her. She didn't trust *me*.

Gritting my teeth, I face Arno again. "Where is his hotel?"

"I don't fucking know." Arno shakes his head. "Besides, the asshole would have moved by now. He isn't stupid—"

"Then where would he go?"

It isn't until Arno cocks an eyebrow that I realize that my fingers are already flexing, aching to rip, tear, destroy. I clench them into fists, but they still fucking shake. Funnily enough, it's *her* face I picture ramming them into, not Stacatto's.

"Where?"

"The fuck if I know," he snaps. Then he seems to realize something, cocking his head. "Dante...you can't really mean to go after her—"

"Your phone." I hold my hand out.

He resists for a second before reaching into his pocket with a sigh. "Son of a bitch. You *are* going after her. That little bitch..."

When he slaps the phone onto my palm, I turn away and barrel through the doors of the bar. Icy rain lashes at the ground outside, smearing the gray horizon. It's already past sunset. How fucking long did Mack and I fight? What seemed like minutes must have translated to hours...

Hours he's had her. Espi claimed that he'd kill her—but I knew better. Vinny wouldn't put his little dove out of her misery just yet, and the caged songbird who tasted freedom surely wouldn't be inclined to remain captive again for very long...

The thought goads my fingers into typing a single number into the keypad, and when a gruff voice answers, I don't waste any time on formalities.

"Where is Stacatto?"

"Ah, Vialle," Van Hallen grunts, sounding too tired to fuck around either. "Want to tell me why my phone has been ringing nonstop with women—all with broken English, mind you—who are more than willing to testify against an illegal sex-trafficking operation?"

I flinch, caught off guard. So the girl's plan worked after all—a victory that will soon be turned against her. For every girl she set free, Stacatto would be sure to make her suffer.

Who knows what the fucker has already done to her. He's had *hours,* after all...

"Stacatto." I clip the name, and it cuts like a whip. "Where the fuck is he?"

Van Hallen takes a second before answering. "Vialle, I wouldn't tell you where Stacatto was even if I knew—but let's say I *did* know," he adds before I can cut him off. "Let's say...*hypothetically,* that I just received a tip that the man bought a house in the waterfront district. Walnut Street. Number two sixteen. And, if this tip panned out, I wouldn't then be an accessory to a crime, now would I, Vialle?"

I hang up. With the address burning in my brain, I cut through Mack's territory, my gaze on the fenced-in perimeter. It's only when a fist rams into my shoulder that I realize I'm being followed.

"Slow the fuck down," Arno snarls, moving to stand by my side before I can whirl on him with a blow of my own. He's wearing a leather jacket over his tattoos, the hood drawn to cover his hair—the same tactics he used when he ran deals for Dino to avoid being spotted. "What? You think I'd let you go after this fucker alone?" He jerks his head behind him to the scattered remains of his crew.

They fall into step like jackals in a pack. I spot Dall and Francisco among them, their eyes sharp, looking eager for a fight.

But then my eyes home in on two figures who don't belong. One of them is just a kid who's clutching his injured hand to his chest and doing his best to fight the pain back.

"Es—"

"I'm coming," he insists before I can say a word. Fuck, he almost sounds like me.

The other figure lingers a few paces behind the others, his cocky smirk bloodied and smug. "Did you really think I'd let you boys have all the fun, Kitty?" he demands, his voice still rough despite the bruising around his neck. He reaches into his pocket and tosses whatever he pulls out into the air only to catch it in a closed fist. "We'll take my van."

"We need a plan," Arno grunts as the van approaches the address Van Hallen gave me—who, at the end of the day, was still a fucking cop. Any other time, I wouldn't go near the place with a ten-foot pole.

Tonight? Tonight, I can't think. I can only taste. My tongue clings to one flavor in particular, and I spit it out onto the floor of the van, not that it helps any. Heroin was easier to come off of than her. On dope, I was meaner, too. Colder, liable to beat the living fuck out of anyone unlucky enough to meet me in the cage.

Now? It's impossible to think above the buzzing. To drown it out, I'll barge in there alone through the front fucking door. I'll drag her out by her hair if I have to. Right there in front of her beloved fiancé, I'll kill the bitch myself—slowly.

I'll make her regret having taken it upon herself to break one stupid fucking promise.

My thoughts drift while Arno plots out a method of attack out loud. "We'll sneak up from behind. Case the property for an hour. Think this through..."

But there is nothing *to* plan. No thoughts to think.

Gritting my teeth, I scan the narrow street, searching for the house of that prick. No matter what he does to her. What he says. How badly he hurts her. How loudly he makes her scream...

She won't ever truly belong to him again. Not if I have any fucking say in it.

"Dante!" Arno snaps his fingers beneath my nose.

It's only now that I realize that the van stopped moving, but he has his arm barred over the door to stop me from climbing out.

"Dante, wait—"

I shove him off and wrench the door open. When my boots hit the pavement, I'm a beast again, aching to kill, tear, rip, bite, destroy.

But, when the sound of sirens reaches my ears and smoke fills my nostrils, I realize I won't have very much left to sink my teeth into.

Nearly a block ahead, a gated townhouse burns beneath the glow of a wild, uncontrolled fire. Firemen attempt to battle the blaze, but I can tell even from here that they aren't wasting too much energy trying. It's a lost cause—the kind of shit that screams "intentionally set."

"We...we don't know if she was even in there," someone says —maybe Espi.

They may not know, but I do. Her scent rides the wind, mingling with the smoke. She was here.

The little bird got tired of waiting for me, apparently; and she set her entire cage on fire.

I've been stabbed before. Shot once. Beaten. Punched. Stomped. None of that shit felt like this does. It's part amusement, part hatred, part fucking rage, and I can't see anything but *black*. Vinny won after all—he took her soul right down to Hell with him.

And all I can do is...laugh.

The sound trickles out of me like blood. First in unsteady drips, and then a steady, gruff stream. I laugh so hard that I have to cling to the van for balance. Then the laughter turns into a different sound—deeper, more guttural—and the hand I brace against the vehicle door becomes a fist.

A hammering thud echoes off the inside of my skull at least ten times before I finally connect it to the metal meeting my knuckles. Again. Again. Again. The blood and the dents beginning to decorate the front of Mack's van are irrelevant. I can't stop fighting. I can't stop punching. I can't stop. Not even as a sharper, higher-pitched sound battles the shouts and curses echoing after every hit I land.

The newer sound is insistent—more annoying than the typical buzzing. A song? I don't know what about it makes me turn and notice Espi's good hand reaching into his pocket, his mouth twisted in confusion as he withdraws a cell phone.

I snatch it out of his grip before he can answer. His little story didn't mention Stacatto giving it back before he'd run. When I scan the screen, the name flashing across it makes me grit my teeth so hard that they crack: *Pyro Girl.*

With my focus on the ruins of Stacatto's latest hideout, I strike the call button and bring the receiver to my mouth. "Dan...Danny?"

"She's alive," a man replies.

Anger nearly short-circuits my brain—but his accent is different from Stacatto's. It's heavier. Eastern European.

"If you want to see her again, you'll do as I say."

I feel Espi's gaze on the back of my neck, but I don't turn around. I swallow hard instead and flex the fingers of my free hand. *Do as I say?* Is the little bitch really worth becoming some asshole's puppet? *Hell no.* But, when my jaw finally unhooks, I spit the wrong word out. "What?"

The man inhales, but the sound doesn't betray an ounce of emotion. He's plotting the next stage of his plan, surprised that I even gave in this far. The girl claimed that Stacatto had a Polish man working for him. This fucker certainly sounds cold enough to have played Arno for the fool at a madman's say-so.

"Come to the riverbank. Alone," he says finally. "Two blocks, make a right, first alley on your left. Leave your men behind—I cannot stress how important that is... I would really hate to snap her neck and throw her body in the river if you cannot comply with such a simple request."

"How do I even know that you have her?" I scan the street and spot a break between two houses where the sunset reflects off the surface of the river. I head toward it and thrust a single hand out behind me to prevent anyone from following.

"You don't," the man replies, his voice steady. "I suppose you just have to decide how badly you want to see her again. Turn left." The command comes before I even reach the mouth of the alley. The fucker must be watching.

Wary, I drag my gaze along the row of houses and empty alleyways but find nothing of interest. He's a slick bastard.

"Take the next right," he says when I reach the end of yet another alley.

The direction is slightly different from the first ones he gave —it was a test, I realize, to see if I'd go charging in with Arno in tow. Still cautious, the fucker leads me in circles to further shake anyone who might be on my trail, but when I finally do reach the waterfront, there's no one in sight.

Before anger can begin to rise up, I hear a voice that doesn't sound like it's coming from the phone.

"Over here."

I turn a corner and finally spot a man standing in the shadows beside a dumpster up ahead. One hand is holding a cell phone against his ear while the other casually reaches into his pocket and draws a gun.

"That is far enough," he says quietly, aiming the barrel over my chest.

Armed with only the girl's shitty knife, I'm the perfect target. I'm also a fucking idiot. Either way, the bastard has another thing coming if he thinks I'll go down without a fight. But, before the thought even fully crosses my mind, the man jerks his chin toward the garbage bin.

"Wait there," he says into the cell phone. Then he hangs up and backs away slowly, never letting the gun slack for even a second. When he's almost completely behind the dumpster, he stoops behind it and reappears with something draped over his shoulder. "Approach me slowly," the man warns. "I will be able to tell if you plan to attack me, and while you may kill me, I'll snap her neck before you can even take the first step."

Shoving Espi's phone into my pocket, I blink back the red threatening to drench my vision. My fingers flex, but I keep them open as I start forward while sizing the other man up with the same scrutiny he's analyzing me with. He's no average fuck, standing at about my height but with a stocky build that betrays a knowledge of hand-to-hand combat. His blond hair is slicked back, his chin sporting a slightly darker goatee. When he comes closer, I recognize the coldness in his eyes as the mark of a trained killer.

"She is alive," he tells me once I see the girl dangling limply against his back for myself. "But I will warn you that she is in bad shape—I only just got her out in time. I will set her down between us. You reach for her slowly."

I don't move until he does what he said. When I crouch beside the woman lying on the pavement, I barely recognize her face beneath the bruising. Stacatto had enough time to do some damage. She's wearing another skimpy, black dress, but it only reveals more battered, broken skin.

"She was badly burned," the man states the moment my gaze settles on the red, blistering flesh spreading from her wrist to her shoulder. "The other arm is broken. Who knows what internal injuries she's sustained. If you do not keep a doctor in your...*establishment,* then I suggest that you get her to a hospital as soon as you can."

I don't answer, prodding the girl's hip with my thumb. Her eyes are closed, her breathing noisy and uneven. She doesn't even cry out when I lift her and jostle the limp arm that even I can tell is definitely broken. She's worse than "pretty bad off," but she's alive...

I'm not stupid enough to assume that it's by luck.

"Why?" I demand of the stranger watching me with an expression I can't read when I toss her over my shoulder.

He shrugs. Then a real emotion taints his features, tugging on the corner of his mouth. "My...my sister was one of the women that you saved." He pauses to let that statement sink in. "Anastasia, a foolish little seventeen-year-old girl who fell for the first man who offered to take her to America 'to be a model.' It wasn't her they were after, however. I have experience in the military, and my...unique skillset makes me a useful commodity." His tone falls flat. He discusses his own value the same way someone might tick off their eye color. "Stacatto wasn't the one who took her—a 'business associate' of his did—but as long as I worked for him, he promised that she would stay alive...even if her soul didn't remain intact." His voice deepens, a gruff note straining the crisp edges. "A life for a life. I assume this makes us even. Besides...a man like Vincent Stacatto deserved to die alone."

I can't fucking agree more.

"I would have saved her regardless," the man adds, "but I cannot pretend that I will not ask you for a favor that I am willing to repay. I need money to send my sister back home —but I am willing to work for it. If you are in need of a man with my...attributes, then call the number in your cell phone. Ask for Gino. With Stacatto dead, I am in need of a new employer, and my loyalty will lie with whoever is willing to earn it..."

I don't say a damn thing, but the man nods as if I've given a goddamn speech.

"And one other thing," he adds, frowning. "That boy. It was implied that he was you when his location was given to Stacatto—"

"Given?"

Something in my tone makes the man nod again, which confirms a suspicion before I even have to mention it out loud. Espi didn't stumble into Stacatto's clutches by accident; someone offered him up on a fucking silver platter.

"The information came from one man," Gino admits. "A Donahugh. I do not know how he came across such intel, but something tells me that it won't be hard for you to track him down and ask him yourself." The words barely finish leaving his mouth before he raises the gun again and backs away toward the nearest alley. "We will part for now. I would suggest that you not follow me."

I turn without bothering to note the direction he heads in. With only the sound of sirens to guide me, I run—straight through the upscale neighborhood and to the smoking ruins of Vinny Stacatto's fucking castle. My gaze latches onto an ambulance as it starts up the driveway, and I pounce on the first paramedic who leaps out. One look at the woman in my arms is all it takes for the man to call for a stretcher.

———

I DON'T BAT AN EYELASH WHEN A COP APPEARS JUST outside the door of the girl's hospital room a little after midnight. Apparently, "car crash" could only explain away some of her injuries, like the broken arm and four cracked ribs—but the lie doesn't cover the burns or her partially missing ear. And, given how close she was "found" near Stacatto's burning manor, I'm not surprised that some skittish nurse called the police.

I'm surprised by which cop has shown up, however.

Meeting his gaze, I shake my head once before he can even take a fucking step over the threshold. Then I rise to my feet, making sure not to jostle the kid dozing beside me. Nothing short of an earthquake could wake the woman lying in the hospital bed with "safe and legal" drugs flooding her system through an IV. Somehow, I still feel her gaze on the back of my neck as I cross the room without taking my own off the man lurking in the hallway.

"Vialle." Van Hallen jerks his chin toward the room, his expression gruff. "Isn't it funny that, not even a minute after you called, we got a tip about a house fire at that very address? Yeah, very funny indeed," he grunts though I don't say a damn thing. "But you know the part *I* find interesting?" He hesitates for a beat as his eyes pierce my own like a laser homing in on its intended target. "That fire was a clear-cut case of arson, but I assume you know that already, huh, Vialle?"

"Are you trying to insinuate something, Detective?" I wonder, keeping my voice down as a nurse scurries by with a clipboard clutched to her chest. "That's what I thought," I reply when he responds with only a lift of his eyebrow. "Well, I guess those Dick Tracy detective skills have paid off for you after all, huh? So, let's just put the case to rest once and for all then, shall we? You're right... I did it." I step forward, kicking the sliding door to the room shut, and then I hold both hands out, baring the wrists. "You got your fucking wish—"

"You can knock it off with the smart-ass 'detective' shit, Vialle," Van Hallen snarls. "And it's *Interim Police Chief Van Hallen* now." He shakes his head, unused to the weight of the figurative crown that's just been shoved on top of it. "Those girls you sent my way had interesting stories to tell. Some of them claimed to be smuggled over state lines for 'parties.' That makes it the jurisdiction of the FBI."

I bristle at the news of FBI involvement. This shit isn't going to go away easily now. Van Hallen nods as if he can read my mind.

"Of course, none of this is official until the press conference tomorrow, but you can cut the fucking heroic act now. I know she did it—*I know she set that fire.* And I'm not going to do a goddamn thing about it, so you can take a step back, Vialle," he warns.

I say nothing, and I don't move a fucking muscle, either.

"I am planning to reopen the Manzano murder case though," Van Hallen continues after a second's pause.

"Why? Stacatto's dead." I spit the words out, though I'm not even sure if I really believe them. At least, in the girl's case, he was alive and well. Killing a monster doesn't erase the scars they inflicted—I know that for a fucking fact.

"Yes," Van Hallen says with a nod. "Dead, but not off the hook. The bastard's organization will feel the legal ramifications of his crimes for years to come—you can bet your ass on that. And I'm sure I don't need to remind you that Stacatto had some powerful criminals in his fold who were complicit in his crimes. It's only a matter of time before they pick up where he left off...like your friend Arno. Let's hope he has seen the light and the Gardai will all suddenly become upstanding citizens—"

"So, if you aren't here to arrest anyone, why the visit, *Interim Police Chief?*" I cut in. "Sending your condolences?"

"Look, I only came here to let you know that she's safe, Vialle," Van Hallen says, his tone softer, and hell, I think he might even mean it. "At least from me. As far as the hospital knows, she's still your '*sister,*' Gabriella Vialle, who was in a terrible 'car accident.'" He scoffs at the lie, shaking his head. "I guess they didn't teach creativity one-oh-one in prison." He starts to head down the hall, but only a few yards away, he stops. "Oh, that reminds me... About *your* case... I did some digging."

A heartbeat later, I'm stone, already contemplating which part of the bastard I'll break first. "Is that so, Detective?"

"Yeah. I looked into the victim's background," Van Hallen admits, oblivious to the darker note in my voice and the way my hands are shaking. "I dug up some old allegations —very old—from a son he had. Seems none of it was founded or even investigated—things like the boy not wanting to strip down for gym class or being jumpy in the showers. Small stuff, but it's clear the system screwed that kid over. In my opinion, if that boy did eventually take a whack at that man with a hammer, no one could blame him—in *theory*. But, even then, something still didn't add up..."

Nearly a full minute passes before he finally shrugs and inclines his head to the door to the girl's room. "I know the kid did it, Vialle. *And,*" he adds before I can even start toward him, my fists drawn, "the case is closed. Sealed. Done. The debt to society was paid...by *you*." He turns on his heel, tugging at the collar of his jacket. "I would say 'see you around,' but quite frankly, I don't want to."

I watch him go, my hands still clenched. The heat surging through my fingertips doesn't fade no matter how fucking tight I grind them together. When I turn and throw the door to the girl's room open, she's still unconscious, but Espi isn't. He's watching me from the bench beside her bed. So far, he hasn't complained about being forced to share the same space as me—apparently, his concern over the girl overrides his hate for me. Still, I don't expect him to speak to me directly the moment I cross the room.

"What did he want?" His gaze cuts over to the doorway. Apparently, an ingrained suspicion of the police is an inherited trait.

"Nothing," I grunt. "But I will say that your little antics with Arno haven't gone unnoticed—"

"I had an audition," Espi blurts out, shifting to sit upright. "At an art school up north. Arno gave me the money for the application process, but I wasn't going to take his charity, so I did the tagging stuff for him as payback. The placement stuff was this week. That's where I was."

I don't move, processing each bit of information. An art school. It's a big leap from "joining the traveling circus," like he'd claimed he would do back when he was a kid. *Placement stuff.*

"So...you got in?"

He shrugs. "Of course I got in. You know anyone else with a colorful, though maybe not entirely legal, portfolio like mine?"

I don't miss the way he glances down at his bandaged hand and winces.

Still, I assume that means he used Arno's tags as part of his "audition." I don't know whether I'm impressed or...relieved?

"So, that's it?" I risk asking. "You're done running with the Gardai?"

"For now," Espi says, but he puts an edge on his tone that warns me not to push the issue.

Talking him out of criminal activity—like a goddamn hypocrite—could come later. I didn't realize until now just how much I've missed this...*talking* to him. Not having him run from me or take a swing. If I had a soul, I might put a name to the emotion swelling in my chest, but I don't have the fucking time.

"She'll be out for a while," I say, nodding to the woman between us. "If you wanted to go back with Arno..."

"Nah." He shakes his head. "I'll stick around until she wakes up. It's the least I could do for her..."

I don't challenge that, but I take up a position on the opposite wall so that he won't change his mind, either. In the dim lighting, I just watch him. Little Espisido's all grown up. Five years have stripped away the little punk who slept with a nightlight to reveal someone who acted like a man. One who talks about getting into art school while sporting a mangled hand. I know I'm partially responsible for the stern set to his jaw and the weariness in his eyes that wasn't there before. I spent years protecting him from whatever I could, but it still wasn't fucking enough.

Apparently, of the same mindset, Espi stares me dead in the eye, crossing his arms over his chest the best he can. "Damn it, Dante, let's cut the shit. I *heard* what that guy said. The cop."

I don't say a damn thing. I can't. The therapy sessions we sat through in prison were more about learning how not to smash a bastard's face in than confronting the past.

"You...you never asked me what happened," Espi goes on. "Not...not even when you saw. You just did what you do best." He swallows hard, and when his eyes widen, I know he's looking back five years ago. All of that fucking blood. "You never even fucking asked me—"

"I didn't want to know," I say before he can even go there. It's the truth.

After all that time…I finally got the phone call I'd been dreading—Espi so fucking incoherent that all he could do was cry into the goddamn phone. I had never experienced that fear—not even for myself. When I got to the house, the bastard was already dead, and Espi was covered in blood.

"I couldn't let you go to… I had to protect… I couldn't protect you from him…"

"He didn't, you know," Espi says softly. "He didn't touch me."

Suddenly, I'm leaning against the wall. When I finally manage to exhale, it's like five years of fear blow out through my nostrils, and my fingers unhook out of fists, numb for once. "Good."

"He…he was drinking, and…he started talking about you."

I barely recognize the sound of the voice that continues to speak.

"*Dante.* How he deserved to have you hate him. All the…all the shit he did to you. How he—" He breaks off, and the kid can't fight one of his old habits back. Tears slip down his chin, and he grits his teeth like he does when he's fighting the urge to cry. "You never told me. I never knew. I thought maybe he just hit you a few times —that's why you were always around. I thought you had it rough when you ran away. That's why you used the drugs and why you fought all the time. I thought that was why you looked like you were dead every time you came around. But…I knew. I knew right then that it was because of *me*."

"Bullshit." Shaking my head, I pull away from the wall. "Espi, what the fuck are you talking about—"

"It was *my* fault." His gaze is on the floor, but he holds his good hand up when I start to circle the bed toward him, and I stop dead in my tracks. "It was my fault. You went there because of me. You tolerated that asshole because of *me*. He was sitting there, wondering if you would ever be able to forgive him, when I couldn't even forgive *myself*. You spent my entire life trying to protect me, and…it was killing you. I didn't…I didn't mean to do it," he croaks. "I just remember shouting at him and s-slapping the bottle out of his hands. The hammer was just lying there, and…"

He stares down at his own hands, flexing his still-attached fingers. "I thought you'd be angry when you saw. I wanted you to yell at me. Hit me. I'd fucked up, and once again, you had to clean my mess. But all you fucking did was make me change my clothes, send me to Arno, and I didn't even know until the next day that you were in lockup." He glances up at me, his eyes shining with hatred. "Even then, you put me first. You confessed without even knowing what the fuck happened. You gave up the rest of your life for me, and *you didn't even ask me why*."

"It didn't matter," I snap. "I would do it again."

Espi watches me for so long that at least three nurses have crept into the room to check on the girl only to dart right back out by the time he finally sighs.

"I know you would...and *that's* what pisses me off."

"Then I suppose you'll just have to be pissed off, then," I counter, not giving a fuck if that makes him hate me even more. "So, you better go to fucking art school and stay out of trouble. You fuck up and I'm the one who will take the fall for you, whether you like it or not."

He doesn't say anything to that, but when I approach the bench and sit beside him, he doesn't run off, either.

CHAPTER THIRTY-NINE

Daniela

I'VE HAD A CLEAR IMAGE OF HEAVEN IN MY HEAD SINCE childhood, thanks to my parents. A devout Catholic, my father entertained this clichéd fantasy of a soul being greeted by angels playing the harp in a pool of white light—and, until now, I never had any reason to doubt that hope.

Reality paints a different picture, however. My heaven is black, and the only serenade I hear consists of angry, masculine voices.

"You think it's that fucking easy?" someone snarls. "You just hand me the reins and I'm what? King for a day until *Daddy* decides to come back home?"

"No," another man growls. "You fucking keep it. I never wanted it—"

"That's not how it goddamn works, Dante! I know you've been on 'vacation' for a while, but there's only one way the alpha stops being alpha. Just ask Dino..."

"Do you really want to try that method?"

The moment that dangerous tone resonates down my spine, I know where I really am. The pearly gates of Heaven must have slammed in my face; this is the devil's domain.

From what I can gather, Lucifer himself and one of his trusted demons are arguing about who really owns the fiery pit.

"I *should* challenge you for it," the first man starts—*Arno?*—but his voice doesn't hold any real aggression. Just...pain? Hurt? Regret?

"You could," the devil concedes. "I won't fucking stop you."

It's more of a dare than a taunt. Tension builds, licking at the silence like flames. Higher...higher...until something has to give.

"Damn it, Dante... Fine," Arno spits out finally. "Have it your fucking way. But, if you think for one second that you can just waltz back in and I'll roll over like a good little boy, then you've got another thing coming. I've been doing just fine on my own. I'm nobody's fucking benchwarmer."

"I don't expect you to be," the devil snaps, but his voice is softer and easily drowned by the thud of heavy footsteps.

What I assume is a door slams shut seconds later and my perception shifts once again. I'm in a room.

When I finally manage to peel my eyes open, I'm blinded by daylight streaming in through a nearby window—not hellfire. My searching fingers deduce that I'm on a bed, and even with my vision blurry, I have no trouble recognizing the dark silhouette lurking beside it.

When he's awake, there is nothing about him similar to the fallen angel I watched sleep. His bulk is glaringly out of place here, and his scars shape everything about him—how he sits, waits, breathes. Scanning his worn expression, I don't see any new scorch marks, however, so I doubt he walked through fire to find me.

But where are we now?

Without saying a word, he waits for me to notice the tubes snaking from my wrist and the bags of fluid hanging from a nearby IV, which answer the question I'm too tired to ask: *a hospital room*. He's not alone, either. Someone is sleeping on a small couch beside him, using their bandaged hand like a pillow. *Darcy*? No, this figure is way too tall, with an unruly mop of black hair...

A flurry of beeping pierces the air—an alarm sounding from the machine monitoring my vitals. It doesn't like how quickly I sit up and struggle to regain control of my heavy limbs.

"Espi?"

The specter on the couch groans, turning his face toward the crook of his elbow. He *sounds* real enough... My brain warns me that it's impossible, but when I blink, he doesn't disappear.

"Is...is he all right—"

"He's fine," Dante grunts, gritting his teeth—but "fine" seems to be the operative word in this equation.

Guilt gnaws at my chest when I take in Espi's bruised face and the mess made of his right hand. He might not be dead, but he survived his trip into hell with plenty of souvenirs.

The thought makes me glance down at my own hand, which is covered in gauze. My fingers seem to be intact, but when I flex them, a dull ache travels up the length of my arm, triggering a wave of memories: *white-hot flames licking at my skin. Smoke. Burning. Death. Dying...*

"How?" I look up while my tongue runs along my sore, cracked lips, tasting blood. "How did I..."

"Gino," Lucifer grits out. "Turns out he wasn't so loyal to your precious Vinny after all." Anger rides every single word, searing hot—though the devil doesn't even seem to understand *why* he's furious as he stares down at his open hands. They're bruised and swollen even worse than before.

Like an arrow to the chest, something warns me that *I'm* the reason. While maybe not through the actual fire, my devil did go through hell, if only to drag his new toy from a rival's grip. Not that it did one damn bit of good.

Despite everything...I'm Lynn again, squashed beneath Vinny's thumb. His death didn't erase my memories. My lungs struggle beneath the weight of them. My limbs burn with the need to escape, but my body... Every cell is too heavy to move.

Did you think it would be so easy, Mi Bella? my old friend taunts from the darkest reaches of my soul. *Think again. I own you...*

Trapped, I squeeze my eyes shut and bite my throbbing lip until it bleeds—anything to be distracted from that hollow, pulsing feeling in my chest. Is it fear? Agony? Or is it merely the knowledge that, alive or not, Vinny will never let me go.

"Look at me."

My eyes fly open at Lucifer's command, and Vinny doesn't exist for the second his gaze homes in on mine—not that the devil's rage is any easier to stomach. I have my own evil to answer for, and Lucifer frowns, both my judge and my jury.

I broke our promise.

I made a liar out of the devil.

I further corrupted his broken soul.

He tallies up my crimes in silence, and Espi's snoring fills the space between us, mingling with the steady drip of IV fluid and the distant commotion of the hallway.

When what feels like an eternity has passed, I can't bear the tension anymore. "Arno...is he okay?" I don't know if I'm really concerned or if I'm just that desperate to say *something*. Either way, I chose the wrong topic.

"Mack wanted him to pay for *your* kill with his life, if that's what you mean," the devil says. His voice is as sharp as the blade we toyed with between us, drawing yet more of my blood.

"What—"

"It's fine," he says quickly. "I handled it."

He handled it, but I don't think it was in a way Arno approved of. *"I know you've been on 'vacation' for a while, but there's only one way the alpha stops being alpha."* What did that mean? I start to ask, but a different voice cuts me off before the words leave my throat.

"You're alive." With one shift of his lanky frame, Espi sits upright, running his unbandaged hand through his hair.

"So are you," I croak once I find my voice again. I can't help the way my eyes dart from him to Dante. Side by side, it's like watching a yin and yang symbol come to life.

Espi's smile lights the room up, contrasting with the devil's permanent scowl—but I'm not sure which expression I find more comforting.

They both eye me carefully, and I must make for quite the sight, because when a nurse peeks her head through the doorway, she makes a show of calling for the doctor.

In a blur of medical jargon, they throw a few terms around like poison darts. *Broken ribs. Fractured arm. Months of physical therapy. Healing. Quiet. Peace.*

When they leave, the only tangible piece of information I manage to decipher is that, after a few days of observation, I'll be "free to go home, sweetie."

Home. It's been so long since I've applied that term to an actual place. Ironically, the only image that comes to mind is of a narrow room with a single bed dominated by a sleeping, imposing figure.

"You got banged up pretty good, Pyro," Espi states with a whistle, drawing my attention back to him. His smile is as bright as ever, though the cut on his forehead ruins the carefree illusion he tries to cast. "The docs think you'll be stuck in here for at least a week. After that..."

He lets the statement hang as if he expects me to dream up a plan of action on the spot. With Vinny's domain in flames, I am "free," after all. When I don't answer, Espi glances warily at his brother.

"If you don't have a place...you could stay with me," Espi says. "Arno got me some digs outside of the city, and I have the extra room."

He fiddles with his right hand while he speaks, rolling the fingers of his good hand over the bandages. I'm so fixated on the unconscious action that I don't realize until he clears his throat that nearly a minute has gone by.

"I, uh… Thank you," I croak out, "but I can't." I've tainted the devil and his angelic cohort long enough—though neither one seems to appreciate my guilt.

"Really, Pyro," Espi starts. "It's no trouble—"

"You have nowhere left to go," the devil says, rising to his feet. There's blood on his shirt. And his jeans. His hands… Noticing my expression, he doesn't try to hide it. He's the beast from the cage again, bearing his battle wounds like medals of honor. "Stacatto's dead," he adds. "Arno sure as hell won't take you in. So, unless you have a better option, I suggest you drop the stoic martyr act and take the fucking offer."

Without another word, he storms out, slamming the sliding door of the room behind him.

"Ignore him," Espi says quietly, but for the first time, there isn't any hostility in his tone when he refers to his brother. "I offered him a spot to crash, too," he admits, watching the space Lucifer left with an unreadable expression. "He turned me down. Something tells me that he'll change his mind though…"

Deep down, I know that, if he did, it would only be to keep an eye on Espi. His absence makes one thing clear: The devil himself wants nothing to do with me.

Three months later

"It's one of the premier musical conservatories in the country," Espi explains, gesturing to the brochure in front of me. "Basically...this place is heaven on earth. You can look, Pyro Girl, but I bet you won't find a better school."

I shift beside him on the couch and peer closer at the glossy cover. The bold font spanning the front of it supports his claim. The faculty contains some of the greatest minds in the classical arts, with a division even devoted solely to the cello.

"The auditions should be a piece of cake," Espi claims as he turns the page to a breathtaking photo spread of a lush, green campus. "I'll help you through it. As for tuition, they offer financial aid, and if you need more help, I can help cover the rest of it..."

I don't interrupt him to ask just how he'll get the money or why he cares. I nod. I smile. I watch him enthusiastically flip through the rest of the brochure, and I try my best to seem as excited as he is. Hopeful. Content.

It's an act I've performed expertly for the past three months. Poor Espi still hasn't seen through it—but the cold, nearly identical gaze watching me from across the room isn't as oblivious.

"I'm so excited," I say, forcing a grin. "I guess this means I'll have to practice more now. I can't wait..." When my voice finally trails off, I doubt I've convinced anyone else in this room of that *but* Espi.

It's a bitter victory. Grinning widely, he's the epitome of optimism, and I feel even worse for letting him down.

"Well, I think I'm gonna call it a night," he says, rising to his feet, though he makes sure to slip the pamphlet onto my lap with a wink. "We'll go over the application stuff tomorrow, all right?"

"All right." I watch him head for the stairs.

Without seeming to realize it, he starts to fiddle with his right hand, and my worn smile slips. The black glove he wears contains prosthetic replacements for his thumb, his index finger, and his pinkie, but after only a month, he hasn't regained much use of the limb yet. I know he's frustrated by the lack of progress, though he does his best to pretend otherwise. The disability hasn't hampered his art, at least. *"I can still wield a spray can with my left hand. Score one for being ambidextrous, eh, Pyro?"*

"You know, Pyro," he calls back, "we might even be able to score a tour this week if we..." Following my gaze, Espi frowns and tucks his hand behind his back. I've been staring for too long. Seconds later, he's already mounted the staircase before I can even choke an apology out. "Night," he calls from the top of them.

"Night," I say in return, but my voice alone isn't enough to drown his weary sigh out.

The house is so small that the faintest sound carries. Sandwiched between two others, it sits on a small street in a suburb about an hour outside the city. The location is near where Espi plans to start school next semester, so I assume that's why he chose it—though I'm not sure how he manages to pay for it. Money from Arno?

Maybe. But I don't dare ask.

Dante's old friend isn't mentioned much anymore—he's become one of the many topics that are tread over eggshells lately. Vinny is another. He may live inside my head, but I still can't voice his name out loud.

It's much easier to pretend—like I do now. Bad things only dwell in the city. The shadows don't exist if you don't acknowledge them. Some nights, I almost succeed in fooling myself...

If only the devil were as easy to ignore.

His eyes follow me when I stand and cross the small living room, skirting the simple furniture that came with the listing: a couch, an armchair, and a coffee table. The moment I mount the stairs, I know he's right on my heels. Like always, he waits until I've crested the top of the staircase, where he watches me enter the room at the end, which I've claimed as my own. When I wrestle the door shut behind me, I don't hear any more footsteps—he'll remain in that spot all night, keeping watch.

I have no choice but to wait him out. Feeling my way through the darkness, I find the small bed tucked underneath the one window and perch myself on the edge of the mattress. My only other belongings are a secondhand cello propped against the corner, beside a duffel bag of clothing Espi found for me, and a pink mirror he hung on the wall to make this room "more girly." From my position, I can just make out my reflection in the moonlight, though I barely recognize the person staring back. Her hair is shorter than it has ever been, barely ghosting her shoulders. There's a scar on her chin and a healing patch of flesh over her right ear. At first glance, she could almost pass for human if it weren't for her eyes. They're too dark. Lifeless.

Her soul has fallen way too far to be of use to anyone now. All she can do now is wait.

It feels like an eternity before the house finally quiets. Espi's snoring trickles down the hallway, and I use the sound as cover when I creep over to the duffel and tug on the zipper. There isn't much inside. Just a few sweaters and a couple of pairs of jeans, but I take the time to fold each garment before carefully packing them back away. It's not long after midnight when I hear someone lumber into the bathroom, and I crack my bedroom door to find that the devil has finally left his post.

I don't stop to feel sorry for myself as I throw my bag over one shoulder and cross the threshold. I've overstayed my welcome in hell. Even the devil himself seems tired of watching me burn. All I have to do is make it to the damn door. One foot in front of the other...

"Going somewhere?"

A heavy hand falls over my shoulder, throwing me off-balance. My foot slips and I have to catch myself against the wall, but the resounding thud echoes like a gunshot. Holding my breath, I look over at Espi's room. Seconds tick by, but his door doesn't budge...

Thank God.

With my heart still racing, I recall the question. *Going somewhere?* "Yes." I take two more steps forward, shrugging off the imposing figure who crept up behind me. I can see the top of the stairs now...

But one shove from behind and I go flying toward them. The scream building in my throat doesn't even have the chance to leave it before I find myself being hauled down the steps after an imposing figure. After dragging me near the cusp of the kitchen, Lucifer comes to a stop, but he doesn't loosen his grip. The shadows bathe him. In the light coming in through the sliding glass door overlooking the backyard, I swear I see them flicker...like wings. I blink, and they disappear, but the fire in his gaze doesn't diminish one damn bit.

"Going somewhere?" he repeats now that we're out of earshot of Espi.

"I didn't want to wake him up," I whisper, explaining away some of the stealth.

But not all of it.

"So you just sneak out," he says almost matter-of-factly. Birds fly. Daniela Manzano runs away when his back is turned.

After three months of apathy, the venom in his tone is a slap. It's reassurance; he really does hate me.

"I...I didn't want to hurt him. Espi," I admit while shrugging the arm with the duffel to keep it from sliding off. "He's looking at schools for me, and he's so excited and…"

"You've been stringing him along this whole time," the devil surmises.

"I…" I've uttered so many lies to myself these past few months that they should just roll off my tongue, but it seems impossible to lie to him. "It doesn't matter," I stammer, glancing over at the front door. "You guys are better off if I leave—"

"Just cut the shit," Lucifer commands, yanking on my arm. "This is about one fucking thing. You still think about *him*."

I turn away again but not quickly enough to hide the guilt that I know crosses my face. The nightmares don't come every night, but when they do, I wake up screaming. Of course he's heard me through the paper-thin walls.

"Yes," I choke out. "I still think about him…" Something about Lucifer's frown makes me add, "I did kill him, after all."

That woman… She didn't sound like me, but Lucifer doesn't seem puzzled by the boast.

"You did," he says carefully. "Having second thoughts?"

"No, he deserved to die," I say so fiercely that my teeth chatter and we both turn to eye the stairs in case Espi appears at the top of them. Seconds pass in silence, and his door never opens. "I don't regret it," I say softly, returning my gaze to the man beside me. "I *don't*."

"Oh, really?" A smile tugs on his mouth. One of those dangerous semi-snarls he wore while facing off against Mack. It's the mark of a wolf who already has his prey cornered before they even know it. "Then tell me something." He jerks his chin to the door. "Why sneak out in the middle of the goddamn night?"

"I...just. I. You... It's not like you even want me here," I toss back.

The devil's eyes narrow. "What the fuck do I have to do with anything?"

"What?" I would laugh if the noise wouldn't wake Espi. What did he have to do with anything? A better question was why this traitorous part of me seemed to believe he affected *everything*. "Because I can't stand living here another second—" I bite the rest of the words off before they ever have the chance to leave my throat. I need to leave. I tell myself that and flex my feet against the floor. *Leave.* But, when I shift to the right, I run into his shoulder.

"Why?" he demands while I stumble to catch my balance.

"Because..."

"Just fucking say it." He takes a step closer—and that one motion has never seemed more dangerous.

I stagger back, grasping behind me with one hand for the wall.

"Because what?"

Good old obedient Lynn would say nothing. She'd bite her lip and hope that her silence would appease him enough to avoid a beating. She might add another lie on top of it all for good measure. *It doesn't matter.*

Broken Daniela is too tired for games. "Because of *you.*"

The devil doesn't know how to process that. His eyes narrow further and crackle with blue fire—hotter than any flames Hell could contain. "What the fuck is that supposed to mean? All *my* fault that you what? Miss that fucking bastard?"

"I don't know." Numb, I stare beyond his head, watching the shadows dance across the backsplash above the sink. This house, with all of its charms, has become a newer, smaller cage worse than any Vinny could ever devise.

That fucking bastard at least bathed his precious, captive bird in attention, however cruel it was. Apart from restraining me when the need arises, Dante won't even touch me. When he does speak, it's to bark out a few simple commands—*eat, sleep, stay, go.* Hell, this...*this* is the longest conversation we've had since the morning I woke up in the hospital.

It shouldn't matter...burn, sting, throb, ache, tear me apart, roll my ruined soul in jagged glass.

The loss of one man's heat shouldn't fucking hurt so much. At the end of the day, the moral of this story is that the devil is harder to withdraw from than heroin. The poor princess can't shake the craving. She can't spend another fucking minute suffocating under the pretense that vanquishing one scary monster was enough to make her whole again.

Because it *isn't*.

The sad truth is that nothing might ever be. Admitting it to myself is a knife through my soul. After five years of torment, freedom doesn't taste as sweet as poor Lynn thought it would.

The devil doesn't seem to realize why I blink tears back. Do I even know the reason? Without Vinny here to cherry-pick what emotions I should feel, I only have a few left to fall back on. Hatred. Loathing. Fear. All three lash out at him like a whip, and my tongue is ready to deliver the sting.

"Maybe...I should have just let him kill me."

I watch in satisfaction as the blow hits its mark. But the devil... He thrives on the violence. One step closer and he has me trapped.

"Maybe I should have killed you myself," he counters.

His heat leaches through my skin, sparking an inferno, and my body doesn't know how to interpret it. I...I can't keep my back from arching. Or my knees from trembling. My core from throbbing...

Loathing. Lust. He splits me apart and watches on as the twisted halves of me go to war.

I've been forced to do things to myself at night other than smother my screams. Shameful, pathetic, twisted things. Did he hear those sounds as well from down the hall?

Looking into his eyes, I can't tell. Either way, he seems fixated on another dilemma.

"You think he's alive?" There is no shred of humanity in his gaze as he shifts his stance, leaving his hands open at his sides.

"He's dead," I croak, watching his flexing fingers, but even I don't believe it. His body may be ashes. Those ashes may be in a morgue—but Vinny Stacatto is very much alive. His soul still lingers...feeding off what's left of mine.

"So they say," the devil agrees, "but...there are rumors."

I suspect that the words are a test. A taunt. He watches my reaction but doesn't seem satisfied when I flinch. My chest contracts, brushing his, though I don't know if he's closer or if I simply stopped trying to shift away. His scent fills my lungs regardless, chasing every ounce of oxygen out.

I look down at the bag dangling from my shoulder. Underneath the clothing are old newspapers scavenged from any store that carries *The City Harold*. While Espi tracked schools down for me, I hunted down every mention of rising crime rates in the city and the names of the bastards who've taken Vinny's place. They were only mentioned in tiny, anonymously quoted fragments, but the mantra became my bedtime prayer. *Piotr Petrov. Wilhem Donahugh. Arno Mackenzie.*

They, and quite a few more, have eagerly picked up where Vinny left off... But none of them comes close to the darker specter who seems to be pulling the strings from the shadows these days. Apparently, even ghosts can rule with an iron fist.

"Yeah. I've heard the rumors," I admit out loud. Do I believe them? I'm not sure.

"And?"

"And..." I lick my lips and consider the question. He seems to want more than a simple answer. "As long as any of those other men exist, Vinny still wins. Even in Hell." I can't tell if acknowledging that sad fact hurts or not. Maybe, deep down, I've made peace with it. I've absorbed it. "Look," I tell him, hiking the duffel higher on my shoulder. "I appreciate everything you've done for me. But I..." My voice trails off, and I seize my moment of freedom by staggering out of his reach. I make it inches from the exit before the duffel seems to fly off my arm of its own accord and hits the floor. "No. On second thought, you know what, Dante? Why do you even care if I leave?" I turn to face him, but his expression is unforgiving. Stone. "Is it because you're worried? Do you really...trust? It all comes down to trust...and the fact that you don't trust me."

The devil says nothing, and I can't seem to shut up. "You guard Espi's door at night like I'm...I'm some kind of threat. You lurk in the shadows, avoiding me, and yet you don't take your eyes off me."

And then it hits me. In the devil's world, betrayal apparently has no distinction—he's treated me the same way he treated the other monster he used to protect Espi from.

"So, what are you afraid of, exactly?" I croak. "Are you afraid I'll tell someone where you are? Someone like Mack? Is that it—"

"I don't give a damn what you do," he tells me, jerking his chin to the door. "So get the fuck out."

I move, but my steps take me in the wrong direction. I'm closer to him. Inches away. On top of him. As battle-worn as he is, he isn't expecting the hand that flies out and catches him across the cheek. The resounding slap echoes throughout the room, but the shock doesn't stop me from hitting him again. And again.

Again.

I punch, kick, slap, scratch, *anything*. The violence is more addictive than the heroin. Maybe this is what Vinny felt— this rage that made him rail against the world. Hitting the devil makes me feel better. For about a second.

It's not as fun when he doesn't fight back though. Not even when I lash at him with both hands. I kick him, and he's stone. I'm hurting myself more than I'm hurting him. Even when I dig my nails in. Even when I goad him on with the words that would have sent Vinny into a blind rage.

"I hate you, you goddamn bastard. I fucking hate you—"

He slams his hand over my mouth, muffling the awful things I'm shouting at him—for Espi, he muzzles me. But, when my teeth cut his palm, he turns my own body weight against me, and I hit the tiled floor on my hands and knees, tasting blood. I try to crawl away, but one of his hands seizes the back of my neck while the other pins me down by my waist.

"Let me go," I croak. I'm *pleading*.

More tears blur my vision, and when I reach back, I'm not sure what part of him I clutch. His chest? No, his arm. He growls when I dig my nails in and try to push him away.

After three tries, he doesn't move—but my body does. Disobedient, it has me lurching closer like a moth to a flame even as the words I spit at him echo with painful clarity. Still broken. Still bitter.

"I hate you. I hate you. Fuck you..."

"Fuck *me?*" a cold voice demands as he hunches over me from behind, slamming one of his hands against the tile in front of me. "I could kill you."

To prove it, he tightens his grip on my throat, caressing my windpipe. *Crushing* it. I see stars. My lungs heave for air, but death doesn't even have the chance to touch me before he lets go.

"Coward," I tell him.

"Bitch," he snarls back.

I gasp as something pinches my shoulder to drive in the insult. Hard. Unforgiving. *Teeth?* I can't decide before his fingers find their way down the back of my pants and graze that space between my legs. When I don't react, he slides one inside—harshly—gritting out a curse at the way I feel—already wet for him, greedily grasping at the digit. Shame and regret don't matter at this moment. My hips jerk, driving him deeper while my nails scrape at the cold linoleum.

This is the only language we know how to speak. Fingers. Skin. Nails. He thrusts his hand, and I lunge forward to bite the arm he has braced against the floor. He deepens his touch... I bite harder. Grunting from the pain, he doesn't let up. He's searching me the same way he did the night with Donahugh, seeking out any trace of another monster. I know before he gives up that he won't find any. If only he could do the same thing to my head—rip Vinny out and leave me hollow. My old tormentor rages from the grave, bellowing in my ear...

"You think," the devil starts, drowning him out and everything else. "You think I was watching over *Espi?*"

I don't like the note of confusion in his voice. If he wasn't guarding Espi's door, then why...

"I don't care." I shake my head, consumed by the hand he still has between my legs. I look up and find three tiny puncture wounds in the flesh of his forearm bared beneath the sleeve of his dark T-shirt. There's a metallic taste in my mouth, but my throat rushes to swallow it down rather than spit it out.

Whore, Vinny would cackle. *You deserve to be used like one.*

But the cadence of Lucifer's breathing makes it harder to hear him. Harder to care. Harder to focus on anything but the searing burn of hellfire. Without warning, he touches me again...and, like a true addict, I can't resist the promise of one last high. My hand finds his, the nails digging in until he retaliates and clutches my thigh so tightly that he breaks the skin. More blood spills, coating his nails and catching on the air like the opening notes of our own fucked-up melody.

I assume he takes my gasp for permission, because the next second, he manipulates me like a rag doll, stripping off the pretty, comfortable clothing Espi picked out for me. My pink sweater hits the counter. My black stretch pants bunch up around my ankles. I hear his jeans come undone. I feel the slick heat of him against my inner thigh, but the bastard waits until I reach back myself and slide my hand along his length before he mounts me, shoving himself deep.

The searing friction ricochets through every nerve ending, but I need him deeper. Harder. Faster. More, more—God, I need *more.* I writhe until he gives in and rides me like an animal right here before the sliding glass door. Any nosy neighbor with good vision could see us. Hear us.

And I don't give a damn.

"More," I rasp. "More, more."

He pivots, swiveling his hips to spark a carnal friction that makes me bite my tongue. It's too much. Not enough, even as my knees are rubbed raw while he lunges to find his own primal rhythm.

We're animals.

But I don't even start to ride that dizzying trip to the edge of insanity until he flips me over, pulling out. Only to wrench my legs apart and slide back in. Slower, this time. Deeper. Harder. His eyes find mine, glowing in the shadows, reinforcing with every thrust just who really owns my soul. I can almost see the letters of his name flashing across my vision like stars. D A N T E...

The brand on my chest is on fire. The blood in my veins simmers. When the fire finally spills over, I can only gasp, digging my nails into his shoulders so fiercely that they break the skin.

Spent and slick with sweat, he gives me five seconds to catch my breath before rolling from on top of me. With my gaze on the ceiling, I expect him to walk away. Instead, he merely waits until my vision clears before rising onto his hands and knees, dragging me closer by my ankle.

It's a familiar scene as he hunches between my splayed legs like a wolf, lowering his head. One brush of his tongue and I croak out the language he made me fluent in.

"Fuck, Fuck—" My voice dies off when he lashes at my throbbing skin, taking his time, heedless of the mess. Lapping. Sucking. Devouring.

Any disgust I might feel is too weak to truly register. I'm riding the high again. By the time my voice returns, I'm already over the edge, and his name spills out like a curse and a prayer.

His lips are still wet when he breaks away, and his mouth finds mine. I should cringe away from the pungent taste his tongue carries when he slams it past my lips—but I don't care. I kiss him back. Bite him back. I dig my nails down his arms, leaving my mark until he takes me again.

Harder. Faster. Meaner. Rougher. *Deeper.*

We may never be fully adept at the art of verbal conversation…but our bodies have mastered it.

I'm sore when he pulls out the final time and paints my stomach with his release. He doesn't bother to rub it in this time. He doesn't have to. When he collapses down beside me, we both know who really owns whom.

But even this moment can't erase three months of suspicion.

"You went back to him," the devil spits out at the ceiling, broaching the topic that I suppose has festered between us since the morning I left him at Mack's. "That fucking bastard. You went back to him."

"I didn't have a choice," I hear myself say, though do I truly believe that? I damn well had a choice—I just made the one that worked in his favor. The act didn't make me a saint—in fact, it made me more corrupt than any fallen angel.

I willingly traded my soul for the devil.

"The fuck you didn't," he snarls. "I would have gotten Espi back on my own—"

"He would have killed you." I let the words hang, but when I hear his mouth open, I reach for his hand and dig my nails into the scarred, callused surface. The remains of our promise leave an ugly mark across his palm, identical to the one on mine. "He would have *killed* you," I croak, surprised that he doesn't try to pull away—not that I could let him go. "He would have made me watch. And I couldn't... I *couldn't.*"

I've stabbed a man to death. Had sex with a stranger on camera. My soul has been stained black with so many crimes, but I couldn't bear to watch *him* die. Maybe that makes me a coward, worse than Vinny. He was sadistic. I'm selfish.

Dante wrenches his hand from my grip only to turn the tables by seizing my wrist so tightly that the bones compact. "So you figured it was easier to let me watch you die," he says in that dangerous, unsteady octave.

"It wasn't how I thought," I croak out when he doesn't say anything else. "Killing him. I thought...I thought it would be easier to..." Move on? Look at my future with Espi at the helm and magically heal like every other damsel in distress did at the end of her fairy tale? Some days, I even longed for that simple, easy bliss. Lynn used to pray for it.

But now...

"Killing him wasn't enough, Dante. Not when there are a million other bastards waiting to take his place. I want..." I scan the ceiling once again while the weight of those two words settles over my tongue. *I want.* A fancy music school or peace aren't enough to satisfy this new creature born in the ashes of Vinny's destruction. "I want to ruin everything he's ever built so that no one can claim it. I *need* to."

The devil stirs beside me, dragging himself upright, but he doesn't loosen his grip. "So, what? You think you can just go back and take on fuckers like Mack on your own?"

"I heard what Arno told you," I admit. They may have been brothers, but even the closest of family didn't enjoy sharing power. "And you have Espi to look after. This isn't your problem—"

"Damn it. Get up."

I blink as Dante rises to his feet and draws his jeans back up. He took his shirt off, however, and I catch a glimpse of the silvery scars left on his torso.

"Now," he snaps when I haven't moved. "Get up."

Wincing, I obey and follow him up the stairs, into the small bathroom. When he flicks the switch, the artificial light washes over our bodies, casting the blood on his arm in stark relief—not that he bothers to even wince as he cuts the shower on. We take turns bathing, and when I'm done, he leaves for a minute only to return with clothes fished from my duffel. The lilac sweater and the dark jeans make for a strange armor against the uncertainty.

In silence, we return downstairs, and the devil opens the front door, marshaling me out onto the front stoop— though we leave my bag behind.

Darkness paints the quiet neighborhood gray, almost swallowing the black truck idling alongside the curb. When Lucifer pulls the passenger's side door open, I recognize the driver and my heels promptly dig into the pavement.

"It's all right," the devil claims while Gino stares dead ahead, his hands on the steering wheel.

"Evening, Ms. Manzano," he greets me, but I can't seem to move until the devil climbs in first, jerking his chin for me to follow.

"It's all right," Dante repeats, and I climb onto the back seat.

The moment I close the door behind me, Gino starts driving.

"You make sure he's secure?" Dante asks him, his voice gruff.

"Of course." Gino shrugs without taking his gaze off the road. There's an ease to his posture that wasn't there around Vinny. Hell, he almost seems relaxed as he blends into the trickle of late-night traffic. "Your *friend* hid him well, but not well enough."

"Good," Dante grunts, flexing his hands in and out of fists. "I hope the fucker's *comfortable*."

"Who?"

Gino ignores me, but Dante glances back, and the dangerous gleam in his eye...

It's terrifying.

It's beautiful.

"Stacatto didn't get lucky," he says. "Someone sold out Espi. I know who."

I don't have the chance to question him before the truck comes to a stop in a narrow alley and both men climb out. Drawing a gun from his pocket, Gino waits near the truck while Dante drags me forward, toward a battered metal door that opens into a small building. It's dark inside, and the stench of rust tickles my nose. I have to feel along the wall with one hand until the moment Dante comes to a stop. He inclines his head toward a single flickering light bulb dangling from the ceiling. There, on his knees, is a man stuffed inside an ill-fitting suit, his hands bound behind his back. In a second, I can place a name to the kneeling figure. *Donahugh.*

"You want to get rid of the bastards who run the city?" Dante questions, watching the man before us with those hellfire eyes. "Then make a choice right now. Either you wait around for monsters like Stacatto to die off or...you *beat* the fucking peace in, blow by blow."

I swallow hard as his words resonate through my skin and settle deep into the remains of my soul. Donahugh spots us and a bead of sweat trickles down his forehead while his eyes widen.

"What...what do you mean?" I rasp.

"Someone gave this fucker a new kind of leverage to barter with Stacatto," Dante says.

"Who?"

He shakes his head. "That bastard is *mine*. But him..."

He reaches into his pocket and shoves something into my hand. I know what it is even before my fingers seek out the familiar shape. My trusty little knife. The weapon is more symbolic, however, compared to what he gives me next. I stiffen. He hasn't taught me how to wield this item yet.

"Like this," he prompts, nudging my fingers into what I assume are the proper positions. Regardless, the weapon still feels heavy and awkward in my grip, not that I let it go.

Instead, I start toward Donahugh. At this moment, I'm not Lynn anymore—but I'm not Daniela, either. I'm not quite sure who this new creature is as she eyes the figure before her, who's muttering curses behind a strip of duct tape sealing his mouth shut.

The bastard doesn't even seem human...

Just a liability. Another potential Vinny. Another danger to some other helpless girl too stupid to know a man from a monster.

Does he *deserve* to die?

Maybe not. After all, the devil taught me that you can't hate an animal. You can only fear it...or "put it out of its fucking misery."

Knowing that, I easily raise my arm and position my fingers over the trigger. A warm hand grazes the small of my back, reinforcing the devil's latest advice. *"Make a choice."*

With him beside me, I find it easier to aim the barrel of the gun straight at the man's head.

Wrapped beneath the shadow of Lucifer's fallen wings, I even find it easy to squeeze the trigger, snuffing out one more monster's life.

But there are plenty more awaiting their turn, and with hell at my back...

They only need to be patient.

The story continues in...
Beautiful Monsters Book 2: Refrain

Hey there!

Thank you so much for reading! If you enjoyed the story, please leave a review and recommend the book to any friend you think would love this twisted world. You'd have my eternal gratitude. Even a short sentence goes a long way!

Then, come join the rest of us dark romance lovers in my Facebook Group where you can get snippets, sneak peeks of upcoming books and even help vote on aspects of future novels.

Come to the dark side:
https://www.facebook.com/groups/lanasbeautifulmonsters/

WANT MORE STUFF TO READ?
Join my newsletter and get a **free book**! Plus, you get to stay updated with any new releases, random giveaways and exclusive sneak peeks!
https://www.lanaskybooks.com/newsletter

Other Novels: https://lanaskybooks.com/

Lana Sky is a reclusive writer in the United States who spends most of her time daydreaming about complex male characters and parenting her Cockapoo Joey. She writes dark, twisted romance across several genres. Her titles include everything from mafia romance to vampires.

facebook.com/AuthorLanaSky

twitter.com/lanasky101

amazon.com/author/lanasky

pinterest.com/lanasky101

goodreads.com/lanasky

instagram.com/lanasky101

bookbub.com/authors/lana-sky